THE

ACADEMY

J.T. PAYNE
RYAN MIX

Rossling Publishers

The Academy
J.T. Payne and Ryan Mix
www.academythebook.com

For more details on the book, its authors, and where to purchase copies, visit www.academythebook.com

Special discounts are available on quantity purchases by corporations, associations, churches and others. For details, contact the publisher at www.rossling.com

Published by: Rossling Publishers
Cover Design by: Kevin Scharfe
Editing by: Barry Napier, Phantom Pen
Library of Congress Control Number: 2015937399
ISBN: 978-0-9962286-0-2 (trade paper)
First Edition

A NOTE FROM THE AUTHORS

We met twenty years ago in a youth group, graduated from a private Christian high school together, then a Christian college, and have remained faithful church-goers throughout our lives. Although this book is a work of fiction, many of the characters and events are inspired by real life experiences. To this end, it is important that we share with you these realities so that they may be put into correct context.

The scandals mentioned throughout the book are fiction, in the fact that neither of us have had personal experience with these type of events in our schools or churches. However from television and radio in the 1990's, the events that take place in this book may sound familiar. Sadly, many of these events happen more frequently than one may think. This story is not based on any one of these circumstances, but is simply inspired by the collective whole.

Many of the positive characters in this book however, are inspired by real people. They are reflections of friends and educators who we had the privilege of growing up with. This book is a tribute to their character. These were the individuals who helped to make us who we are today.

Both of us wanted this story to be as genuine and thought-provoking as possible. With this in mind, we placed the story in the 1990's. The world felt bigger and unexplored then. Our lives felt more innocent and authentic. In keeping with this sentiment though, we did not create a protected fantasy world in which our characters could live. This is the story of a very imperfect world - the one Jesus came to save. Therefore, we would like to make you aware that some of the subject matter and language in this story may be uncomfortable.

We'd like to dedicate this novel to the friends we grew up with and the families we now have. Thank you for your support and love. We hope that this story will challenge you to question why you believe what you do. The most rewarding answers come from asking the most difficult questions. The beauty is in the struggle.

- J.T.PAYNE & RYAN MIX

CHAPTER 1

My grip grew tighter on the hardened steel blade as blood began to drip from my trembling hand. I didn't feel pain until I saw the blood, gasping as I surveyed the damage. The razor-sharp blade had made a clean, effortless slice, exactly as it was designed to do. I had nicked a vein, and a substantial one at that judging from the look of the crimson river forking between my fingers. Grabbing a monogrammed towel that sat on the rack, I wrapped my left hand tightly with my right, my knuckles blanched white.

It was these unforgiving straight razors. This wasn't the first time I had accidentally cut myself with one and probably wouldn't be the last. The proper way to use a straight razor was the last thing my grandfather taught me before he died. My grandpa took pride in a good shave, and out of respect for the man I once loved, I carried on the tradition.

It was foolish of me to pick today, of all days, to use it, though. I had been rushing in the face of jet lag ever since my plane arrived just an hour before, and I was already late. I should've known just to play it safe with a disposable.

I turned on the faucet and ran some cool water over the cut, the shaving cream on my face getting colder. A little filet of skin lashed wildly in the cold stream. In the mirror in front of me, I saw a man of thirty-eight. His face seemed old - tired beyond his years. He was not as in-shape as he once was. He thought he had come to peace with what he had done two decades before. He thought time healed all wounds. But now, being back here, those feelings had rushed back as they surely had for everyone who he'd soon be facing. It had never been his intention to hurt any of them. But as he used to say, intentions are meaningless.

My cell phone vibrated in my pocket. It was my wife.

Are you on your way?, the text read.

Heading out the door in a few. Probably 20 minutes away, I replied.

I walked over to the bedside phone and dialed '0' to the

concierge at the front desk. A few scattered clothes spilled out of my wife's suitcase, which sat on the edge of the bed.

"Hi, could I schedule a cab for this evening?" I asked. "I'm headed to the Clanton Grand. I'll be down in the lobby in five minutes."

The front desk operator confirmed my reservation so I thanked him and hung up the phone.

Throwing a bit of putty in my hair and a bandage on my hand, I adjusted my bowtie and checked my reflection in the mirror again. I closed my eyes and took in a big, slow breath of air.

"Ok, here we go," I muttered.

The hotel seemed surprisingly quiet. It wasn't until I reached the lobby and looked outside that I realized it had begun to storm. Violently. The cab was already waiting outside the automatic doors with its hazard lights reflecting the pounding showers all around.

"It's only going to get worse," the bellman told me as I looked out. "Are you ready for what's coming?"

His comment took me off guard as I didn't realize he was only speaking of the weather.

"Thank you. I'll be fine," I said, pulling my coat above my head to prepare for the dash to the waiting cab. The driver stepped outside with an umbrella and opened my door. It was pouring rain. Sheets of water blanketed the street, the taxi, and the mood.

"Evening, sir," I said to the driver. "The Clanton Grand, please." I had to shout in order to be heard over the pounding rain as I ducked into the car.

The storm was muffled inside the cab. We pulled out onto Windsor Avenue and then onto Milton Road, a familiar street that I hadn't seen in quite some time. Outside, the colors smudged and ran together through the taxi's window. The rainbow of lights streaked across the pavement, stretched and skewed by refraction as the car rocked gently over the old cobblestone streets of downtown. I rhythmically twisted my cell phone in my hand, one of my many nervous habits, while my mind continued to race. Lightning cracked from above. The storm was getting worse.

My phone vibrated a second time. My wife again.

Are you close? People have been asking about you. I felt my face flush and neck began to burn with pins and needles. This was really happening.

Turning into the Clanton Grand Hotel, my eyes seemed momentarily dazed, as if seeing it for the first time. It has always been a beautiful place - a southern guest house at its finest. Pristine white pillars and ivy-covered brick overlooked the winding river that carved its way through town. On summer nights, front-porch guests could enjoy a performance of crickets and fireflies from its nearby banks.

The taxi pulled up to the front steps, and when it stopped, I realized that I was nearly an hour and a half late. I took another deep breath, then thanked the driver and handed him a twenty. After opening the door, I quickly hopped a puddle and made it to the metal awning, the rain pounding against it like machine gun fire. One by one, I ascended the stairs and could already see them: my peers, my classmates. The ones I had known and the lives I had interrupted.

Jessica Tinsley was speaking with Aaron Sinclaire in the lobby. People I assumed to be their spouses stood by with drinks in hand. I sucked in one more big gulp of air, wishing there was someone beside me to help soften the nerves. But I had experienced loneliness before. My life was defined by it. There was no turning back now. They deserved an explanation.

I opened the doors. Jessica and Aaron stared; politely pretending my entrance wasn't surprising. They quietly smiled and nodded, as did I.

As I awkwardly moved past them and towards the main ballroom, the music and commotion grew louder. I began to see more of them. Their faces were different—worn and older. No one looked the same. Even more, I recognized those who were not there, those who would not dare return to this place, and those who were no longer with us.

Looking up, I saw the banner hanging directly above them. It made me wonder if this was, perhaps, a very bad idea. Perhaps this was a mistake all along. I had put this in the past, but now the past stood before me in bold, red Helvetica.

CHERRYWOOD CHRISTIAN ACADEMY CLASS OF 1996
20 YEAR REUNION

It was like a tombstone, its epitaph marking what had died

and when it had passed. My high school had long since been put to its grave and I was the one with blood on my hands.

"Sylas Ernst. I thought you'd be the last guy to come," a voice from my right stated. I turned toward it. An older Grady Sites just stood there, looking at me.

"Grady!" I stopped, fearing that out of all the people in this room, I could've wrecked his life the most. "How you been?"

"I'm ok. I'm going by Gradon now, but you can still call me Grady," He laughed. "Got two boys now, so I certainly can't complain."

"Oh, what are their ages?"

"Ten and seven," he replied.

"That's wonderful." I didn't know how to say anything else. There were so many questions I had for him, but no tactful way to ask them. We spoke pleasantries until he said something that caught me off-guard.

"I'm glad to see you're still alive," he stated.

"Yeah. Me too," I replied with a laugh, unsure if he was joking.

He nodded his head, and putting his hand on my shoulder, leaned in and whispered. "It's easier to forgive an enemy than to forgive a friend." He leaned back away from me and squeezed my arm. "I'll see you around," he added with a smile.

If his quote by William Blake was true, then I knew I would be just fine. After all, it seemed that I had very few friends in the room that night besides Grady. I had really only kept up with one or two people from high school, so I knew very little about the aftermath and how it had affected everyone who had been involved. I had purposefully stayed off of Facebook and any other social networks when everything had come out; I just never developed an interest.

With hesitation, I looked around and began to survey the room. People were starting to notice me a bit more. They were murmuring and whispering among themselves, just like I had seen them do so often in high school. Then, out of the corner of my eye, I saw a figure walking towards me. I turned to see a man my age with deep lines of worry on his face.

I recognized him right away and a lump formed in my throat. It was my old friend, Shawn. He approached me slowly, and I couldn't help but smile at him. "Man, it's good to see you!" I said, reaching out my hand for a handshake, I was relieved to at least have one person there who I loved and trusted.

"It took you long enough to get here," Shawn said, accepting my hand and shaking it. He then went one further and pulled me in for a hug. "How was your trip?"

"Long," I answered as I unintentionally got a whiff of Shawn's breath. "You drink scotch now?"

"Shhh," he said in a joking fashion. "You want some?"

"No, thank you. Where's - "

"Your wife? She's over there somewhere."

Shawn and I kept in touch every so often but I never realized how deeply he was bothered by what had happened. I didn't really think it affected him that much at all. Or perhaps, more precisely, I never realized how much he drank to deal with his past hurts. I saw it in him then, though. It was in his eyes, a hazy sort of detachment that went hand in hand with the smell of scotch on his breath.

"People were wondering if you were gonna show tonight," he said.

A tremendous crash of white light and earth-shaking thunder broke outside, causing the lights to flicker. I scanned the room and saw the back of my wife in her beautiful red dress. I could recognize her silhouette anywhere, even in a darkened room. A second bolt of lightning struck and at once, there was darkness. I closed my eyes as the voices grew around me, each person speaking louder to make their voice heard above the others. Chairs and dishes were clamoring together as some people stumbled toward the red glow of the exit signs.

My mind raced back twenty years to a scene of pandemonium much like this one. It was the night of our senior year homecoming. That night so many years ago would set in motion events that would change everything about me. It was the beginning of my story; the story of what made me who I am. I stood in the darkness and allowed the memories to rush over me. Time slowed to a crawl as my mind drifted away from the present and back to where it all began.

For the Academy and one of its students, it was the beginning of the end.

CHAPTER 2
20 YEARS EARLIER

"Where is Roscoe!?" Shawn asked worriedly. "It's already half-time!"

"Calm down, he'll be here," I said.

"I guarantee he's trying to get with some girl."

"Yeah, I wouldn't be surprised. Who do you think he's trying for this time? Donna?"

"What about that sophomore with the wooden foot?"

"Meredith?"

"Is that her name?"

"Yeah, it's Meredith and she doesn't have a wooden foot. She has scoliosis."

We were in Mr. Wagner's old tobacco field some twenty yards away from the football stadium. The field served as an overflow parking lot for the football games. It was set lower than the actual football field by about fifteen feet, a rather steep incline and a menacing fence separated the two fields. From the stands, it was nearly impossible to see the majority of cars parked there.

"Do you think anyone noticed the tarp?" he asked.

I looked over my shoulder to the tarp in question. It had been placed on the ground behind a row of cars, an eight-by-ten foot construction tarp, green to match the few patches of grass left in Ol' man Wagner's field. Surely, no one had given it a second thought.

"No one cares," I answered. "It just looks like some landscaping work or a pile of mulch or something."

Homecoming night was always my favorite time of the year, and tonight was no different. It was our senior year and the whole school had turned out for tonight's game. The Cherrywood Saints were battling against their nemesis, the East Creek Devils. Perhaps it was the simple paradox between the two team names that began the rivalry, but time only served to make things worse.

The night was crystal clear. The bleach-white lights of the stadium made a stark contrast against the warm lavender glow of dusk to the west, the only light left in the nearly blackened sky, while the moon was just a sliver of silver on the eastern horizon. The cool wind blew my hoodie gently as the smell of nachos and onion rings flooded the air. Even though I was never much of a football fan, which, for a Southern boy was almost as blasphemous as smoking in church, football season was still my favorite time of year.

"I'm going to go grab a hot dog," I said, trying to take Shawn's mind off of Roscoe's tardiness and ultimately, our imprudent plan. "You want one?"

"I guess, but no onions."

"Right, got it." I said, starting towards the steep hill.

"You forget something?"

I turned around slightly confused until I saw what he was holding. It was my old SLR; a beautiful Canon Camera I had shot with for years. My family had never had much money but my mother still found a way to buy me that camera for Christmas a few years ago. Over time, working at Mr. Winter's print shop, I had been able to purchase more and more lenses. As my skills grew and developed, so did my equipment. I never went anywhere without my camera, and although my friends teased me about it, they also respected me for it.

Photography was something that I was truly good at. This was not a thought created out of arrogance. I knew it in my heart, without anyone else telling me. Grabbing the camera from him, I checked the frame count to see how many I had left: seven.

I grimaced. Luckily, there were two more rolls of Kodak 400 in the front pocket of my hoodie—more than enough to capture tonight's memorable events.

"Don't start shooting and forget my hot dog," Shawn called after me.

Shawn and I had been friends for years, and unlikely ones at that. His father was a distinguished lawyer, often handling high profile cases at the state and even national levels. Although too prominent to be on staff at Cherrywood, he was the first to be called if the Academy or its board members ever required legal services, which they often did. Cherrywood took pride on a stature of propriety and great expectations. It went without saying that in order to maintain a certain image, you gain enemies along the way.

The similarities Shawn and I shared were few, but the bond

they gave us was strong. Intelligence and perspective were what tied us together. We thought of ourselves as free thinkers, not persuaded by what most people thought was cool. Shawn did have his limitations, though. He grew up privileged, and because of that, was not able to find joy in the more simple things of life. Camping, fishing, and hiking were all foreign concepts to Shawn and therefore I sought out other friends to fill in the gaps Shawn left. By all accounts, most would consider Shawn and me to be good kids, but when viewed from the conservative and legalistic standards of the Academy, we lived on the fringes. In this way, we were able to, at times, cheat the system and manipulate the odds in our favor, much like we were planning to do that evening.

After entering the stadium, I trudged down the side steps and onto the field. I was allowed to be down there since I was often taking photos for the yearbook. No one ever thought twice when they saw me. I spotted my friend, Cameron Fosjord, warming the bench, and as I started to approach him, saw the football coming directly at me out of the corner of my eye. A player from the Saints snatched it out of the air, and immediately, one of East Creek's largest players, Topher Landau, tackled him to the ground.

"Nice hit," I said, barely loud enough to hear myself say it.

I had known Topher long before he had ever stepped onto a football field. We were childhood friends, but time had a way of changing people. For Topher, time had hardened his heart and numbed his need for education. He had become a bully, a selfish young man who won friendships and enemies from fear alone. My attempt at a compliment was due to a rumor that Topher would be transferring to Cherrywood.

A devil in saint's clothing, I thought to myself.

I turned my attention back to the bench.

"Cameron!" I shouted a few feet back.

Cam stood out easily enough, as his uniform was impressively white and clean. I was sure he had not played a minute in the game. Last year about this time he would have been covered in grass stains but this year, Cherrywood was blessed with some impressive talent. They were calling this year "The Dream Team" and businesses from all around the state were lining up to advertise at our events. Sponsors' advertisements had always hung from our bleachers or been printed in our bulletins but this year this space was prime real estate. Cam turned around to see me pretending to photograph the game.

"We still on for the fourth quarter?" I asked in a strained whisper.

"Yeah man, we're still good. I'll give the signal."

"Cameron!" the coach shouted. "Cut out the chit-chat and get your head back in the game. You're going in!"

"Right Coach!"

"Let's go Cameron!" I shouted in the toughest voice I could muster. "Yeah, go our home team! Yay football!" I was clueless to the sport and everyone around me knew it.

I walked off the field and towards the concessions, along with dozens of other fans leaving their seats. The line for hot dogs stood about sixteen people deep due to the slaughterhouse occurring on the field. The Saints were up by thirty-four points with eight minutes to go in the third quarter. Boredom was starting to set in as the crowd was now focusing on the quality of the plays rather than the plays themselves. Short runs and passes were merely inducing a golf clap while only the long bombs and crushing sacks garnered school spirit. Saints fans had seen blowouts before so they were used to mingling and killing time during games.

Cafeteria Cathy, a spunky eighty-year-old school lunch lady with a smile held firmly in place by Polident, finally called for my order. Even here, getting a hot dog during the football game, it seemed it was impossible to get away from the faces of the staff you saw every day at the Academy.

The night had gotten into full swing and quite a few people were already leaving, which I knew would complicate our plan. None of us had expected a shutout of these proportions.

Hot dogs in hand, I walked down the embankment to the overflow parking.

"It's about time," Shawn stated from the hood of his car.

"Sorry, the line was really long," I said handing him his dog.

"How much time left in the game?"

"The clock said 2:18 when I left and I think there is one more section to play," I said also climbing onto his hood.

"Section? You mean quarter. So we've got what, like twenty minutes?"

"I dunno. Probably."

Shawn was as clueless to the sport as I was. We both felt that football was a pointless sport to learn. It was a sport that you'd most likely never play again after high school or college, and if you did get that far, you were left with a bad back, sore joints, and possibly the inability to perform long division. Sports like tennis and golf are mocked in high school but those are the sports you can play throughout your life. I liked tennis and smacking golf balls around at the Locksboro Country Club driving range, although I was not really that good at either one.

"Did Roscoe show up yet?"

Shawn shook his head, noticeably irritated, with a mouthful of chilidog.

Roscoe was an important part of our plan but if he went AWOL, like he had done before, Shawn and I could probably still pull this off by ourselves. Our idea for tonight was simple: to celebrate Cherrywood's victory and the homecoming of our honorable alumni with a favorite display of the fans. We would gladly take on the task of organizing a grand celebratory event so our beloved institution would not have to foot the workload, the necessary paperwork, or the bill. Not to mention, many high level contributors and directors were at tonight's game so we wanted to make sure they saw what a dynamite school this was. It was charitable and we loved to give....and blow stuff up.

Reading the warning labels on fireworks is important. Not that you're going to do what they say but because they'll tell you what the firework does. For example, "Warning: Emits Showers of Sparks" might leave you disappointed. But "Warning: Explosive" will definitely not. Teenagers living in North Carolina know full well that the fireworks in our beloved state leave a lot to be desired. We have the sparklers, black snakes, crackling balls, and those little tanks, but if the most a firework can do for you is give you third degree burns, it's not good enough. Luckily, there is a solution and it's as simple as a car ride to the state's southern cousin.

South Carolina has the good ones, the ones directly from China where not all of the warning labels are in English. The ones where just lighting the fuse alone can send you running for the Neosporin. And you can get them anytime you want, not just two weeks before the Fourth of July from some little roadside pop-up shack. They've got the huge firework stores that are open all year— the ones that are painted bright yellow, have a huge attention grabber like a life-sized fiberglass dinosaur. These are the stores that are always running some sort of 'Buy 2 get 1 free' deal and stock enough explosives to level a small city.

Two weeks prior to the homecoming game, we made a road trip to Big Tom's Fireworks Emporium in Lewisville, SC. We used Cam's fake ID to buy a sizable collection of pyrotechnics. Then we grabbed a piece of plywood and some cardboard tubing to create a rather impressive self-contained fireworks display. We spent all of last Saturday in Shawn's mom's garage carefully designing a network of interconnected wicks to create a domino effect that would allow all our fireworks to be ignited with one simple fuse. The display would be timed to go off right at the game's end to add another level of excitement to the already enthusiastic atmosphere. It was a stunt that involved illegal explosives, crowd endangerment, disturbing the peace, and a whole slew of other charges, but it's not like we had malicious intentions. We were just teenagers with time and creativity.

"There he is!" Shawn exclaimed.

Roscoe waved from atop the embankment, on the other side of the fence. A sigh of relief came over both of us. Shawn waved back and we both hopped up from our perches and made our ways towards him.

"Way to cut it close!" Shawn exclaimed when Roscoe joined us.

"Sorry guys. I was talking to Tracy," Roscoe replied.

"Traaaacy!" Shawn and I replied.

"Sylas thought you were with Meredith," Shawn said.

"The girl with the wooden foot?"

"Unbelievable," I replied.

"Are you guys still doing this?" Roscoe asked.

"You mean are *we* still doing this?" I asked. "Yeah, it's still on."

"How much were those hot dogs?" he asked.

"Three bucks. Chili is free."

"Crap."

Roscoe never had any money. He was famous for bumming money off friends but always managed to pay it back. If you lent Roscoe money, you could never tell when you would get it back but when you did, you would always get the exact total down to the penny.

"Did you guys talk to Cam?" Roscoe asked. "Are the fireworks here?"

"They're here. Everything is set up and Cam is good to go. Looks like he finally got some playing time."

"You don't think we're gonna get caught, do ya?"

"You can't even think like that," I replied. "We're good."

"Well, we all probably shouldn't be standing here looking all sketchy," Shawn observed. "Can you see Cam from here?"

Roscoe took a moment to spot number 77. "Oh yeah, he's sitting on the bench again."

"Ok, we're gonna go. Where are you gonna stand?"

Roscoe moved around to get a good visual on Cam and the parking lot. He studied the area before saying, "I think right here is good. Is there enough light here to see me?"

"Yeah, you should be fine." I said. "You know the signal, right?"

"Yeah, I got it."

"Ok, we're gonna go," I said. "See ya on Sunday."

"Good luck guys," Roscoe said holding two thumbs up.

We all tried to conceal our mischievous grins as we returned to our respective posts. We had this all planned out. Cam was the inside man. He would let us know the perfect time to engage. Roscoe was the messenger, I was a lookout, and Shawn was the detonator. Once the device had been activated, we'd split up and not see each other until church on Sunday or school on Monday. There were a lot of eyes around so maintaining our innocence with solid alibis was crucial.

When we left Roscoe and headed for the woods, there were about ten minutes left in the fourth quarter. The score was 59 to 17 and people were already leaving. The stands would have been nearly empty by now if it weren't for the crowning of the Homecoming King and Queen after the game.

We had set everything up along the woodline, just on the edge of the field. It was close enough to the stadium to have the effect we needed but still disguised enough to be overlooked. I waited behind some cars, close enough to be within whisper range, while Shawn hurried over to the device.

"You're clear," I whispered.

He pulled back the tarp and folded it. It was a masterpiece. Cardboard mortars stood in perfect alignment, resembling a lethal pipe organ and all were intricately connected to each other through a series of interwoven wicks and fountains. The full sheet of OSB plywood was thirty-two square feet of colorful rockets, Roman candles, mortars, fountains and other flammable propellants ready to dance and scream with the kiss of a flame. It was a contraption Wiley Coyote himself would be proud of.

Shawn could see me, I could see Roscoe, and Roscoe could see Cam. Cam would be the one to initiate the operation by holding his helmet in the air above his head. It was a gesture that we felt would be easily dismissed by the crowd but one that was unmistakable to notice. As we waited for the signal, a car making its exit from the lot flashed its lights in our direction. For a split second, both of us were completely illuminated. We froze, petrified. Nothing happened. The vehicle completed its turn and left. We nervously waited for what seemed like half an hour but it was probably only a few minutes. Then I saw Roscoe's fist high above his head. Cam had given the signal from the field.

"Ok, go!" I exclaimed in a whisper.

Shawn flicked his lighter and ignited the cigarette. We had done some extensive experimentation on cigarette burns and discovered that it takes about eleven minutes for a cigarette to burn down to its filter. Confident with this knowledge, we stuck one of Shawn's stepdad's cigarettes on the end of the main wick. With the amount of timeouts and plays in the game, this should put the first fireball over the stadium at about the time the clock reached all zeroes.

Shawn darted back from his position. "It's going!" he exclaimed.

"Ok, see you at school," I replied tapping Shawn on the back.

"Get some good photos," he said.

"Ha! I'll try!"

Shawn hurried to his car and I made my way towards the main entrance. I looked up to see if Roscoe was still at his post. He was gone.

I gripped my hand on my SLR to keep it from swinging back and forth from my neck. My pace was much faster than I wanted it to be. A steady stream of people were leaving the unguarded stadium entrance, their hands full with fold-up stadium chairs and Saints paraphernalia. In the distance, Shawn pulled his white '94 4Runner out of the lower lot. I pushed my way through the main gate and immediately started to make the crowd my alibi by doing what I don't like to do; spurn people on to give the yearbook a big smile. I much preferred candid snapshots to keep my photos looking different than every other family scrapbook and the interior of every girl's locker. But I needed those people to see and remember me. Stumbling through the crowd, I wildly snapped one shot after another, giving little thought to composition or focus.

Cam was warming the bench again, and from this side of the stadium, I had a perfect view of his face. I snapped a picture of his anxious expression in front of the dwindling time clock, knowing our masterpiece would detonate any second. Every so often he'd look around to try to spot one of us. He never saw me.

After making my way back down to the front row of bleachers to grab a seat along the field, I asked a man to pardon me so I could squeeze by a few spectators to the vacant middle of the bench. I had annoyed everyone around here enough to be remembered. Now it was time to enjoy the festivities. Cam was watching the clock even more frequently now. I grabbed a few more shots of the game, and after a Saint interception, the ball was now back in our possession. The Devils called a timeout, which received grumbles and some chants for the Devils to warm up the bus.

I looked at my watch. It had been roughly ten minutes since Shawn had lit the fuse and there were still several minutes left in the game. Cam was now focused exclusively on the time clock and the sky above the stadium. Zooming my lens in to try to get a reading from his face, I could see a mix of nervousness and a devilish smirk on his face. Cam and I had been friends for years so I knew by his face that he had underestimated the amount of time left in the game. If East Creek hadn't used their timeouts, which I'm sure Cam didn't think they would, his guess probably would've been pretty close.

I turned back to the crowd, and in an instant I saw her. Natalie stood at the very end of the stands close to the marching band. She rocked back and forth blowing gently on her hot chocolate. I couldn't help but grab a quick photo. Her big doe eyes blinked gracefully, and then almost instinctively she looked in my direction, as if feeling my eyes on her. I was completely flustered, waving at her nervously with a smile, putting my head down in embarrassment. For that one moment I had completely forgotten about our-

SHHEEW, SHEEW, BACCACK!

Our bottle rockets were the first to go. The stadium paused for a moment, wondering what exactly they just heard.

BA-BA-BA-BA-BAPP...firecrackers emulated the sound of machine gun fire from below the field. A few teenyboppers screamed while the rest of the crowd attempted to locate the small infantry unit that had apparently just opened fire. Players on the field slowly stood from their crouched positions. Forcing a straight face, I kept snapping photos.

THHUUB, THUB – the sweet bass sounds of mortar ignitions. Then, *BOOOM, BA-BOOM*...color bursts and pounding explosions shot through the goal posts filling the sky high above the end zone. The stadium was stunned with awe and confusion. I thought of Shawn and how he would have loved to see the grandeur of this rebellion. Cam was wearing a huge smile, as was I. Roscoe probably was too, wherever he was. A baby cried, to which I responded with laughter. Whispers filled the crowd as fans struggled to figure out what was happening. No one knew if they should be excited or fearful.

I was bursting at the seams as I listened to the stream of conversation around me.

"Was this supposed to happen?"

"I don't know."

"I think it's a prank. I don't think they'd be doing this in the middle of the game."

As others began to reach the same conclusion, Larry Bellfield, a marching band trumpeter and junior class clown, playfully blew out the notes to "Stars and Stripes Forever" which caused a chuckle to run through the crowd. Some even started to applaud. The reaction was exactly what we wanted, even though it came in a roundabout sort of way. The moment, however, would become very short lived.

On the other side of the distant fence, Donald Fench, a janitor at the Academy and volunteer at the football games, dropped over the embankment wielding a shovel. He was headed towards our launch pad but from my angle, that's all I could see. In less than a minute, the mortars that had been exploding high above the stadium dropped within feet of the crowd. Fireballs were now firing directly overhead. Explosive color and ash peppered the stands. Our homecoming game was now a warzone.

The whistling mortars were deafening as a firestorm blasted

its way through the chainlink fence sending sparks everywhere.
The crowd was in an uproar, running and seeking shelter wherever
they could. Rockets pounded the Will Call booth. Mothers raced
for their children while some fans dove under the bleachers for
cover. A lone child stood in the grass simply wailing and wetting
himself. I was also in tears, but from laughter. This was a
photographer's dream and I couldn't change rolls fast enough. I
wish we could have all been together for this. Shawn would be
furious that he wasn't here. Roscoe was probably freaking out
somewhere but I knew Cam and I were having the time of our
lives.

Donald had tried to extinguish our creation using the only
resource he had around at the time. Destroying the set-up may
have worked if we had not so carefully instituted a multitude of
fail-safes. Each mortar had been rigged by at least three fuses,
ensuring that each and every rocket, mortar and fountain would
fire successfully. We had no intention of our device ending up like
a string of Christmas lights where if one goes out, the fun stops.
Apparently, all Donald did was dislodge the device putting himself
and everyone else in danger.

BWEEP, BWEEP, BWEEP...a rocket hit a car, sounding the
alarm. The dry autumn leaves of a decorative shrub caught on fire.
Screaming mothers overpowered the high-pitched shrieks of
whistling rockets.

I had blasted through all rolls of film in my hoodie and at this
point, could merely watch and enjoy the chaos as everyone
suddenly recalled techniques from every action movie they'd ever
seen and attempted to utilize them to their best physical abilities.
Old people maneuvered their Power Scooters down the single
handicap ramp like a Tokyo raceway, while fat people ran faster
than I'd ever thought was humanly possible.

The night's final bombardment came from a single firework
nicknamed "Armageddon". It cost us a pretty penny and certainly
lived up to its name because the firestorm it showered upon
Clanton Stadium was truly apocalyptic. The bombardment of
explosives shot through the fence and lit up the field. It was as if an
army had taken over Old Man Wagner's tobacco field and was
advancing towards higher ground. Blasts that shook your core fell
from above, and showers of colorful hellfire continued endlessly as
ash pelted the crowd below.

My smile quickly faded as I began to realize this prank had gone too far. The joy of the event had quickly begun to darken as the unrelenting thunder of rockets pounded overhead. The once jovial crowd was now truly terrified - some injured. Then as quickly as it started, it was all over.

An eerie silence filled the stadium. A high pitch tone rang in my mind. I looked down to see Cameron who was still wildly laughing, not realizing the change in mood. His expression dampened quickly when he finally began to look around and observe what I had noticed. Our senior prank had gone too far, and the horror was written on everyone's face. This had never been our intention, but as I would come to understand, intentions are meaningless.

CHAPTER 3

I sat at my desk, forehead beaded with a cold sweat. Wiping my palms on my pants, I looked down and saw that I was wearing jeans, not the navy or beige khaki pants required at the Academy. What had I been thinking this morning?

A blurred figure passed by me. Somehow I knew it was the teacher distributing this morning's calculus quiz. I looked at the page, but try as I might, I couldn't make out any of the numbers or letters. I began to breathe heavier without realizing it. My nose started to run and because I had no tissues, all I could do was wipe it on my sleeve. Some people were starting to take notice.

I then realized that the teacher was unfamiliar to me. Who was this new redheaded instructor? A substitute perhaps. Miss Myers must have been sick. Then the redheaded instructor noticed my pants and just as she was about to speak, there was a knock at the door. She turned quickly to open it. It was Principal Sites. Without acknowledging the substitute's pleasant *hello*, the Principal turned and looked at me.

"Sylas," he said in a simple and stern voice. "Sylas," he repeated.

I fought hard to ignore him. I wasn't going to take the rap for all of this. "Sylas, come on now, enough of this, time to wake up!"

I gasped heavily as my eyes opened in an instant.

"Sylas," my father said. "The wind blew the power out last night. Your alarm clock didn't go off. It's seven o'clock. You need to hurry or you're going to be late for school." His voice was coming from downstairs, yelling up at me.

I unwrapped myself from my pile of blankets, damp from my nightmare. The power outage had turned off the small space heater in my room, which was an absolute necessity in my family's old house. The alarm clock on my nightstand blinked a bold, green 12:00am.

I placed my hand on the plate glass window to see how cool it was outside. It was surprisingly cold, so I opted for my commissioned navy blue school sweater to accompany my uniform. After slipping my pre-tied school tie over my head, I double-checked my pants. They were the correct beige khakis.

The old grandfather clock at the bottom of the stairs moaned and creaked with each passing second. It ticked its discomfort and tocked its old joints just as our old pre-war house seemed to do. After just building a fire in the fireplace, my father sat as he always did, in his worn armchair, listening to a cassette tape of a pastor from the 60's since he believed modern preachers were too soft.

"Thanks for waking me up," I said on my way to the kitchen.

"It is my duty."

I had always found my father's communication cryptic and arduous. Anyone else hearing this response would have gone on their way, puzzled, but unconcerned. For me, accustomed to hearing him speak in guarded dialect, I knew he meant more than what he let on. In this case, he was referencing a poem by Ellen Sturgis Hooper, one that he quoted from frequently.

I slept, and dreamed that life was Beauty;
I woke, and found that life was Duty.

He believed that life was built out of obligation and duty. In all he did, my father provided for his family, clothed his children and gave of his time not out of love, but obligation. This giving out of obligation, in turn meant he expected certain things in return; a conditional sense of love to match his own, compliance to his wishes, and an unwavering respect for authority. Obligation and duty consumed my father's life, but he never took the time to finish the poem and therefore had never understood what it was truly saying. He lived his life according to his own viewpoint of the world, of history, literature and most dangerous of all, Scripture. He became a god unto himself, blinded by his own twisted conscience.

"Thank you, nonetheless," I said, "It would look bad if I was late today."

"What's important about today?" he asked.

"Oh…I am pretty sure I have a calculus quiz first thing."

"Calculus?" he said, with a slight scoff. "Okay then."

He had never taken calculus, or any advanced math to my knowledge. He grew up on a farm in the rolling hills of Pennsylvania, the son of a New England shipbuilder. However, my father decided to go to seminary, doing the only work he believed to be harder than building ships or tilling the field: reaping lost souls.

"I may need to stay after school for a bit," I said trying to change the subject.

"Why is that? I need you here at home."

"For the yearbook," I said. "I'm supposed to photograph Oak Ridge Bakery and Sanderson's Hardware for their advertisements in the sponsors' section." My father began to shake his head looking down at his Bible, thinking of what to say. "I made a commitment to my teacher. It's my obligation." I said these last bits as an attempt to reason on his level.

He stopped shaking his head, and turned to me. "Your obligation is at home, not wasting your time taking pictures for those people."

"Please don't be like that, Dad. Not everyone at Cherrywood is against you."

My father had applied to the school as a pastor on staff at Cherrywood. Truth be told, he'd applied to numerous pastoral openings across the south, from Virginia to Mississippi. He was always encouraged by the quick reply he received as they looked upon his credentials and found his cover letters to be saturated with teaching and scripture. The problem always came during the interview when the church would try to get to know him better. An introvert to the core, my father deflected questions about his past and personal life and would almost instantly begin to point out faults in those around him. I always thought my father would be a better evangelist than a pastor. I fully believed he had the capacity to show up to a church any given Sunday, preach fire and brimstone and frighten righteous God-fearing people to empty their pockets so that he could do the same thing next Sunday one town over. My father, however, lacked the wherewithal to be a pastor, to be a shepherd to his flock, to nurture them and love them unconditionally. He was unable to relate to those around him and that was why he left those who spoke to him as confused and empty as I believed him to be.

"I'll come home when I'm done and then I can help you with whatever you need," I said. I knew my father did not need my help. He simply wanted me to be there so he could control that portion and time in my life.

"Do what you have to," he said.

That was all the permission I needed. I grabbed my book bag and an English muffin from the kitchen and darted out the door. "Love you, Dad!"

"Take care," he replied.

This was another of his all too common replies. I was out of my father's will, and therefore I knew I was outside of my father's love. Sad to say, I had become very familiar with this over the years.

It took a few moments to get the old '84 Chevy Nova started. I usually had to give the engine a little gas to help it turn over. As I drove to school, I tried to push my father's words out of my mind. He made me feel so simple, as if I was willing to go along with whatever Mr. Winters and the other board members of the Academy needed. I knew that at the Academy one hand washed the other, and if I was going to get ahead and be successful I would have to play by the rules. That meant fulfilling obligations and using my photography skills to make the Academy look good. In turn, perhaps I would receive a letter of recommendation to an art school or receive an apprenticeship in Charlotte or Raleigh. It wasn't until I was pulling into the parking lot that the realization of what had happened Friday night hit me. The school - faculty and students alike - would probably be buzzing with rumors.

I was seventeen years old, just one of seventy-two seniors at one of the most privileged high schools in the state. Although my folks paid my tuition and I made good grades, I still felt like I was bottom shelf and lower tier. An outsider would have seen me as very fortunate to be where I was, but the Academy had a way of making you know your place, as it saw fit. I was able to attend there only by the sweat of my brow and skin of my teeth. Attending Cherrywood meant that you were virtually guaranteed to find one or two college scholarships and it also earned students more respect in the community.

The rules, however, were very rigid. Your actions were often called into question and your choices often judged. For students new to the Academy, the rules seemed overwhelming but for those of us who began our time there as freshmen, we felt comfortable.

We were also just as comfortable bending the rules, and at times, breaking them. There were rules and then there were rules on how to break those rules. Out of the seventy-two students in our class, only a handful of us understood the latter.

I entered through the west entrance of the school, as I had always done during the last four years at Cherrywood. The school had an ivy-league look about it; buildings made of some sort of colonial brick or stone, columns, hand-made ironwork and a cherub-laden fountain in the middle of the courtyard that, once a year, some student from somewhere would dump a bunch of dish soap into, turning it into a foaming cauldron.

Passing through the bustling halls and scampering underclassmen, I made my way up to my homeroom on the second floor. Overhearing gossip words like "explosion" and "police" seemed to make my fears that much more real. I glanced out an arched window at the top of the staircase to see a dense fog lifting in the courtyard. Briefly, I wondered if I would ever see this view again. Perhaps there had been a hole in our plan that we hadn't managed to root out.

At that moment, I felt a hand on my right shoulder. My face turned pale as my eyes widened with fear. It was my classmate Grady's grandfather, but in that moment I saw him only as Principal Sites. His face was stern, focused, and displayed yet another emotion I was somewhat surprised by: sadness.

"Sylas," Dr. Sites said flatly, "Come to my office, please."

"Yes, sir," I said over the lump quickly forming in my throat.

Blood began to rush to my head at a rapid pace as I followed him. My heart pounded as my face burned with worry. What would I tell my mother? What would my father do? Through the window blinds of the administrative office's oak door, I saw Miss Crisby, the secretary, sitting at her desk. She raised her head and gave an empathetic nod as she pursed her narrow lips. She stood from her desk and opened the door for the principal and me. This was not good. If even cold-hearted Crisby felt pity for my plight, no doubt I was in a heap of trouble.

"Miss Crisby, would you mind joining us?" the principal asked.

"Of course sir," she replied grabbing a notepad and a record book as she got up from her chair.

As I moved from the reception area towards the principal's

office, I began to feel the full power and control that Principal Sites held. The hallway leading to his office was covered in old photographs of him with various heads of state and an unmistakable picture of him shaking hands with former president Ronald Reagan. He had lived a very extraordinary life, and it appeared that he was using his final years to give back to the school. The hallway seemed to narrow as we stepped closer to his office door. Principal Sites, walking a few paces in front of me now, turned back to me as we approached his office. The rotund figure, dressed in a dark charcoal suit, stood patiently waiting. His cheeks sagged gently, tugged down by the passing lot of years. His hair was stark white.

"Hurry up then," Ms. Crisby said, nudging me from behind. I realized I had been moving even slower than I had previously thought.

Principal Sites opened the door to his office and stretched out his arm. "After you, Sylas."

"Thank you, sir." I swallowed hard, my mouth now void of all moisture.

"Take a seat," he said while he shuffled papers off his cluttered desk. "I have to apologize, this morning has been very busy for me. Where did I put--? Ah! Here it is. So…my grandson tells me you're the best photographer we have on the yearbook. Is that true?"

Completely caught off guard, I said, "That's very gracious. I don't know if I am the best, but I—"

"I appreciate your modesty, son. That's very admirable. This weekend we are hosting the Southern Hope Foundation fundraiser at the Clanton Grand Hotel…"

The Southern Hope Foundation was a charity organization that the Principal and a few other church board members had started on behalf of the school years ago. Some of its more notorious campaigns included establishing orphanages in Africa, providing meals for needy families in our community, and even providing free scholarships for underprivileged students. Principal Sites remained very humble about it, always contributing its generous missionary efforts and humanitarian outreaches as coming from the students of Cherrywood Christian Academy and never taking any credit for himself.

"…Governor Hawkins will be there, Ronald Harris, the

Chief of Police, and several other prominent people in the community. One of the missionaries who we have been supporting is here in town but his visit is short lived. I had hired a photographer to shoot the event for a little publicity, but unfortunately he called me over the weekend to cancel. Most of the other photographers in town all seemed to be booked with weddings, and one fellow I found in Raleigh who was available, was just way too expensive. I thought about Ms. Turner, your yearbook teacher, but, just between us...," he leaned forward in a whisper. "Grady has shown me some of your work and I personally like yours better. Plus she's a bit of a talker, and I need someone to work," he said out of the corner of his mouth.

A small snicker escaped Crisby's lips. Principal Sites looked over surprised. "I am so sorry," she whispered in her thick Carolinian drawl.

"Don't tell her I said that, although she'd probably agree with me," Sites said with a chuckle. "Would you be interested in shooting the event? Are you busy this Saturday around four?"

"Yes, sir." I said. "I mean no, sir. I'll photograph the event if you like. I'm not busy."

"It won't just be you, I am sure. Not much happens around here, so I am sure Channel 6 will be there, but you will be representing us. Think you can handle it?"

Ms. Crisby smiled and nodded her head at me with pride, seeming to have known all along.

"Wow! Gosh, thank you! I thought something was wrong. Ms. Crisby, you seemed so saddened when I first walked in the office." I immediately regretted talking out of turn, and feared that a discussion about the fireworks would surface. Her smile vanished and a look of concern came over her face.

"Yeah well, we're just dealing with a tough issue this morning," Sites interrupted. "Anyway, you have everything you need for the shoot this weekend?"

"Yes, sir."

"Good. Just bring us the receipts for any film purchases, and we'll reimburse you."

"Ok, I will!" I stretched out my hand to happily shake his for the opportunity.

"Ms. Crisby," Sites said, "if you would be so kind as to write an excuse to homeroom for Sy, I would appreciate it...Oh Sylas!"

Principal Sites said stopping me from fully opening the door.

"Yes, sir?" I answered.

"About Friday night. You don't know anything about that fireworks incident, do you?"

My vision blurred and I unknowingly inhaled as I tried to swallow, nearly choking myself. "No, sir....I was just taking photos when it happened."

There was a long pause as he studied my face. "Mmm. Eventful weekend, that's for sure," Principal Sites said, breaking into a smile. "Ok, that's all. Thank you, Sylas."

"Thank you, sir."

I turned and closed the door gently behind me. I still couldn't believe what had happened. Knowing that I had dodged a bullet, I was even more excited to realize that I would be able to add the governor and his family to the list of individuals I had photographed. I knew that in photography, especially starting out, it was not always about the quality of the photograph you produced, but the subject itself.

An announcement was made during lunch that a special chapel assembly would be taking place the following period. Usually reserved for Wednesdays at this time, the students would meet together for a time of prayer and reflection, paired with a message from the principal, guest speaker, or selected faculty. Whenever a special assembly did not fall on a Wednesday, however, it was generally bad news. It was a way for the principal to call the entire school into his office and that day, and most of us knew why.

From lunch, Cam and I headed to our chapel building, which shared a wall with East Wing and was designed to resemble a country wedding chapel. Cameron was the son of Clanton Baptist Church's audio/video technician. Clanton Baptist was the church affiliated with Cherrywood and Cam's father had worked there for eight years.

Cam wasn't your typical jock. He played sports, but he appreciated that I didn't care about most of them. He was one of the few cool kids to actually hang out with my group of friends, and in doing so, afforded me opportunities that I wouldn't have had otherwise. I got a behind the scenes look at the world of sports and popularity inside the Academy. I was protected from harm by Cam alone and knew that if he removed his shadow of protection from me, I would be at the mercy of the rest of the football team. He and I rarely talked about football or sports. We spent our time on the riverbanks, hiked trails, and made discoveries in our own backyards. He was a country boy at heart, and although he also lived a childhood filled with silver spoons and golden opportunities, he remained humble, simple, and kind.

Cry for Love, the new song by Michael W. Smith, was playing through the chapel sound system as we entered the auditorium. Playing upbeat, contemporary Christian music to begin a church service in an attempt to invoke excitement was a favorite technique of our school chapels and church youth groups. It never really worked for most of us, but it was a good try. The idea behind having chapel once a week was to keep us filled with the Holy Spirit and growing closer to the Lord. Tragically, for many of us, attending a church service during the week and one on weekends was sometimes an overload, despite the intentions of our leaders.

Golden rays of sun blended seamlessly into hues of jewel-toned light through the stained glass windows of the theatre-style chapel building. Each of us dropped our books, purses or backpacks onto or underneath a wooden pew and instinctively remained standing as our music teacher and school worship leader took the stage.

When the worship song ended, Principal Sites took the stage and then paused for a moment before asking: "So who made it to the Homecoming Game on Friday?"

Most of the student body, with nothing to fear, let out a jubilant cheer. Cam and I looked briefly at each other with nervous smirks. Several aisles over, Roscoe was visibly tense.

"Congratulations, Saints! Another dominating victory! We are what, six and o now?" he asked rhetorically. From the congregation, Tyler Sammons yelled, "Seven!"

"Seven and o, excellent, excellent! And Michael Bosley and Tina Garbaro, the new homecoming king and queen!" The student body cheered gingerly.

"And then of course, who could forget our famous fireworks show?" Dr. Sites stated as if it were not a question.

A mix of responses came from the students. Some whooped

and hollered. Some laughed. Others mumbled among themselves. Although I was still impishly smiling, I could feel more nerves creeping in. Cam remained confident though and kept his head forward, like he knew something I didn't. Dr. Sites' mood turned stern.

"Bear with me for a moment, I've got a few things I need to go over. For those who did not attend the game, I am sure you have heard what I'm talking about. I'm sure there have been a few rumors circulating over the weekend so let me silence a few of them and state that this was not an event planned by the staff but rather, this was a prank. This stunt was childish, caused several minor injuries, and showed a decided lack of character and maturity."

Cam and I looked forward to Dr. Sites, not allowing the words to break our poker-faced stares.

"May I remind all of you that pranks like these are not just dangerous and illegal but they also reflect a bad image on you, this Academy, and the God we serve," Dr. Sites continued. "Imagine how hard it would be for an employer or teacher to trust you if you did something like this? This could ruin relationships, maybe job opportunities, and our witness to others.

He paused for a moment to stare into the crowd to make sure we were all intently listening to his reprimand. We were. Then he changed moods once again.

"On to other matters. I'd like your continued attention for a moment. The fireworks display wasn't the only incident we had over the weekend. I'd like for us to come together as a school and pray for one of our fellow students. We were notified this morning that Rachel Ellis, a senior, is in the ICU today. Rachel is going through some tough times and needs our love, our support, and our prayers. "

A few heads turned, including mine, and some whispers escaped among the crowd. Cam leaned over and whispered in my ear, "Rumor has it she tried to kill herself."

I said nothing.

"Her father found her in the bathtub," he added. I gave him a confused look as he slowly gestured a slicing motion over each wrist.

My heart broke for her, although I didn't know why. Rachel had been my lab partner in Freshman Earth Science and also a classmate of mine in Calculus. She was a nice girl. She wasn't the most popular kid in school but she wasn't disliked by anyone. Kinda like me, I guess.

The crowd grew silent as Dr. Sites tried to find the words he was looking for.

"You know...when a person..." Dr. Sites stammered for a moment. Collecting his thoughts he began again. "When people try to escape their problems in a dangerous way, it usually means that they feel they have no other way out. And I'm sure some of you know Rachel very well so right now, especially, it's important for us to make her feel that she's loved and valued. And that's important to remember for all of you. High school can be tough, believe me, I've been there. But all of you are highly valued, and we as the administrative body will do everything we can to make sure you recognize that. So please, if you do know Rachel, maybe find some time to visit her, write her a card, do something to show her that she is loved. Let's go to God right now and ask for healing for Rachel."

Dr. Sites led us in a prayer for Rachel and asked God to help his students make good decisions. I agreed with him. Our fireworks stunt, although impishly well intentioned, was not a good decision. It had turned out to be far more disastrous than we planned, and it could have been a lot worse.

Chapel came to a close with softer, introspective music playing in the background. In the next aisle I saw Natalie Benson slowly filtering out of the auditorium with the exiting crowd of classmates. I had first noticed Natalie last spring at a soccer game. She had transferred to Cherrywood that year but, after she refused the initial advances of all the jocks going after the fresh meat, she was still on the market. Natalie was one of the stars of our women's soccer team. I guess she had been in gymnastics for most of her life, which really gave her a strong athletic advantage. At least, this was the scoop I got from her best friend when I started researching my newfound curiosity. After I first noticed her last spring, I did about one week of due diligence and confirmed that I indeed had an official crush.

"Ok, see ya later," I said to Cam, ducking out early to try to score a moment with her.

"Alright, see ya," he replied. At least, I think that's what he said. I was kind of paying attention to something else.

I casually pushed my way through the crowd. Playing it cool was important at this stage of the game. If I trampled over the crowd to get to her, I would look desperate and lose what few cool points I had. But if I didn't move quickly enough, she'd vanish into her next class without a trace. I kept careful track of the progress both of us were making and estimated that, by the time our respective rivers of students flowed together, we'd bump into each other before exiting the building.

But then my calculations came askew. A kid in my class had broken his leg three weeks prior racing his BMX bike and was on crutches. When he slowed down her line, I decided to briefly step out of mine to tie my shoe. Of course, it was already tied, but one can never be too safe.

This did just the trick. I jumped back into the exiting mass and Natalie did the same, entering into the main flow of students just a few feet in front of me. I enjoyed watching her hair sway back and forth as she walked. I could almost smell her shampoo. Outside, the sun reflecting off of the white sidewalk created a blinding light as if we were approaching a doorway to heaven. Natalie was the first to step through the door. I squinted to allow my eyes to adjust. She looked back at me and smiled. This was the chance I had been waiting for.

"Happy Monday," I gracelessly muttered. She smiled again. I dropped my head in embarrassment. That was a train wreck. I turned and walked towards my class and she walked towards hers.

I had blown it.

CHAPTER 4

The weather Saturday evening was perfect. Indian summer had come a little early this year, and with it, brought bright colors and short-sleeved temperatures. I had been on many photography assignments before, including a few wedding gigs, but this one felt the most official. Entering the Clanton Grand Hotel reception area, I was met with tall cathedral ceilings, marble floors, and exquisite hardwood furniture. A chandelier the size of our kitchen dangled from the massive ceilings and sparkled and glimmered from every angle. Moving my camera bag higher onto my shoulder, I proceeded towards a white paper sign that read "Southern Hope Foundation Fundraiser Suite Banquet Hall Four."

A few other black-tied guests walked in that direction. They looked rich, defined by wavy salt and pepper hair, expensive glasses, fancy ball gowns, and grinning faces. I felt underdressed and insignificant. I was merely the hired help and hardly that. Just a poor kid from across the river struggling to create a life for myself.

Around the corner and into the expansive banquet hall, most guests were hobnobbing with drinks and laughter. From the looks of the décor, fancy attire, and whimsical people, one might find it hard to believe the old saying that claimed money couldn't buy happiness. The most popular area of the room seemed to be the non-alcoholic cash bar, but the reception table came in a close second. I found a place in line and patiently waited for my turn to receive my table assignment.

"Name?" the lady asked when it was my turn.

"Sylas Ernst," I replied. "With an E."

"Ernst…" the lady mumbled as she scanned the guest list.

"I'm the photographer."

"Mmmm…I don't see you…let me check over here," she said as she grabbed another list. "You're the photographer?"

"Yes, ma'am."

"Ok, I don't see you on the service list…" she stated as she grabbed a third list.

"I'm here by request of Dr. Sites."

"Oh, Charles!" she said warmly. "Of course, let me see what I can do."

"Thank you, ma'am." A small line started to gather behind me. I already felt underdressed and out of place; now I was beginning to feel overlooked and in the way.

"Table Eighteen," she said with a smile. "There are still a few open chairs there."

"Ok, thank you."

I worked my way through the crowd in the ballroom. The stage was situated in the center of the room with life-sized PR photos of African orphans and the charitable work that Southern Hope had done. I snapped a quick photo of a well-to-do elderly couple examining the photographs with unbelieving eyes. On either side of the stage sat about thirty neatly set tables with an arrangement of sunflowers, Gerber daisies and roses as the centerpiece of each one.

Along the other side of the ballroom was an assortment of gift baskets, artwork, and prize items all generously donated by local businesses to support tonight's charity. Some of the more prestigious items were a sleek blue motorized scooter with whitewall tires, a brand new set of Titleist golf clubs, and a year membership to Locksboro Country Club. Invitees crowded around the tables eyeing up the different goods for auction and placing bids on their top choices. Out of curiosity, I stepped over to see the top bid on the scooter. I was a bit surprised to see it was only $75 so I wrote down my name on the sheet of paper and decided to gamble my savings, a hard-earned $225. I'd be ok with helping out a charity and winning a scooter for a really good price.

Surprisingly, I only recognized a handful of people in the room. I expected to see more people from school or church, but it seemed like only the affluent of our community were invited.

Governor Hawkins was there joking with Mr. Korta, a Cherrywood and Clanton Baptist board member. "Usually, I'm asking if I can count on people to vote for me," he was saying. "But this time, you can count on my vote."

"Sylas!" a man called from over my shoulder while I snapped a candid photo of people musing over the silent auction items.

I turned around to be surprised by Shawn's dad, Bruce. "Mr.

Lessner, hi!"

"You're taking pictures tonight?" Bruce asked.

"Yes, sir. Just building up my portfolio."

"Good to hear. There are some big players here so hopefully they'll make you look good."

"Yeah, I hope so."

"I saw you eyeing that scooter, did I not? Place a bid?"

"Yes sir."

"You bid more than my $50 bid?"

"I did, but if it makes you feel any better someone had already outbid you by $25."

"No kidding? Well if you are trying for it then I won't bid anymore."

"Thanks," I said, not knowing quite else what to say. Mr. Lessner or any other person here could buy that scooter outright. For me, this was my only chance to own something that nice.

"Well, I don't want to take you away from your job. Good luck and I'll see you around."

"Yes, sir."

Shawn's dad was a prominent member of the community so it came as no surprise that he was invited to this event. Bruce took a no-nonsense approach to life, love, and religion, or lack thereof. He did not give much time to feelings, and very few saw him for the man behind the briefcase. Shawn's mother left him years ago. She said that Shawn's father had changed, but Shawn had known early on the type of man his father was. That led him to held tight to the relationship he found with his mother, who had been his best friend until we met six years ago.

I moved out into the hallway to take more candid photos. The elevated mood made my job easy. There was no shortage of smiling and candid faces. Wearing a neat black tuxedo and honorable black tie, Principal Sites was talking to a guest when he spotted me snapping his photo.

"Sylas! Come on over, I want you to meet someone," he commanded.

"Hi, sir," I said, extending my hand for a handshake.

"Sy, this is Joe Knowles. He's a world-famous photographer."

Joe laughed. "I wouldn't say world-famous."

"This is the best photographer we've got at Cherrywood," Dr. Sites said. "He's taken some incredible photos."

Joe reached out to shake my hand. "Wow, the best in the school!"

"I don't know if I'd say that," I humbly responded. "Pleasure to meet you, Mr. Knowles."

"Joe flies all around the world photographing for magazines and everything," Dr. Sites said. "Celebrities, famous travel destinations, you name it."

"Mostly editorial stuff," Joe corrected.

"Cover of *Time* and *Newsweek* type stuff," Dr. Sites replied.

"Wow! That's amazing!" I said.

"If you're the best in the school, I'd love to see some of the photos you take of this event," Joe said. "I'll be back in December to snap a few photos at Senator Warren's Christmas ball and could use a second shooter. Maybe if your work is good enough, you could lend me a hand."

"Really? Yes, sir. I'd be happy to let you see my work. How should I get the photos to you?"

"Why don't you just deliver a few to Charles - "

"Yes, I'd be happy to pass the photos along," Dr. Sites interrupted.

"That'd be great!" I said. "Thanks!"

"You're very welcome. I look forward to seeing your shots."

"Of course! Well, I better keep shooting then," I said to which they both chuckled.

As if I weren't already excited to be photographing this event, I was now infused with even more passion to get some great material. After another twenty minutes or so, the emcee, an anchor for the local WSBT-6 channel news team, tapped on the microphone from inside the ballroom.

"Ladies and gentlemen," he said. "Ladies and gentlemen, if you could please find your seats. Dinner will be served in five minutes."

If most of these people were like me, they were starving but in order to maintain elegance, they moved slowly to their seats as not to let it show. The beautiful part about photographing an event where dinner is served is that no one wants their picture taken while they are eating. So when dinner is announced, my camera can go down and my fork can go up. It's one of the greatest perks about being a photographer, and my personal favorite.

Shortly thereafter, servers came out with house salads

followed ten minutes later by juicy cuts of tenderloin steak and broiled salmon. I could usually only afford to eat this well a few times a year. When the server placed the juicy cut of steak topped with asparagus and a red wine crème sauce in front of me, a bittersweet feeling of joy and guilt came over me—joy that I would soon be able to stuff my face with a most delicious assortment of food, and guilt that those orphan kids in the pictures probably never would.

As the servers were returning to clear the dirty dishes from the tables, the emcee once again took the stage. "How about that meal? Give the kitchen staff a round of applause," he stated as the room began to applaud. I returned my napkin from my lap onto the table and grabbed my camera again. Quietly, I moved along the perimeter, snapping pictures swiftly and without drawing an ounce of attention from the crowd.

"As most of you have already seen, we have so many wonderful sponsors to thank for helping make this evening a reality. I'd first like to thank the many generous businesses and individuals who donated all of the items up for auction this evening." He paused to let the crowd applaud one more time. "Of course, Clanton Grand has graciously allowed us to host tonight's event in this exquisite ballroom." Another round of applause. "And then our Platinum sponsors; Illustra, Pine House Financial Group, and Lakeside Chevrolet." Their logos appeared on the screen behind the podium while the crowd took another few moments to applaud.

"While these businesses are instrumental in providing the support for this event this evening, none of us would be here if it weren't for our next speaker. A man who needs very little introduction but I'll give him one anyway. He has a doctorate from NC State in Educational Leadership and Administration, served as a missionary in Cambodia for five years, was a public relations coordinator for U.S. Senator Mike Cooley, is currently Head Principal of Cherrywood Christian Academy and co-founder of the Southern Hope Foundation. Ladies and gentlemen, please welcome to the stage Dr. Charles Sites."

The crowd stood to recognize Dr. Sites as he stepped onto the stage and shook the emcee's hand. Appreciatively, he took the podium and paused for a moment before politely motioning for the crowd to take a seat.

"Thank you, Glen, and thank you all. Give yourselves a round of applause; you're the ones buying these items tonight."

"Six years ago a few friends and I came up with this idea to start a charity, but we wanted to take it one step further. We wanted to give the charity to a bunch of kids. We wanted to give credit for everything that the Southern Hope Foundation accomplished to the students who attend Cherrywood Christian Academy. My thought was that if the students feel like they weren't just going to school, but they were going to an institution that makes a difference, they would perform better and help to build some of the change that we so desperately need in this world.

"It was a long shot, but you know what? It worked. Our students are of a higher caliber than others their own age, because they have a higher calling and a higher purpose. So it comes as no surprise then that this year's class has a higher collective GPA than we have ever seen at the Academy and higher than any other school in the county!"

The crowd erupted in applause and stood again. I snapped pictures wildly, and then, with the dexterity of Billy the Kid, reloaded my camera with a fresh roll of 36 to shoot once again.

"We've done something for the students at Cherrywood to make them believe that they are a part of something big. This higher calling that we work each day to instill into these young minds translates to success both academically and athletically. Our scholastic scores are in the top fifth percentile in the state, and forgive me for shamelessly plugging our athletic program, but our championship football team remains undefeated!"

The crowd, still on its feet, laughed and applauded again. I maneuvered past a few tables to get a different angle of the stage. "I know we're here tonight to support Southern Hope, but as someone who is playing both sides of the field, I can tell you that this foundation is doing more good than you might realize. We're giving kids futures, not just overseas, but in our own community. I can't thank you enough for supporting such an important program, so allow me to introduce missionary and boots on the ground, Jeremy Maitland, to tell you what the kids of Cherrywood Christian Academy have done!"

Still standing, the crowd applauded again. A man stepped onto the stage and shook hands with Principal Sites. He looked familiar, but I couldn't pinpoint where I'd seen him.

"Thank you very much," he said as he took the podium. He turned around to applaud the Principal. "And thank you to Charles and the kids over there at Cherrywood Christian Academy. He's done an incredible job." More applause.

"Thank you," he said nodding as the guests slowly began to take their seats. "As Charles said, my name is Jeremy Maitland, and I'm the Overseas Representative for the Southern Hope Foundation. On Wednesday we returned from a month-long assignment in Nairobi, Kenya where we are continuing our work with an orphanage that we helped build just over five years ago. Kenya has about one million orphans, most of them orphaned due to AIDS. In fact, Kenya has the third highest number of HIV/AIDS orphans in the world. Five years ago, we partnered with a few other organizations to build our orphanage, and within just three months we were caring for over four hundred children."

A projection screen lowered behind him, the lights dimmed, and a slide show presentation began. The first few slides revealed some disturbing images of the living conditions in Kenya: kids sleeping on the street, orphans playing in a sewage ditch that ran through the middle of the city, and bone-thin children and animals drinking the same muddy water. It was heart-wrenching to see those conditions and hear Jeremy explain the poverty and hopelessness that those kids were facing on a daily basis. The crowd was silent and glued to Jeremy's presentation. Then a photo of a dirty little boy staring blankly into the camera appeared on screen.

"This is Kutu, but we called him Rusty," Jeremy said. "He is four years old and his parents both died of AIDS. When we found Kutu, he was living at the landfill just outside of the slums and was surviving on scraps of food that he would find among the trash. He was frightfully malnourished and on the brink of death."

A few gasps and disturbed faces emanated from above the tables. Jeremy changed the slides a few times to show Kutu's life at the orphanage. "He was treated with vaccinations to spare him from diseases like giardia, malaria, and typhoid and given his very first toy, a blue softball, which he takes with him wherever he goes."

In the next slide, Kutu was singing and playing a tambourine.

"Kutu is six now and has been with us for two years. He loves to sing, so every Sunday at show-and-tell time, he always sings and plays the tambourine. Usually he sings the same song over and over but all the kids love Kutu. He has made such a big impact on everyone there."

The crowd smiled fondly, and several of the ladies wiped away tears. I grabbed a few photos of the emotional presentation, the audience, and Jeremy. "When you donate funds to help continue the work of Southern Hope, you help save children like Rusty. It's because of you that we are able to help so many and on behalf of these children, I thank you from the bottom of my heart. Please give generously tonight and thank you for your support."

Once again, the crowd stood to its feet and applauded. The lights came up as Jeremy walked off stage and shook hands with Principal Sites, who was sitting at a front table. I squeezed the shutter at the perfect moment. This could have been the best photo of the night.

The events continued for another hour. A professional auctioneer directed a live auction of some other high-dollar items, all in all raising around $20,000. After the winners of the silent auction were announced, it was disclosed that close to $50,000 had been raised for the Southern Hope Foundation that night. The mood was excitable and the atmosphere encouraging. The fundraiser had been a monumental success.

After I packed my camera bag and headed to the lobby, I was finally able to ignore the demands of work and let my mind reflect on the inspirational evening. I hoped to be like some of these men when I got older. Most of these guests had created successful businesses and were using that success to further other humanitarian efforts. Tonight was not about religion. It was about doing good. One man paid $10,000 for a local artist's painting, simply so that he could help those less fortunate. That kind of money was something my dad had to work half the year for, and with my part time job, it would take me nearly a full year. I hoped that one day I could display the selflessness and generosity that some of those men did.

A voice from behind me broke me away from my thoughts.

"You can pick up the scooter anytime next week, Bruce."

I turned around, a bit unsure of what I had just heard.

"Thank you, Miles. I know my girlfriend will love it," Shawn's dad said while he turned back around to coincidentally catch my gaze.

"Sylas!" He said walking towards me. He leaned over my shoulder and talked softly into my ear.

"I stopped back by the table. You had already been outbid, so I took another shot at it. I ended up getting it for about half the price of retail!"

"That's great." I said, trying to sound excited for him.

"I'm sorry Sylas, but it's all about the orphans right? Well, I'll see you later, big guy. Tell Shawn I said hello."

"Big guy?" I repeated back to myself.

I pushed open the large front door and zipped my jacket up a little tighter. As I meandered through the parking lot to my car, my mind started to reflect on something else – the slideshow. Perhaps it was because I was a photographer or maybe it was because I was a bit more observant than most, but something about it struck me as strange. The photos didn't seem to have any similarity to them. Some of them were brilliantly composed and taken with high quality lenses. Postcard photographs of giraffes, villagers, and the picturesque savanna. Yet others seemed to be taken with a disposable point-and-shoot, like they were merely vacation photos taken by an amateur. Jeremy told us that the team's photographer took the photos, but they clearly did not have the markings of one common artist.

Blink 182 blared from the speakers and startled me once I started the car. I quickly turned down what my school would consider musical contraband and threw the camera bag and tripod onto my passenger seat. But just before leaving the parking lot, another curious thought came to mind.

Jeremy had showed pictures and slides for about twenty minutes to explain what he and his team were doing in Africa. He said he had been there for a whole month. But out of the fifty or so photos in the presentation, why hadn't he been in a single one of them?

CHAPTER 5

Shawn and I had pretty similar schedules, partly because of careful planning but mostly because of dumb luck. Shawn had already gotten to Mr. Oakridge's fourth period Bible class before me, so he saved me a seat in our usual spot—far right of the class, four rows back, on the opposite side of the room as Grady Sites. I liked this point of view because it allowed us to observe everyone in the class, their expressions, and at times, their confusion.

"Good morning, my free thinkers," Mr. Oakridge said walking through the door and commanding the attention of the whole class.

Mr. Oakridge, a late thirty-something nonconformist with a neat goatee, stylish glasses and hip collection of ties and sweater vests, was different from any other instructor at the Academy. He had a charismatic way of speaking to say the least, jumping from celebrity impressions, to every type of humor imaginable. But Mr. Oakridge's teaching style wasn't the only thing that set him apart. In a sea of creamy white-faced faculty, Mr. Oakridge was profoundly black. We were a bit unsure how he became an instructor here. Usually the jobs went to individuals with the right name, right pedigree, or right credentials. Mr. Oakridge had none of that but did possess an unwavering love and dedication to his students. In an occupation that can become so muddled with meetings, regulations, curriculums and salaries, he never took his eye from his purpose of helping his students learn.

"Jessica Tinsley," Mr. Oakridge shouted.

"Eeek!" Jessica squealed dropping her books with astonishment. The class laughed at her startled response.

"What do you believe?"

"Uhh...what?" she replied perplexed.

"Fair enough, let me phrase my question a different way. Why do you believe what you believe?"

"Like...what do you mean?" she questioned nervously.

"Do you believe in Santa Claus?"

"Nooo..." she said apprehensively. The rest of the class sat confused and shared her nerves. All of us hoped that he wouldn't call on us next.

"Why not?"

"Umm, I...I don't know. My mom told me he wasn't real, I guess..." she stated with nervous laughter.

"Why doesn't your mom think he's real?"

"Probably because she's the one who hides the presents."

"Santa's not real?" Jonathan Farlow sarcastically remarked. Some of the class spurted guarded laughter.

Mr. Oakridge smiled and then turned back to Jessica. "What if he just doesn't come to your house for some reason but visits everyone else's? What if you've just been naughty? Why should you believe your mom?"

"I don't know..." she said, stumped.

"Michael. What do you believe?" Mr. Oakridge asked his next helpless victim.

I turned around to watch Michael Simmons squirm.

"I-I believe the sky is blue." Michael stammered.

"Interesting approach," Mr. Oakridge paused for a moment. "Do you believe, or do you know?"

"I - I know it's blue," he said with hesitant confidence.

"Really? How?"

"Yeah, because I can see that it's blue."

"How do you know you're not color blind and that the sky is really green?" Mr. Oakridge fired back.

"Because I can see other things that are blue and other people agree with me."

"How do you know all the people who agree with you aren't color blind?"

"Because...they're not..." Michael answered with confused hesitation.

"But can you be absolutely sure?"

Michael considered his words very carefully but ultimately was left with a simple answer. "No," he admitted.

"Mr. Jonathan," Mr. Oakridge said, turning towards Jonathan Farlow, sitting motionless in his seat. "You were so anxious to talk before. What do you believe?"

Without blinking, Jonathan stared into Mr. Oakridge's eyes and semi-jokingly said, "Jeeesuus." Every kid in the class knew that this was the textbook, Christian response to almost any spiritual question that you didn't know the answer to.

"Splendid! Please tell me, how did you arrive at this conclusion?"

"I just did."

"Do you believe He exists or do you know He exists?"

"I know He exists."

"No you don't," Mr. Oakridge shot back, leaving the classroom silent. "How do you know He exists?"

"Well, from what you teach us," he remarked humorously. The class laughed.

"So you believe everything that you're told?"

"No."

"Why do you believe what I say then?"

Kayce Hall threw up her hand.

"Yes, Miss Hall, perhaps you could shed some light on this conversation."

"John 3:16. 'For God so loved the world that He gave his only begotten Son, that whosoever *believes* in him shall not perish—'" She made sure to put special emphasis on the word 'believes' in an attempt to make her point more valid.

Mr. Oakridge smirked and turned his back on Kayce, reaching for a brown book from his desk. After taking a moment to find a dog-eared page he read, "He sent the Messenger Muhammad reciting to you the distinct verses of Allah that He may bring out those who *believe* and do righteous deeds from darkness into the light. And whoever believes in Allah and does righteousness - He will admit him into gardens beneath which rivers flow to abide therein forever. Allah will have perfected for him a provision. Surat At-Talaq 65:11."

The entire class was even more deathly silent than before. We had never heard such words spoken. Even I felt a bit uneasy in his classroom. Where was the fun-loving teacher we all knew and loved?

"Most of you probably drove here today. Do you know that you will be driving home again this afternoon? Do you know if your car will be in the parking lot this afternoon? Do you even know if there will be an afternoon?" He paused and silence filled the room like some heavy invisible presence. "No, you don't. You believe that all these things will happen because they've been happening for weeks; so you've got good reason to, but you don't know for sure. You put your faith in these things just like Jonathan puts his faith in Jesus and Michael has faith that the sky is blue. Does Michael have good reason to believe the sky is blue? Sure. He sees it, everyone else sees it, science says so, and no one thinks otherwise. So he's got good reason to believe that the sky is blue. Does Jonathan have good reason to believe in Jesus?" He shrugged his shoulders and said, "I don't know."

He made his way around the classroom, and stood beside my desk. Then, in barely a whisper, he began to address the class again.

"Every worldview gives promise to something. My question remains: why do you believe what you believe? Many of you have grown up believing the words preached in this book," he said holding up my worn copy of the Bible. "But why? Because it was taught to you by your parents? Jessica's parents told her Santa wasn't real, but we just found out that she doesn't know if they are right or not. What if you were born Muslim and you learned this book instead?" he said holding up the book he had just read from. "The passage I just read was from the Quran. How many of you have ever read it?"

Not a single hand was lifted.

"Here is a better question," he added. "How many of you have read this book?" he said holding up my Bible again.

Two people slowly raised their hands. I wished with all my heart that I was one of them, as Mr. Oakridge returned my Bible to my desk and walked back to the front of the class. "Two of you, out of twenty-eight have read this book, and yet all of you put your faith into it."

I looked around the room and I realized that I was the only one still making eye contact with Mr. Oakridge. The rest of the class hung their heads in guilt and reflection.

"Why do you pick that book to believe? Why not the other? Why neither of them? Socrates said, 'The unexamined life is not worth living.' We are told in first Peter to always be able to give an account for what we believe. By the end of this year, I hope you are able to do just that."

Charity England raised her hand timidly.

"Yes Miss Charity?"

"I believe in God and the power of Jesus Christ to heal a person's life because of the change I have seen in my father. He used to be angry and bitter but after he found salvation, he was a different person."

The story tugged on Mr. Oakridge's heartstrings—we could all see it—and he cracked a smile because someone was finally speaking from their heart and not from their well-rehearsed mind.

"That's referred to as experiential evidence and under the right circumstances, can build a strong case for what you believe. Thank you for sharing."

Charity smiled timidly and rested back in her chair.

"Okay," Mr. Oakridge said. "Things have gotten a little heavy this morning. I think we need to mix things up a bit here. Everyone pair up with someone next to you."

Dennis Weaver began to turn around to me, and in an instant I turned back to Shawn. "Wanna be my Par—"

"Yep!" Shawn said interrupting me. I had paired up with Dennis before on an English assignment and was left doing more than my share of the work. I was not going to repeat that.

Mr. Oakridge grabbed a small blue velvet bag from his vintage brown leather attaché case. "I've got fourteen different faith systems in this bag which make up the majority of the worldviews out there. Most any faith system about where we came from, what we're here for, et cetera, can be derived from these major ones. And just like how we need to have faith even in something as simple as driving home this afternoon, each one of these religions or worldviews requires faith. None of these are absolutely provable. So starting now, we are going to try to break down which one of these might be right. Hopefully one of them is because if no one on earth has the correct answer, we're probably all in trouble.

"Now once you pick a worldview, it is your responsibility to thoroughly read up on what you believe if you were to subscribe to that way of thinking. From there, you will submit a thorough outline of each of your belief systems. Then, after everyone has presented, the whole class will attack your worldview like a gang of spider monkeys to see if it has any validity. To make things a bit simpler for you, we will cover each of them in class, one by one starting next week with Atheism. Till then, I checked out at least one book from our library on each worldview to give you each a jumping off point."

Mr. Oakridge started in the front of the class and weaved his way in and out of the rows, although curiously skipping by Shawn and me. When everyone else had selected a worldview from the bag, he looked back at me and remarked, "Did I forget you guys? I'm sorry."

Swinging back around to me, he held out the bag for me to reach inside. There was only one piece of paper left. I removed the yellow slip of paper and unfolded it carefully. To my surprise, there was scribbled a belief system I didn't expect: Christianity.

I had been working for Mr. Winters for a little over two years. Winters' Printing, owned by Cherrywood board member James Winters, had a long history with Cherrywood and Clanton Baptist. All of the church's promotional materials and bulletins, as well as our high school yearbooks, made up a sizable portion of Winters' business.

My first two summers were spent stuffing envelopes and folding mailers. Then, when Mr. Winters agreed to allow me to work for two hours after the school day, I graduated to packaging and processing orders. When a client would make an order and the graphics team had laid out the images, I would be the one to organize the work order in the system and send it through the manufacturing process. Most recently, I was allowed to process my own film, which for an artist, was a huge perk. I had 100% control over every image that I ever created, which is something very few photographers can say.

At work, I developed the high-profile film that I shot that weekend, along with the low-profile film I shot at the homecoming game. I was anxious to get home and show it to my mom whom had always encouraged my photography. She was cleaning in the kitchen when I arrived home, and my dad was sitting in the living room watching the news.

"...A new bill could require more detailed accounting requirements for businesses and charities when filing their state tax returns this year, but not all business owners are pleased with the added government watch..." the local news anchor droned as I walked in the door.

"Hi," I greeted.

"Sylas," my dad said acknowledging my presence from the

couch.

From the kitchen, my mom answered, "Hi, Sy. How was your day?"

"Pretty good," I replied.

Halfway into the kitchen, my father called me back. "Take a seat, Sylas," he said.

He turned off the television with the remote while our dog Buck stood up from the floor next to my dad and walked towards me. I scratched Buck's chest and rubbed his belly as my father began.

"How have you been?" my dad asked.

Once again, this was another question that seemed innocent enough, but had the potential to turn the conversation sour very quickly. Although, I believe at times he genuinely wanted to help me, his idea of help was to pinpoint flaws in my life and give Biblical instruction on how to remedy my misguided ways. As always, I had to choose my words very carefully.

"Fine. School is busy," I said.

"Spending enough time in prayer?"

"Um, yes."

Somehow this question always took me off guard. Prayer was a personal thing to me, which I usually did in the car, the shower or a walk in the woods. Having someone address such a personal topic made me feel a bit uneasy.

"Martin Luther once said, '*I have so much to do today that I'm going to need to spend three hours in prayer in order to be able to get it all done.*'"

"I guess three hours of prayer is doable when it's your job," I mumbled.

That came out the wrong way. My father was raw about not having a church of his own and my comment just added salt in to the wound.

"It *is* my job, Sylas," he replied noticeably upset, "and it should be yours, too. You need to focus on what is most important in life instead of running around all the time with your friends. I can teach you some things, you know, if you weren't too hard-headed to learn them."

My father stood up and childishly walked into his bedroom. Under my breath, I muttered, "The apple doesn't fall far from the tree."

I shook it off, relaxing my shoulders as I walked into the kitchen to greet my mother.

"Hey Mom, I developed the photos of the governor and everyone I took on Saturday. Dr. Sites is gonna show them to a guy I met who takes photos for *Time* and *Newsweek!* If they're good, he might even let me shoot with him! Do you want to see them?" I asked her.

"Oh, you did? Of course, let's take a look at them."

My mother had been a nurse for nearly forty years, most of which had been spent in nursing homes and long-term care facilities, caring for the chronically sick and terminally ill. A plump and happy-go-lucky sort of woman, her profession reflected her character. She was selfless and as my father continued to look for a church to call his own, she was the primary provider of the family.

After she scolded me for throwing my backpack on her freshly cleaned kitchen counter, I dropped my bag to the floor and grabbed out the four envelopes of prints, making sure to keep the homecoming photos still hidden.

"Ok, here is the ballroom," I started, showing her the first photo I had taken of the Clanton Grand ballroom.

"Oh my. That's gorgeous. What is all that stuff back there?"

"Those are the silent auction tables. They had a lot of things for people to bid on."

I continued to explain the night's events, showing pictures of the Governor, Mayor Bishop, and perfectly timed photos of people laughing and enjoying themselves.

"This was the Representative for Southern Hope giving the main presentation," I said, introducing the photos of Jeremy Maitland. He just got back from a missions trip to Kenya and showed a slideshow of his trip."

"Oh, look at that little boy in the picture," she said fondly.

"Yeah, that kid's name was Rusty. Kulu or Kotu or something, in his language. He was one of the orphans that Southern Hope's orphanage helps. They found him in a garbage dump and gave him giardia and malaria vaccines and stuff to help save his life."

"Oh, wow. They probably didn't give him giardia vaccines, but that's really great," she said still looking fondly at my well-composed photo within a photo.

"I'm pretty sure that's what Jeremy said. Why wouldn't they have given him a giardia vaccine?"

"Because there's no such thing," she chuckled, looking up at me, then back down at my photos. "There's no vaccine for malaria either. Just pills."

Puzzled, I responded, "Hmm. Maybe I misheard him. Anyway, this is the last part of his presentation. Look at this photo of Jeremy shaking hands with Dr. Sites."

"Oh, that's a good one."

"Yeah, it's my favorite, too."

I continued showing her the rest of my photographs without giving much thought to anything else but homework and snacks the rest of the evening. It wasn't until I was lying in bed that evening, looking up at my lath and plaster ceiling while waiting for sleep that my mind started churning again.

Something about Jeremy's presentation still seemed off to me. I couldn't put my finger on it. I thought he mentioned malaria and giardia vaccines, but I could've been wrong. But he definitely wasn't in any of those slideshow photos, which...I don't know...was still a little weird to me. And then that got me thinking about something else. I had seen this guy before. But where? I felt like it was recently, too. I mulled it over in my head for a minute but couldn't figure it out. Pulling the covers up closer to my head, I buried my head deeper into my pillow, already feeling my eyes getting heavier.

The homecoming game! The homecoming game? Is that where I saw this Jeremy guy? The thought snapped me awake with a surge of adrenaline.

I quickly threw my head back up. It seemed like I might have asked him to move when I went to sit down on the bleachers. He was sitting on the aisle, and when I asked him to "pardon me," he looked up and we made eye contact. But that doesn't make sense because he said that he got back from Kenya just a few days ago; on Wednesday, I think it was. I guess I could have misheard that too, but I thought he said Wednesday. Still, I'm pretty sure I remembered seeing him at the game last week.

I jumped out of bed and turned on the lights. Wearing nothing but my wife-beater and boxer shorts, I went over to my cluttered desk and found the packs of photos I had developed from the game. I always kept all of my photos in chronological order so I opened up pack number two and started to rifle through.

Finding roughly the moment in time that I thought I saw

him, I carefully went through each one from the time we lit the fireworks until the very end. At the moment when I entered the opposite side of the stadium and began taking pictures wildly in order to uphold my alibi, that's when I found him.

In the background of one of my crowd photos, dressed in a Saints' sweatshirt and far away from any staff or faculty, exactly where I remember seeing him, was Jeremy Maitland. He wasn't in Kenya last week.

He had been right here in Clanton.

CHAPTER 6

My father graduated seminary yet ironically never went to church with us. Actually, he hardly went to church at all. He said it is because Pastor Samms' teachings were not Biblically sound, but I surmised that he just didn't like people.

My mom and I walked the white sidewalks to Clanton Baptist Church, passing by our Lead Pastor Samms' sleek Mercedes S-class; a gift he had sheepishly accepted from the board after Southern Hope and Clanton Baptist finally completed construction on their Kenyan orphanage earlier that year. Cherrywood was labeled as a Christian school and not segmented into a denomination, but the church affiliated with it was proudly Baptist.

Cherrywood Christian Academy initially started as a church ministry back in the 50's, before it broke off and became its own entity thirty years later. Many of the school board members also served on the church board. It was the largest and most expensively constructed church in town and very mainstream compared to the other sleepy chapels around. Joel Samms, the trendy-looking pastor in his mid-forties who lived in luxurious Breaker Heights Estates, always bragged that everyone in town was a member since their membership numbers and Clanton's population were roughly the same. That was about nine thousand people, but I know that they fudged the books a little. My brother was still listed as a member even though he moved away three years ago.

Clanton Baptist had a regular Sunday attendance of nearly two thousand, which met during two separate services. They had three different youth groups for various age levels, twelve or more different community outreach programs, and the excitement inside was palpable. The décor, music, and even the technology were state-of-the-art. Joel often used PowerPoint, which was cutting edge technology, to display his teachings on a big screen. It was very modern which was no doubt the contributing factor to Clanton Baptist's status as the largest church in the region.

The upbeat music blared out of the front doors like a rock concert when my mom and I approached. There were always two people to greet guests at the front door. One was handing out church bulletins and the other shook your hand to welcome you which, having a nurse as a mother, I found rather disgusting, actually. The greeter had touched everyone's hand in the entire church and probably spread more germs than the puking babies in the nursery. However, you still had to be cordial and accept his handshake.

"Do you have any hand sanitizer?" I asked my mom as we entered the main foyer.

"I think so," she replied as she rummaged through her purse.

We meandered among all the smiling, freshly-showered people into the main sanctuary where the worship team, a group of twenty-and-thirty-somethings, rocked out on stage to an overplayed worship song. The stage was decorated differently that week with sleek looking geometrical shapes illuminated by changing colors of light to accompany the music. Everyone in the congregation was clapping their hands to the beat and delighting in the emotionally charged atmosphere. Like the chicken and the egg question, I've always wondered which came first: the belief or the emotion. Was the congregation really excited to be in church, and the large production was simply a reflection of that? Or was the congregation being emotionally stimulated and egged on by the grandeur of the whole thing?

Glancing around the room, I saw a few of the church regulars. In the front row, the next aisle over from the sign-language interpreter, sat Edmund McBryer and his mother. Edmund, with his chubby frame and thick, brown-rimmed glasses, lived near Roscoe in the only completed house of the failed subdivision of Glenwood Estates. We hung out in the subdivision often and were actually planning to meet there that afternoon. None of us knew quite what was wrong with the mentally impaired Edmund. There were rumors that he was an autistic savant. Other people cruelly called him a retard. As a grown man who enjoyed spending his time with the kids at the public pool, playing mini-golf or grabbing snow-cones with his mom, his hobbies also left some church members wondering if he wasn't perhaps somewhat of a pervert as well. Whoever he was, he was extremely OCD, needing to sit in the same pew and always arrive exactly twenty-five minutes before the service every single Sunday.

We got through four or five worship songs, all taking us on the emotional journey from joyful to contemplative to victorious. I was never really that big on singing. I wasn't that good at it and didn't do it very often so singing in church always felt a little off to me. Still, I went along with it because I thought it was what God wanted. Wearing blue jeans, stylish shoes, and a fashionable dress shirt, Pastor Samms walked out on stage as the last song came to a climax. The excitement was palpable, the crowd was charged, and it felt like we were about to watch *American Gladiators*. He tapped the worship leader on the back and charismatically spoke into his small headset mic—the type that an infomercial salesman would wear.

"God is so good, isn't he?" he rhetorically asked the congregation.

He received a few yeses and a lot of confident mm-hhmms from the crowd.

"Isn't he?" he rhetorically asked again in a louder tone.

The crowd grew louder with emphatic agreement.

"God, we come to you today as your humble servants," he started in prayer, closing his eyes. The rest of us also all instinctively bowed our heads and closed our eyes.

After he finished praying, he proceeded to give an entertaining, yet somewhat shallow message from the book of Acts. I never understood why Mr. Oakridge's Bible class and church could feel so different, yet teach from the same material. I also didn't understand who decided that twenty minutes of expected singing followed by a passing of the offering plate and a forty-five minute guilt-inducing sermon was the appropriate formula God wanted us to follow on Sunday mornings. But that's how it was, and that's how it had always been.

No one asked questions. We just followed along and went through the motions.

The failed housing development of Glenwood Estates, which we fondly dubbed "Chernobyl," was a fifty-acre parcel of land that a local contractor began to develop back in the 80's, maybe even around the same time as the Ukrainian nuclear plant disaster. It was our home away from home. When the contractor died shortly after the project began, his five adult children inherited the land, but while they feuded over how to divide the property among themselves, construction halted, leaving a suburban ghost town.

The acreage had been cleared and marked for roads, sidewalks, and utilities, but tall grass, weeds, and saplings had long reclaimed it. Only eight homes had been started in the subdivision, but most of them stopped at various levels of construction. Wild vines seized the brick pillars and windows. Every house was desolate except for one: 18 White Birch Lane.

That was Edmund's place, where he lived with his mother. It was the only home in the development that was both completed and purchased by a third party. There were no vines on that house and no overgrowth in the front yard. Edmund's OCD kept it a snapshot of Stepford perfection among the decaying shell of a community.

Chernobyl sat behind Roscoe's neighborhood, and as the leaves continued to fall from the trees, it could be seen increasingly clearer from his back porch. Often calling on Roscoe's dad for driving assistance, Edmund loved Roscoe's family, especially his little sister Lily. He had seen her grow from babyhood, and six years later he was still smitten by her rosy cheeks and gap-toothed smile. Occasionally, Edmund would give her a gift from his toy collection. This often needed to be supervised, as Edmund did not know that sewing needles and a half-used box of aluminum foil weren't appropriate gifts for a kindergartener. Being the kindhearted people they were, the Martins were always very welcoming of Edmund, although Roscoe never fully trusted him.

About a hundred yards away from Edmund's house and only a short deer trail away from Roscoe's backyard sat a partially completed starter home. The abandoned shell of a split-entry style house had been framed, roofed, and securely wrapped in Tyvek. Quality dual-pane windows and steel exterior doors had been installed to keep it secure shortly before it had been abandoned nearly nine years ago. We had known about the ghost town and this house for years, but it wasn't until our sophomore year that we finally developed the courage to step inside. We first started by brazenly slipping in through an unlocked window until last year when we finally became so comfortable that we bought a new lockset at Sanderson's Hardware and changed the lock, enabling us to come and go as we pleased. It had become our grown-up fort and a retreat from parents, school, and responsibilities.

"Shawn and Cam are already over there," Roscoe said as he met me in his driveway while I parked my car behind Shawn's. He was waiting at his house for me to arrive so we could both walk over to Chernobyl together and join the rest of the guys.

Roscoe's real name was Jake Martin, and he was one of the best guys I knew. He got his nickname because when he was a freshman, he saw a postcard somewhere of the gorgeous Beartooth Mountain Range near Roscoe, Montana. From that day on, he continually promised himself that he would visit there someday. He was honest and although at times socially awkward, he kept his word and truly had a good heart. I once saw him give his sandwich to a kid who just got his stolen from a bully. Roscoe was one of the kindest guys I knew, but he did have some quirks. For instance, he could be irrational. If something set him off, then he would snap. He was not very brave, but when he was angry nothing could stop him. Much like the character of Two-Face from my old Batman comics, Roscoe's heart could turn at the flip of a coin.

One time when we were sophomores, Roscoe saw some bullies making fun of his little sister, Lily. Lily was born with very poor eyesight and was just a few steps away from being considered legally blind. She wore large, coke-bottle glasses that allowed her to see but sadly were entirely too large for her face. Roscoe had always been protective of his little sister, but because of her failing eyesight, he felt an even greater sense of duty.

The minute he saw them picking on her, Roscoe bolted towards the bullies without thinking, dropped his backpack, and began cursing like a sailor. It was a total disaster. He lifted one kid up by his throat before slamming him back down, and then when the bully's two friends got up and tried to escape, he grabbed a nearby chair and hurled it at them, knocking another one to the ground. I had to grab his arm and yell at him for a moment before Mr. Hyde finally left him and Dr. Jekyll returned. He was suspended from school for a week for that. He would've gotten expelled had it not been for my heartfelt testimony that he was merely protecting Lily. He had developed a little more self-control as the years passed by, but I would always worry that someday he would do something that my best heart-felt testimony wouldn't fix.

When we finally made it to Chernobyl, we found Cam and Shawn hanging out on the old plaid, wool couch we had rescued from a dumpster earlier that summer. Their feet were propped up on the makeshift coffee table that we had assembled from an old wood pallet and four five-gallon buckets, and they were munching on Pringles and Gushers.

"What took you so long?" Cam asked. "Come on, we want to see the pictures."

I pulled the much-anticipated photographs from the Homecoming Game out of my backpack, and we all quickly crowded around the couch to take them all in.

For about five minutes, we eagerly browsed through the pictures, starting with a photo of Shawn and Cam unloading the fireworks contraption and ending with a picture of a terrified fat man running with his jelly rolls frozen in time. We were in tears from laughter, and I was enjoying the comedy, although I had already spoiled this moment for myself by peeking at a few photos while they were being developed.

"That is freakin' awesome!" Roscoe declared, distributing high fives, when we had gotten through the last envelope. "Well done, everybody. And none of the faculty know anything, do they?"

"Not a soul," Shawn said.

"Actually, hold on," I said. "There's one more thing that I want to show you guys." I reached into my backpack to find another packet of photos. "I took some photos at that Southern Hope Fundraiser last week, ya know?"

"Oh yeah, my dad won a scooter or something at that thing," Shawn said. "How did that go?"

"It was good. Mostly just a bunch of rich people." I thumbed through the photos from my backpack as I continued, "So the keynote speaker there was a guy named Jeremy Maitland. Anyway, he's the Representative for Southern Hope, ok?"

They were all paying attention to my story as I found the photo I was looking for. "That's him right there," I said showing them a photo of Jeremy speaking on stage at the charity event. "He told this story about how he was living in Kenya for a month on this missions trip and working with the orphanage that they started over there...the orphanage that Pastor Samms was raising money to buy solar panels for last Spring. Hey Roscoe, can I see those photos right there?"

"Yeah sure," he said, tossing me the pack from the homecoming game that he had still been holding.

"And check this out," I added. "He said he got back from this trip on Wednesday. Like, not this past Wednesday but the one before that. Well, hold on one minute," I said while I took some time to find the photo that I was looking for. "Here we go. Look right here." Holding up the photo of Jeremy at the homecoming game, I pointed to him in the background and exclaimed, "Look. He's right there!"

They didn't seem as shocked as I thought they'd be. They mostly just seemed confused.

"The homecoming game was two weeks ago," I said, hoping they'd catch on. "Five days before last Wednesday when he said that he got back from his trip!"

"Whoa, that's weird," Roscoe replied.

"So?" Shawn questioned.

"Well, obviously he wasn't in Kenya if he was at the game."

"Maybe he got his days mixed up."

Cam took a closer look at the photo and replied, "I've seen that guy before. Yeah, his photo is on the Wall of Fame outside the locker room. He used to play football for Cherrywood, I think."

"Really?"

"Yeah. Back in the 80's or something. I didn't know his name though."

"There were a few other things that seemed off, too," I continued. "He said that Southern Hope helps give kids malaria and giardia vaccines, but my mom just told me that there's no such thing."

"Really?" Roscoe asked.

"Isn't giardia when you get the runs from drinking river water?" Cam asked. "They call it beaver fever, right?"

"Yeah. So there's more. He showed a bunch of photos in this presentation he gave but he wasn't in a single one of them. Why would a guy who lived overseas for a month not have any photos of himself?"

"Maybe he was the one taking the photos," Shawn mused.

"No, he said that they were taken by the team's photographer. And what about this?" I went on, suddenly finding it very important that they understand my concern. "If your mom took a photo and I took a photo, could you tell which one was mine and which one was hers?"

"Yeah. Hers would have her thumb in front of it," Shawn joked while we all laughed.

"Exactly. Because each photographer has their own look, right? Well, these photos were all very different. Some were really high quality, and others kinda stunk. I don't think they came from just one guy."

"Hey, you know what else is kinda sketchy?" Cam interrupted. "Did you know they're kicking Rachel Ellis out of the Academy?"

"What? Why?!" Shawn asked.

"Yeah, my dad heard from someone at school that since suicide is self-murder, the board won't allow an attempted murderer to continue studying at the Academy."

"Attempted murderer?" Shawn exclaimed. "It was a cry for help, not an act of violence!"

"Attempted murderer is *really* harsh," I answered.

"That's bogus. She obviously needs love; that's what Dr. Sites said in the assembly. Why aren't they offering that?" Shawn asked.

"This wouldn't have happened at a public school," Shawn surmised.

"You don't think so?" Roscoe said.

"It shouldn't happen at the Academy either," I said. "It's a Christian school; it should be better, not worse!"

"I know. I think it's lame too, but that's what I overheard," Cam said.

After a moment of silence, Shawn spoke up. "You know," he said, "my guess is that they weren't as much worried about the idea of murder as they were about the negative portrayal of it. They don't want anything considered sinful tied to their name."

"Isn't it a greater sin to cast out someone who is hurting and in desperate need of help?" I asked.

The dark shadows on the floor started to lengthen as the sun began to set. I was saddened to find that the drama of school had found its way here. I wondered how the halls of the Academy still seemed to find their way into our hidden, protected oasis.

The next day at school, I had hoped Dr. Sites would have been in his office when I proudly delivered the final prints from the Southern Hope Banquet. He wasn't, so I had to leave them with Mrs. Crisby. Hopefully, I'd get some feedback on them soon.

A few hours later, I decided it was time to attempt talking to Natalie once again. Usually, she made it to her locker at exactly 1:54 after acting as teacher's assistant to Mrs. Jenkins. Each teacher got one free period to grade papers, and they were able to choose one student, usually with an interest in academics, to help them. Natalie wanted to be an elementary school teacher, which was totally hot.

Once she got to her locker, she would swap out some textbooks, give herself a quick look-over in her magnetic locker mirror, and take off to Social Sciences. Sure, it might be a bit creepy that I knew these things so well, but I make no apologies.

There were only a few fleeting moments during the school day where I could get the chance to see her, and that was one of them. She was a little late, or maybe I was a little early, because as I strolled passed Locker #185, she wasn't there. She hadn't even entered the hallway yet, from what I could see.

Swallowing the lump in my throat and trying to overlook the butterflies in my stomach, I stepped out of line and used the old search-through-my-bookbag-like-I'm-looking-for-something-until-she-comes trick. Leaning against Locker #188, I unzipped the old Jansport book bag and fumbled through some papers from History, a report that I was working on for Biology, an envelope of photos for Yearbook, and a few gum wrappers.

As I went through my bag, Natalie entered the hallway and started coming my way. My heart started to beat faster as I continued to rummage through my backpack. Imaginary items can sometimes be tricky to find.

"Hi," I casually said as she walked passed me, her hair in a simple scrunchie-tied ponytail.

"Hi," she replied with a smile.

Hesitating for just a moment, I mustered up the courage to blurt out, "I didn't mean to wish you a Happy Monday the other day."

"What?" she asked.

Already feeling flabbergasted, I tried to harness my confidence. "I mean, I was just going to say "Hi" but I guess I thought "Happy Monday" was better for some reason. Don't worry, I know I looked totally stupid. It's cool."

She giggled and replied, "You didn't look stupid."

"No, I did. It's ok. I've accepted it."

"Well, you didn't look *that* stupid."

"Thank you. You're too kind. Your name is Natalie, right?" I asked, wanting not to seem oblivious, but also not wanting to look too eager.

"Yeah. And yours is Sylas?"

"You can call me Sy. Sylas is my grandfather."

She politely snickered again as she dialed her locker combination. I paused for an awkward moment and then interjected, "Are you going to Nate Sanchez's Day of the Dead party?"

"Umm...I don't think so. I heard some stories about that from last year. Not my cup of tea. I think my cousin is having a Halloween party, so I'll probably go to that."

"Oh that's cool. I love this time of year because there are so many good holidays. You just go from Halloween into Thanksgiving to Christmas, one right after the other."

She opened up her locker and replied, "I know, me too."

I couldn't tell if I was annoying her, or if she was enjoying the company. I stammered to keep the conversation flowing. She kept focused on the task at hand, never fully ignoring or engaging me.

"My favorite is Christmas, though. How about you?" I asked.

"Yeah, me too. I love Christmas. Although I'm biased because it's also my birthday," she said with a snicker.

"Oh really, it's your birthday!?"

"Yeah."

"That's cool."

She swapped a neatly labeled three-ring binder from her backpack with one from the locker. "Yeah, it's not bad, I guess. Although I wish it snowed more here on Christmas. I love Christmas lights and how they reflect off the snow. And I love white birthdays," she giggled. Then she asked me, "Are you going to the East Creek game on Friday?"

In all honesty, I hadn't planned on attending the game, but it sounded like she did so I replied, "Y-Yeah, I think so. You?"

"Yeah, I'll be there. Should be fun. Well, I better go," she said.

As she swung her hand up to close her locker, she accidentally knocked over her binder and sent a small stack of papers floating to the ground. "Oh!" she responded dropping to the ground to pick them up.

"Here, let me help," I offered, also kneeling down.

"Thank you. I have to return these to Mrs. Yelski."

"Did you help grade these in Mrs. Jenkins's room?"

"Yeah. I'm her Teacher's Assistant."

Grabbing a small pile, I noticed a quiz that Topher Landau had taken resting on top. Several of the answers were left blank, and one which asked what century the Canterbury Tales were written in was marked 19th.

"19th century?" I said chuckling. "Canterbury Tales were written a hundred years ago? I guess Topher won't be our valedictorian this year."

She snatched the papers from my hand, visibly irritated with my comment.

"You don't know what subjects different students struggle with," she said.

"Oh. I'm sorry. I hope that wasn't offensive," I said quickly.

"Learning is different for everyone. It's fine, Sy," she replied restacking all the papers and standing back up. "Well, I should go. See ya later."

"That was rude of me," I pleaded. "I'm sorry."

"It's ok. Maybe I'll see you at the game."

"Ok, yeah. I'll definitely be there," I replied attempting to remove my foot from my mouth. I don't think it worked. The successful conversation we had was lost, and my last impression tactless. That had quite possibly been strike number two.

CHAPTER 7

At 5:10 on Friday, I returned home from work and rushed to get ready to leave again for the game. My mom and I usually returned home from work around the same time, although tonight it would seem that I had beaten her to it. Throwing my backpack on the kitchen table, I opened up the freezer to see if there was something I could quickly pop in the microwave before heading out. My father shuffled into the kitchen just as my mother opened the front door.

"Hi, boys," she said as she draped her coat over the banister and walked into the kitchen. She looked exhausted and visibly worried.

"Hi, hun," my father said turning around.

"Is something wrong?" I asked.

She smiled tenderly and shook her head.

"Helen, did you pick up Buck's dog food like I asked?" my dad said.

"Shoot. I forgot. Are we completely out?"

"Yes, that's why I asked you to pick up more."

My mother reached for her coat until I interrupted her and offered to go once I finished nuking dinner. It seemed like she had a long day. She thanked me, then my dad and I had a brief argument about me driving to East Creek all by myself that evening. My dad's temper seemed to be growing shorter, just like the autumn days were. My mom eased the tension by reminding him that the Martins were going to drop off Lily to be babysat any moment.

Dad had always been very fond of Lily. I'm sure it was mostly because she was well mannered and adorable, but I had always suspected that it was also because she was still young enough to dutifully obey him, something his older children generally did not. The three of them usually played games when Lily would come over. During those times, Dad seemed to have more fun than he had in years, even since when I had been that young.

"How was work, mom?" I asked grabbing the blistering, spewing goo out of the microwave.

"Oh, I don't know. It wasn't great. One of my patients is pretty sick."

"Aren't all your patients pretty sick?" I asked.

"Some of them, but this one was actually improving."

"So what happened?"

"Well, she's had a history of atrial fibrillation. It's an irregular heart rhythm. Nothing too serious, if managed properly. She was taking this medication to help regulate her heartbeat, called amiodarone." As she spoke about it, it became clear to me that mom needed to get this off her chest.

"Anyway, her family came to visit yesterday from Florida and brought her some seafood. I think she got food poisoning because she was vomiting and just miserable. I hated to see her like that. I couldn't find a doctor, so I thought I would give her something to help stop her nausea. It was so stupid; I shouldn't have done it. I didn't have an order for it, but I didn't think it would be any big deal. I thought I would be able to get an order afterwards. It was just stupid."

I hated to see her beat herself up over this, but I wasn't sure what to say.

"What happened?" I asked. "Was she allergic to the medicine?"

"No. It stopped her heart."

"The anti-nausea stuff?!"

She nodded. "We performed CPR and got her heart working again, but she was transferred to the Intensive Care Unit."

"How did that happen?"

"The doctors said it was the combination of amiodarone with the ondansetron. He said he never would have written an order for that, that he would have substituted something else."

"So is everything gonna be ok?"

"I have a meeting with my manager and risk management and the corporate attorney on Monday. I hope so."

"Do you think anything's gonna happen to you?"

"I don't think so. The patient is fine, but it's just all so worrisome. It was a foolish mistake on my part. I shouldn't have done that. Her daughter is worried sick."

I squeezed my mother's hand and then gave her a hug. "Don't

worry about it, Mom. It was an accident. If the patient is fine, you'll probably be fine too."

I had finished my dinner and dumped my empty tray in the trashcan. Grabbing my keys from the pegboard, I told her, "I'll just run out and grab the dog food, then I'm headed to East Creek."

"Ok, honey," be safe, she said with a kiss.

"I will. Be right back."

It broke my heart to see my mother like that. All she wanted to do was to help that poor woman. But sadly, I knew that most people in our culture cared more about lawsuits than acknowledging a simple mistake.

Kroger was only a few blocks from our house, and as I pulled into the parking lot, I was surprised by how busy it seemed to be on a Friday evening. Then I realized why. Adjacent to the grocery store was New Life Women's Clinic. It was the place that did the mammograms, the gynecology, and all that other lady stuff. Filling up their parking lot were two large crowds, most of which probably parked next door at Kroger, both yelling back and forth at each other and waving brightly colored signs.

The skirmish noise was almost impossible to ignore after I stepped outside of my car. Both opposing forces were shouting mostly unintelligible commands at each other, with the occasional word like 'murder' or 'child' wafting through the crowd via megaphone. Clearly, neither group was listening to the other, and a poor, lonely police officer stood between them like a dodgeball referee trying to keep the confrontation from getting physical.

As I rubbernecked the battle, I soon realized that this was an abortion demonstration with the pro-life and pro-choice armies standing in fuming opposition to one another. I couldn't help but feel the passion that both sides had for their beliefs. They both thought that they were doing the right thing and each person firmly believed the other side was wrong. How could you fix that? How could you even begin to make one side think about things from the other perspective? They were both so deeply entrenched in their own way of thinking that they saw the other as the enemy.

Then, while walking under a fiery red maple tree, I immediately recognized a blue sedan in the Kroger lot that I had not seen at school in nearly two months. I knew whom it belonged to, and she was sitting inside. I tapped on the passenger window and tenderly waved. A puffy-eyed Rachel Ellis looked up and smiled at me, fumbling for her keys to turn the car on and roll down the power window.

"Hi, Rachel!" I said when she finally got the passenger window out of the way.

"Sy! Are you here protesting this place, too?"

"No, just stopping by Kroger to get dog food, actually. Then heading to the East Creek game. What's going on?"

"This clinic recently started performing abortions."

"Oh. Were you protesting?"

"No...just dropping off a friend to pick up a prescription."

"That's nice of you. Are you feeling ok?"

"Oh yeah. My allergies are terrible right now. Tree pollen."

"I didn't think pollen was supposed to be bad this time of year."

"I'm weird, I guess."

"Ehh, that's too bad," I said empathetically. "Hey, I heard about what happened and everything. I'm sorry about all that; I had no idea."

"Oh thanks, but that's ok. It's actually a really good thing. I was able to enroll at the community college early and started taking some college classes."

"College, already?"

"Yeah, just some basic stuff; Biology, English, College Algebra."

"Well, you were always really smart."

"Thanks!"

"No, seriously. When I was told you weren't coming back, I freaked out. I didn't know how I was going to pass Calculus without your help!"

"That's sweet. You're smart, Sy. I'm sure you'll do fine."

"You think so? Well, thank you. It's good to know someone believes in me."

"And hey, if you ever need a tutor, you can always come by the college. You could probably even sit in with me in one of my classes."

"That'd be awesome."

"Yeah seriously. Here's my number if you ever want to take

me up on it."

She found a piece of scrap paper on the floorboard of her car and scribbled down her phone number. While she was doing that, I noticed something else on her floor. It was a pamphlet from the clinic titled *What to Expect*. Probably just something one of the demonstrators handed out.

"So, what do you think about all this stuff?" she asked handing me her phone number.

"What do you mean? Oh, the protesters? I dunno," I said with a shrug. "Doesn't seem like it's working too well...whatever it is they're trying to accomplish."

She giggled. "I mean, do you think a woman has a right to choose what she does with her body?"

It seemed like an odd question. Being from a Christian school, I would've thought her to ask the pro-life version of that question; do I believe abortion to be wrong?

"Well, abortion is certainly not like getting a tattoo, that's for sure," I said.

She giggled again at my dark humor.

"Ya know," I continued, "it's not hard to understand that a pregnancy will eventually produce a full-grown, unique human being so if a woman alters that, they are actually controlling someone else's body, not just theirs. Someone else's life, for that matter. But on the other hand, if human life is just a byproduct of this environment and evolved along with everything else, any human - even an unborn one - is just another valueless accident and means nothing. So...killing it is just another form of population control, I guess. I don't know."

She thought about that for a minute. "See Sy, you're smart. You'll do fine in Calculus," she joked.

"I do have one other piece of wisdom to impart to you, though," I said.

"What's that?"

"If you're allergic to tree pollen, don't park under a maple tree."

She laughed and nodded. "Good advice," she said.

"I gotta go, but it was great seeing you. And hey, I'll definitely give you a call if I need some help with Calc. Thanks again!"

"You're welcome," she said. I waved as I headed back to Kroger, regretting that I wasn't halfway to East Creek already.

Something told me that Rachel wasn't telling me the whole truth, but it was her truth to tell. I was starting to wonder what the truth in my own life was anyway, so I knew I was the last person who deserved to make a black and white statement. I just wanted Rachel to know that she had my support. More than anything, that is what I felt she needed.

It was another twenty minutes before I was able to drop Buck's new food off at my house and get on the road. I didn't really have the money to drive fifty miles away, but seeing Natalie and salvaging my dignity seemed more important at the time.

I showed my media pass and walked in through the front gates about fifteen minutes before the game started. Everything was unfamiliar. The only things I recognized were the blue and white towels and other accoutrements of the Saints scattering the opposite side of the field, so I headed towards them. On the field, a few of the Saints' cheerleaders were checking each others' hair and getting ready for the game. I asked Heidi Jackson if I could set my stuff next to their bench and got the a-okay.

The yearbook photographer shtick was my alibi tonight. It wasn't that I didn't want Natalie to know that I drove all this way for her. It's just that if she did, I might look desperate or creepy, both of which I had already demonstrated and didn't care to repeat. One more strikeout would most likely seal my fate with her for good.

The Saints had not arrived to the field yet. They would most likely all run out just before the game started to an unreceptive arena only to be upstaged by the entering Devils with their uproarious crowd, glitz, and fanfare. That would probably be the only victory cheer the Devils would have all evening. The Saints were predicted to dominate yet again.

The Saints finally ran out, followed by the Devils, and after that, everything went exactly as I had suspected. From my vantage point on the field, I glanced around both sides of the stadium hoping to catch Natalie's face but had no luck. To pass the time, I played along with my story and grabbed some shots of the dramatic entrances, then the coin toss, then the kickoff. Mike Conrad received East Creek's kick and ran it up to the thirty-yard line before being tackled. The game was barely underway, and I was already bored.

I wandered around by myself for the entire first quarter. I grabbed a hot dog then came back down to the field and claimed an open stadium folding chair a little bit before halftime. Natalie was nowhere to be found. The Saints' bench was just a few feet to my left, and I could overhear their conversations, which included everything from motocross to cheating on an English test to the cute cheerleaders on the other team. Having very recently transferred from East Creek, Topher knew the down and dirty about each girl and was pointing them out to his new teammates. It caught my attention so I zoomed in my lens for a quick peek. He was right. There were several really cute ones, and after my window-shopping, I panned my lens over to the East Creek players. I made it halfway through their bench when I immediately stopped, dead in my tracks.

Standing behind the opposing team's bench was none other than Mr. Jeremy Maitland.

I felt like a hunter who had suddenly spotted his prey. My adrenaline spiked up, my heart rate doubled, and I sat up at attention. I had been trying not to overthink this Jeremy thing, but now that the opportunity had presented itself, I found myself surprisingly curious. And oddly enough, this was the second time within a month that I had spotted him while photographing a football game. I watched him for a moment and then the photojournalist in me had a thought. If my curiosity about him was somehow justified, it would be good to have some supporting evidence. So I snapped a photo.

Like a seasoned marksman, I immediately tried to steady my camera. Jeremy was well-dressed and talking to one of their players. Number 38, to be exact. I watched the interaction for a moment through my viewfinder and then Jeremy shook 38's hand. I snapped another photo. He walked away and 38 turned back around to watch the game. I followed Jeremy in my lens. He casually walked along the sidelines, like he was out for a Sunday stroll. He didn't clap or cheer or smile—he just walked to the stairs and resumed his place in the crowd.

I took a mental note of where he was sitting and got up from my post. Walking down the sidelines, I went directly to the concession stand to buy a game program. Setting down my camera on a nearby picnic table, I fumbled through the black and white pages to find the Devil's roster. Player number 38 was Brian Fitzpatrick, a 6'1", 195 lb. junior who played middle linebacker for East Creek.

I dog-eared the page, then took a quick glance across the field to make sure Jeremy Maitland was still in his seat. He was indeed still there.

I turned back to the concession stand and saw that two middle-aged men were standing in front of it watching the game, casually chatting among themselves. One of them was wearing an East Creek Devil's sweatshirt.

"Good game, huh?" I butted in, clearly not thinking about my opening line.

"What game you watching?" the bald one asked me. "That dern Cherrywood pays off their players or something. Can't never beat 'em."

"Yeah. Frikin' Saints," I said. Then, never one for the art of segues, I added, "You know anything about Brian Fitzpatrick?"

"Do you go here?" the man in the Devils shirt asked.

"Yeah," I lied.

"You go here and don't know much about Fitzpatrick?"

I knew my lie was hasty. "Well, I just transferred last week so I don't really know much of anyone." I quickly covered the lie with a laugh.

"Ahh. No, don't know a lot about him," the man said. "I think my boy has a class with him. You know Jeffrey Walker?"

"No, I don't."

"Oh well, that's my kid...Yeah, Fitzpatrick is good at what he does, that's all I know. Pro'ly make MVP, if I had to guess."

I looked back to the stands and saw that Jeremy Maitland was getting up from his bench.

"Ok, great," I said. "Well, I gotta go. Have a good night."

I moved quickly behind the end zone toward the opposite bleachers, never taking my eyes off of my target. Jeremy walked down near the field again, although this time he turned at the bottom of the bleachers to take the stairs to the exit. He then vanished underneath the stands. I reached the Home team side of the field and also ducked under the stands, in pursuit. Frantically glancing through the passers by, I spotted him about fifty yards away as he pulled a lighter from his pocket to light the cigarette that dangled from his lips.

"Excuse me?" I asked when I finally reached him, slightly out of breath from my aggressive power walking.

Startled, he embarrassingly jerked the cigarette from his mouth and replied, "Me?"

"Yes, sir. I'm sorry, I don't mean to bother you, but I had a question for you. My name is Chris Lambert, and I'm doing a story on Southern Hope for our school yearbook. I saw you speak at the Southern Hope Fundraiser a few weeks ago and was wondering what your experience in Kenya was like?"

"Oh yes," he replied dropping his cigarette and extinguishing it with his foot. "I'm sorry, it's a nasty habit I've almost got licked...uh, I actually never went to Kenya."

His matter-of-fact reply completely shocked me.

"I'm sorry," I said. "You said you never went to Kenya?" I stumbled a bit in my speech, suspecting that was always the truth but not expecting he'd just come right out and admit it.

"No, actually. So, this is for your yearbook story, huh?"

"Uh...yeah."

"That's great. That's great. I was into photography when I was in school. Don't do it as much as I'd like anymore..."

"So why did you tell people you went to Africa with Southern Hope?" I asked trying to keep him on track.

"Oh, I'm sorry. Yeah...sorry I don't have any information about Southern Hope for your story. They just hire me as a spokesman every once in a while to speak on behalf of the missionaries that can't be in town to speak at those types of events. I just read the scripts they give me."

"Southern Hope gave you a script?"

"Yeah. It was just to help the audience connect more with what they were doing over there. At least that's what they told me." I noticed right there under the stands that he was a very down-to-earth guy, completely different than the shady conman I had imagined. Our conversation felt genuine, and he seemed real.

"But they called you a missionary for Southern Hope," I went on. "And didn't you say that *you* went to Kenya? Wouldn't they be sort of misrepresenting the facts if they wrote that in a script for you to say?"

It was then that, on the far end of the bleachers that I got a fleeting glimpse of Natalie passing by. It was absolutely terrible timing. I had so many more questions for Jeremy but knew I had to cut them short.

He answered, "I think they just called me a representative. I wasn't a missionary. And no, I never said that *I* went to Kenya personally. I was just speaking on behalf of the administration like, 'we' as Southern Hope went over there, 'we made a difference' - stuff like that.

"Oh, ok," I said, suspecting that he was, in fact, telling the truth and that I could have been overanalyzing everything from the beginning.

"Well, I gotta get going. Thank you for your time." I rushed before almost darting off. But then, just before I turned around, one last question popped into my head.

"Actually, can I ask you one more question?"

"Sure."

"I was taking photos of the game just now and saw you on East Creek's sidelines. What were you doing down there?"

"Oh, about ten minutes ago? That was just a family friend I was saying hi to."

"In the middle of the game?"

"Yep."

"Ok. Well hey, it was great talking with you. Sorry to barge in on you and leave so quickly. Have a great night."

"You too. Have a good night, Chris."

I grabbed the camera, which hung from my neck and started to power walk again.

Now searching for Natalie, I couldn't get over the fact that Jeremy had been surprisingly pleasant to talk to, although he still left me with suspicions. He said Southern Hope had asked him to speak at fundraisers before. What was so hard about getting a real missionary to speak? People from church always seemed to be going on missions trips. And I still didn't buy that those slideshow photos were from one photographer, even if that is what the scriptwriter wrote.

I reached the end of the bleachers and quickly scanned the stands. Luckily, I wasn't too late, and I noticed a familiar ponytail bobbing around the bleachers near the fifty-yard line. My heart fluttered as I watched Natalie walk up the bleachers by herself and take a seat. From my angle, she had disappeared into the crowd, but I did know that she was in row H, towards the aisle. I took a mental note of her exact location and immediately turned back around in the direction I had come from. I headed directly back to the concession stand with a plan in mind.

"Could I have two hot chocolates?" I asked the girl at the concession stand when it was my turn to order.

"Sure. That'll be three dollars," she said.

Digging into my pockets, I found the last few dollars I had, which were only four. She handed me the two steamy beverages, and I gave her three of my last four bills.

"Thank you," I replied swinging the camera over my shoulder and grabbing the drinks with both hands.

My plan was to walk to the very top of the bleachers, cross over to the aisle on the forty-yard line, then down to row H. I felt that this come-from-behind tactic would be much more surprising and less intimidating than if we had seen each other coming from a distance and awkwardly waited until I arrived. Plus, I was nervous and wanted an exit strategy in case I decided to bail.

Walking up the side stairs and across the top of the bleachers to the forty-yard line, I kept rehearsing in my head what I would say to her. *"It's a little chilly out so I brought you this"* or *"Here's something to show that I'm not a jerk"* were my top two lines, but I didn't care for either one of them. I didn't have anything solid nailed down before reaching the aisle. I stood at the top for a second to scan the crowd and identify the back of her head. Then, taking a deep breath, I started my descent.

I was at row P when I finally spotted her again. Although to my surprise, in this sighting, she wasn't alone. Kevin Thompson, a good-looking soccer player, was sitting next to her. As I watched, he turned and whispered something in her ear. She turned back to him, laughing at what he said, and flirtatiously slapped him on the shoulder.

My heart sank. I knew I had missed yet another opportunity. This time, though, it might've been for good. It was my own stupid fault. Pausing in the middle of the aisle several rows above, I turned around. Sitting next to where I stood was a middle-aged man wearing an East Creek sweatshirt calmly watching the game.

"You want a hot chocolate?" I asked him.

CHAPTER 8

In second period English the next Monday, Ms. Yelski was already handing out the quizzes we had completed on the Canterbury Tales - the same one that I stuck my foot in my mouth with Natalie the week before.

I got a 96. Not bad. When she placed Topher's assignment on his desk though, I was expecting to see a 50 or something because I knew he bombed it. I saw Natalie's familiar markings written in red, but curiously on the top of the page, was written an 85 in black ink. I squinted for a closer look, making sure I wasn't reading it wrong.

I was right. Topher got a 'B'.

Mr. Oakridge's class was unlike any other I had ever been a part of. Faith, ethics, and commonsense were called into question. Absolutes were antagonized by relativity. Laws appeared to bend if not altogether break, and as the students opened their minds to question why, they were rewarded with a greater understanding of the world around them.

When Bible class rolled around, Jody Webber and Matt Young were the first to present their reports to the class. Their belief system was a big one: Atheism. It was probably one of the most popular worldviews out there, and maybe because it started with an "A", Mr. Oakridge made them go first.

Jody took the podium first while Matt sat at the folding table next to it. The rest of us kicked back to watch their performance, thankful it was their turn and not ours. Matt spread out his papers like a lawyer preparing for a deposition. Jody glanced at him as if waiting for permission to start. She then looked at Mr. Oakridge. After he nodded, Jody cleared her throat and began.

"There are a plethora of religions in the world, and all of them claim they have the correct answer," she started. "However, they all contradict each other, and as I'm sure we'll find out in this class, they all can't be right. But they can all be wrong."

She stopped and looked at the class hoping to see the powerful impact that their first opening statement had made. It didn't seem to work as they had hoped; we all stared blankly back. She awkwardly looked back down at her paper.

"Why does there have to be a God? Why does there have to be a Holy Book? What if there isn't? What then? Atheism is simply the belief that a God, or gods, do not exist and there are many different reasons for believing so. First, world religions contradict themselves."

It was clear that Jody was nervous, as she never looked up from her paper the entire time. Other than stumbling on a few words, she made some excellent points.

"There are hundreds of religions in the world," she continued, "but no two that are the same, meaning that the very greatest number of religions in the world that can be correct is only one. However, even within these religions there are differences. Hasidic Jews, Reformed Jews, Theravada Buddhists, Mahayana Buddhists, Pentecostal Christians, Baptist Christians and on and on. So from the one religion that might be correct in this world, you would still have to narrow that down to the correct denomination in order to have a chance at finding out what the truth is. They all claim that their way is correct, but the only way you can know for sure is to have faith in it. Atheists state that the probability of one of these denominations getting it right out of the thousands that think they are equally right but must be wrong, is far too unlikely, and therefore all are wrong."

She went on to explain that most religions attribute the idea of power as well as moral goodness to their God; however, she argued that this concept alone is contradictory because if a god is so good and powerful, why can't he seem to eliminate the suffering that happens in the world? Much of that suffering has even been caused *by* religions, from the Crusades to the modern-day battles in the Middle East between Jews and Muslims. She also explained that even though most religions claim that their God created the universe, science has proven that there was no creator but rather that life evolved. The theory of evolution is much more widely accepted by scientists and scholars than the theory of creation, so since there is no evidence that a supernatural deity or an afterlife exists, we can assume that life on earth is merely a natural occurrence, and there is simply no reason to believe in the supernatural.

Her points made perfect sense, and I couldn't help but find myself somewhat intrigued.

"Unlike most religions," she continued, "Atheists are not out to convert anyone to our way of thinking. We don't use aggressive methods or even the force that a lot of religions do. Religions give a lot of people hope, and we see nothing wrong with allowing people to believe whatever they want to believe, as long as they don't hurt anyone in the process. However, most atheists believe that religions *do* cause harm by impeding popular science, social development, and world peace, so we will speak out. Ultimately, because we are merely natural beings, we will all end up in the same place, and therefore our goal as atheists is to simply live a harmonious existence. There is no need to believe in atheism, but based on the scientific evidence available and the contradictions among religions, there is also no need not to."

Jody finally looked up from her report, neatly tapped her papers on the podium, and took a seat.

"Whoa…who still believes in God now?" Mr. Oakridge sarcastically asked the class. He began to applaud. "Well done. Excellent. The bar has been set, class. What do you think? Do you think they're right?"

A few people defiantly shook their heads. Most of us didn't know how to respond so we kept our mouths shut.

Ever since I had spoken with Jeremy that weekend, something had seemed very off to me, and I really wanted to know what it was. It was probably nothing, but people have told me before that I can overthink things. I just want to understand everything; it was apparently just part of my nature. I'm sure there was a reasonable explanation for why Southern Hope hired a spokesman like Jeremy, but until I found it, it would remain a nagging curiosity rattling around in my brain.

One day after school, I decided to stop by Southern Hope Ministries. The administrative office was easy to miss with only a humble banner that read "Southern Hope Foundation" over the doorway to the drab commercial office space. I guess whenever I heard Pastor Samms or Dr. Sites talk about Southern Hope, I always assumed it would be located in a more official looking building.

Inside was even worse. It was like a cheap Chinese restaurant with a few fake plants used poorly in an attempt to add life to the waiting area and a front desk that looked like it could be knocked over by a rogue wind. It was a valid attempt at trying to appear professional, but they could not hide that they were operating on a nonprofit's shoestring budget.

There were two things from my visit that stood out to me as odd. The first thing was what I saw before I walked inside. Sitting by a side door on the outside of the building was Bruce Lessner's blue scooter with the whitewall tires. I didn't have the foggiest idea why Bruce would be there, or even why a highly respected legal professional would be seen riding around town on that thing.

And the second thing that stood out to me was one of the photos on the wall of the reception area. When I walked inside the building, Janelle Samms, Pastor Samms' wife, was manning the reception desk while the receptionist was taking a restroom break. She greeted me cordially, but when the receptionist returned allowing Janelle to leave, I began asking about volunteer opportunities. The receptionist pointed to a photo on the wall of a group of volunteers that just got back from a missions trip to Kenya; the same trip that Jeremy Maitland was portrayed to have gone on.

In the photo, I noticed a woman who regularly attended Clanton Baptist Church. The receptionist told me her name was Brandi. I immediately asked myself, "Why would Southern Hope use Jeremy Maitland as a spokesman instead of someone who actually went on the trip? And why would a speechwriter include glaring errors about giardia vaccines when they could've just asked someone like Brandi what really happened over there?"

I hoped this would be one case in which the monotony and routines of church would play out in my favor and I could talk to Brandi about her experiences that Sunday.

Lily really wanted her big brother to take her trick-or-treating that year, so being the stand-up guy that he was, Roscoe didn't make plans for Halloween and did just that. Shawn, Cam, and I however donned our adult costumes for Nate Sanchez's Second Annual Day of the Dead party. Cam was dressed as a 1970's tennis player with short shorts, big hair with a vintage polo shirt and racquet. Shawn didn't put much thought into his costume and just grabbed a mask from Spencer's. I wore a black plastic trashcan over my body and a gray trash can lid on my head to resemble a roll of film.

Nate Sanchez's Day of the Dead party was a mix of our American Halloween and his Hispanic heritage Day of the Dead rituals. Overall, it was mainly just an excuse for a bunch of us to get together to look and act stupid.

"Hey do you guys know if Natalie and Kevin Thompson are together?" I blurted out while waddling up to Nate's house.

From inside his rubber mask, Shawn's voice echoed apologetically, "Aw man, I didn't want to tell you. I think they are, bro. I heard Amanda Fogle talking about it."

Disappointed but not surprised, I shrugged. "That's what I thought."

"It's never over, man," Cam said. "You can get in on that whenever you want. She doesn't have a ring on her finger."

"Yeah, I saw them flirting at the game last Friday."

"You went to the East Creek game?" Cam asked.

"Yeah."

"Why didn't you say hi? I didn't see you?"

"Don't worry about it. It's not over," Cam encouraged again. "Kevin's arrogant. She'll realize that soon enough and you'll look even better," Shawn said.

"Thanks, man. Oh, ya know who else I saw at the game last weekend? Jeremy Maitland."

"Really?" Shawn asked.

"Yeah. He was on East Creek's sidelines talking to one of their players during the game."

"I asked a few of the guys about him and Topher knew who he was," Cam stated.

"Topher knows him?" I asked.

"Yeah. He said that he was the guy who helped him get into Cherrywood."

"Get into Cherrywood? What does he have to do with Cherrywood?"

"I dunno. That's just what Topher said," Cam mentioned opening the front door to the buzzing house. The party was loud even from the outside.

Nate's parents owned a successful travel agency so they were often gone enjoying the perks of their enterprise. The cool kids from school, mostly athletes and class clowns, walked around with goofy costumes. Everyone was all loud mouths and big smiles. There were several good costumes, although most were just quick purchases at Salvation Army and the local costume rental shop.

Inside the kitchen were a few selections of beverages, about a quarter of which were legal for minors to consume. Nevertheless, most of my peers were sampling all of them. If the cops showed up, we would all flee like cockroaches and the ones who got caught would just lie about going to a Christian school so they wouldn't suffer the scorn of the Academy.

Joey Ryan, Cherrywood's quarterback and one of Cam's football buddies, greeted Cam with a hearty laugh. "Dude, that costume is killer! Nice legs there, bro!"

Shawn immediately spotted a girl he had the hots for and tossed us aside like a gospel tract in a bag of Halloween candy.

"Thanks, bro!" Cam reciprocated.

"What are you supposed to be?" Joey asked me. "Oscar the Grouch?"

"No, I'm a roll of film."

"Pff, I think you look better as Oscar...Hey, hold up, hold up," Joey said as he turned to the counter and poured two shots of tequila in red Solo cups. Turning back to Cam, he handed off one of the drinks.

"Cheers, buddy, " he said as he downed one shot while Cam took the other. I was a little disappointed that Cam had obliged so eagerly but he was a big boy and could make his own decisions.

"Sorry man, you want one?" Joey asked me after the fact. Luckily I really, really did not.

"Nah, that's ok. Thanks," I said.

As the night went on, I witnessed a smiling Nate Sanchez and his homecoming queen girlfriend, Angela Garbaro, walk out of his parent's bedroom. Their costumes were slightly more disarranged than they had been when I had seen them earlier.

A little later, four football players and three cheerleaders came down from upstairs, all overly giggly and talkative. Their demeanor had changed in the time they had been up there, and while I certainly had very little knowledge of these sorts of things, I couldn't help but think they were on something even more illegal than our under-aged libations.

Within a relatively short period of time, Cam had become intoxicated and discovered an open door to the basement. I followed him to make sure he didn't get into trouble, and as we descended the stairs into a dungeon-like unfinished cellar, we found five more partiers lounging around in a thick skunky haze. They had cracked a window in hopes that the marijuana smoke would escape but it still enveloped the basement like a fog.

"Let's ask Fosjord," Topher told Brian Hartman, a Cherrywood lacrosse player who was munching on Cheez-its. Their eyes were glazed as they smoked on an old ratty couch.

"Cameron...Why is there so much suffering in the world, man?" a high and enlightened Topher asked. "People just hurt each other for no reason. Why would God allow that to happen? Do you think He's even there?"

"Have you guys been down here the whole time?" Cam asked.

"I'm gonna go," I said to Cam.

"No, no. Don't go," Topher said. "Oscar the Grouch, you can answer the question too."

"I'm a roll of film. I'm not...nevermind."

"Wouldn't life be so much easier if you just didn't believe in God?" Topher posed. "If you didn't believe in any religion, your life would be so much better. There are so many stupid rules and crap that go along with religion. If you just didn't believe that, you'd be free."

After rolling my eyes, I responded, "Choosing not to believe in a religion is still a belief. You believe that religions are wrong, which in and of itself, is still a belief system that you need to defend."

"Wait. What?" Topher asked, trying to grasp the depth of my statement.

"But seriously. What if there is no God?" an equally high Brian Hartman asked. "He doesn't show up in pillars of fire anymore like He did in the Old Testament. Prob'ly cuz He's not there. Dude, a pillar of fire would be so sweet."

"You think there's a God, Fosjord?" Topher asked.

"I dunno. Pro'ly," Cam slurred.

"How 'bout you, Oscar?"

I thought about the questions I'd always had about God - about why He calls himself a jealous God and then later on in the Bible He says that jealousy is a sin - about why He seemed to have a temper in the Old Testament and had the Israelites brutally kill all kinds of people, including men, women, children, and livestock. I thought about Matt and Jody's presentation.

"I don't know," was my simple but surprising reply. "I'm gonna go back upstairs. Cam, you gonna stay here?"

"Yeah," Cam replied as he took a seat on an old rocking horse. I paused for a moment to hear Topher pose one more question.

"Okay, here's another one for ya. Why doesn't God let it rain in places like Africa, where people are dying of thirst? He's got total control of that. Now do you mean to tell me that there is a designer out there brilliant enough to create this world, including the rain, but He can't or won't even turn on the faucet every once in a while to save the people he claims to love? Because if so, He seems either incompetent or evil. Either way, why would I want to associate with that?"

Everyone was quiet. I always thought of Topher as a dumb jock, but marijuana allowed him to speak brilliantly. No one had an answer for him - especially not me.

"I'm gonna go. See you guys later," I said as I walked back up the stairs still pondering the surprisingly stimulating conversation with a bunch of stoners. Recently, it felt like my childhood faith was being called into question more and more. I was growing tired of feeling unstable.

Upstairs, it was the same old scene. Most of my other peers were wasted, and it felt like I was a witness to some strange disease—a disease that left everyone around me totally moronic with no control over their minds or bodies. I stood in a sea of people who were simply trying too hard. And somehow, by some strange twist of imagination, that was cool.

The currency in high school is *status*. It's all about who's cool and who's not, and if you're cool, you can buy just about anything. Being invited to Nate Sanchez's Day of the Dead party was cool. Not being invited was not. It should follow then, that I should've felt privileged to party with some of the most popular people in school at a rich kid's house. But I didn't. I felt out of place.

It had started to rain outside, and about ten minutes after I had come back upstairs, I bumped into Topher who had just come up to use the bathroom.

"Your boy's got the spins," he told me.

"He's got what?" I asked.

"I told him liquor and pot don't mix."

I went back downstairs to see what Topher meant and found Cam puking in the corner, wearing only his boxer shorts and a blue construction tarp. Cam had decided to join in on the marijuana and had thrown his clothes outside so his parents wouldn't smell the weed. Already being hammered, it was only a short time later when he found himself with a case of the spins and began hurling on the concrete basement floor.

For the slim few who could remember the events of that night's party, the memories weren't worth it. The undisciplined behavior of almost everyone there left social stains on their character and barf stains on the Sanchez's leather couch. I took off my costume and found a bag to line my trashcan with so Cam could puke inside it while I drove him home. His soaking clothes still remained outside of the Sanchez's basement window. Shawn had sobered up and followed behind me to give me a lift after I dropped off Cameron. The two of us snuck Cam into his bed, and I left my trashcan by his side. Then we locked his bedroom door for him and snuck back out of the house. If his parents found out what he had done, he'd certainly face much steeper consequences than the hangover he was already destined for.

I'd never seen him like the way he behaved at the party. It was sad. I've always looked up to Cam. His confidence, charisma, athleticism, and looks were supreme qualities. But by the end of that night, he hadn't even been able to form a cohesive sentence, smelled like vomit, and was nearly naked shivering inside of a dirty tarp. You always want to think of people at their best but can't forget them at their worst. And from the times I've known Cam, this was his worst.

CHAPTER 9

The next day I was hanging out with Roscoe on his back porch. It was around nine o'clock at night and we were engrossed in a somewhat philosophical discussion, which I had initiated earlier, since the questions Topher asked the day before still had not left my thoughts.

"I think it all comes down to your upbringing," Roscoe said, leaning back and resting his elbows on the railing behind him. "My dad was raised in a Christian home, I was raised in a Christian home, and my kids will be raised in a Christian home. But if you're raised in a Muslim home, you'll probably be brought up believing that, and you just didn't get so lucky. It's like if you're born in America, you got lucky but if you're born in a Third World country, you just weren't as lucky. You can't control it."

"No, I don't think it has anything to do with luck," I argued from a chair with my feet resting on the wrought iron patio table. "Look at us right now. If I came up with a reason to believe Buddhism was a more logical belief system than Christianity, I'd probably become a Buddhist."

"No you wouldn't."

"Yeah, I would."

"You'd really just throw the Bible out the window and start praying to Buddha or whatever?"

"If I felt that Christianity was not the – " I stopped immediately. Taking my feet off the table, I slowly sat up in my chair and stared intently out into Roscoe's dark backyard.

"What?" he asked. I stood up to look over the railing and kept staring in the same spot. "You see something?" he asked.

Along the woodline, near the deer trail to Chernobyl, I could see a figure standing there. I never would've noticed it if it hadn't moved. I moved closer to the edge of the deck, attempting to get my eyes out of the glare of the floodlight and adjusted to the darkness. Deer were frequent visitors to Roscoe's house, but this shadowy figure wasn't a deer. It was too slender, and it only moved once. My eyes were adjusting, allowing me to study it closer.

"There's someone out there," I said in an excited whisper.

My eyes finally adjusted enough to identify the image. Chills ran down my spine when I realized that it was a man. He was standing still. Just standing there staring straight back at me.

Suddenly terrified, I whispered to Roscoe, "There's a guy out there watching us!"

"What?" he replied, quickly swiveling around to peer out into the yard.

I kept watching him. He kept watching me, completely unmoving. "There's a dude right there!"

Roscoe took a moment to locate the figure. The man on the edge of the woodline moved an arm.

"Holy crap!" he exclaimed as he jumped back in fright. "Hey! What are you doing?!" he added. The figure didn't respond.

"Who are you?!" Roscoe shouted again. Still no response. The man turned to walk along the woodline; not away from us and not towards us—just parallel.

"What are you doing out there?" Roscoe shouted again.

A light came on in his neighbor's house after its owners were apparently disturbed by the shouting. The man at the treeline stopped a few steps later and turned back towards us. Once again, he just hauntingly stared.

Roscoe turned to me and said, "Dude, I'm freaked out."

"Maybe we should call the cops," I suggested.

"Should we go grab my dad's gun?" Roscoe asked. Then from the distance, we heard the man begin to mumble.

"Wait, wait, wait…he just said something," Roscoe said. "*WHAT?*" he shouted to the figure. We waited nervously for an answer. The reply was faint but chilling.

"Is Lily home?" he muttered.

"What the -" Roscoe blurted out as he stumbled backwards.

I reached for the screen door, ready to go inside and grab a phone or a gun, whichever was closer.

With a face drained of color, Roscoe looked at me and said, "He asked for Lily!"

"D'you know if Lily is home?" the voice faintly asked again.

I paused, recognizing the voice. "That's freakin' Edmund," I said.

"Edmund? You sure?"

"Yeah, I recognize his voice."

"Is that you, Edmund?!" Roscoe shouted angrily.

"Is Lily home?" he asked again.

Roscoe snapped his head to me. His eyes were hollow with rage, his face confirming that he too had recognized Edmund's voice.

"Get off my lawn, retard!" Roscoe shouted as he raced over to the stairs. In one of his rare but most defining character traits, he had snapped and lost all logical reasoning abilities. He was acting out of pure emotion. It was only the second time I had seen him like this. Both times were when he felt his little sister was being threatened, and both times I was scared. He was a mad dog off his chain, and I could not control him.

Roscoe raced down the stairs of the deck.

"Roscoe!" I shouted to him as I chased after him. He was in attack mode and had given no thought to the idea that Edmund could, in the unknown darkness, be dangerous.

"Don't you ever mention my sister's name again! I will frikin' end you, you pervert!" he shouted as he hit the grass and started running towards Edmund.

"Jake! Stop!" I pleaded calling him by his real name like everyone else did as I arrived at the top of the stairs. I stopped, knowing that I'd never catch him, and even if I did, he was too large and enraged for me to stop him. Behind us, the light upstairs in his parent's bedroom came on. In the woods, I could hear the snapping of sticks. Edmund was running away.

"Run 'tard! I will end your life if you ever come looking for my sister again!"

"*JAKE!*" a deeper, louder voice shouted from above my head. His dad had awakened and opened his window. Like a trained puppy, Roscoe halted immediately.

"Get in the house!" his dad demanded.

Roscoe shouted from the backyard in response. "There was a guy out here trying to get Lily!"

Slower and sterner, Mr. Martin ordered, "GET. IN. THE. HOUSE. NOW!"

With his head down and tail between his legs, Roscoe obeyed. I stayed silent. He walked up the inclined yard to the base of the stairs. His dad was still staring through the window screen from above, wearing both an angry scowl and his bathrobe. Roscoe glanced up at me with an ashamed look.

"I gotta go," he simply stated as he walked passed me at the top of the stairs.

"See you tomorrow?" I quietly asked.

"Yeah."

With his head down, he opened the screen door. Another light came on in the hall upstairs. He vanished inside, leaving me on the cold, dark porch. Every so often, I could hear the rustling of leaves and the snap of a stick as Edmund found his way back home through the woods. I was still frightened. Usually, Edmund appeared to be harmless, but one could never tell. Clearly, he had a few dim bulbs upstairs and that lack of brainpower is exactly what I thought could make him a very real threat.

With one hand in my pocket, I reached out to release the latch that secured the fence gate. I closed it behind me as I walked around the side of the house to my car. All was quiet again. It was unclear as to exactly what Roscoe was experiencing inside the house, but it was safe to say it wasn't fun. I had never heard his dad yell so angrily. It was completely outside of his character. Mr. Martin was always a very mild-mannered man, but it seemed that perhaps Roscoe possessed some of his father's hidden traits.

The next day at church, I found Cam in the bustling church foyer. My mom was already sitting down in the sanctuary, but she wasn't saving me a seat or anything. She was considerate enough to know that even though I loved her dearly, a senior in high school didn't always want to sit with his mommy during every service.

The dynamic between Cam and me had gotten weird over the weekend. We had been very close through most of high school, but Cam was starting to change. I know he'd drunk alcohol before and may have even tried pot, although he never told me. But he'd never let those vices take him over like they did that weekend. It was more than the illegalities of the stuff that bothered me. Cam gave up control to some extent. And that seemed like a very slippery and dangerous slope.

"You ok, man?" I asked him.

"Yeah, why?" he asked.

"Well, I didn't want to say anything around the guys, but you were kinda out of control this weekend."

"Out of control? What are you talking about?"

"Dude, you were drunk and high and basically naked. What's up?"

"Nuthin'. So what?"

"Well, I mean, it just doesn't seem like you, that's all."

"It's me, bro. Still me here."

Joey Ryan spotted Cam and came up to him in time to break up our deteriorating conversation.

"Sup, man," Cam said to Joey as he shook his hand.

"Heya, bro," Joey reciprocated. He then looked in my direction and gave me a simple, "Hey."

"How's it going?" I replied.

"You study for that test tomorrow?" Cam asked him.

"Nah. Yelski's a joke," Joey laughed. So did Cam.

"Where's your new girl?"

"I'm meeting her later," Joey responded.

Cam was obviously more entertained with Joey's conversation than with mine. I scanned the room and started looking for Brandi, the lady from the Southern Hope pictures.

I didn't know the slightest thing about her, so I didn't know if she had kids she'd be dropping off at children's church, or if she had a husband, or anything. I barely remembered what her face looked like, so if she cut her hair or changed her appearance in some way, then I could sit right next to her and not even know it. Then she walked in the door on the other side of the busy foyer, fortunately looking exactly the same as she had in her photo.

"Hey, I gotta go talk to someone real quick," I told Cam. He didn't seem to hear me, so I just left.

Brandi was looking down at the bulletin after I worked my way through the crowd to her.

"Excuse me," I started. She looked at me wondering who I was and what I wanted. "By chance, is your name Brandi?"

"Yes," she replied.

"Hi, my name is Sy. Did you happen to go on a missions trip with Southern Hope recently?"

"Yes," she curiously replied again.

"Oh awesome. I'm sorry to bother you, but I saw your picture in the Southern Hope office and was wondering how the trip was. I might be interested in volunteering and was hoping to get some more information."

"Oh ok," she answered with a smile. "It was good, I guess, for a missions trip. I had never been on one before, so I didn't really know what to expect. Are you thinking of going on the next one?"

"Possibly," I lied. "So what did you do over there?"

"Well, originally the plan was to install solar panels at the rescue mission, but that didn't happen."

"Rescue mission? I thought you went to the orphanage."

"That was the plan, too, but there was some civil unrest going on at the time, so we were told the orphanage was too dangerous to visit. The place where we stayed was actually a rescue mission that was built by a church in Nashville, but they still had quite a few orphans there, as well."

"Did you meet Kutu?"

"Who?"

"Rusty?"

"I don't know who that is."

Things were rapidly starting to feel more and more out of place.

"You said you were supposed to install solar panels," I began. "Why didn't that work out?"

"The team couldn't get them through customs, I guess."

"You tried to carry them on your plane?"

"We didn't," she said with a chuckle. "A group leader for Southern Hope was supposed to work with a shipping agency to get them to Kenya, but it was like they hit a brick wall."

"That's awful."

"Yeah, the country can be pretty corrupt. It's sad. The mission was disappointed too. They had been without power for some time, but while we were there, they were able to get one of their generators working. There was still a lot of work that needed to be done at the mission, so we helped out the best we could."

"How many people went?"

"Just five of us."

"Including the Southern Hope staff, too?"

"No, just five volunteers. The Nashville group picked us up at the airport. They dropped us off, too."

"So there was no team photographer?"

"No, I don't think so."

"Yeah, Southern Hope really didn't have as much

involvement as I thought they would have, but it was still an incredible trip. You definitely need to go. These kids will change your life. They have nothing, and yet they are the most gracious people I've ever met."

"That's really cool."

"Yeah, it was amazing."

"It sounds like it! I wish you had been back in time for the fundraiser."

"Fundraiser?"

"Yeah, it was a couple of weeks ago. I was told that no missionaries were there because they were overseas or not available. That's why they had a special speaker."

"Well, I was definitely back, but I wouldn't call myself a missionary. I was just a volunteer. Maybe I just wasn't what they were looking for. Well anyway, I'm sorry, but you'll have to excuse me; I'm meeting some friends inside. Do you have a place to sit?"

"I do, thanks."

"It was a pleasure talking with you, Sylas."

"You too, and thanks for the information."

"You're welcome."

When the service began, my brain kept turning in circles. Things were strange. Southern Hope was much smaller than anyone had expected, and even their own volunteers were surprised at their lack of influence. It seemed a bit implausible that all of their misdirection in regards to their size, capacity, and capabilities could be attributed to pure exaggeration. And why have a spokesman talk about helping an orphanage when they really volunteered at a rescue mission? Who cares what kind of building it was? It's all charity.

Throughout the sermon, my mind continued to take a series of sharp turns. I thought about my friend Cam and then my missed opportunity with Natalie. I then turned to more trivial fare, wondering if I should go home for lunch or just grab something from Finchies after service.

Then my thoughts took an unexpected turn. In the foyer before the service began, Cam had asked Joey if he studied for the test in Mrs. Yelski's class tomorrow. I found this odd because there wasn't a test on Monday in Yelski's class. It had already happened last Thursday...for non-football players, at least.

It brought to mind how Topher got that 85 on one of Mrs.

Yelski's quizzes. And that reminded me of the East Creek game when Brock mentioned that he had cheated on an English test.

A bit unnerved, I couldn't help but wonder if Mrs. Yelski was also involved in some questionable activity.

Recklessly blindsided by the idea that Mrs. Yelski was possibly giving athletes such as the football team an unfair advantage in class, I decided to see if my hunch was correct. The next morning in her English class, I strategically sat one chair ahead of where I usually sat. Then when Topher entered the classroom, he sat in his usual spot, which was now catty-corner to me. He looked at me and nodded as if to instruct me not to say anything to anyone about the marijuana. I nodded back, not even caring about that at the moment.

It was announced in a previous class that we'd be having a reading test that day. About half of the time, Mrs. Yelski would have us grade each other's tests while the other half of the time, we'd simply pass our papers forward to have her grade them. When she did have us grade each other, she generally used her trademark phrase of "pass 'em back," which meant to pass your quiz to the person behind you to have him grade it. Today, I was merely hoping to get lucky.

She distributed the tests, and the room stayed quiet for about twenty minutes as we answered the questions about our assigned weekend reading. When Yelski suspected all of us to be complete, she said, "Everyone done? Ok, pass 'em back."

I breathed a sigh of relief. Luck was on my side.

Topher passed his test back to Judy Wilson, and Will Rose passed his to me.

"Could you trade me?" I whispered across the aisle to Judy, offering Will's paper to her. "I can't read Will's writing."

The girl looked puzzled but obliged and slipped me Topher's paper. This was my chance to see what kind of student Topher really was. Even before Yelski read the answers, I knew Topher got several wrong. I took out a piece of paper and started making notes as Yelski read off the correct answers. Overall, he only answered 11 out of 20 correct. He got a 55. He failed. I noted the date and his grade and the subject of the test, in case I ever needed to reference this again.

That was my control test to see if my hunch was correct. I expected to pass Mrs. Yelski's test, but unfortunately, I didn't expect her to pass mine.

CHAPTER 10

Grady and I said hi to each other as we both entered Mr. Oakridge's Bible class around the same time. Shawn was already sitting down, and before I dropped into my chair, I said, "Dude, I talked to that lady from church yesterday about the missions trip she went on with Southern Hope."

"Ok?" he replied seeming only mildly interested.

"She said they didn't work with that orphanage like Jeremy said in his speech. She said that none of those solar panels made it over there!"

"Whoa, whoa, slow down. What solar panels?"

"Remember the ones the church was trying to raise money to buy last spring? They purchased those solar panels to help power a rescue mission, but they never made it to Kenya. She said they got stuck in customs."

"Weird. Those solar panels cost what, like twenty-grand or something?" Shawn asked remembering the figure Pastor Samms had been trying to raise from the church.

"Yeah, something like that."

"I wonder if there's a way to look at the records of Southern Hope."

"Like the financials?"

"Yeah. Twenty G's is a big chunk of change that's probably gonna show up somewhere. At least you can see if they even purchased them."

"Yeah, that's good. How would we do that? Would we need to break into an office somewhere?"

"You might. I'm not," Shawn said.

"Man, I feel like everything is turning upside down."

"Don't get too dramatic, Sy. You're probably overthinking this Southern Hope thing anyway."

"Yeah, but that's not the only thing that feels off: Mrs. Yelski is curving grades."

"What?"

"Yeah, she lets football players take tests later and gives them better grades than what they actually earn. I just set up one of Topher's quizzes during second period to confirm my suspicion."

"Huh?"

"Good morning, class," Mr. Oakridge said, greeting everyone as he entered the room.

"Topher failed a quiz the other week, and when he got it back, she put an 85 on it," I said, my voice lower now that the teacher had arrived. "I graded one of his quizzes this morning and know that he failed that, too. So when he gets it back and it's not an F, I'll know for sure she's curving them."

"You're jumping around way too much, man. You're going from this Jeremy guy to Southern Hope to Mrs. Yelski; you're all over the place, Sy."

"Ok, settle down, class. Settle down," Oakridge commanded.

Shawn leaned in and whispered, "You're probably just getting paranoid now, man. I'm sure everything's got some sort of explanation, but you're on edge and starting to see stuff that's not there. I'd just focus on one thing for now, if I were you."

Mr. Oakridge stood in front of the class and took charge by simply standing there. "Today we will hear from Kendra and Susan on Hinduism," he said. Right away, Kendra Hollinsworth and Susan Joy stood from their seats.

The advice Shawn had given me was good. There were so many moving parts, so many stupid little things that probably weren't connected at all that I didn't know anything about. I needed to focus on just one of them. And that's what got my brain re-centered, honing in on Southern Hope again and specifically what Shawn had said about finding their financials.

Beverly was one of the only middle-aged women who I would consider a friend. She had a dark sense of humor, had been divorced twice, sported a large tattoo of a butterfly across her chest, and often shot rabbits from her garden with a BB-gun. She was the accountant for Winters' Printing, and in the brief moments we shared between obligations at work, we'd often engage in lightly teasing someone around the office or superficial flirting. I was always joking with her, but sometimes I got the feeling that she wished I wasn't.

On the afternoon just before Winters' closed for Thanksgiving weekend, I poked my head in Beverly's office as she was trying to figure out what the new invention of electronic mail was and how to use it. I casually brought up the topic of accounting and asked her how nonprofit organizations work. Eventually, I steered the conversation toward my true intentions of learning more about the different nonprofit regulations and she told me about Form 990, which was the tax return for nonprofits. Form 990s, she told me, can be made public upon request. This form would allow me to see if there were any discrepancies in Southern Hope's records. Anyone who wished to see a snapshot of how a particular charity was operating could request this form from the IRS. I lied and told her that I was working on a school project for an economics class, and she dug through a large book to find the document and mailing address needed to request the form. She printed a few off for me, which I thanked her for, and then I stayed in her office a few more minutes. I stayed mostly out of obligation and regret, to make her feel that I had not simply used her. We complained about the new clock-in policy and the rainy weekend before I headed back to my desk to finish out the day.

With work and school behind me for Thanksgiving break, I finished one last chore to hopefully put my mind at ease. Returning home that evening I filled out a document Beverly had given to me called Form 4506-A, which would request the tax returns for Southern Hope. I slid it into its envelope, planning to mail it on Black Friday when the post office would resume deliveries again. I wasn't sure how long the whole process would take, but knowing the efficiency of the federal government, I didn't expect to receive my answers quickly. I addressed the envelope and placed the stamp, but just before I licked it shut, I thought of something.

Southern Hope was a familiar name around the church. Endless fundraisers for the Kenyan orphanage, as well as other charitable ventures, were all put on by Clanton Baptist. So I put the envelope back on my desk, grabbed the second form, and began to write. I decided I would also request Form 990 for Clanton Baptist.

Because my dad was being his typical antisocial and domineering self, he issued a decree that we were not driving back home to visit the family that year for Thanksgiving. He was a Republican and his brother Paul was a Democrat, which meant that most holiday gatherings usually ended with some sort of political argument regarding which party Jesus would belong to if he were on Earth today. Paul only lived a few towns away from his parents in Pennsylvania and was going to be at Grandma's that year, so Dad decided not to visit. My dad, permeated with holiday cheer, allowed me to go if I drove myself, but I didn't have the gas money.

Thanksgiving came, and while my friends were all celebrating with their families, I was left in the cluttered dining room with my parents. My two older siblings drove to Grandma's instead. My brother Jimmy lived closer to her anyway, and my sister Sarah was a social butterfly who loved being surrounded by lots of family. My mom made a turkey with some boxed stuffing and gravy. I heated up the canned beans and cranberry sauce. My dad slept in his easy chair while the radio played some static-laden old gospel music station that I never knew existed.

While my mom was working on the turkey, I decided to call grandma's house to wish them a Happy Thanksgiving.

"Yello," my Uncle Paul answered on the other end of the phone.

"Happy Thanksgiving, Uncle Paul! This is Sy."

"Hey, Happy Thanksgiving to you there, Sy. You staying down there with the old man in Clanton?"

"Yeah, the parents and I are down here. I would have loved to come up if I had the gas money."

"Tell your pastor I still haven't gotten my gold plaque," he said. "Maybe he'll get it for me for Christmas."

"Ok, I will," I chuckled politely. Uncle Paul had held a grudge against Pastor Samms for about eight years, ever since he donated around $2,000 to help the church build the North Wing which was now being used by Cherrywood Christian Academy. Pastor Samms had sent out mailers and spoken at conferences, asking for donors to help complete their facility. Donors who gave $2,000 or more were promised two gold plaques in their honor, one to be affixed to the wall of the North Wing and the other to keep as a thank you gift. There were no gold plaques anywhere to be seen in the North Wing.

"You wanna talk to Grandpa?" Uncle Paul asked.

"Yeah, if he's around."

"He's right here. Hold on."

After a slight pause and the jostling of the phone on the other end, grandpa picked up the phone.

"Happy Thanksgiving, slugger," my grandpa said. Of all the people that I would miss that year, he was number one. My grandfather was a kind man and soft-spoken, unlike my father. My father was the oldest of two children, the son his parents had wanted through years of trying to have children. He was doted on far more than his younger brother, who came as an anticlimactic surprise four years later. The favoritism my father received created quite a bit of tension between them. At a young age, my father began to believe that the world revolved around him, but as he grew older he soon found that, in fact, the world was merely passing him by. My grandfather loved my dad, but was the first to admit that he spoiled him when he was younger.

My grandma walked every day and was in great health, so she'd be around for many more years. But Grandpa's heart was failing and everyone knew it. I felt certain that the next funeral I attended would be his. It made me resent not being able to see him, and not for the first time made me angry with my father for being so stubborn.

My lonely Thanksgiving came and went. Black Friday marked the start of the Christmas shopping season, and since school and work were both closed that day, my boredom took me to the church. I'd seen a flier somewhere advertising a bake sale raising money for a youth group trip some girls from school were going on just after Christmas.

The church lobby was humming with bright faces and delicious smelling treats as some volunteers were starting to decorate it for Christmas. There were several booths with various sweets available for purchase, and to my surprise, Natalie just so happened to be one of the volunteers. She was wearing an apron, had her hair pulled back in a bun, and was picking up several dirty bowls and trays from one of the tables when I arrived.

"I didn't know you baked," I cautiously said to her as I approached her booth.

"Sy, how are you? How was your Thanksgiving?"

"It was good. How was yours?"

"Mine was good, too."

"Do you need any help with those?"

"Uh, sure...if you want to. I'm just taking them back to the kitchen to clean."

"Wait. Are you guys baking fresh cookies as we speak?"

"That's the best way to sell them!" she replied with a smile.

"Well in that case, let's get these to the kitchen," I said grabbing a few bowls and making her laugh.

The empty church kitchen was bursting with the wonderful, fragrant smell of fresh chocolate chip cookies and cinnamon—a scent that always reminded me of Christmas.

"Mmm, they smell good," I said taking the dishes to the sink.

"They've got five more minutes," she said looking inside the oven.

"So you just need these washed?" I asked, pointing to the bowls.

"Yeah, you can put them there. I can do it."

"No, that's ok. I'll help. I spent a whole summer washing dishes at Denny's, so I'm kind of a professional."

She giggled.

"So you're raising money for a youth retreat?" I asked.

"Yeah. A bunch of girls are going to rent a cabin up at Casper Mountain and do some snow tubing and have a Bible study and stuff.

"Oh, that sounds nice."

"Yeah, it should be fun."

"Is Kevin here with you?" I asked nonchalantly.

She paused to consider the right phrasing. "No, he's not here."

I paused for a moment, not sure of exactly how I'd come across so far. Then I started in again with the awkward but nagging question, "So are you guys still together?"

She paused again before saying, "Yeah, sort of."

I hesitated before responding to that. Things were starting to feel tense and weird.

"So... are you a good baker?" I said, quickly trying to break the tension.

"I'm ok. Although cookies are pretty easy to make."

"Not for me. I can barely make a peanut butter and jelly sandwich. But I can buy cookies."

"Are you gonna buy some of our cookies?"

"Absolutely! I once bought three boxes of girl scout cookies from a girl because she was only three boxes away from earning a badge."

"Maybe she just told you that to sell the cookies," she joked.

"That little jerk!"

We both laughed again. The tense moment had passed, and things felt right.

I began to fill the bowls with hot water as Natalie walked up next to me and handed me another empty dish.

"Thanks a lot for helping with this," she said in a surprisingly serious tone.

"Sure. It's my pleasure."

"You're a good guy."

I smiled and went back to scrubbing the dishes. It was a very simple statement but some of the nicest words I had heard in a long time.

"Do you need these pans over here cleaned, too?"

"Um, yeah, but you don't have to do them. I can get those later," she said as she picked up a towel and started to dry the freshly cleaned dishes.

"Nah, I don't mind."

I grabbed a large baking dish, and as I maneuvered it into the sink, the still running faucet caught an odd angle of the pan and reflected spraying water all over the counter, including Natalie and me.

"Whoa! My bad!" I exclaimed, quickly reaching to turn off the faucet. "Sorry about that."

"I thought you said you were a professional," she joked.

"I'm a little rusty, I guess. This thing won't even completely fit in the sink! How am I supposed to clean it?"

"You wash one side at a time, silly."

"Well, that just seems inefficient."

Suddenly, Natalie dusted a wet towel across my face. It caught me completely by surprise, causing me to drop the pan loudly in the sink.

She laughed playfully and said. "Sorry, I guess I'm a little rusty drying dishes, too."

I also broke out in laughter.

We spent an hour together that day. Finally, I was able to make the impression that I had wanted. I helped her as she baked five more batches of cookies, and we talked and laughed about things that probably wouldn't have been funny to anyone else. I looked forward to the next time we would be together and prayed that it would come soon.

As it turned out, Black Friday was really nice that year.

CHAPTER 11

Second period English class came bright and early the Monday we returned to school from our long holiday weekend. Mrs. Yelski opened the class with prayer as usual. With this formality over, she then grabbed a stack of papers to return to us. She must have used the long weekend to catch up on some grading because she was returning a few quizzes we had taken, some from several weeks ago, including the quiz I had used to bait Topher with. When she handed mine back to me, I saw that I had earned a 95; I'd only gotten a single question wrong.

Topher's came shortly after, and I made sure to pay careful attention. Over my shoulder, I watched him flip over the small stack. An essay he had done a few weeks ago earned him an 83. Then he turned over that quiz. It was still marked with my familiar corrections, but interestingly enough, the 55 that I had written on top of the quiz had been changed to an 85 with the stroke of a pen.

I clenched my teeth. I didn't understand why she had done it. I hoped that she had a reasonable explanation for doing such a thing, but whatever it was, it seemed wrong and especially harmful to students like Topher who didn't realize how academically hindered they were. I knew something had to be done about it, and although I cared little for Topher, I didn't want him to get in trouble. He was being cheated out of an education, though. I actually felt pity on him.

As the rest of the quizzes were being handed out, I decided to go directly to Dr. Sites during study hall and let him know what I had discovered.

On my way to fourth period Bible class, I happened to spot Natalie at her locker. Kevin was there too, and they weren't giggling like I had seen them do before. So many times in high school it feels like you need to be very strategic with how you come across to other people. But this was not one of those times. In fact, I felt like being genuine. I didn't know if it was a bad strategy or not, but I didn't want to overthink this. I simply wanted to tell her what I felt.

"Natalie," I said to get her attention as I passed by.

She smiled and said, "Hi, Sy." Kevin also looked at me. I had no idea what he thought about me, and it didn't matter.

Nodding to him out of respect, I turned back to her and said, "It was really great seeing you at the bake sale Friday."

"It was nice seeing you too," she answered.

"Have a nice day." I gave her a smile as I continued to class.

Again, I don't know how that came across to her or Kevin but it didn't matter. That's what I felt and that's what I wanted to say.

I was looking forward to Bible class because I hadn't talked to Shawn since before Thanksgiving break. I had accumulated some information to tell him since then but as I walked in the room, I immediately noticed a strange man sitting at Mr. Oakridge's desk. A white man.

"Who's that?" I asked Shawn as I took my seat.

He just shrugged. The class was still talking amongst themselves as the bell rang, still waiting for our teacher to arrive.

"Good morning, class. My name is Mr. Huxley, and I'll be your new teacher from now on."

The class mumbled even louder. Ross Josef spoke up, asking: "What happened to Mr. Oakridge?"

"Mr. Oakridge has parted ways with the Academy and will be pursuing another career path." Shawn and I looked at each other in confusion. A few of the other students groaned.

"It sounds like he will be missed," Huxley said. "Unfortunately, life can sometimes have other plans for us."

"Was he fired?" I whispered to Shawn. I only got another shrug.

"How was everyone's Thanksgiving?" Mr. Huxley rhetorically asked. "Did anyone do any traveling?"

"Was he let go?" I boldly asked, ignoring his pandering question.

"I'm not at liberty to discuss that."

"That's a yes," Jonathan mumbled from across the room.

"Why?" I asked again.

"I never said he was let go, Sylas. I just know that he parted ways; I don't know the details. Now I know we've got a month to go, but we're almost into a whole new year, so we're going to take a fresh new start and begin with the Book of Proverbs. Everyone please open your Bibles to Proverbs One."

I leaned over and whispered to Shawn, "How did he know my name?"

Shawn looked as surprised as I and just shrugged again. It seemed to be his answer for everything that day.

Most of us reached for our Bibles, although with hesitation. As we did, Angie Simons spoke up. "Mr. Huxley? Will we still be working on the assignment that we had been doing for Mr. Oakridge?"

"Oh. What assignment was that, dear?" he responded.

"We were dissecting the different religions of the world."

"Oh good. I thought you were going to say dissecting frogs because I believe that's a different class," he lamely joked. A few laughed nervously as the tension began to dissipate.

"Actually, now we will be transitioning and looking at a few different books of the Bible. We're going to start with Proverbs. Most of us have memorized some verses from Proverbs, or read it occasionally, but Proverbs was written by Solomon, one of the wisest and richest men to ever live. Ms. - what was your name again?"

"Angie," she responded.

"Ok, I'll get your names down soon, I promise. Angie, would you read Proverbs 1:1 for us?"

"It seems like he has your name down already," Shawn whispered.

As soon as the bell rang, Shawn and I immediately convened.

"You think Mr. Oakridge got the boot?" he asked me.

"Kinda seems like it, but how did that guy know who I was?" I replied stuffing my Bible into my bookbag.

"I dunno, man. That was bizarre."

We both slung our backpacks over our shoulders and entered the hallway, heading to our lockers and next classes. "I'm gonna talk to Dr. Sites this afternoon. I'll ask him about Mr. Oakridge."

"Why are you talking to Sites?"

"Yelski is curving grades. I was right."

"So you're going to go tell Sites?"

"Yeah."

"Are you sure that's a good idea?"

"What do you mean?"

"Are you sure it's worth it?"

"Worth what? It's wrong. I'm not doing this to gain anything."

"Yeah, but you might lose something," he pointed out.

"Like what? No one will know it was me except for you. Don't tell anyone, ok?"

"If someone does find out though - like Topher, probably - you might lose a whole heck of a lot. And he'll be the one to take it."

I shifted the weight of my book bag back up onto my shoulder. "It's not right, Shawn. Someone's gotta know what she's doing. Even if Topher does find out, one day he'll realize I wasn't doing it to hurt him. He's not the one cheating, here - he's being cheated. You think colleges are going to give him a free pass?"

"Okay, fine. Just remember I tried to warn you, because this will come back to bite you."

I hated to go against what my best friend thought, but I knew that alerting Dr. Sites was the right thing to do.

I wasted no time. Immediately at the start of sixth period study hall, I told the teacher that I had to go to the office. He granted me permission even before the bell officially rang to start class. I was about to just do an about-face and exit when I saw Roscoe wave me over from his seat.

I walked over and he quickly said, "Hey, I got something to tell you that you'll want to know about."

Already feeling a lot of time and emotional pressure about dropping my bombshell on Dr. Sites, I nodded but cut him off. "I got something to tell you, too," I said, "but I gotta go real quick. We'll talk later, ok?"

"Ok. Make it quick though."

"You got it," I assured him as I turned to leave the room just as the final bell rang.

I was very nervous. This was the first time that I had voluntarily gone to the principal's office and one of the only times since elementary school that I was preparing to tattle on someone. I knew that even though Dr. Sites would most likely remain very professional about the whole thing, I'd be a target. Also, if Yelski got fired, she would always wonder who the student was who ratted her out. Word spreads fast at the Academy. I would be naive to think that she would never discover it was me. But I also knew right from wrong, and this was the right thing to do.

I slowly pushed open the door to the office. Ms. Crisby looked up from her desk.

"Hi, Ms. Crisby. Is Dr. Sites in?" I respectfully asked.

"He's on the phone right now. Is there something I can help you with?" she answered in her Carolina drawl.

"Actually, no. Sorry. It's pretty important. It's regarding student safety, and it's kind of a private matter, if that's ok."

"Ok. That'll be fine. If you'd like to take a seat, I'll let him know you're here when he's off the phone."

"Ok, thank you." I obliged by taking a seat. I sat there for roughly ten minutes, just listening to the monotonous ticking pendulum clock that sat behind the main counter and Ms. Crisby taking phone calls. My stomach was tied in knots. The waiting only served to make me that much more uncertain of my decision.

Then, seemingly out of nowhere, a deep voice called my name.

"Sylas," Dr. Sites said startling me as he walked out of his office. "I hear you've got an issue you'd like to discuss with me?"

He reached out his hand to offer me a handshake, to which I accepted and replied, "Hi Dr. Sites. Yes, sir. This is pretty uncommon for…"

"Come on in, and have a seat in my office," he said as he escorted me to his office. Once inside, he invited me to have a chair while he rounded the other side of his executive, wooden desk. I obeyed and took a seat in one of the two chairs facing him.

"Thank you for taking the time to see me, sir."

"Sure thing, Sy. What's going on?"

"This is kind of uncommon for me because I am not usually a tattle-tale," I said. He listened closer and let me continue. My heartbeat was still at a rapid pace. "I think I have some information that you might want to hear. And please, I implore you, don't tell anyone I was here. Would that be ok, sir?"

"Alright then. What is it, Sylas?" he agreed cooperatively.

"I just want to let you know so you can make your own judgment on how to handle the situation. Just please forget you heard anything from me."

"Ok, what is it, Sy?"

"Well…" I took a deep, nervous breath. "I think there is a teacher here who is falsifying certain grades."

He raised his eyebrows and listened closer. "Really? Who?"

"Mrs. Yelski, sir."

"Mrs. Yelski? Why do you think that?"

"Well sir, several weeks ago I accidentally saw a classmate's test before it was graded, and I know that he got a lot of the questions wrong. I actually got a 97 on that assignment, so I know that I knew most of the answers, and this particular student didn't. Well, when he got the assignment back, he got an 85, which was really curious to me because I knew that he didn't get that many right."

"Who was the student?"

"Do I have to say, sir? To me, I feel that the teacher is the one cheating the student – "

"I understand. First of all, thank you for coming to me about this. You are doing the right thing. However, this is somewhat serious, and as I investigate it a little further with Mrs. Yelski, I want to make sure I'm referencing the correct information."

Hesitantly I said, "It was Topher Landau."

"Ok," he said appreciatively. "Were there any other incidents?"

"Well, the first one struck me as strange, so I paid attention to a few more of his assignments just because we sit near each other. I even graded one of his papers one time and took notes to make sure I wasn't falsely accusing anyone of anything." Reaching into the front pocket of my backpack, I pulled out my completed quiz that Yelski handed back earlier that morning along with the folded piece of notebook paper with the notes I took on Topher's quiz last week. "Here you go, sir. This is a quiz we took last week in Mrs. Yelski's class that I just got back this morning. I got a 95 on this one, so I only answered one wrong. And this will show what all the questions and correct answers were."

"Well done on the 95."

"Thank you. And these were notes I took last week when I graded Topher's quiz. These were all the answers he wrote down when I graded his quiz, and you can see that he got nine out of twenty wrong, but like I said, I don't think Topher should get in trouble for any of this."

"And you took these notes because you already had a hunch that something wasn't right?"

"Yes, sir. I wouldn't have done this if I didn't think there might've been something going on."

"Ok. And you say that Mrs. Yelski gave him a C on this assignment, instead of an F?"

"Yes, sir. We got these quizzes back this morning, and I definitely saw that his was marked with a C."

"Hmm...You're very observant, Sylas. May I keep these for now?" he asked referencing my quiz and notes.

"Would you mind making photo copies? I just feel like I've kinda put my neck on the line here."

"Of course, we can copy these. Do you know of any other teachers doing something similar to this?"

"Not that I know of, but I haven't been paying attention to any others."

He shook his head in disbelief. "Well...I certainly thank you for trusting me with that information. Thank you very much, Sy. I really appreciate it. And don't worry, I'll keep our little chat in confidence."

"Thank you, sir."

"Do you need a hall pass or anything?"

"No, this is my study hall."

"Ok, well thank you again."

"You're welcome, sir," I said feeling good about what I had done. I could tell Dr. Sites really appreciated it, too. Just before I got up to leave, I remembered the other thing I wanted to ask about.

"I just have one more thing, sir."

"Yes?"

"Was Mr. Oakridge fired?"

Dr. Sites looked a little ruffled. It was clear that he had not been expecting such a question. Searching for the right words, he answered, "Mr. Oakridge is a great man, but the board felt that some of his teaching material wasn't in line with the doctrines we hold to at Cherrywood. But after expressing our concerns with him, he left on his own accord. It was less than an ideal situation. He was a good man. We hated to see him go."

"Were they talking about that belief assignment we were all working on?"

"I'm sorry, Sylas. I really can't discuss any further details. But as I said, it was ultimately Mr. Oakridge's decision to leave."

"Oh," I said, disappointed. "Well, thank you for your time, sir."

I grabbed my bag and started for the door.

"Hey, I should be thanking you!" he said standing as he reached out his hand. I accepted his handshake, and Dr. Sites escorted me back out to the front entry, stopping at the copier to make copies of the notes I brought.

It was unfortunate that Dr. Sites had a board to answer to. I could tell he didn't want to see Mr. Oakridge go either.

Just before we parted ways, I thought of one more question for him. When he handed me back the originals, I asked, "Have you ever heard back from Joseph Knowles regarding my photographs? He had mentioned a potential opportunity for me to work with him."

"Oh yes. Joe. Of course. Ya know, I showed him the photos, and he didn't want to hurt your feelings, but - I'm sorry - he said that you have great talent and to keep honing your craft, but your style wasn't quite to the level he needed at this point. I'm sorry. He thinks you do fine work. He said to keep it up and you'll go far."

I was bummed, but I had known all along that it was a long shot anyway. "Oh, ok. Well, thank you for everything, sir. Have a good day."

"Of course, Sy. You're a good man. Thank you as well."

The relief I felt after leaving the office far outweighed the disappointment I felt about the Joe Knowles opportunity. I had done the right thing and had survived it. That was enough of a reward for me.

There was still about fifteen minutes left in sixth period, so I returned to study hall. The room always stayed quiet so the class could study, which made it very difficult for Roscoe and me to continue our earlier conversation. We both had some pretty meaty information to share, and we didn't want to keep it to ourselves for another twenty minutes, so I turned my chair to face him, like study-hallers often do. The teacher didn't care which way the desks faced, as long as we didn't disturb anyone and returned them to their original positions at the end of class.

We looked directly at each other, our desks touching to form a usable-sized surface. Then Roscoe took out a picture from his backpack and slid it across to my desk. It was a picture of him in hunting camo kneeling behind a six-point buck that he must've gotten over the weekend. I smiled and gave him a thumbs up, to which he did the same. Then I took out a piece of paper and a pen to write the words: *Where did you get him?* - before sliding the paper and photo back his way.

He grabbed his own pen and replied: *My grandpa's place. Thanksgiving morning.*

He slid the paper back.

I replied: *Nice. From your tree stand?*

Yup. That's not the big news though. Natalie's single.

I was shocked. *Really?* I wrote. His big news completely trumped mine.

She and Kevin broke up this morning.

You sure?

Positive. You gotta seize this opportunity. She's not going to be single long.

The bell rang, giving us the freedom to talk normally again as we walked to our next classes. Roscoe and I got up from our seats, rearranged our chairs, and left. He finished giving me the details on Natalie and Kevin. I then told him what I had seen in Yelski's class and what I had done about it. Hearing that Natalie was back on the market was the only bright spot of that depressing Monday. With impending semester exams, a missed opportunity to work for a photography legend, and the open case of fraud that I had uncovered, this was not a good time for my focus to change, although it had to; I probably wouldn't get a second chance to tell Natalie exactly how I felt about her.

CHAPTER 12

Upon arriving to work one day, I found a sticky note on my computer screen asking me to stop by my manager, Mike's office. I knocked on Mike's door and was promptly invited to have a seat in front of his desk.

"Sy, thanks for stopping in," Mike said.

"Sure thing," I said. "I saw the note you left for me."

"Yes, of course. Thanks for coming." He shuffled some paperwork on his desk, the whole time never really looking at me. I had a bad feeling. "Hey listen, I don't want to take up too much of your time, and I'm sorry this has to come a few weeks before Christmas. Please don't take any of this the wrong way, but, um...Jim and I were talking, and we're going to give you a new position."

"Ok," I said, clearly confused.

"We're going to have to transition you back to your previous job in packaging," he explained. "You've done an excellent job for us before in that department, and you already know the ropes, so I think we're going to ask you to fill that role again for us."

"In packaging? Am I not doing well processing orders for you?"

"No, no! It's definitely not that. You're doing great, actually. It's just that, Jim and I know you're in your senior year at school, and once you graduate, you'll probably be going off to college or at least starting work in your field of studies. As much as we'd like to keep you forever, we know that you'll probably only be with us for a few more months. Therefore, we've decided to start training someone to take over your position, so that when you move on, we can have someone in place who is all ready to go."

Not really understanding their logic but still thankful to have a job, I simply said, "Ok. But nothing else is going to change, right? My pay and hours will still remain the same?"

"We're still more than happy to work around your school schedule. Yes, your hours will still remain the same.

Unfortunately, the packaging positions do not pay at the same rate as your current processing position, so we will ask you to accept the current rates for the packaging department."

"So...you're giving me a pay cut?"

"Like I said, please don't take any of this the wrong way. It's not personal; it's just business. If you could take a half hour or so to clean up your work area, and then I'll just have you get with Sam to start for the day. We want you to stay, I hope you don't think we don't want you to. We just have to make preparations in case you decide that working in a stinky, old print shop after you graduate high school isn't for you."

"You're working here," I jabbed. He shook it off with an embarrassed chuckle.

"Thank you for your understanding, Sy. Feel free to come back to me with any questions."

"Alright," I said rather flatly as I took the hint and left his office.

I had hid it well in his office, but I was actually pretty furious. Demoting me made no sense. I could've quit at any time over the past three years. What made them concerned now all of a sudden? Plus, high school graduation wasn't until next June, and it certainly didn't take someone seven months to learn my job. Still, Mr. Winters gave me the job, and he could change it or take it back, if he wanted. It didn't make sense, and the $1.50 per hour pay cut just added salt to the wound. At least I had a job, though, which was something not everyone could say.

Shawn spent weekends at his dad's place in the gated community of Locksboro Country Club. Bruce's gorgeous three-story condo on the water-speckled fourteenth fairway came with a membership that included pool, tennis, and driving range amenities; golf course membership was extra, which Bruce had, but Shawn didn't. Mr. Lessner lived the coveted bachelor life. Mid-40's, good health, plenty of money, a girlfriend, life on a golf course, and no rules. It was no wonder that we enjoyed hanging out with Shawn on the weekends. It gave us a peek into what to expect from the good, lawless bachelor life that would be waiting for us in later years.

We spent a lot of time at the Country Club pool during the summers to mingle with the beautiful elite. But when the scorching summer heat dwindled, we'd often hack around on the tennis courts and driving range. None of us were very good at either sport, but we liked to continually sharpen our skills. On the Saturday after my demotion at work, we spent a good hour abusing Shawn's driving range access. Shawn was the only one of us with decent form. The rest of us were just trying to crush balls as hard as we could, putting ourselves and everyone around us in danger. Eventually, the whole experience deteriorated to a golf ball kicking contest before the manager asked us to leave.

Indoor activities consisted predominantly of Super Nintendo. None of us were big gamers, and about the only time I ever played video games was over at Shawn's dad's house. Super Mario Cart was a favorite. It had decent graphics and just simple racecar action with no heavy, technical maneuvers to get bogged down with. It's what we ended up playing as that day came to a close.

"You guys want some drinks?" Shawn asked as he headed toward the kitchen.

"What do ya got?" Roscoe asked.

"Is everyone cool with Dr. Pepper?" Shawn shouted.

"I just put those in there a minute ago, so they're probably not very cold," Mr. Lessner said to Shawn from the kitchen where he was hooking up a new cordless phone that he had just brought home.

Shawn came back balancing four Dr. Pepper cans.

"They might not be very cold, so you can go grab some ice if you need to," he said. I handed my controller to Roscoe and popped open my soda. Shawn's dad was right. It was lukewarm.

"I'm gonna grab some ice, anyone want some?"

Cam replied, "Yeah, I'll take a glass if you're going back."

Roscoe and Shawn were already engaged in battle on the screen, so they didn't hear me.

"Hi, Mr. Lessner," I said entering the kitchen.

"Hi, Sy," he answered after looking up from the installation instructions.

"New phone?" I asked.

"Yeah. It's got more buttons than I need, though."

"Looks pretty, though," I said reaching for two glasses in the cabinets. Bruce chuckled.

"How'd your photos turn out from that fundraiser a while ago?" he asked.

"Pretty well, I think. Hey, you weren't at the Southern Hope Foundation a few weeks ago, were you? I saw your scooter there."

"My scooter? No, I never rode that darn thing anyway. Hard to believe there's two of those contraptions around town. So how's school going?" he asked.

"Good" I replied. I grabbed the glasses and closed the cabinet. Then I decided to make the moment of small talk more beneficial. I wasn't due to race again for another few minutes.

"Actually, I have a question for you. Did Shawn tell you about this project we were doing in Bible class?"

"No, I don't think so."

I should have known. Shawn never talked to his dad too deeply, so I wasn't surprised.

"Well, we were basically breaking down all of the world's belief systems and religions and stuff," I explained. "We were sort of defining what we believe and why."

He raised his eyebrows and replied, "Sounds like a good class."

"It was, yeah. We're not doing it anymore because they got a new teacher recently, but I'm still thinking about the assignment. Shawn and I actually were assigned Christianity, so that's kinda fortunate, I guess, but it's also kinda weird. I've grown up in a Christian environment and have been exposed to all of this stuff all my life, so it's hard to tell if I've just been conditioned to believe this stuff, or if I actually know it's true. I just wanted to get your take on it because I know how you prove and disprove things for a living."

He set down his phone instructions, probably eager to take a break from the frustrating task. "What do you mean by *stuff*? You were conditioned to believe this *stuff...*"

"Well, like the Bible, God creating the universe, Jesus dying for our sins and all that."

"Ok."

"And I'll admit, there's some weird ideas in there, but it all kinda makes sense, I guess."

Bruce was staring at me in confusion, waiting for me to come to a solid point. I was waiting for that, too. I'll admit, I didn't fully think this spur-of-the-moment conversation through and was kind of intimidated talking to Mr. Lessner. He was a professional litigator and had been known to destroy people in a courtroom. The kitchen setting we were in was certainly much more preferable to me, but I still formulated most of my thoughts while in his presence by looking anywhere but into his confident eyes.

"I mean, let's take the talking snake in Genesis, for example," I went on. "Satan entered a snake and convinced Eve to eat a forbidden fruit. That sounds pretty weird, but no one can really prove it or disprove it so you gotta take it with a grain of salt, right?"

"I suppose."

"I guess what I'm asking is how can you really prove or disprove that this belief system that I've grown up with is true or not? Like, in school, we learn about Noah's flood and God creating the universe and everything, but they don't teach that in real school or in the real world."

"So, for your assignment, you needed to explain why what you've been brought up to believe is true?"

"Yeah, I guess so."

"Why are you still thinking about the project if you don't need to do it anymore?"

I put the glasses that I was still holding onto the counter. The conversation was moving along rather quickly.

"Just...can't get it off my mind, I guess."

It felt a bit odd to open up to Shawn's dad, but perhaps it seemed a bit easier due to the fact that I was unable to talk to my father about such things. My father was not one to question the Scriptures or hear my point of view for that matter.

"I hear ya. Well let's break this down," Mr. Lessner began. "You brought up a good point about how some Bible stories can't be proven or disproven, so what can you really do with that? Not much. So let's look at what can be proven. Science can prove things. Reason, observations, experience - this is all provable stuff. And I might add that I don't always prove things or disprove things in my job. A lot of things can't technically be proven or disproven. I can't technically prove to you that I drove back from the store today, because you didn't see me do that. But I can show you my car in the garage; I can show you my car keys and store receipt in my pocket. You can obviously see that I'm here; you know that I can't fly, so based on that evidence, you can deduce that I most likely drove here today. That's what we must do in life. We take the most plausible evidence and piece it together to form our belief system."

This made sense. I was listening more intently now as he continued on. "Ok, so you mentioned that Christianity teaches that God created the universe, but the "real world" teaches evolution as the cause, right?"

"Yeah."

"Well, science is very evidential, so let's look at that."

I knew that Shawn's dad wasn't a strong Christian, if one at all, although he often referred to himself as one. He seemed like a good man and very successful, but church wasn't really his thing.

Bruce began by telling me why he didn't necessarily believe that one God created the universe, and he even explained why. He used the analogy that if he built a car from scratch, he'd have so much pride in it that he'd be tinkering on it all the time. If there was a Being powerful enough to create this world, why does He never seem to interact with it afterwards?

I kept listening. It was all making sense. He explained that animals, like Darwin's finches, have been observed adapting to their environment by evolving different body structures, and even though major evolutionary changes like evolving from one species to another, for example, have never been officially observed, there is still plenty of other evidence to suggest that these types of major changes have happened in the past.

Humans share ninety-eight percent of their DNA with chimpanzees. Dolphins and whales have five bones in their pectoral fins just like mammals have five fingers. Most every living creature operates the same way with eyes, noses, livers, hearts, and other common elements. The fossil record indicates that lower life forms appear in the bottom, earlier rock layers, and as the layers increase, so does the advancement of the fossilized creatures inside.

He explained everything very clearly, and based on the evidence available, deduced that evolutionary theory seemed to be the most plausible explanation for life. Along with his earlier analogy about the creator and the car, he had a more logical, scientific, and observable argument for evolution over anything else.

His reasoning made total sense, and it left me questioning my own even more than I had been already.

I was silent for a moment after he finished explaining. Then I replied with, "Do you think God could've started the evolutionary process?"

"Like a best-of-both-worlds type thing? I suppose *a* god could've started it, but the God of the Bible probably didn't because the Bible clearly states that God created all things like we see them today in a week," he paused with a smirk. "That contradicts evolution, so probably not."

"Now, I'm not suggesting that you don't listen to your teachers or anything. That's not what I'm saying at all. I'm just suggesting that you consider outside evidence. Your school teaches that in Genesis, a loving God created the universe from scratch, but then just a few chapters later, he's killing them all with a flood." He paused with eyebrows raised. Another valid point. "Again, I'm not saying don't listen to your teachers. But just think for yourself. What makes the most sense based on the evidence *you* see?"

I guess that is what Mr. Lessner's opponents usually felt like. He clearly stated his premises for his beliefs, gave reasonable evidence to support them, and pretty much stopped me in my tracks.

"So can I ask you this?" I replied. "Evolution probably doesn't involve a god. But do you believe in one?"

This question seemed to make him uncomfortable. He leaned back to support his weight on the kitchen counter and tilted his head to search for the best approach.

"You know, Sy...I do, but not the way you do. I don't think god is an actual being who can create or do things like you and I can. I think he - or it - is more of a state of mind. A lot of people call it Mother Earth, the Universe, morality, whatever you want. I think god is what you make it. But please don't think that I have anything against Christianity or the Bible or anything. Religions have done more good for the world than bad, I think. I know they get a bad rap sometimes, but I think more charities have been started in the name of religion than wars have, so I have nothing against them. And I also really appreciate the level of education and opportunities that Cherrywood provides. That's why I send Shawn there. This report you were working on seems like an excellent exercise."

"Yeah, it was. The teacher was awesome."

"I also appreciate your asking me. It takes a lot of guts to interrogate a lawyer. I respect that. Thank you for your honesty."

"Sy, you're up," shouted Roscoe from the living room.

"Ok, I'll be right there," I replied. I then turned back to Mr. Lessner and said, "No problem. Thanks for talking."

"Anytime. If you have any more questions, feel free to let me know. I'll shoot straight with ya."

"Ok, thanks."

I headed back into the living room, my thoughts rattled enough to completely forget about my cup of ice.

Another week passed and mid-term exams were just around the corner. Teachers were gearing down their lessons in preparation for midterms, followed by the Christmas break. I had passed Natalie a few times in school but never quite made any more progress than that. My friends were pushing me to make a move on her fast, but I had developed a pretty solid idea of what I was going to do and how I would do it. The only problem was that it was going to require two more weeks. The nail-biting question was whether or not I could afford to wait those two more weeks, or if someone else would get to her first. If I could hold out, I was virtually a shoo-in. But if not and another guy swooped in, then I was done for. I decided to wait.

After school one very average Thursday, I wandered to my car after classes. Nothing had been out of the ordinary for the entire day until I found a note tucked under my windshield wiper. It was a folded piece of college-ruled notebook paper. I opened it up, and to my horror, read:

Here's a news story for you: Nosy yearbook journalist gets his teeth kicked in for investigating the wrong people.

I was terrified. I quickly looked around. Students were milling about, flirting, and driving away. Nothing was different. No one was watching me. I looked back at the note. It appeared to be male handwriting, and the torn three-holes in the side of the notebook paper suggested it was a student who ripped it from his notebook. But who? What could this mean and why now?

I didn't tell anyone about the note right away, not even Shawn. My initial thought was that it had come from Topher. Maybe he found out that I dropped his name to Sites. But I was pretty confident that it wasn't his handwriting. I kept my head low for another few days, just thinking and observing. For the life of me, I couldn't find anything out of the ordinary. No one was watching me, acting threatening, gossiping, or anything.

One Saturday, on a bold whim, I pulled the phone book out from the kitchen drawer. I scanned the white pages and then scribbled down an address that had come to mind. I didn't pay attention to the phone number. What I had to say wouldn't feel right coming over the phone, so I got in my car and headed for the address.

I scanned a map from my glovebox that I had draped over my steering wheel. Caverns Creek Road was over on the west side of town in a new subdivision that was developed a few years ago. Once I re-folded the map to the best of my abilities, I put the Nova in reverse and backed out of the driveway.

153 Caverns Creek Road was a quaint, modest home. The yard was neat, as were most of the houses around the area, and a simple American flag hung from a porch column. I could've parked in the driveway, but I stayed on the street and respectfully followed the sidewalk up to the house. I took a deep breath and rang the doorbell. A few moments later, a young girl cracked the door and peeked out.

"Hi, is your dad home?" I cheerfully asked.

She nodded and ran back inside, leaving the door ajar. A few moments later, I could hear heavier footsteps inside, and Mr. Oakridge, my beloved former Bible teacher pulled the door open.

"Sylas!" he said, surprised to see me.

"Hello, sir. I'm sorry to drop in unannounced."

"How did you know where I live?"

"The phone book. I took a guess."

"Oh. Well, it's nice to see you. Would you like to come in?"

"No, that's fine. I don't want to impose. I know you weren't expecting company. I was just wondering if I could talk to you for a minute."

"Sure, what is it?"

"We miss you at school. Everyone does. It's just not the same really, without you there.

"Thank you Sylas, that's really nice of you to say." I could sense that Mr. Oakridge knew that I was stalling.

"They said that you decided to change career paths."

Mr. Oakridge looked down at his house slippers. He said nothing to this, and as far as I was concerned, it was enough.

"They fired you, didn't they?"

He looked rather stunned. "Is that what they told you?"

"Not directly, but I figured it out. Dr. Sites said you left on your own accord, but I don't think you would've just voluntarily done that. They forced you out, didn't they?"

He paused for a moment. "I'm gonna grab my coat. It's chilly out here. Hold on."

He ducked back inside and closed the door. I took a seat on his front step. After a few moments, he came back out wearing a coat and a pair of unlaced boots. Completely shutting the door behind him, he took a seat on the banister next to the stairs.

"It was their decision," he said. "They hired me, and they had the right to fire me."

"But it wasn't because of you, was it? It was something else, right? Something on their end."

"I hope so. I thought I was doing a good job."

"You were! You were awesome. What was the real reason they let you go?"

"Sylas, I think it's really nice of you to come here to see how I've been doing, but I'm not really into mulling over sour grapes. And no disrespect to you, but I don't think it's the most appropriate thing to discuss with a high schooler."

His defenses were up and rightfully so. I knew how he felt in some small way, just having received a demotion at *my* job. I knew he needed my empathy over my pity.

"But you never treated us like we were high schoolers. You taught us to be more than that and to challenge what we believe and what we were told. I can respect your willingness to bury the hatchet, but I can't help but think there might be something else going on."

"Sylas, I'm not going to talk badly about anyone or gossip."

"No, I know. I'm not asking you to, sir," I said. I know I had made this already very uncomfortable for him. I thought for a moment on how I was going to make it right while still getting the answers I was looking for. "Do you know a Jeremy Maitland?"

"Jeremy who?"

"His name is Jeremy Maitland. He does some stuff for the football team."

Mr. Oakridge looked uncomfortable. "I might've heard of him, but I don't know."

"How about Mrs. Yelski? What do you know about her?"

"She's a fine teacher and a nice woman." He then paused for a moment and then added, "Sy...be careful."

"About what?"

"About talking too much. God gave us two ears and one mouth for a reason."

I wanted to say something else, but took the advice he had just given me and kept my mouth closed. After a moment, he began again.

"Sy, you've got a lot of guts coming here. A lot of courage to speak your mind, but sometimes your mind can wander. I've seen it. Just be sure it doesn't take you down a path you can't come back from. Don't spook the prey. Don't be hasty."

Thoughts raced through my head, but I was unable to pinpoint one to bring to the tip of my tongue. It was like an expressway of thoughts and feelings zipping by me, and I was not able to find the right words. I didn't even know where to begin.

Mr. Oakridge sighed again, his breath clouding the air in front of him. "You're really bright, Sy. I've always known that about you. That's why I gave you that assignment on Christianity."

I was confused. "You didn't give that to me. I picked it, right?"

He smiled. "Do you think I accidentally forgot about you when I was distributing those?"

I thought back to the time when he passed out beliefs for us to choose from and when he seemingly passed by Shawn and me. He continued, "You were the last to pick from the bag, weren't you? It was just a simple sleight-of-hand trick. Magicians do it all the time. I had you choose that card."

"You wanted Shawn and me to have the easiest assignment?"

"You're kidding, right? Sylas, how long have you spent thinking about that project I gave you?"

I began to piece together the hours at the library and at home, the phone conversations between Shawn, and the discussion I had with Mr. Lessner just one week before.

"Exactly," he said before I gave him an answer. "You're an over-thinker. You're bright, Sy. You notice everything. You pick up on everything. You think about everything. Anyone else would've just regurgitated what they had learned in church for the past eighteen years, but that's not what I wanted. I needed someone to think it through. That's why I gave that card to you, and I think that's why you're here."

I wisely continued to listen, utilizing the wisdom of the two ears and one mouth approach.

"Things at the Academy aren't always what they seem," he continued, "but by you coming here, I know you already know that. Just be careful, okay? Make your moves very carefully."

Mr. Oakridge put his arm around my shoulder and gave it a squeeze, then headed for his door.

"I found this note on my windshield the other day," I blurted out, handing him the folded note from my pocket.

He just paused to think after he read the message. I abruptly added, "And I know Mrs. Yelski is curving grades. Dr. Sites knows, too."

"How do you know Dr. Sites knows?" he asked me.

"I told him."

Mr. Oakridge dropped his head.

"What?" I asked. "What's wrong?"

Taking a moment to formulate the correct words, he responded, "This coming year is going to be very different for you now, Sy, and no advice I can give you will change that."

My neck burned with pins and needles as painful goosebumps covered my arms. Mr. Oakridge thanked me for coming and returned back inside. I sat alone on his front porch for a moment. The solitude was chilling; it was a feeling with which I would soon become all too familiar.

CHAPTER 13

It was the first night of Christmas break.

"Is this gonna be too cheesy?" I asked holding an extension cord and three Walmart bags, each stuffed with packages of one hundred-strand Christmas lights. I held a grand total of nine hundred lights in all.

"Grow a pair, dude," Cam said. "She knows you like her. Now you just gotta own it." He was searching in his pocket for his keys while he spoke. Being on the church staff, Cam's dad had a key to the sanctuary, so when his dad got home from work earlier that week, Cam ran out to Sanderson's and had a spare key made.

Once he found the key, he placed it in the lock and was rewarded with a big *CH-CHUNK* as the push bar on the inside of the door engaged. The door unlocked.

Cam slowly pushed it open and peeked inside. A few exit signs and ambient streetlights from beyond the stained glass windows were the only lights within the church lobby. The large sanctuary did not have an alarm system. The only security for the campus was a hired cop who patrolled the grounds every hour or so. Perhaps the cost of a security system was too expensive for these large, historic buildings, or perhaps the residents of Clanton wanted to believe there was no need for one in their safe, humble town. Either way, breaking into the sanctuary was as easy as spending less than a dollar for the key at Sanderson's.

"When is she coming?" Shawn asked, holding some of the pieces of black foam board that I had crafted earlier that day.

"Nine-thirty," I replied.

"That's in what, two hours?" Cam asked.

"About an hour and forty-five minutes."

We walked through the lobby and into the cave-like theater. On stage, the decorations formed eerie silhouettes. They were figures of men and ambiguous shapes; any one of them could have been watching us.

"Wait here while I try to find the lights upstairs," Cam said.

When Cam was younger, he would often hang out with his dad in the sound booth. When the sermon was boring, his dad would even let him operate some of the equipment, so he had a good knowledge of which knobs and levers did what.

The dark objects on stage grew larger as Shawn, Roscoe, and I moved down the dark church aisle towards them. I had seen them many times in the daylight and knew what each one of them was. I had participated in the Christmas Cross, the annual Christmas pageant put on by Cherrywood Baptist, every year in middle school, and the stage setup had never really changed much. As I studied the shapes in the dark, the stage lights came on.

"Does that work?" Cam shouted down from the sound booth, his voice echoing throughout the massive, open room.

"Yeah, that's probably good," Roscoe answered.

The three wise men watched us from stage left while a full-scale manger and its animal inhabitants stared from stage right. Elaborately hung Christmas lights and festive decorations adorned the stage all around us. These were the tried and true representatives of the Christmas Cross.

"So where do you want to tie this string off from?" Roscoe asked.

I surveyed the set design. "Uhh, maybe from the top of that building over there to that balcony," I said pointing to one of the plywood cutout stage props. "What do you guys think?"

Shawn yelled to Cam, "Stay up there! We're gonna tie off from the balcony!"

We spent the next hour and a half rearranging and adorning the stage. We used baby Jesus' manger and a plywood cutout camel to climb onto the roof of the stable and managed to successfully tie one end of string while we pulled the other end up from the opposite balcony.

When the job was done, I realized that this was going to be epic—for good or for bad. There was no playing it safe this time. We were all hanging in the balcony, judging the belching contest Cam was having with himself, and looking at our handiwork. Cam and Shawn had sprung for a soda from the break-room vending machine. Roscoe didn't have any money, and I was too nervous.

"It's quarter after nine, guys," I said. "Should I go?"

"Yeah, go outside and wait for her," Cam replied, his feet propped on the pew in front of him.

"Ok. Turn the lights off," I told Cam. "Are you guys ready?"

"Are you?" Roscoe fired back.

I took a deep breath and replied, "No, but here goes."

"Good luck, man," Shawn said.

Cam started to chant: "Sylas…Sylas…Sylas…"

The rest of the gang joined in. I grabbed my jacket and walked down to the main level and quietly out the front door. It was chilly outside. The clouds formed a haze around the moon. We weren't lucky enough for a Christmas snowstorm, but one could hope.

For fifteen minutes I paced outside, blowing steam out of my mouth like a train engine. Then she showed up, right on time.

She drove a new yellow Jeep Wrangler. It was a generous birthday gift from her parents, but I never heard her brag about it. Even with the hard top on, you could tell a fun adventurous girl was inside. You can tell a lot about a girl by the car she drives.

"Hi!" she greeted me kindly after she had parked her car. All of the other times she responded neighborly to me, but this time she actually seemed happy to see me. I felt instantly warm. "Why did you want to meet here?" she asked as she opened the door.

"I want to show you something," I replied.

"Ok."

"It's inside," I motioned as we walked towards the sanctuary.

"Is it open?"

"Yup."

I grabbed the cold, brass door handle and opened it up. My heart felt like it was about to beat out of my chest. The lights in the sanctuary were dim, just enough to see the familiar Christmas Cross decorations. I could see Cam's faint silhouette in the sound booth and a brief glimpse of Roscoe before he ducked behind a doorway. Fortunately, she never saw either one.

"Ok, I've got something that I want to show you. Follow me."

"Ok." she responded curiously excited. We walked to the middle of the sanctuary, standing directly toward the familiar stage.

"Ok, now close your eyes," I instructed.

She paused, smiled and then agreed. "Alright."

She put her head down and closed her eyes. I immediately signaled to Cam who engaged the lightboard and then ducked out of sight.

"Ok, open them," I said.

Slowly she opened her eyes and looked up. A huge smile appeared on her face and she started to laugh.

Artificial snow fell from the ceiling as the stage lit up with a vast array of colorful lights that had been prepared by the church and strings of Christmas lights that we had all feverishly pre-hung just hours before. The lights all connected at center stage where, our thirteen pieces of black foamboard all hung about ten feet in the air, filled with Christmas lights that spelled out "HAPPY BIRTHDAY."

"Oh my gosh!" she exclaimed as she cupped her hands over her mouth and started to laugh.

"You told me that you love Christmas lights," I said.

She laughed. "This is so cool. Did you do all of this?"

"It was my idea, but I had some help setting it all up."

"Unbelievable," she replied. "This is seriously the nicest thing anyone has ever done for me."

I didn't say anything. I just smiled as our eyes locked.

"Wait a minute...how did the lights come on? Are your friends here now?" she asked.

"Guys!" I shouted. "You can come out."

"My friends Cameron, Jake, and Shawn helped me," I told her. "You know them, right?"

"Happy birthday, Natalie," they shouted one by one as they emerged from hiding.

"Oh my gosh, thank you all so much!"

"It was all Sy," Roscoe said from the balcony.

It was about this time that I became extremely nervous. My friends were not supposed to be watching me from the balcony. I wasn't supposed to feel this extra pressure. But now was the moment that I'd been waiting for. Now I had to ask the question that I've been thinking about for the better part of this semester.

"I...I just wanted to tell you Happy Birthday."

"Well, that is the coolest birthday present ever. Thank you."

"So...you're not going home for Christmas this year, huh?" I was fumbling and I knew it.

"Not to my dad's, no. Can't afford the airfare."

"Oh. This is the best I could do as far as Christmas lights. If I could, I—"

"He likes you, Natalie," Cam brazenly shouted from the

balcony. I turned red, and Natalie smiled. It was a smile that told me that she already knew.

"He would like the chance to get to know you better because he thinks you two have a lot in common," he continued. I was visibly embarrassed although I can't say that I was upset. Cam was doing a great job, and as long as I could deal with the embarrassment, he was making my difficult job easier.

"He had a really great time working with you at the bake sale, and he thinks you're hot," Roscoe blurted. Everyone laughed but me.

"He's one of the best guys I know, and he'd just like a chance to get to know you better," Cam said. "At least give him a shot. There's no harm in trying."

I was flattered, but knew that I needed to be my own man at some point. "Thanks guys," I said. "I'll pay you later."

Everyone chuckled.

"They're right," I said to Natalie. "I've had a really nice time getting to know you in the few times that we've interacted, and yes, I do think you're very attractive. I was just wondering if you would be open to the idea of getting to know each other better. I really like you."

It was all out there. I did what my friends instructed and just put it all on the line. Playing coy didn't work before.

"So, are you asking me out?" she smiled.

"Uh...yeah. I guess that's the gist of it."

"Then sure. You're cute, and I wouldn't mind getting to know you better, too."

I smiled. "Thanks," I said, not knowing what the correct response would be. "So...I can hug you now, right?"

She laughed. "Yeah."

I laughed too. My friends clapped, and I let them know I appreciated them by fist-pumping the air behind her back.

"So, umm...this is awkward, but...I gotta clean this stuff up," I said.

"I'll stay to help you clean," she said. "Can we get a picture first though? Does anyone have a camera?"

My friends and I smiled and chuckled. "You picked the right guy, ma'am," Roscoe said.

"Yeah, I got one," I said. "It's in my car. I'll go get it."

It was about 11:30 and I was on cloud nine when I packed up to head home. I couldn't stop smiling. Everything had gone perfectly, and I still couldn't believe that I was dating Natalie Benson. After I jammed the foam board letters and Christmas lights into my back seat, I started the car and fiddled with the radio, looking for some festive Christmas music to echo the feelings that I was bursting with. I found one of those stations that played Christmas music twenty-four hours a day during the month of December and "O, Holy Night," one of my favorite songs, immediately flooded the car.

On the way home, I jubilantly sang along, albeit off-key, with the lyrics. My commute took me past First Clanton Bible Church, a small humble church with an even humbler lighted nativity scene. As I pulled into my driveway though, the joyous Christmas spirit started to quickly unravel. On the curb still covered in Christmas lights was our family's Christmas tree.

I opened the front door which was no longer wearing its festive wreath to find my mother sitting on the living room floor in her pajamas packing up many of our childhood ornaments and stockings.

"What's going on, Mom?" I asked quietly.

"Oh hi, Sy. I'm sorry. Your father cancelled Christmas this year."

"Cancelled Christmas? What does that even mean?"

She was trying to hold back tears. "Jimmy and Sarah aren't coming home this year. Jimmy will be with his girlfriend's family, and Sarah is going to Grandma's, and your dad thinks that since you spend most of your time away from the house and with friends, his children don't value this family so he's canceling it."

"Seriously? Why did he throw away our tree? It's artificial!"

She chuckled through a falling tear. "Shh...he's in bed. You know your father. When he gets mad at something, he can go overboard."

"So, what, we're just not exchanging gifts and pretending that Christmas never happened?"

"I'm so sorry, Sy. I really wish I could get you something. I knew exactly what I was going to get you, too."

"Why do you put up with this mom? Why don't you leave

him to be miserable on his own?"

My mother shook her head, as she wiped the tears from her eyes.

"I can't do that, Sylas. I can't. You kids deserve better than that. That's just how he is sometimes. Besides, I can't handle the idea of being alone."

"You're not alone, Momma. I would never let that happen. Dad is a lonely, miserable man who wants to make everyone feel as bad as he does."

"That's enough of that," she said, doing her very best to sound strong. " I don't want to hear you talk that way. I'm just sorry that there won't be a Christmas this year."

"Mom," I said shaking my head. "There's still going to be a Christmas. It's still Jesus' birthday. Santa and his reindeer are still going to fly on the twenty-fifth. The only place it won't exist is in Dad's heart, but I am very sorry that he took the joy of giving away from you this year."

She dropped her head and continued her task of wrapping one of my childhood craft ornaments made from a Kerr jar lid and pipe cleaners.

"I'll be back later, Mom."

"Where are you going? It's almost midnight!"

"I'll be back. It'll be ok."

From our curb, I furiously grabbed a few of the light strands that still entangled our fake tree along with some of the Christmas decorations that used to adorn our front porch. Tossing them in the back seat of my car, I drove over to that drab little manger scene at First Clanton Bible Church.

I stayed out in the cold until 3 a.m. glamming up their meager display. When I was done, the church landscaping, manger, and trees shone with life and excitement while the big, black foam board letters of Happy Birthday hung brightly over baby Jesus. I stepped back to admire my handiwork and snap a photo, but I couldn't help but think about my family.

There comes a time when Christmas really has nothing to do with the presents you get or the ones you receive, as clichéd as that sounds. Those are simply mementos of a genuine love between family members or friends. I felt bad that my mother's joy of seeing her children happy on Christmas morning was taken from her. I couldn't have cared less about the gifts themselves. I felt sorry for my mother and pity for my father. He missed more than just the meaning of Christmas; he missed the meaning of Christ. I was used to dealing with his demeanor the other three hundred and sixty-four days of the year, but somehow the coldness in his heart seemed to break mine just a little more that Christmas.

CHAPTER 14

The minivan pulled up to a quaint farmhouse. A few pieces of rusted farm equipment were scattered around the property. Up in the hills and back roads of southern Virginia, Roscoe's grandparents had a storybook place to come home to for Christmas. The color palette of the surrounding woods was very dull, a stark contrast to the bright red barn and vibrant decorations on the house. There were no white Christmases around here, just gray trees, brown leaves, rusty tools, and a pale sky. The Christmas décor was simple, yet meaningful – a candle in each window, a wreath on the front door, a modest tree in the living room. The warmth could be felt through the drab and drizzly afternoon. The coziness was tangible.

"Here we are," Roscoe said as he slid the side door of the van open.

"Nana!" Lily exclaimed rushing past me as her grandma appeared on the front porch, wrapped in a shawl.

I had told Roscoe of my dad's decree this year, and without hesitation, he invited me to spend it with his family, who couldn't have been more supportive. This was a bittersweet moment for me. It was a snapshot from a Rockwell painting—the scene of a joyous, family Christmas homecoming, even though it was not my own. I helped Roscoe and his dad unload the presents, luggage, and shotguns from the back. Mr. Martin and his brother were avid skeet shooters and were planning a bit of target practice.

The house was warm and cozy but slightly cluttered. Stacks of *Lady's Home Journals, Readers Digests,* and cookbooks were piled next to an old organ, while handmade wreaths embellished with cloth flowers garnished the wall above the old instrument. The opposite wall was filled with a cascade of family pictures.

In the living room a collection of Raggedy Anne and Andy Dolls - some of which must've been older than my father - sat on a shelf in the corner. Two dusty whitetail deer heads hung on either side of the TV, which was playing *Rudolph*, the Christmas

Claymation, on a very low volume. A fresh Christmas tree stood proudly in the center of it all.

Roscoe introduced me to his grandparents, his aunt, uncle, and two cousins who would also be staying for Christmas. I smiled politely at everyone, hoping those sweet people would learn nothing about the pain I had left at home, particularly the disconnect between my father and me.

Grandma Francis had a big crock pot of beef stew waiting for us. The beef came from their farm, and the stew was better than anything I had ever tasted. I hated to rush it, but Roscoe and I were in a hurry to get outside. Any Southern boy can tell you there aren't many finer things in life than riding four-wheelers, and there were two of them sitting in the barn. One was his grandpa's, and the other belonged to one of his cousins who was storing it there while he was deployed with the Navy. We reasoned that it was not good to let a vehicle sit for too long without use, so we felt like we were doing his cousin a service.

We tore around the sixty-acre property for about an hour, wiping our runny noses on our sleeves, until my four-wheeler ran out of gas. We left it where it sat, and I hopped on the back with Roscoe to go grab a spare gas can from the barn. Even though I was missing spending time with my brand new girlfriend and even my own family this Christmas, doing thirty miles per hour across an open cow pasture and power sliding on a dirt road was something that couldn't be replaced.

Roscoe's family spent a mellow Christmas Eve just visiting and enjoying each other's company in the living room. They were all devout Christians, so the background music of Christmas songs, prayers around the table, and just all-around positivity was infectious. My family was also Christian, but our holidays never felt like that.

Roscoe and I bunked in a spare bedroom that his grandma had turned into her sewing room. He selflessly let me use the air mattress while he stole a few couch cushions to make up his bed.

"Do you miss Natalie?" he asked as we were preparing for bed.

"It's weird," I said. "I've liked her for so long that it doesn't even feel like we're actually together. So, yeah I want to be around her, but I'm just used to still being single."

"Yeah, I can see that. I'm a little jealous, man. I wish I had a good girl."

"Dude, don't worry about it. You're a great catch for some girl. And let's be honest with ourselves...how many high school relationships actually work out?"

"Yeah, you're right." He paused briefly to unfold a blanket and drape it over his cushions. "Is it weird to be staying here for Christmas?"

"Kinda. I've just never stayed at anyone's house for Christmas, but I'm having a ton more fun than I would be at my house, though. It's mainly weird to have been adopted by someone else's family for Christmas because my family doesn't value it."

"Yeah, that stinks."

"And the really dumb part is that this is what Christmas is all about, ya know? I feel so bad for my mom right now, and my dad, I suppose. He calls himself a Christian but doesn't even see what Christmas, or Jesus, is all about: the generosity, love, compassion, all that stuff."

We laid there in the darkness that night as we let our minds race. Above all other things from my childhood, it was those close times with my friends that I missed the most. As years passed by, deep conversations changed to lighthearted pleasantries, friendships became distant and superficial. Today, we rarely ponder the importance of each passing day, but that night I shared with Roscoe, we shut the world out and opened up our hearts to share our deepest fears, our darkest thoughts, and our greatest doubts.

"You ever wonder what's different about Christians?" I asked.

"What do you mean?"

"I mean, they...or we...call ourselves Christians, but how are we any different from everyone else?" I asked. "Sure, we believe in God, but most people believe in God. Most people believe in Jesus too - he was a real guy. But we believe that He died for our sins, and if we accept that, we'll have everlasting life? So what's the big deal? We just take it one step farther from everyone else, which may or may not be true to begin with. But how does that make a difference? We still got some scriptwriter at Southern Hope writing a speech to deceive donors. People like Mrs. Yelski are manipulating students' grades. Christians like y'all, who are incredibly loving and invite me to be with you on Christmas, yet there are Christians like my dad who went to seminary but cancels

Christmas. My father wants to be a pastor, but what kind of pastor does that? I don't know, man. It just seems like Christianity can mean different things to different people, but if it's that subjective, what's the point in it anyway?"

"If it makes you feel any better, I think Christmas originally started as a pagan holiday," Roscoe said.

"Great, even less reason to be a Christian," I joked. "You ever wonder about the whole thing though? I mean, what significance does Christianity have? The Bible says, "For the wages of sin is death," and, "all fall short of the glory of God." So all humans are born with a sin nature. We were never given a choice to sin or not to sin. We were programmed to sin. So why would a loving God create us, knowing that we are completely programmed to sin and fall short, so that if we literally did nothing, we'd be tortured in hell forever? That's like tying someone to a conveyor belt with a saw blade at the end and giving him only one ultimatum to save himself. That's what movie villains do. Why would a loving Creator do that?!"

Doing his best to avoid a large theological discussion, he answered, "Well, His ultimatum was love. He sent His son to die in our place. That's what Christmas is."

"But why even need to do that in the first place? Why would God create an awful place like hell to torture people there who don't accept the only option He gives us? The world's worst prisons aren't even that bad. What if a person in Cambodia or someplace never hears about God? What then? Or what if he does, but he can't understand the Christian missionary, so he doesn't fully comprehend it? Why would a loving God torture someone in hell for all eternity?"

"Well, God doesn't want us to go to hell. He wants us to be with Him, and He's given us a method to do that."

"Yeah, I know He doesn't want us to go to hell. But it's still there. You ever heard of Pascal's Wager?"

"Mmmm...no."

"I hadn't either before our assignment in Mr. Oakridge's class. Basically, Pascal says that it's safer to believe in God because if He does exist, you'll go to heaven, but if He doesn't exist and you're wrong, you'll just die normally like everyone else. But if you choose not to believe and you're wrong, you'll suffer in hell. So basically, believing in God is the safest option. But taking this bet, so to speak, has no appeal to rational thinking and integrity. You're just taking the coward's way out and hoping you get lucky. If God does exist, why would He let someone into heaven who apparently just beat the system and torture some Pigmy in hell for not understanding what the Christian missionary was saying? There's no logic in any of that!"

"Well, we can't understand the mind of God."

"I don't have to understand it, but it just doesn't seem like a perfect nature to me. The concept of hell doesn't make me like my concept of who God is, and some of what I read in the Bible doesn't make me like who He used to be."

"Like what?" he asked hesitantly.

"Like condoning slavery."

"I don't think it actually *condones* slavery."

"Slaves, obey your earthly masters with deep respect and fear. Serve them like you blahty-blahty-blah, something Christ. Ephesians 6 something or other. I memorized that in AWANA. Sort of. But America has made slavery illegal. In the book of Acts, it says to obey God's law over the laws of man. So is America going against God's will? Does God want me to go out and pick up a slave or two?"

"You want to know what I think?"

"What?"

Roscoe responded by letting out a massive fart.

We both cracked up. He knew I had a tendency to overthink things and wanted to keep Christmas Eve light. I couldn't help but think he sometimes appreciated my crazy rants. Perhaps it made him feel a bit more normal. I, myself though, couldn't help but feel blessed exactly where I was that night. Whatever this was - whatever made Roscoe's family who they were - that was what I wanted to surround my life with. Their genuineness and unconditional love made me want to know more about who they were, what they believed, and what they stood for. I never had that feeling or desire toward my father.

These were the thoughts that followed me as I fell asleep in my valley of inflated vinyl. I must have slept soundly because the next thing I knew, Lily and Roscoe's younger cousins were knocking on our door at the crack of dawn.

Downstairs everyone was milling around and hemming and hawing over what was under the tree. I cordially wished them all a

Merry Christmas, and after grandma had forced Roscoe and me to eat a delicious bowl of oatmeal, we were ready to open the Christmas gifts. We sat around the room and went in a semi-organized fashion, opening gifts and watching others open theirs. Roscoe's family got me a stylish new coat. This made me slightly embarrassed to only be able to afford for them some decorative candles. Mr. Martin got a new skeet thrower from his parents, and his brother got him a brand new box of clays.

Being big kids themselves, Mr. Martin and Uncle Dave were anxious to play with their new toys, so they got the guns and targets together as Grandma went back to preparing Christmas dinner and Roscoe's mom helped Lily put together her new dollhouse.

A half hour later we threw the guns, targets, and new trap thrower in the back of Uncle Dave's pickup and headed out to the field where Roscoe got that six-pointer. Roscoe and I bobbed around in the truck bed as it rolled through a small, wooded trail to a secluded pasture. Uncle Dave parked the truck on the edge, and Roscoe and I hopped over the sides.

We all started working together to get things ready. Roscoe set up the new skeet thrower while his dad got out the few twelve and twenty-gauge shotguns. His uncle laid out the different boxes of shotgun shells - some were store-bought and some were handmade - and a blue box of random leftovers from previous shoots. We all agreed to let Mr. Martin have the honors of blasting the first target, so he grabbed his gun of choice and a set of ear protectors.

"You ever shot skeet, Sy?" Mr. Martin asked me.

"Nope, never have."

"Oh, you'll love it. It's a lot of fun. Hand me five of those shells, would ya?" Mr. Martin asked.

"Here you go," I told Mr. Martin as I handed him a few rounds.

"No, those shells from that box. I'm starting with the twelve-gauge."

"Oh sorry," I said realizing I had accidentally handed him some twenty-gauge shells.

"Yeah, won't be that fun if you get those mixed up."

Roscoe had already armed the thrower and nodded to his dad that he was ready. Mr. Martin smiled and nodded back, his hearing muffled by his ear protectors. Putting his pump-action twelve-gauge up to his shoulder, he took a minute to line up the barrel and remove the safety. Dave and I covered our ears.

"Ok, pull!" he shouted.

Roscoe yanked the slick new rope, and a clay target was launched from the shiny, metal arm. It quickly soared away from us, and within seconds Mr. Martin thunderously annihilated it in mid-air.

"Woo-hooo! Merry Christmas!" he shouted.

The rest of us hollered and applauded. We each took turns shooting and releasing from different angles and with different guns. Mr. Martin and Dave only missed a few out of the many that they shot at. Roscoe had shot clays before, so he hit about six. I was pretty sure I missed all of my targets, but everyone said that I got a small piece of one. I think they were just trying to make me feel better.

The rest of Christmas Day was spent enjoying a delicious turkey dinner then cutting down a tree that was growing too close to the chicken coop, dismembering it into firewood and burning the branches and leftover Christmas wrapping paper in the burn pit.

We left Grandma's the next day. It was probably the greatest Christmas I'd had in years, and it wasn't even with my own family. I was happy to be going back to see my mother and my new girlfriend, but truth be told, I was not happy to be going home.

The first date I had with Natalie came the evening after I got back from Roscoe's. It was still hard for me to comprehend that we were together or that Cam was right about my having a chance with her. We went for milkshakes to The Cobbler Hotel café, located in downtown Clanton. I had never been there before but quickly found that although it didn't have all the grandeur of the Clanton Grand, it was still pretty nice. Old red brick covered the surface of every wall and daguerreotype photography accented the exposed black water pipes and Edison bulbs.

I talked her into ordering a Hawaiian pizza for us to split even though she had never tried one before. It turned out that Natalie didn't like pineapple on her pizza, but I thought the fact she had tried it merely at my suggestion was pretty cool.

We spent about two hours talking. She told me how she came to live in North Carolina following her parents' divorce and what brought her to Cherrywood. I told her a little bit about my family, although I left out quite a few details about my dad. Eventually we made it back to our cars, and I thought long and hard about how I could sneak a kiss with her, but I wussed out at the last minute and just kept it safe with a hug. Still, it was awesome. I was dating Natalie Benson. Life was good.

Mr. Oakridge was right, though. The coming year would be very different for me.

CHAPTER 15

We returned to school on Wednesday, January 3rd, and there would only be half a week of school before heading into a weekend again. Everyone wore the new jackets, shoes, backpacks, and other Christmas gifts that they had received over the holiday. I couldn't relate to that. Natalie was the best part of that short week for me. Word was slowly starting to circulate that we were together, which I didn't mind at all. No longer being seen as a yearbook nerd, but rather the boyfriend of an attractive athlete was a very welcome change. It was also something that I wasn't used to yet.

Other than those few small changes, school was pretty typical for that half a week. Yelski was still there, Mr. Oakridge still wasn't, and it was just a matter of getting back into the class routine before the weekend.

When that Sunday rolled around, my mom and I went to church and sat in our usual spot. After worship, Pastor Samms strolled somberly onto the stage and took the podium.

"I hope everyone had a pleasant New Year's," he started softly. "I want to thank God for this new beginning." He looked down at the podium a lot, and it was clear that he was referring to notes. He wasn't the fiery, excitable Joel Samms that we were used to.

"Today, and for the rest of this month, you're going to receive the message from our associate pastor, Ken. I'll be taking a sabbatical for a few weeks to reconnect with God and my family. I want to apologize to all of you, including my wife, for my absence. As a leader of this church family, I feel that I should first make sure my own family is properly cared for before I can properly care for all of you. I'd like to humbly admit to you today that I have failed in that area. When I return in February, my message will be on forgiveness. Thank you."

The congregation started to mumble as Associate Pastor Ken Portney took the podium. It wasn't until after the service, once word had started to spread, that the reason for Joel's sabbatical was aired. Apparently, he had found out that his wife had been cheating on him. It was sad, especially since lovable Janelle was usually at church every Sunday, welcoming guests and praying with visitors. But what was even sadder was that this was becoming far too common. Not the adultery, but wrongdoings in general. I was surrounded by it: in my Christian school and my Christian church, by people who claimed to be living Godly lives. It was in a place where it wasn't supposed to be.

For me, church was once a comfort, a reverent and respectful time to worship and to learn. But in recent months, it had become a place where I felt more and more uneasy. During the summer I had stopped into the vintage furniture store beside Mr. Winter's print shop on my lunch break. They were selling a one-of-a-kind floor lamp from the 40s. I kept my money, knowing I had to save it for the offering plate at church. Two weeks later, I saw that lamp on stage at Clanton Baptist. My sacrifice - my offering - had been used to buy a simple stage prop.

I began to think that perhaps my father was right about church, although perhaps slightly off in his reasoning. Over the months, I had found myself passing the time during the church service by filling in every letter "O" on the church bulletin with the golf pencil placed in the back of the pew in front of me and watching for Edmund McBryer to complete his weekly ritual of asking Jesus into his heart.

I began to feel for Edmund. I realized that he and I both longed for the truth, and I doubted either of us was fully getting it.

The next day in English class, Mrs. Yelski wasted no time. At the start of class, as we were preparing for our first quiz of the new year, she commanded, "Pencils out, books away!" I put my book under my chair and reached down to grab my pencil from my backpack.

"Make sure to keep your eyes on your own paper," Yelski continued. "If I catch anyone looking at anyone else's quiz, there will be consequences." I was slumped over grabbing my pencil, but as I sat back upright in my chair, I looked forward to notice that Mrs. Yelski was looking directly at me.

"Does everyone understand?" she said, still looking at me. I was unnerved. Was she talking to me? She started to walk by the students in the front rows and passed out the stacks of quizzes. After everyone had received them, she ordered us to turn our papers over and begin.

I answered the first few questions but responded to a gut feeling and looked up towards the front. Mrs. Yelski was watching me. Her face was unmoving, even as we made eye contact. I was under her suspicion. It was all the proof I needed; she had probably figured out that I was the one who turned her in. Degraded, I focused on my work and finished my quiz.

After we were all finished, Mrs. Yelski announced her famous, "Pass 'em back." This time, however, she had something extra to add. "Pass them directly back. Not forward. Not to the side. Pass them to the person behind you. Those of you in the back row, pass yours forward to those in the front."

Everyone obeyed, and the quizzes from the back row students came forward. She read out the answers while I graded Will Rose's quiz. He ended up getting an 85. We passed the completed quizzes forward for her to collect, and while she made her rounds collecting those, she also started to hand out the results of the semester exams that we had taken just before break. My exam came about halfway through the dispersement and floored me. At the top was a grade I hadn't seen since middle school when I missed an entire month because I got mono.

It was a D.

Natalie approached me at my locker after English class. Seeing her was a pleasant surprise that I wasn't used to. The delight didn't last long, though.

"Why did you tell people we slept together?" she asked abruptly and angrily.

"What?" I was genuinely shocked.

"Melanie Dunaway said that you told a few people that we slept together over Christmas break."

"No I didn't! I didn't even try to kiss you on New Years to respect our relationship. Why would I say that?"

"They said that you told them we got a room at The Cobbler and hooked up. How would they know we went to The Cobbler,

Sy?"

"I didn't tell anyone that! I didn't even tell Shawn or Roscoe or anyone!"

"Now people think I'm a slut!"

"Natalie, I didn't tell anyone anything like that! I don't know why people would think that I did!"

I tried to squash that ridiculous rumor for another minute before she stormed off just after the bell rang. It was ludicrous. How would an unbelievable thing like that even start? Everyone knew Natalie was a wholesome girl. Even when she had been with Kevin, who would've been much more likely to score with any girl than I would have, there hadn't been any rumors like that.

Third period History was a blur to me. All I could think about was that awful grade in English which I was certain I hadn't earned, and that slanderous rumor about Natalie and me. Sex was strictly forbidden at Cherrywood. We all knew it happened, but it was still against the rules. Something like this could not just damage our reputations as Christian students, but quite possibly our futures as well.

These thoughts carried over into fourth period Bible class - the corruption, my environment, my beliefs. It was hard for me to sit in Bible class. Mr. Huxley never provoked us to think. He was wasting my time as far as I was concerned. I'd already heard these stories before, and nothing I was learning was new. It was so disconnected from reality. We learned about the Bible, but we never learned about life. I felt the same about church. We learned that God loves us, but we didn't learn why we should believe in a God in the first place.

"Mr. Huxley?" I asked raising my hand. I was bored and I wanted to make things interesting.

"Yes, Sylas," he responded.

"Do you believe in God?"

Stunned, he answered, "Yes of course. Why would you ask a silly question like that?"

Most of the class turned around to look at me. I knew that question would turn heads.

"Why?" I asked.

"Why do I believe in God? Sylas, I don't think it's fair of you to take up valuable class time with silly questions."

"Why is it a silly question? People ask that question to

themselves every day. Is there a God and if so, why?"

"Well, of course there is a God. How old are you? Eighteen? You've been coming to church and this school and learning for eighteen years that there is indeed a God. Why don't you tell me?"

"Science says there's not," I argued. "Millions of brilliant people around the world say there isn't. None of us have ever seen Him. Why do you believe something different from what modern science says?"

"Because modern science is wrong."

"That's obviously a logical fallacy, sir. Calling something wrong doesn't make it so."

"Sy, I'm not going to have this discussion right now. We're discussing Malachi today, not God."

"We can't discuss God in Bible class?" I was being obnoxious on purpose and everyone felt it, especially Mr. Huxley. I think in an effort to shut me up, he did something interesting.

"Ok, Sy. Why don't you tell me why there is no God?"

"Ok. Modern science. It clearly says that there is no designer of the universe. Pretty black and white."

"No, it's actually pretty gray. If there is no designer, why do we even have a universe at all?" He paused to let his point sink in. "The delicate balancing act that this universe needs to even stay in existence is so unbelievably sensitive that the mathematical probability says there should be *no* universe rather than *some* universe."

"Yeah, but if you throw Scrabble tiles in the air long enough, eventually you'll get some words."

Grady piped up from the front of the class. "Yeah," he said, "but our universe isn't made up of just a few random words. It's an entire set of Encyclopedia Britannicas. What are you doing, man? Why are you asking these questions?"

"Because we never talk about them. When's the last time Pastor Samms talked science in church? This is our world; the Bible needs to connect with it otherwise we're just living in two separate worlds."

"Where did the Scrabble tiles come from?" Michelle Hodges asked.

I was getting the class into a frenzy - exactly what Mr. Oakridge would've done.

"They've always been there," I snapped back. "They just

didn't start assembling until sixteen billion years ago."

"So you're saying the universe is infinite then?" Mr. Huxley asked.

"It could be."

He smiled. "No it can't be. Since it looks like we're playing by the rules of modern science, scientists have discovered a while ago that the universe is expanding. So if it's getting bigger and bigger, all you have to do is rewind the tape to watch it get smaller and smaller. Eventually, it will stop at zero, which is the beginning of time. So the universe is not infinite. Ninety-nine percent of scientists will agree with that one."

"Yeah, Scrabble tiles can't just form out of thin air, so where did they come from?" Michelle asked again, pleased that someone else had reinforced her point.

"Where did God come from?" I shot back.

"Sy, cut it out," Shawn said to me from the next aisle. I looked over to see my friend embarrassed and annoyed. "Seriously, just stop." For the first time, I could see my frustrations making me a target and disrupting those around me. I looked back towards the front. Grady raised his hand.

"Yes, Grady," Mr. Huxley said.

"Time and space were some of the parameters God created for the universe to exist, so He transcends them. Scrabble tiles, on the other hand, don't. They needed something to bring them into existence."

Grady looked at me, waiting for my argument.

"Just having a friendly debate like Mr. Oakridge used to do," I said with a fake smile directed towards the class.

Most of my peers forced a smile too, but all seemed to breathe a sigh of relief. They seemed to buy it. I still wasn't satisfied, but they didn't know that. Yeah, several of my classmates impressed me with their reasoning skills, and quite a few of them made some points that I hadn't even thought of before. But I was still struggling.

"Well, Sylas, you certainly got us all into thinking mode, but we're not in Mr. Oakridge's class anymore; we're in mine," Mr. Huxley said. "So we're going to get back to Malachi. Please try to read the room before you do something like that again. I appreciate the discussion, but this wasn't the time."

"Yes, sir," I said.

A few of the kids looked back at me again. I looked over at Shawn and saw that the look on his face seemed to ask: "*Why did you do that?*"

"I was bored," I whispered with a shrug and a wink. Try as I might, I felt my earnestness change to apathy as I no longer cared what the faculty thought of me. I had lost respect for them, and I cared little if they lost respect for me.

When the bell rang and we all got up to leave, Shawn immediately came over and asked, "Are you alright?"

I smiled and said nothing for a moment. "People are saying that Natalie and I slept together, which is horse crap. I don't even know why a rumor like that would start!"

"Did you?"

"No! And you know that test we just took in English?"

"What about it?"

"I got a D."

"I thought you studied."

"I did. Yelski low-balled me."

"Are you going to talk to someone?"

"Like who? Dr. Sites?"

Shawn stopped packing his books to give me his full attention. "I don't know what to say, man. That sucks."

"You don't have to say anything. I'll say it for you. You told me so."

Shawn looked down at his book bag. "Well, hopefully we'll have a snow day soon. They're calling for it to start Wednesday afternoon."

"I'll catch you later," I said, walking out of the classroom.

That Monday ended worse than it had started, and Tuesday picked up from there. The rumors about Natalie and me were spreading wider. Now the entire football team and several of the other athletes and jocks were starting to tease us about having sex. Perhaps it was something that the jealous Kevin Thompson perpetuated, but the taunting wasn't letting up. If this rumor got around to either Natalie's parents or mine, especially my dad, it could be devastating.

The weatherman was calling for a nor'easter to dip down far enough to hit us within the next day or so. Snow days were rare in my neck of the woods, but the mere thought of them brought hope and joy to students anxious for a day off.

I felt my mind growing weary, unable to find a place to recollect my thoughts and breathe. My school was filled with liars and cheats, and my home was filled with judgment. I needed some time away from the noise. More than anything, I wanted to separate myself - if even for one day - from a school I had nearly lost all respect for.

CHAPTER 16

Snowfall is pretty rare in North Carolina. We'd usually get a rumor of a flurry at least once a winter but most of the time, it usually just stayed at that. Still, it never failed that the talk of snow would have news stations buzzing and townsfolk bustling out to the store to grab their fresh rations of milk and eggs in preparation for the impending natural disaster, which was never more than an accumulation of two or three inches of snow.

The snow was predicted to fall Wednesday afternoon so, of course they closed school early in the morning in case a rogue flake should fall early and devastate the town. Shawn brought his Super NES back to his mom's house and he, Roscoe, and I played *Street Fighter II* and watched a few movies from Blockbuster most of Wednesday before a few heavy, wet flakes started to fall around dinner time. After supper, I called Natalie to talk things out. We talked for an hour or so, and she finally realized that I would never say those things about her and that the rumors were not started by me. We made tentative plans to go sledding the next day if we got enough snow. I was happy that we were back to normal.

Roscoe and I crashed at Shawn's that night, and when we woke up the next morning, there was a debilitating two inches of accumulation on the ground. All schools were clearly canceled Thursday as well, which left a bunch of Southern kids with a hallowed snow day. It was an especially significant snow day because it actually involved snow. The roads were extremely dangerous, not because of the snow, but because of the Southern drivers who didn't know how to drive in it. I gave Natalie a call that morning, and we all quickly coordinated a 10 a.m. meet up at the edge of Old Man Wagner's field - the absolute best sledding spot in town. None of us had actual sleds since there was hardly a use for them, so we had to improvise with what we had.

There were a few other Cherrywood kids on the long and open hill when Shawn, Roscoe and I showed up with a blue pool raft, a rubber inner tube, a large cardboard box, and a plastic laundry basket. Because none of us had true snow gear either, we were lucky that Roscoe had nabbed some Saran wrap to try to waterproof our jeans. A few us wore windbreakers and other water-resistant fabrics over cotton sweatshirts and jackets.

The pool raft and cardboard box were destroyed almost immediately after we began sledding, and as the day went on and the temperature continued to rise, our clothes got wetter and wetter. On one run, I happened to meet Ray Grenlichten at the bottom of the hill. Ray was a cocky little baseball-playing sophomore, and one of the popular kids from his class. He had just made it down the hill on a skateboard deck. He was a few inches shorter than me and was like one of those annoying Bull Terriers who wasn't very big, but still looked intimidating and barked a lot.

"Hey bro, I heard about you and your girl up there," he said with a devilish smile. "Props for tapping that. She's fine."

He raised his palm for a high-five. I walked over, as if I was going to smack back. In a sense, I did. I shoved him as hard as I could, knocking him to the ground.

"She's not like that, ya little punk!" I shouted. I don't think I would've reacted like that if this was a first occurrence. However, I had been bottling up my anger about this infuriating rumor for the better part of a week and had taken enough. It simply came out of nowhere, and I was letting it out on someone weaker than I was.

"Whoa, dude!" he exclaimed from the ground. "Chill. Save your energy for your lady friend."

I lunged at him again, and he stuck his feet out to stop me. I'd never been in a fight in my life, and I don't know why I picked then to start. In my carelessness, I slipped and fell to the ground. Ray took instant advantage of this and rolled over, trying to pin me there. Before he could grab hold of me, I took a cheap shot at his crotch, which dropped him to the ground.

"Sylas, chill!" Roscoe shouted pulling me off the ground and holding me back. He must have witnessed the scene escalating from the top of the hill and came whizzing down on the inner-tube.

After Roscoe and I made it up to the top of the hill again, I told Natalie what had happened. I thought she'd be honored that I stood up for her, but she seemed bothered instead. I wanted to ask her why, but I didn't press it. I didn't want to take the chance of pushing the matter and bringing it all back up. I hated to see her like that, but what was done was done, and I couldn't change it.

Natalie walked back to the cars and chatted with some of her friends. I thought that maybe I should go after her, to understand what she was feeling, but I let her go.

In hindsight, that was probably not the best decision.

Roscoe and Natalie's parents had both told them to be home by lunchtime, and they left earlier than the rest of us. Because neither Shawn nor I were given any such instruction, we jumped in the car and headed over to Finchies, a favorite little hole-in-the-wall diner that probably should have been condemned by the health department, but had an amazing chili corn chip queso pie.

We dropped our winter gear and ourselves in a booth, and in less than a minute, our order was placed and each of us was sipping on a Mountain Dew. I was still fuming from my altercation with Ray, but that wasn't the breaking point for me. My feelings had been bubbling up for months; Ray had just tipped them over the edge.

But at the core of it all were the questions and struggles I'd been facing - the problems with my dad, with my school, and with my faith. I had tried to open up to Roscoe about my thoughts over Christmas break, but a well-timed flatulent interjection cut the conversation short. Since then, I began to find more clarity.

"So what's going on with you?" Shawn asked over the table.

"It's all a bunch of bull crap, man. I don't believe in this stuff," I stated.

"Believe what?"

"What we were taught growing up."

I could feel Shawn trying to find the right words to say to comfort me, but somehow I felt as though he shared my feelings of doubt. "I don't believe in God," I said as the words fell out of my mouth like bricks. "At least not the God we learned about growing up. It's just a fairy tale."

"The Bible?" he asked. Shawn was used to my out-of-the-blue tangents. He had learned to just go with them.

"Yeah, or at least how it is being used. People just manipulated an ancient book to fit their cult or maybe just the biggest game of Telephone in history. It just got ridiculously distorted with time. I mean, how can this possibly make sense?

The Southern Hope Foundation was, and maybe still is, deceiving its donors. Our Christian teachers are manipulating their students' grades. The pastor's wife is an adulteress, and my own father, an ordained pastor, can't seem to contain his judgments long enough to help people who are actually hurting. Where is God in Pastor Samms' fancy house or million-dollar Clanton Baptist? Instead of helping a hurting girl who tried to take her own life, Cherrywood expelled her to clear its name. And it did the same with Mr. Oakridge. They preach that the world is lost, but why is it that a lost world often shows more mercy than they do? There can't be a God who can allow such evil to continue in His name. Why would there? I'm tired of buying into the lie, man."

I heard Shawn let out a deep sigh. I continued with my rant.

"Why is it that the only place you learn that God created the world is in church? Schools, museums, the Discovery Channel...they don't teach that. Why? Probably because it's just a comforting fairy tale for the gullible but has no basis in the real world. One of the plagues God sent through Moses was to kill all of the Egyptians first-born children! He has Joshua wipe out the entire city of Jericho, including all women, children, and livestock. And we're told to love a God like this?"

"And what about what Topher said: Why doesn't He make it rain for those kids all over the world who are dying from dehydration? They just need rain and He won't or can't do it. That's either evil or incompetence."

"When did Topher say that?" Shawn asked.

"At Nate's party. He was high. Everyone claims that their God is the correct God. Muslims, Christians, Hindus, African tribes, ancient Greeks - they all believe that their way is right. It's a pacifier, that's all it is. Just a child's pacifier. The idea of a big jolly man in the sky looking over us makes us feel safe, so we buy into it. Nobody knows, though. "

Our waitress came back with our food and a smile. "Here you are boys," she said. "Chili chip pie and here's your chicken tenders, sweetheart. Anything else?"

"Can I get some ranch?" Shawn asked.

"You got it," she said and headed away.

"So what do you think it's about?" Shawn asked me.

"It's not about anything, I guess. If there is no right or wrong, then there is no truth. We are born, we evolve a bit and die.

Nothing else."

"Kinda scary to think that way isn't it? That this is all there is?"

"Well, yes and no, I guess. If there is nothing else, then we have nothing to fear because once this life is over, we will no longer exist. Our minds will stop. We will be finished. That sounds peaceful compared to the alternative."

"Which is?"

"That most will die and be separated from a supposedly loving God for all eternity."

"That does stink."

I chuckled, "Yes, yes it does. I mean, you were working with me on that religion assignment for Mr. Oakridge. What do you think?"

Shawn sat up in his seat. "I mean, I've never been buddy-buddy with the whole idea. I just go to Cherrywood because I got a better chance of getting into Stanford. I don't really care either way."

The waitress swung back by with Shawn's ranch and the checks.

"We can't be the only ones who feel this way, right?" I asked.

"Heck no. Nobody knows, man. It'd be nice if there was something else out there. It would stink if this was all there is. But we're all just grasping at straws and hoping for the best."

"Do you think maybe Christians are wrong, but maybe another religion has the right answer?"

"Could be," he said thoughtfully. "But I think most of them teach similar things. Like, their way is the right way, and others are wrong. Maybe it's like Matt and Jody said in their presentation. What if they're all wrong?"

"I guess we're all in for the same fate...Islam teaches that you get seventy-two virgins after you die. Let's go with that one. That sounds pretty cool. Better than a harp and a yellow brick road."

Shawn laughed. "I'd be ok with seventy-two virgins. Does the Quran say if they are hot or not?"

"I would assume they are. It's Heaven. I'm sure Allah only lets in attractive people."

"We're definitely in then," Shawn joked. "I mean look at us!"

"For sure. No question."

"But then you gotta wash your feet all the time and pray to

Mecca five times a day. I don't know if it's worth it."

"Yeah, I'm not that dedicated. What about Hindus? They don't believe in any one God and basically say it doesn't matter what you believe. It's all about karma and reincarnation and crap."

"But if you can believe whatever you want, what happens when two people believe conflicting ideas?"

"Yeah, two opposite things both can't be right which, if that's what Hinduism teaches, seems contradictory. So that one doesn't make sense."

"What about Mormons?" Shawn asked.

"I'm not sure about Mormons," I said. "Gotta do more research. Although, didn't Joseph Smith start that one? Wasn't he just a regular dude like a hundred years ago who said God talked to him or something? Sounds kinda fishy."

"Yeah, seems sketchy. I don't know if I buy it." He paused for a moment and then added, "Well...that settles it. Religions are stupid."

"Yup. Religions are stupid."

"So...what now?" Shawn joked.

"I guess we could just sleep through Bible class and get drunk on the weekends."

"Cheers to that," we both said, toasting with our Mountain Dews.

"Speaking of getting drunk on the weekends," he said, "Cam told me about this party tomorrow night. You wanna crash it?"

"Sure. I have no convictions to stop me," I joked.

I loved having friends like this, where I could be completely open and honest with them, and they would let me process the information freely. If I tried this with my father, he would've quoted seventeen verses about salvation. The funny thing is though, that quoting Scripture only works for those who believe it. And I certainly had my fair share of doubts.

Some long-haired kid who I had never seen before, was standing outside the house smoking a cigarette and holding the universal symbol for a crazy party – a red Solo cup. I double-checked the house numbers to make sure it was the right place.

"Is Cam Fosjord here?" Shawn asked him.

"Don't know. You can go in."

La Bouche's *Be My Lover* thumped out of the door and filled the anonymous dark house as we walked inside. Shawn found a kid from his Marketing class and started talking. I kept moving inward. I had been there less than a minute, but I could tell just by the looks of the house and the atmosphere that this wasn't a rich kid's party anymore. This was different. It felt much darker...and I liked it. A few people who I recognized from school, mostly athletes, were in the kitchen. They were all laughing and doing shots. Lined out on the kitchen table were bottles of Pepsi, two empty bottles of Canadian whiskey, bottom shelf vodka, endless Pixy Stix candy wrappers, and a few other low-grade alcoholic drinks.

I hung out at the party mainly just trying to fit in. I talked to Shawn off and on for another half hour or so. Neither one of us had seen Cam yet.

I quickly figured out that this was the sort of party where things deteriorated quickly. Some foul-mouthed tattooed kid puked in the sink, and Tommy Danielson, a soccer player, had his tongue down another girl's throat, even though he had a girlfriend. No one seemed to care. That was the thing. No one cared about anything: their reputations, their grades, their health, their beliefs. Sure, my beliefs had changed, but I still cared about how others perceived me and how I perceived the world and myself.

I guess I was alone. I was getting used to that feeling.

I asked the longhaired guy where the bathroom was, and he said, "Down the hall on the right," without looking at the hall or me. I found the hall and pushed open the first door on the right. It was not the bathroom but a bedroom. Three guys and a girl were inside. I recognized most of them. Two of the guys were Cherrywood football players and the girl was a cheerleader. One of the football players was especially significant to me.

It was Cam.

The other two had their noses on the dresser. The girl was laughing and Cam, without caring who I was, shouted at me. "Get Out!!"

"Sorry," I shamefully said while closing the door. It took me a second to process what I had just seen. Nothing they were doing in the bedroom was sexual. They were doing coke.

The next door over was the bathroom, which I entered and

shut the door behind me, completely stunned. When I turned on the light, I was even more startled. A guy was passed out in the bathtub. A syringe rolled around the vinyl floor.

"Geez...Hey! Wake up!" I shouted.

He didn't move.

"I need to pee here; let's move it!" I shouted, shoving his shoulder. He remained lifeless, so I checked for a pulse. He was still very much alive. I pulled the curtain, picked up the syringe with a wad of toilet paper, and tossed it into the trash. Then I lifted the toilet seat to do my business, knocking a metal spoon onto the floor.

After washing my hands, I splashed cold water on my face, not knowing what to do next.

"Hey moron!" I shouted at the guy again. Still nothing. Giving up, I grabbed him by his belt and turned him on his side; a lesson I learned from having a nurse as a mother. I went outside like it never happened. Cam was talking to Shawn in the kitchen. I walked in and he made eye contact with me before finally coming over.

"What are you doing here?" he asked.

"I got invited. Why do you care?"

"Who invited you?"

"Shawn."

Cam looked backwards at Shawn, and then turned back to me. "This party isn't for you."

"Why not? Because I don't do blow?"

"That's exactly why, Sylas," he snapped back. "You don't do it, but you love to look down on anyone who does!"

"Whoa, I didn't say that at all, Cam. I just don't need to do that stuff."

"And you think I do?"

"Dude. Chill. I didn't say anything like that."

"Then why are you here, Sy? Why are you here?"

Shawn interjected, trying to salvage the situation. "Dude, we just came to hang out. Not a big -"

"I wasn't talking to you!" Cam shouted, which quickly shut Shawn up.

"I came to see you, man," I said. "To hang out." I kept my voice low and somber, trying to calm him down. I felt as if I could feel Cameron's heart beating out of his chest. As I looked at him, I saw a vein pulsating on his forehead.

"You want to hang out?" he rhetorically asked before turning around to grab a smoky nub out of some kid's mouth. "Hit this," he challenged, shoving the joint in my face.

"No!"

"Hit it!"

"I'm not doing that, dude. Get it out of my face!"

"Dr. Sites don't care. He knows about this stuff. He doesn't do jack about it, so do it."

"What?"

Cam grabbed me by the arm and swung around behind me to try to force the blunt into my mouth. "Come on, bro!"

"Get off me!" I yelled, wriggling out of his grasp while he let out a deranged laugh.

"You are freakin' high, man," I said. "You're messed up."

"WOOOO!" Cam maniacally shouted.

"Get help, man. You need help," I said walking away from the madman who had once been my friend. "I wanna go, Shawn. Can we go?"

Shawn nodded and walked with me to his car. We left the party amid slack faces and expressionless eyes.

"I didn't know the party was gonna be like that," Shawn said. "You alright?"

"Not really," I replied as we got into the car.

Cam and I had been friends since middle-school, but that night, the friendship ended. He had changed. We were both struggling with something in our lives, but we both had totally different ways of coping with it. Losing a friend is always hard. It's like a death in the family. I realized it for the first time that night.

A few summers ago, my family took a trip back to our hometown in Somerset, Pennsylvania and passed by our old house where I grew up and spent my childhood. We parked the car on the edge of the road and kept the engine running. My father pointed out the changes the new owners had made: new trees that had been planted, old shrubs that had been removed, the clutter in the lawn, and a newly paved driveway. I stared blankly at that house. It felt familiar but also strangely different. It had been changed by those who now lived in it. The house was locked up tight, the curtains drawn, my memories trapped inside. As we pulled away, I knew I had to say goodbye to all that I knew to be familiar in that old house. It was a feeling I had forgotten about until now.

"So long, old friend," I said in a whisper.

And with that, Shawn and I drove away.

CHAPTER 17

Natalie and I had already made plans to sit around and watch Brat Pack movies all day on Sunday after church. When I got back home and ate some lunch, I grabbed the phone and took it into the laundry room. I quickly dialed the number that I had memorized and waited for her to pick up.

"Hello?" her soft voice answered on the other end.

"I have two bags of microwave popcorn with our names on them," I said with a cheesy smile.

"Oh hey, Sy."

"When should I come over?"

She paused. "Hey, um...I don't know if you should come over today."

"Why not?"

"Hey listen, Sy...I've been thinking, and...um...well, there's just been a lot of things recently that have made me think that...maybe we just don't, uh, really connect on a deep level, ya know?"

"What?" I said stunned.

"I mean...I have fun with you and all, but I've kinda been wondering if that's enough...I mean, please don't take that the wrong way, but...I don't know. I'm just not sure if I can really see a future with us."

"What are you talking about?"

"I mean, when we worked together at the bake sale and what you did for me on Christmas was so sweet. You were such a nice guy back then, and I think that's the guy I really connected with."

"Back then? What do you mean, *back then*?"

"Well, I mean, now that we've gotten to know each other a little better, there's just been a few things that I don't really know if I could see myself with. I mean, you were really aggressive with Ray on Thursday. You didn't need to attack him like that."

"I didn't *attack* him!"

"And I heard about you at that party Friday night. I know

what happened there, and I don't want to have anything to do with someone who does that sort of thing."

"I didn't do drugs, Natalie."

"That's fine, but you also said that you didn't tell people we slept together; but everyone says you did."

"Not everyone says that...and the ones who do are just spreading rumors. I never would've said anything like that!"

"I just...I just think that we've only been together for a short time, and in that time I've seen some of your actions that make me question if our relationship will work. I just don't see what I thought I saw in us. I think we should take a break, Sy."

I was shocked and had to pause for a moment. "Take a break. What does that mean?"

"I think we could still hang out every once in a while, but we should probably also be free to see other people."

"So....you're breaking up with me?"

She paused again. "Kind of, I guess. I'm really sorry. I really wanted it to work."

"I shoved Ray because he was talking bad about you! I was standing up for you because that's what boyfriends do," I exclaimed defensively.

"I know what Ray said, and you didn't have to start a fight with him for that. I'm sorry, Sy. I'm sorry, ok? I just don't know if this will work right now."

I started to get misty-eyed. I've been broken up with before, but it was only by middle school flings that didn't mean much. I had genuinely thought that this relationship with Natalie felt real. "Well, I'm sorry for disappointing you, Natalie."

"Sy, stop. You're a great guy. I just think we need a break, that's all."

We talked a while longer, and when we finally hung up, I punched the ironing board, knocking it to the ground, which spilled a bag of dog food. Unable to stop the onslaught before it overtook me, I went up to my room and cried it out.

Natalie was my first love - and I lost her. But this time, it wasn't because another guy got to her first. It was because of me. I had failed. And it was my fault that she was gone.

I didn't talk to anyone else for the rest of the day. I stayed in my room and finished a few homework assignments. The next day, I woke up a bit earlier than normal and laid in bed, dreading school. I was over it. My mother tried to convince me it was senioritis, but I knew it was something more.

Perhaps I'm sick, I thought to myself. *Yes, that's it. I'm sick. Not physically, but emotionally, mentally, and perhaps spiritually. Perhaps I should self-medicate with one day of truancy.*

But my mom wouldn't have it. She made sure that I went to school, and an hour later I found myself pushing open the door to the Academy, dejected, lonely, and miserable.

I saw the normal, typical things: all of my peers milling around throughout the hallways, grabbing books from their lockers, flirting with each other and smiling as if it were just another day. Several of the people I watched had been at the party three nights ago with their faces in a toilet or someone else's mouth. And Natalie was somewhere around here, too.

This wasn't worth it. I didn't want to be here. I didn't care about the consequences. Before I even stepped into the hallway or made eye contact with a single person, I turned around and left.

With my backpack slung over one shoulder and my Dayminder opened in front of my face, I stopped at the pay phone by the gym. I dialed the number that I had scribbled down a while ago and listened as it rang twice.

"Hello?" a young woman answered.

"Hi. Rachel?"

"Yes?"

"This is Sy Ernst. I hope I'm not calling too early."

"Sy! What a surprise. How are you?" Rachel Ellis asked.

"Do you have classes today?"

"Yeah. At ten. Why?"

"I know this might be super weird...but can I come?"

I had only been on the CCC campus once when they were hosting a middle school science fair several years ago. Taking the main entrance to Clanton Community College as Rachel had directed, I immediately saw the Tancely Learning Annex on my right where we had arranged to meet. Sure enough, after I parked my car and walked inside, Rachel was waiting on a wooden bench, looking shockingly different than when I'd last seen her at the abortion rally.

"Hi Rachel," I said as I walked towards her.

"Hi Sy," she said with anticipation. She knew what my reaction was going to be.

"Oh my gosh, you're pregnant!" I stated. Her surprising pregnancy was impossible to miss.

"Yeah…"

"How far along?"

"About five months. Did you just come from school?"

"Yeah. How'd you know?"

"You're a little overdressed."

"Oh, right," I said, remembering that I was still wearing my school uniform. This was highlighted even more as another guy walked by me wearing torn jeans, flip-flops, and a Simpson's T-shirt that read, "My Drinking Team has a Bowling Problem." I took off my school tie and jacket and loosened my collar so as to just look like another preppy college freshman and not like a student from Cherrywood.

"So why did you want to come here today?" Rachel asked me.

"Well," I paused searching for the right words. "I'd rather learn with honest sinners than fake ones."

"I got ya. Well…it's cool of you to come. My first class starts in twenty minutes. It's just Bio 101," she said as she wobbled to get up from the bench.

"You need some help?" I asked, my eyes again going back to her pregnant belly.

"No, I'm ok. Thank you."

We walked to the class and took seats in the middle of the room. Since we had arrived early, we chatted for about fifteen minutes about life, our mutual disappointment with Cherrywood, and her upcoming baby shower. I couldn't help but be impressed by how far Rachel had come. This same girl, just months before, had been so depressed that she had tried to take her own life. She had been exiled from her school but in spite of that went on to get her GED, was now a college student, and soon to be a single mother. It seemed that there was no limit to how determined and resilient this girl was. I felt a great deal of respect for her in that moment, as well as another feeling I had not yet identified.

In the midst of all of this, the professor walked in. I have never been one to stereotype people, but if there was ever a secular, probably liberal, college science teacher, he was it. Most likely a hippie earlier in his life, disheveled grayish-red hair circled his nearly bald crown. A goatee covered the lower half of his face. He wore loafers and a mismatching, outdated attempt at semi-professional attire. He rummaged around in his briefcase, checked his pockets for something, and then seemed to have located it inside his case.

"Ok, everybody," the teacher started. "We're picking up on page 293. I'll give you a minute to get there."

All the students, including Rachel, rummaged through their belongings to open their science books. He made a few opening remarks about parking and the faulty thermostat in his office and then started with, "Tetrapods came on the scene around three hundred and sixty-four million years ago."

He fired up the overhead projector and located a handful of slides in his briefcase. I eagerly found a piece of paper and a pen from my book bag and started taking notes. "Now in your books, there are a few photos to help illustrate. We can start seeing the transition from ray-finned fish to lobe-finned fish starting in the late Devonian period, around three hundred and seventy million years…"

He went on to show a few slides and talked for ten minutes on the transition between the different fish, how they go from ray-finned like the typical smallmouth bass that we catch in the Cape Fear, to lobe-finned fish. Whales, for example, curiously share the same skeletal hand structure as human hands. I wrote it all down as fast as I could; I eagerly wanted to learn this stuff.

I wanted to learn it for one very simple reason: if evolution is true, then the Bible isn't. There are no two ways about it. The Bible teaches that God created the universe. It teaches that He created earth and light *before* He created the sun and a bunch of other nonsense that contradicts evolutionary theory. But if it didn't actually happen that way, then the Bible was wrong about at least one thing. And if it was wrong about one thing, then it was most likely wrong about other things, as well. Regardless, if the Bible was wrong like I was hoping, then my questionable belief in it could finally and definitely come to a welcome end.

I listened to the professor for a few more minutes as he

explained how the fish fit into the fossil record and corresponded with the different prehistoric time periods. He explained the different periods and how fossils form over millions of years, and he touched on the Cambrian Explosion, which was when a bunch of fully formed fossils mysteriously appeared in the fossil record all at once. That could've been due to the rapid increase in oxygen that began around seven hundred million years ago, which fueled the movement of evolution of more complex body structures, as he explained. Or it could have been due to the Biblical flood, which killed a bunch of animals all at once. The oxygen thing was pure speculation as no one could have any way of knowing that for sure. On the other hand, a global flood was recorded in many ancient writings around the world.

Still, it was a toss up.

The more I listened and wrote and the more the teacher spoke, the more questions kept piling up in my head. With everything in me, I wanted to believe that the Bible was wrong. But I also needed to be intellectually honest with myself. I felt that I was at a perfect neutral point. On the one side, I had grown up my entire live believing in God, but on the other side, I really didn't want to believe in Him anymore. My mind was completely open.

And I believe that's why I raised my hand.

"Yes," the teacher said, responding to my raised hand. Rachel looked at me very surprised.

"I'm just confused about something. You mention how the fossil record is the series of rock layers where you can basically see the earth's timeline and how things happened, right?"

"That's right," he said, as if I was born yesterday.

"So it's kind of like counting the rings on a tree then, where the oldest layer is on the inside, or bottom, and the youngest layer is at the top?"

"More or less. Yes, we can use that analogy."

"Well, I was reading a book and it mentioned how fossilized sea creatures have been found on mountain tops all over the world. But if that's true, these sea creatures, which are some of the earlier and older forms of life, would actually be in a higher rock layer than the younger fossils. And a mountain, by its very nature, has more rock layers than the valleys below so I just don't see how you could accurately establish a realistic timeline of events this way, because there seems to be no uniformity or consistency to the

Earth like a tree would have."

"Well, did you miss my lecture on that topic several weeks ago? About how tectonic plates pushed the mountains upward?"

"Oh, I'm sorry. Yes, it would seem that I did miss that discussion."

"Ok then, well try to make it to class more often, but scientists have also used various dating methods to identify the age of these rock layers. Once we determine a reasonable age, we can deduce the age of the fossils inside and then use that information to piece together the strata around it."

"But…wouldn't that be circular reasoning, sir? They date the fossils based on the age of the rock layers and the age of rock layers are determined by the age of the fossils?"

He stopped, as did the class. "Let's just stay on schedule and get back to the lecture, ok? Feel free to come see me after class, and I can share some more information with you," he said.

Noticeably perturbed, he went back to his overhead projector. He was a long way from Mr. Oakridge. He didn't seem to appreciate open discussion either.

"What are you doing? You're not even enrolled in the class," Rachel sharply whispered to me.

"I just wanted to know."

"Just don't get us kicked out. This class is a prerequisite."

I was the only one in the class to ask questions that day. I noticed something strangely similar about CCC and Cherrywood. Just like at the Academy, the students there just wanted to get in, get out, and go on their way. They didn't care about challenging or even understanding what they were being told. They simply chose to believe it so that they could continue on with their lives. What was being taught at the Academy as well as what was being taught at that local community college was in complete opposition, but in both places it was believed with the same blind acceptance and apathy.

The class ended, and Rachel and I headed out.

"So what do you think of college so far?" she asked.

"Eh…I think I ended up with more questions than answers, actually," I chuckled. "It probably sounds weird, but I want to know why I believe what I do instead of believing a collective society's best guess, ya know?"

Rachel nodded.

"I really appreciate you letting me tag along," I added.

"Well, I'd say you could come to my next class, but I don't think you'd like it."

"Why not?"

"Because it's Women's Studies."

"Ah. Gotcha."

"You can come if you want," she said hesitantly.

"No, that's okay. That'd be weird."

"Yeah, probably," she said. "Do you just want to meet at the cafeteria for lunch?"

"Sure. Where?" I asked. "And When?"

"Noon in the cafeteria, behind the band room. It's behind the 'Legalize Pot' display. You can't miss it."

"Noon, lunchroom behind the pot. Got it. Hey, let me at least walk you to class. Do you need any help with anything?" I asked, again referencing her maternal condition.

"You're sweet, but no. I'll be fine."

"Are you nervous that you're going to be a mom soon?"

"Actually...yeah, but excited too. I've got a name picked out already."

My mind wandered for a second. Rachel said she had been pregnant for five months, which meant she would have known about it when I last saw her back at that abortion rally in October. Then I remembered the pamphlet that I saw on the floorboard of her car. I also remembered her puffy eyes that she told me were due to pollen. I suddenly realized why she was there, and it wasn't to drop someone off at the rally as she had said. She was there for something much, much different.

I just stood in place, my eyes blankly staring at the floor.

"Sy. Are you ok?" Rachel asked.

"Uh...yeah," I said snapping back into character. "What are you going to name him?"

"It's a girl. I'm going to name her Hope."

"Perfect," I said.

I got a really good feeling when I heard that name. It felt like I had known about it much longer than for that moment. That little girl would have a mother who would take on the world for her. I had no doubt of that. She was already doing it.

CHAPTER 18

While Rachel attended her Women's Studies class, I meandered aimlessly around campus, eventually landing in the Applied Sciences Building where, wafting from one room in particular, came a wonderful smell: warm cinnamon rolls.

I leaned against the doorway and looked inside as a number of people scurried about a relatively small room. One class was finishing and cleaning up, and another class was setting up to begin, I stood there, absorbing the sights and sounds. The level of care these students provided was a far cry from the haphazard debacle of my sixth grade Home-Ec class.

"You!" a young man said, at the back of the class, pointing directly at me.

"Me?" I asked, looking around to see if he was surely talking to someone else.

"Yes, you! Come here! Please, come!" He emphatically waved me over to him. "What's your name?"

"Sylas."

"Sylas, hi! I'm Dillon, and I could really use your help right now."

"Sure thing," I said, having absolutely no idea what was about to be asked of me.

"Oh my God. Thank you so much!"

Dillon immediately began pulling out cutting boards, pans, and pieces of charred wood, frantically putting each in what seemed to be a pre-arranged order. Then he accidentally dropped his knives on the floor and with them, also dropped an F-bomb.

I looked around, not used to hearing profanity spoken openly in school. No one even noticed.

"So, uh, how can I help?"

"Dammit! Dillon shouted, cursing his knives again. He piled them into the sink. "Mind washing these for me? Just a quick rinse. And with this one, try not to submerge the handle okay?"

"Ok," I said, a little nervous about what I had just gotten myself into. I stuffed my folded school jacket and tie under the workstation and got busy.

"My boyfriend was supposed to be here today. He promised," Dillon started.

"Boyfriend?" I asked a bit unsettled.

"Excuse me, *ex*-boyfriend! Not anymore. We're so splitsville its not even funny. Last night we ended up getting in this huge fight, and then he just gets up and leaves. Just walks out. Who the hell does that?"

"That stinks," I said trying to empathize, while still being a bit uncomfortable.

"You have no idea, but thank you so much for stepping in. Seriously, I can't do this without you."

"What exactly are we doing?"

"My mid-term project. Cedar-seared Ahi-Tuna with a ginger-balsamic glaze, paired with a roasted duck confit, and heirloom vegetables." He said it all so fluently that it almost seemed as if it were all one word.

"Okay. I understood cedar."

Dillon laughed nervously.

"I thought we were making cinnamon buns."

"Pfft!" Dillon said laughing. That was last class, intro to easy-bake-oven or some crap like that.

"So what class is this?"

"Cul 245: Advanced Gourmet & Culinary Practices."

"Wha-? I...I can barely make a TV dinner."

"You'll be fine. I'll tell you everything you need to know. I will be doing most of the work. I just need you for some basic cutting, mixing, and stirring to make sure I don't burn anything."

"Dillon, I'm just not sure if I can really help you here."

"You can. I'm really sorry to throw this onto you Sylas, but I've got no one."

I could sense the desperation in his voice. I fought the part of my father in me who wanted to tell Dillon about the dangers of homosexuality and recite First Corinthians to him. But that didn't matter right now, and the best thing I could do for him was to help him.

"Here goes nothing," I said, laughing nervously.

"That's the spirit! Nothing to lose, baby! Nothing to lose!" He made a few more statements, all dotted with some cleverly placed profanity.

I laughed, feeling myself relax in Dillon's presence. I wasn't used to his profanity, his lifestyle, or his culinary skill set for that matter, but all at once I found myself taking a step back and putting myself in his shoes. Who knows what brought Dillon and me together that day. If a person believes that the world is a series of meaningless events, then perhaps our encounter meant nothing at all. But I felt as if there was a deeper purpose for my being there.

The next hour passed in a blur - from filleting the fish to simmering sauces to stirring for half an hour at a time and to making sure a gentle simmer did not transform into a rolling boil. Dillon took great care with each step he executed. His attention to detail was unlike anything I had ever seen. It was only the last fifteen minutes that we even began to cook the fish itself, the main part of the dish.

"Do you know the hardest station to work in a proper kitchen?" he asked.

"Dishwasher?"

"Sauce," he said, drizzling the seared golden tuna with the deep crimson glaze. "The chef in charge of preparing the sauces for each dish has the absolute hardest job in the kitchen. It takes patience, skill, and above all, an immaculate palate. If the sauce is too heavy it overpowers the food; too light and it is negligible and worthless."

Hearing Dillon talk about the intricacies of being a proper chef intimidated me, so I stood in silence, unsure of what to say.

"I work at The Starboard," Dillon said. "The head chef makes me prep sauces sometimes. It is *so* stressful."

"That's a pretty fancy place," I said, surprised. "You're a waiter over there?"

"No, just a line cook, but I want to be sous-chef someday...How many pieces of fish have you tried in your lifetime?" he asked.

"Um, none worth remembering, I guess."

"Exactly. That's all about to change," he said poking a piece of the fish with a fork and cupping his other hand underneath to make sure no sauces dripped. He offered it to me as a mother would offer food to her child, or a flirtatious wife to her husband. Although meaningless, I was extremely uncomfortable with this gesture. Not wanting to offend him though, I opened my mouth and sampled the tuna. Perfection.

The bell on our table dinged, a sign that our time was up. The shrill sound paired with the symphony of flavors inside my mouth made my hair stand on end. Goosebumps covered every part of me. The professor, a thin elderly woman with a heavy English accent, approached our station. Dillon reached for the plate on the left, then at the last moment, chose the plate on his right. I saw no difference between the two. They both looked identically perfect.

"Lovely job with presentation, Dillon," the instructor said.

"Thank you, chef," he replied.

"Who is this young fellow?"

"This is my sous chef for the day."

I was caught off guard, my mouth completely full. The chef looked down under the table at my school jacket.

"I didn't realize today was a holiday for Cherrywood," she said, "but it would seem very fortuitous for Dillon that you were here."

"Cherrywood?" Dillon asked.

"A-minus, Dillon," the head chef commented. "The duck is just a bit dry, but wonderful job overall."

When she left, Dillon turned back to me and asked, "You go to that Christian high school? I thought you were in college."

"High school," I said.

"Are you gonna tell me I'm going to hell?"

"No."

"What do you mean 'no'?" he replied.

"I just wanted to help you. You said you needed help."

Dillon took a step back, realizing he was out of line. "I'm sorry. That was rude," he said sincerely. "Oh my God, thank you so much for your help today, Sylas. You were so great."

"You're welcome, Dillon. Nice job on the A."

"A-minus."

"Who's counting?"

"Hold up," he said taking out a piece of paper and writing down some digits. "Here's my number. I want to return the favor, so give me a call if you need any help with anything, ok? Moving, changing a tire, whatever. And I'm not hitting on you. I'm serious. Give me a call if you need anything."

"Thanks, Dillon. You don't have to feel like you owe me anything. It was my pleasure."

"Just keep it, ok? Seriously, just let me know if I can help."

"Well, thanks! That's very nice of you. It was great meeting you."

"You too. Thanks again so much. You're a life saver."

After I shook Dillon's hand and parted ways, I wandered across the courtyard to the cafeteria, being guided by two large neon posters that read: "NORML. Legalize it!" Glancing around the courtyard, I saw other signs for Greenpeace, PETA, and the like. These organizations were foreign to me. I'd heard of them before but had simply lumped them into a class of secular worldviews. Not seeing Rachel after I entered the cafeteria, I decided to get in line and order a tray of food.

As I stood there, I thought about why Dillon was so quick to ask if I was going to preach hell to him. I'm sure most Christians had mistreated him. He had likely been hurt in the past and was quick to judge Christians, much like I was initially going to judge him.

Regardless of our backgrounds or current worldviews, we weren't so different after all.

I arrived home around three o'clock following a very pleasant hour spent talking with Rachel after her classes. It was one of those refreshingly vulnerable conversations that you wouldn't think you could have with a mere acquaintance. She opened up to me later by telling me that she tried to commit suicide as soon as she found out she was pregnant. She felt her parents, who were staunch conservatives, would've been livid that she had sex out of wedlock, so at the time, taking her own life seemed like her only way out. I wondered how many times the legalism of religions made others feel the same way. It made me think of Dillon again, and I felt bad for him.

With only half an hour before I had to leave for work, I walked in my front door holding my bookbag and the stack of mail that I had just rescued from the packed mailbox. Two large white envelopes stood out in the stack of letters and junk mail. The envelopes were addressed to me with the return address declaring that they were from the Internal Revenue Service.

I ran up to my room and took a pocketknife from my motley bowl of office supplies to cut the first envelope open. Inside was a neat stack of papers filled with IRS tax jargon. *Return of Organization Exempt From Income Tax* was stamped at the top, and below that was a series of columns, numbers, and rows that confused me at first. The first one read *Southern Hope Foundation,* so I browsed through it. The numbers were complete gibberish and not worth my scrutiny with such little time, but about seven pages in was a list of officers and employees of the company. Jeremy Maitland's name was listed. They called him a 'Key Employee.'

At work I punched the time clock, greeted Tony the warehouse guy, and then immediately took the envelopes in to Beverly.

"Hi, Bev," I said as I greeted her.

"Well hello, toots," she said in her gravelly voice. "Whatcha got there?"

"It's actually something I was hoping you could help me with." I opened the one envelope to show her what was inside as she reached for her reading glasses. "This is something I'm doing for school," I said as I showed her the Southern Hope forms. "It's...a project for journalism class."

"Journalism?"

"Yeah, photojournalism actually," I lied.

She nodded and looked the first return over.

"I'm doing a story on non-profit spending. They said I could use Cherrywood Church and the Southern Hope Foundation as examples, but I don't know how to read this stuff."

"So what do you need to know?"

"Well, I just need to know the numbers and specifically if anything looks strange to you. I'm taking my inspiration from that big United Way scandal that happened last year. I'm doing a story on how most charities operate."

"So you just want me to look these over and make sure your pastor isn't sailing around the Caribbean, right?"

"Yeah," I politely chuckled, knowing she was making a joke but thinking it may not be that far off.

"I'll put these in my purse and look over them tonight if that's okay."

"Absolutely, that would be a huge help."

It was an odd feeling, coming back to the Academy after my ramble into college life. I felt like I had grown; changed in some way. I liked it and wanted more, but for the time being, I knew I had to stay confined within these halls. I felt imprisoned by the Academy's walls and looked forward to graduation when I would be able to put this place behind me for good.

On my way to first period Calculus, Jesse Gilder, a lacrosse player, smiled at me as he tapped his two straightened index fingers together and remarked, "It doesn't work this way, dude." He laughed as he walked by me.

I didn't know what he meant so I just blew it off and kept going. Jessica Smith and a few other volleyball chicks watched me as I walked past. Jessica started whispering to her friend Amber.

I didn't understand what that was all about until fourth period History. After I found my usual seat and dropped my backpack below, Terrance Hoziah, one of Cam's football buddies and my classmate who sat two seats behind me, commented, "Have you always known?"

I turned around, still unsure if he was talking to me.

"Me?" I asked.

"Yeah. Is that why Natalie broke up with you?"

"What are you talking about?"

"Ya know..." he snickered.

"No. No, I don't."

"Have you told your parents?"

"Told 'em what?"

"Ya know..." he responded in the same snarky tone.

He was obviously trying to annoy me, so I turned back around.

"Most of us already knew," he responded from behind. I swiveled around again.

"What are you saying?"

"You know..." he responded again in the same exact irritating way as he had twice before.

"Seriously. I don't know, so please stop."

"Dude...you're a nancy boy...It's ok. My second cousin is a queer. There are others around."

"You saying I'm gay?!"

"Have you always known? Nature or nurture - what's your

assessment?"

"Shut up, Terrance. I'm not gay!"

"That's not what the word on the street is. A little birdie told me that you skipped school yesterday to bake cookies with your boyfriend."

"What?"

"Yeah. They were probably fabulous," he said with a sinister laugh. Hilary Modahey came in and took her usual seat between us, thankfully blocking our conversation. I turned around to end our dialogue and was completely flabbergasted. He must have meant that someone saw me yesterday with Dillon. Jesse's inappropriate gesture earlier finally made sense. Once again I sadly felt much more loved from a bunch of secular heathens than I did by my own religious peers.

I found Roscoe by his locker after class.

"What's up, man?" he said as he saw me approach.

"Hey, dude. Hey, have you heard what people are saying about me?"

"Yeah, Natalie broke up with you. Dude, that stinks!"

"Yeah, that. Actually, I meant the other thing they are saying about me."

"Uhh...yeah, Kaitlyn Benedict said you were in her mom's class yesterday.

"Who?"

"Some junior looking to gain a little collateral at the expense of your reputation. She's been telling everyone that you and some other guy were pretty cozy, feeding each other and what not. Is it true? Cause if you are gay, that's fine, but you should know that you and I are never gonna happen. I know you want me."

"What?!"

"I'm sorry, I'm just busting your chops. It's just a stupid rumor. No one really thinks you're gay."

"Shh," I said trying to quiet him. "Yeah, I went with Rachel Ellis to CCC."

"Why?"

"I just wanted something different. Yeah, I was in a cooking class, but it was just because Rachel had a Women's Studies class that I didn't want to go to. It was more boredom than anything."

"Well, she said that you were having fun with this guy who's a huge flamer."

"Yeah, his name was Dillon. So what?"

"I know, that's what I've been telling people. So what?"

"Have people been saying stuff to you?"

"It's whatever, man. People are always gonna give others a hard time."

"Why is it a big deal?" I asked. "Who cares that he was gay? He's just a person."

"Don't worry about it. It's just stupid drama. Hey, I gotta get going to class though. Got a big test today."

"Ok, that's cool. Good luck."

"Thanks," he said as he closed his locker. "See ya later, man."

"See ya," I said.

I quickly found myself wishing for the good old days when the only slanderous rumors about me were of me scoring with my hot girlfriend. But those rumors had morphed into something completely different and unsettling. Now I was fighting the odious story that Natalie broke up with me because I was gay.

The day got harder and harder for me. I saw Natalie in passing. She apologetically smiled. I nodded. The new rumor followed me like a plague. Yearbook class was my long-awaited sanctuary, and it couldn't get here soon enough.

When I closed my locker after grabbing my seventh period government book and my camera, I turned around to be startled by Dr. Sites who appeared to be watching me.

"Are you going to Yearbook class now?" he curiously asked.

"Yes, sir," I nervously replied.

"I'm heading up that way too. You mind if I walk with you?"

"Uhh...Sure."

"Great," he said as he sidled up beside me, and we both awkwardly started to move in that direction.

"We missed you here at school yesterday, Sylas."

My tension instantly doubled. "I'm sorry, sir. I had a prior obligation."

"A prior obligation? Sounds pretty important. What was this prior obligation?"

I knew that he already knew. He wouldn't have been talking to me like that if he didn't suspect something. "College, sir."

"College?"

"Yes, sir. Clanton Community College."

"You skipped school to go look at a community college? Are you thinking of enrolling?" His tone indicated that he already knew the answer.

"Maybe."

"Maybe?"

"I don't know. I'm sorry, sir. I shouldn't have done that without permission."

"And did you meet anyone interesting at college?" I knew where his questions were leading, so I met them head-on.

"Yes, there were a few nice people. I met this one guy who needed help on a cooking exam, so I gave him a hand."

"Cooking, huh? Do you enjoy cooking?"

"Sort of."

"My wife loves to cook. I don't care for it so much, but lucky for me, I like to eat." I chuckled politely. "What other things do you enjoy, Sy? Photography, right? You obviously like photography."

"Uhh...yes sir. I do like photography."

"Yeah, your photos are quite good. Did I ever thank you for the photos you took at the Southern Hope Banquet?"

"No, I don't believe so. That's fine though. It was really my pleasure."

"Oh well, the photos were excellent. I think Southern Hope has used a few in their promotionals. Thank you for taking those."

"Really? That's cool. I'm just glad you asked me."

"You take a lot of photos, don't you? You get to see a lot of the stuff going on around here?"

My body was getting hotter. "Yeah, I like taking pictures."

"And you're very observant. Mrs. Turner showed a picture you took at the homeless shelter of that mother and daughter. Very touching moment."

"Well, thank you sir." We had entered the expansive courtyard by this time, and migrating students were now much more sparse. We made our way over to a set of unoccupied benches, and as we took our seats, I couldn't help but realize that we were now completely alone.

"Sy, I know you skipped school yesterday without permission, and I've heard about the types of people that you were associating with. That's a concern for me. But it's also come to my attention that you've taken an interest in finance and are doing a story on accounting for your photojournalism class. What class might that be for? We don't offer a photojournalism class as part of our curriculum."

My heartbeat tripled in speed, and I swallowed a big lump in my throat. I stayed silent but unwittingly stopped moving.

"Sy, you're very observant. And if you look closely, you might notice things that don't make sense by themselves."

"Yes, sir."

"Right. I don't know what kind of details you're picking up on, but you're never going to know what the big picture is if you just look at small little snapshots. So let me tell you what the big picture is, Sy. Cherrywood Christian Academy, Clanton Baptist Church, Southern Hope Foundation, and all of the other programs you've grown up in are doing a darn good job at furthering God's kingdom. We're influencing lives, leading people to Christ, and making a huge difference in North Carolina and throughout the world. If you have any questions about Cherrywood, the church, or Southern Hope, just come ask me. I'm an open book."

He paused for a moment and took a deep breath. I was preparing for him to hand down his punishment for my actions.

"I tell ya what," he continued. "Let's forget this whole thing. We'll call it a lapse of your professional journalism, as long as you agree to come to me with any other questions you have about me or my responsibilities. Does that sound fair?"

"Yes." I stammered with a guarded smile. I certainly had plenty of questions I wanted to ask him, but I remembered what Mr. Oakridge had told me. I knew I couldn't trust the man.

"Good. Now I'm going to encourage you to keep challenging yourself with your photography, but please use conservative discretion in your endeavors," he said, patting my leg as he stood up. "You better be heading onto class."

He took two steps before turning back around with one final thought. "Oh, and please be sure to use conservative discretion in your new friendships as well."

That statement boiled my blood. Dr. Sites knew nothing about Dillon or me and had no right to be so judgmental. I knew he had cornered me for a reason. If there was nothing to hide, then we wouldn't be having this conversation. He was playing mind games. So I decided to go all in.

"I do have a few questions for you, actually. Why did you fire Mr. Oakridge but keep Mrs. Yelski? Why was Rachel Ellis kicked out of Cherrywood when you discovered she attempted suicide? And what ever happened to the solar panels for the African orphanage?"

My words froze him, and I immediately regretted speaking out of emotion. He turned his head slightly, standing nearly at attention with arms at his side. Then after what felt like an eternity, he spoke.

"Why did your mother give a medication to her patient without an order from a doctor?"

He never fully turned around to face me. He simply faced forward again and walked away.

I was floored. I was speechless and more frightened than I had ever been in my entire life. How did he know about my mother's mistake? I never fully realized the reach of his power and influence. If I had, I think I would've done things differently.

I had wrestled with the Devil in the courtyard and the Devil had won.

CHAPTER 19

I was terrified for a month after that encounter. Dr. Sites knew everything. He'd known all along. I didn't tell anyone what had happened. At work, Beverly the office accountant denied telling anyone about the tax returns I had her look over. Although a bit kooky at times, she seemed genuine, and I felt as if I could trust her. She told me that nearly every night she went directly home to her three cats, drank two glasses of *Franzia,* and was in bed by nine. No one could've possibly seen or known about her involvement with the tax returns. Still, for her safety and for mine, I had her take a break from looking over them. I didn't want to bring her down with me.

I kept my head down and just fumbled through the motions for a while, still trying to identify the answers, both in my school and in my home life. I visited Mr. Oakridge once more during that time and told him about my brush with Dr. Sites. He was surprised it didn't come sooner. I also told him about my college experience, and we got to talking about Rachel, Dillon, and CCC Bio 101. The theory of evolution was still a stumbling block for me. This is where it all seemed to hinge. If I could demonstrate that there were no supernatural elements and that this world was all there is, religions would therefore become useless to me, and I'd be free. However, if pure naturalism was too far-fetched, I would clearly need to understand the idea of a supernatural much better than I currently did. Mr. Oakridge let me borrow a science book from his library in order to aid my process.

Around the end of February, when Spring was just starting to flirt, I grew restless. The Academy was winning with each passing day. Mrs. Yelski continued giving me sub-par marks, the gay rumors were still floating around, and Dr. Sites still had me under his thumb. Natalie had moved on and was already dating someone else. Cam had completely gone off the deep end. He was a party boy now, and we lost virtually all of the common bonds that connected us. Like a bull elephant confined to a circus ring, I became frustrated to the point of aggression.

A part of me knew I should simply fly under the radar and just do my time. Still there was another part of me that could not stand to be walked over and silenced out of convenience. That was the part I listened to.

One day at work, I decided to find out exactly how deep the rabbit hole under the Academy went. I stepped back into the accounting department at Winters' Printing and waited until Beverly and I were alone.

"Beverly," I said in a whisper, "could you finish taking a look at those tax reports for me when you have the time?"

"You changed your mind about it?" she asked. "So you're gonna do it now?"

"Yes ma'am. Do you still have those files?"

"Well, let me see," she said getting up from her chair and checking the top of her unorganized file cabinet. She thumbed through a stack of papers and found them towards the bottom. "Here they are. Do you need them back?"

"Actually, could you explain them to me? I think I'm ready now."

"I don't know what you're looking for, but I can explain some of the numbers to ya. Just give me one second."

I waited patiently in the doorway while she finished typing out an email.

"Ok, I think I sent it. Or I just deleted it. Either way, it's gone," she joked as she swiveled around in her chair to grab the forms from the top of her filing cabinet. "Pull up that chair."

I did as she asked, pulling a chair over in front of her desk. She placed the forms in front of me and proceeded to explain each one briefly.

"Ok, I'm not sure what you're looking for, but I'll go over each page, and then just stop me if you have questions. Ok, we'll start with the church. The front page here is just a summary of everything. Here's their name, their EIN number over here; you can see that they are a 501(c)(3) organization, and then these are just itemized breakdowns of their financials. Here's Reverend Samms' signature here and then the signature of their accountant at the bottom."

She spent the next few minutes explaining all the different checkboxes and information that they reported. A few pages in was a list of all the officers and employees of the church.

"Here is where they report the different officers and their salaries and everything. Your pastor makes a pretty good living. $350,000 per year right here. Not bad."

"He makes that in a year?" I muttered out loud.

"Looks like I should start preaching more."

A few more pages in was a more detailed breakdown of the revenue and expenses. As she was explaining a few of the numbers, I asked, "What's this $37,000 expense?"

"That looks like they purchased a company vehicle," she said. "See, you can see that they started to take the depreciation on it over here. They got some big expenses that they've reported, but I don't see anything out of the ordinary. They receive a lot of tithes and donations, so I'm sure they just let that money flow right back out to purchase hot meals and the other outreach programs that they had. Although, I did see one interesting expense, though. Look at this." She pointed to a number about halfway down the page. "It looks like they spent $62,140.85 on professional fundraising services. But then take a look over here," she stated while opening up the Southern Hope Foundation's tax return.

Taking a minute to thumb through the pages, she stopped on one of the pages and pointed to a line item. "This $62,140.85 was received as revenue over here. It would seem that Clanton Baptist hired Southern Hope to do $62,000 worth of fundraising work for them. I guess that's not unheard of, but you'd wonder why they needed to hire Southern Hope. Aren't they just a subsidiary of the church?"

"You mean, like, Southern Hope is just a spin-off organization? Yeah, pretty much."

"Right, so why would a big church like Clanton Baptist need to hire its smaller daughter company to fundraise for them? It would seem like Southern Hope should pay Clanton Baptist for the fundraising services, not the other way around."

Deep in thought, I replied, "Yeah, that makes sense. The church is always touting Southern Hope. You don't hear it going the other way too much." Still surveying the strange numbers, I asked, "So what's this big expense up here?"

"This is just all the grant and assistance money they gave to some state government programs. A lot of nonprofits will usually help give support to some government programs that might help further their cause. These are some big numbers though. Almost a quarter of Clanton Baptist's revenue."

"Yeah, that's a big chunk."

"Sure is. Other than that, I don't see anything too bizarre."

"Beverly," Mr. Winters said, poking his head in from the doorway. "Do you have the new quarterly ledger? Oh, hello, Sylas."

"Just about, I should have it to you by five," she said.

"Hello, sir," I responded.

"Perfect," he said. He glanced once more at me, before heading back to his office.

"Do you have any more questions?"

"What? No, I don't think so," I said, my train of thought broken by Mr. Winters' interruption. "I'll go home and look at these tonight, and I might have questions for you tomorrow. Is that ok?"

"Yeah, that's fine. I hope I was helpful."

"Yes, you definitely were. Thank you very much," I replied as I scooped the papers from her desk.

"Anytime, sugar. Good luck with your assignment."

My mind kept churning while I folded and packaged some freshly printed brochures for a medical company. Almost a quarter of Clanton Baptist's revenue went to some governmental organization. That's a huge number. Half a million bucks could have done untold wonders for the needy in this community and abroad. Why send it to Raleigh? I tried to think back on how the church or school could possibly have any government involvement of any kind to warrant spending a number that big. Then I remembered Governor Hawkins at that Southern Hope Banquet. He said something to Mr. Korta about being able to count on his vote. What could that mean?

A few minutes later, a wild concept came to my mind.

I went back into Beverly's office. "Heya, Bev. Got one more thing to ask of you."

"What's up, sweetie?"

"You can access the internet on your computer, right?"

"Oh honey, don't ask me to do anything like that. I just learned what an inbox is; I wouldn't have the slightest clue on how to use an inner-net."

"Can I show you?"

"You can try."

I moved around behind Beverly's desk and found the Internet Explorer icon on the bottom left of her screen. We made some small talk while the thing loaded, making the awful squealing sounds of a trapped pig. I typed the words: *NC bill about tax return reporting.* I recalled a news story a while back that reported on a new bill which would require business and charities to report more information on their state tax returns.

The proposed bill was called SB-348. It would have increased this year's state tax returns by three additional pages of more detailed disclosures and accounting to allow the state government an even more in-depth look at how businesses and charities do their books. If there was anything fishy going on with the tax returns I held in my hand, I'm sure the authorities at Clanton Baptist or Cherrywood wouldn't have been in favor of a bill like that.

Reading further into the article, I saw what became of that proposed bill. The governor had vetoed it.

It was the very next day that I came home to find my mom distressed.

"How could this happen? Why would they bring this up now?" my mom was frantically asking my father as I walked in the door. They were both standing in the kitchen when I came home from work. My mom was the most upset I had ever seen her.

"I'm going to give them a call," urged my dad. "Who is the guy I should ask for?"

"No, no. Don't call. You can't call them directly anyway."

"What's going on?" I asked as I walked in the kitchen."

"Oh hi, Sylas. How was school?" my mother asked trying to force a smile through teary eyes.

"Mom, what's wrong?"

"They're bullying your mother at work," my father said anxiously pacing back and forth.

"What do you mean?" I asked.

My dad thought for a moment about what he should say. "Do you remember a few months ago when your mother was worried that she accidentally gave one of her patients the wrong medication?" he said.

"Yeah."

"Well, the hospital has re-opened her case and has given her a suspension."

I was stunned. Dr. Sites had been serious. "That happened six months ago, and your patient is ok!" I said angrily.

My father had slowed his fly-like zigzagging throughout the kitchen and finally settled on the kitchen doorway to lean on.

"So what happens now?" I asked.

"Now, I wait," my mother said.

"Wait?"

"Yeah. Until they call me," she replied nodding.

"Are you gonna be ok?"

"We'll have to be."

"What do you need me to help with? I'll work more hours at the print shop," I said. "I can get a weekend job. What do you need me to do?"

"Sy, God bless you," my mom said as she started to tear up again. "We'll be fine."

"No, I want to. Just trust me. I think I know something about this," I said.

"You know something about this, Sylas?" my father said leaving his post.

I stopped, realizing the extra large can of worms I had just opened. "I know why they're doing this," I softly said.

"Why who is doing what?"

Pausing for a painfully long time, I replied, "Dr. Sites. It's to get back at me. It's because of me. I did this…But I'll make it right. I'll start working extra until it gets solved. I can drop out of school and go full-time at Winters'. Whatever you guys need."

"Sylas, what are you talking about?" my mother asked.

"He's doing it to get back at me for what I did. What I said."

"Sylas, are you saying you have something to do with your mother getting in trouble?" my father asked angrily.

"No…but yes. I didn't mean to do anything to hurt mom. I didn't think it would."

"I don't like the way you're talking, boy," my father said stepping closer to me. I tried to regain my footing and move out of his path. "What did you do to Charles Sites?"

"Nothing. I was just asking questions. He's not a good person, and I found out and now he is using mom to get back at me."

"He's not a good person? Funny, I think I said the same thing to you last fall before you started taking pictures on the weekends for that man. Now you've gone and stuck your nose into his business where it doesn't belong, and he's taking it out on your mother!"

"I'm sorry, but can't we tell someone?"

"Who? Who? Please tell me - who in the little town of Clanton can we tell to make this go away?" my father shouted.

"Anyone, everyone, someone!"

"Yeah! And then what? What will happen? Who will believe a disgruntled, backsliding, disrespectful kid over someone like Dr. Sites?"

The room fell quiet, deathly still from the storm that was over and before the one that was about to erupt.

"Get out."

"What?" I said confused.

"You heard me. If what you say is true - that you brought this on your mother - I want you to stay as far away from her, from me, and from this house as possible!"

I looked at my mother, her face half-buried in a dishtowel. Buck barked and whimpered uncontrollably.

"Mom, I'm so sorry. I'm sorry."

"Do not call us or write us or visit us or contact us in anyway until I say otherwise. Not so much as a postcard. You brought the Devil to my doorstep, and I want no part of it. Get out!"

My father grabbed me by the arm and started ushering me out of the house like a bodyguard.

"I'm sorry, Mom! I'm sorry!"

"Sylas!" I heard her scream from the kitchen, sobbing uncontrollably.

My father shoved me out of the door and threw my backpack on the front lawn. Buck snuck out of the house with me.

"Buck! Inside, now!"

Buck looked up and whimpered, not wanting to leave my side. My father walked over and grabbed him by the scruff of his neck. Buck let out a yelp as my dad pulled him back inside and locked the glass door. I picked my backpack off the lawn and walked over to my car. On the other side of the glass door, Buck pawed, trying to escape, as my mother stood next to him and cried into her dishtowel.

I started my car, and with one last wave I drove away, unsure of where to go.

CHAPTER 20

There was really only one place I could think to go to. Shawn's life was already sort of unstable with his time split between his two parents, and I hadn't spoken to Cameron in weeks. Pulling out of my driveway, I turned left down my street toward Roscoe's.

I took another deep breath after I parked on the street being careful not to block in their new SUV. Their family's old minivan sat on the street just in front of me with a "For Sale" sign placed in the back window. I remember having a lot of good times in that van. Car rides with Roscoe, his little sister, Lily, and his parents to grab ice cream or a burger had been common before the two of us got our licenses. I missed those simpler days before life got complicated. I left my belongings in my car. Since I had not yet been asked to stay the night, I did not want to invite myself or assume anything.

I shook off the last hour and tried to put on a genuine smile. I knocked cheerfully. Roscoe's father opened the door.

"Sylas! Good to see you! Are you here about the van?"

"The van?"

"Oh, your father called earlier this morning about purchasing it. He's not with you?"

"Oh, um, no sir. I'm actually just here to see Jake."

"Alright then, come right in. You'll have to forgive me; I am just finishing up dinner. I think Jake is upstairs."

"Thank you, sir."

I started to climb the stairs as Jake met me halfway.

"Hey man! What are you doing here?" he asked cheerfully.

"Just passing by. Hey, can we talk upstairs?"

"Is everything okay?"

"Yeah, fine. Just…can we go up to your room?"

"Sure thing."

"Dad, when's dinner gonna be ready?" Roscoe shouted down.

"About ten minutes. Sylas, you wanna stay for dinner?" Being a restaurateur, Mr. Martin's dinners were always the best.

"If I'm not intruding, sir."

"Not at all. I'll call you both when it's ready."

"Thanks, Dad." Roscoe replied as we entered his room.

"So what's up?" Roscoe asked. Before answering, I shut the door behind us.

I pulled his desk chair out and sat down as he collapsed onto his bed. "Well. I'm not quite sure how to say this."

"Just say it."

"Ok...I just got kicked out."

"Of school?" he shouted.

"No."

"Your house?"

"Yeah."

"What did you do?"

"It's a long story."

"So what's the short version?"

"I got kicked out."

"Alright, the medium version then."

I stood up and began to pace around the room. I anxiously grabbed a Nerf basketball Roscoe had for his plastic hoop that hung from his closet door.

Tossing it up and down a few times, I began, "Things at school are pretty bad."

"Are you failing?"

"It's not my grades." I took another moment to find exactly how I wanted to phrase things without making him upset, knowing he had a short fuse.

"There are certain people at school who I believe don't want me there."

"Like who? Topher?"

"Most likely. But that's not who I am talking about."

"Teachers? Mrs. Yelski?"

"Yeah, probably her too, but I'm not talking about her either."

"Then who?"

I paused for another moment before I cautiously said the words, "Grady's grandpa."

"Principal Sites?"

"Yes."

"Why does he want you out of the school?" he replied in a

whisper.

"I think I know too much."

"About what?"

"About him."

"What do you mean?"

I heard a thump from downstairs and a bit of clanging. Roscoe's father was pulling out dishes to set the table. I grabbed the desk chair and scooted it close to Roscoe's bed. "You can't say anything to anyone."

"Okay, what is it?"

"I mean it, Roscoe. I know you like to chat with some of the guys on the football team, but you can't tell them this. Don't say a word to a girl you're trying to impress. No one. Get me?"

"Okay," he said solemnly, realizing how serious I was.

"He's not the person you think he is."

"Principal Sites?"

I nodded. "The Academy, the church, Southern Hope. There's a lot going on underground there."

"Underground? Like what?"

"Well, I first thought it was just that Jeremy guy, but it turns out he's nobody. I think they're just using him as a pawn, and he might not even realize it."

"Why would you think that?"

"Because I got a hold of the tax returns for the church and Southern Hope. Dude, they're doing some shady stuff with money, man. Like laundering it or something."

"Money laundering?"

"I don't know, but they listed Jeremy as an employee when he says he doesn't work there. They were passing stuff from the church through Southern Hope, and I think they paid off Governor Hawkins for vetoing a bill."

"What are you talking about?"

"Ok, so my mom made a mistake at her work about six months back. Nothing too serious - everyone is fine. Dr. Sites approached me about a month ago and basically threatened me if I didn't stop looking into his business. He brought up my mother's mistake she made at the hospital in a threatening way. Like, you had better stop coming after me, or I'm coming after someone you love."

"Are you serious? A month ago?"

"Boys," Roscoe's dad called. "Dinner's ready!"

"Be right down, Dad!"

"I found out that thing about the governor yesterday. Now all of a sudden my mom's case got re-opened, and she was suspended from work. That's why my dad kicked me out. I told him it was my fault, and that's why he told me to leave."

"Man, I'm really sorry."

"So that's the medium version. I'm my family's pariah, and now I'm homeless.

Roscoe stood up from his bed. In his face, I saw that he felt a taste of what I was feeling: helplessness and confusion, encased in equal parts of fear and anger.

"You think they paid off the governor?" he asked.

"I'm not sure if they paid him off or heavily influenced his decision. The bill that he vetoed would have required more detail when filing state tax returns, and if they're doing some shady stuff with money, of course they'd want him to veto it!"

"I gotta tell my dad about this."

"No," I said sharply. "You promised."

"Sy, I think my dad could really help on thi--"

"Roscoe, no. This thing has gotten too big. It's a cancer that eats up anything in its path. My mom has already been suspended. How soon would it be before your father's restaurant is closed up? I just need some time to think and figure out exactly what I'm going to do. Can I trust you to keep my secret?"

He nodded, seemingly deep in thought. "Let me talk to my parents," he said. "You can stay here until we figure something out."

"You sure that'll be alright? I'm not sure how long it will be."

"Trust me; let me do the talking."

"Boys! Now! Dinner is getting cold," Roscoe's mother called.

"Yes, ma'am!"

"Come on, let's eat," Roscoe said. "I'm starving."

We made small talk over the kind of home-cooked meal that seemed too good to be true. As I took a bite into the fresh hot cornbread, I felt an unexpected emotion come over me: envy. I wish I had Roscoe's life, his loving family, and even his height. I suppressed the feeling strongly, telling myself that I needed to be grateful for their kindness, but the feeling lingered on through my attempts to ignore it. Eventually, Roscoe brought the conversation around to me.

"Oh, hey Dad. So, um, Sylas has roaches."

"What?" I said, unsure where he was going with this. Roscoe gave me a sharp look, as Roscoe's mother unintentionally made a sickened face. "Oh, right. Yeah. I do."

"I'm sorry to hear that Sylas." Roscoe's father said. "Has your father contacted an exterminator?"

"Well, only Sylas's room has roaches," Roscoe said. "The rest of his house doesn't, but his dad contacted the exterminator and said they just need to bomb his room."

"Bomb?" Roscoe's mother asked.

"Yeah, with chemicals."

I closed my eyes, humiliated and furious at the stupidity of Roscoe's plan.

"So just your room has the roaches, Sy?" Mr. Martin asked.

"Yes sir." I replied, knowing I wasn't able to jump off this moving train now.

"So, is it okay if he stays here for a couple days, or at least tonight?" Roscoe asked.

I could feel Roscoe's father staring at me. He didn't buy it. I knew he was smarter than that, but I also knew he was too kind to further humiliate me.

"I don't think so boys, it's a school ni--" Roscoe's mom began.

"It's okay, honey," his father spoke up. "I think it will be alright."

I glanced up to see Roscoe's father signal to his wife to look at me. I immediately looked back down at my plate.

"Alright then, I suppose it's okay. At least for tonight."

"Thank you," I replied, looking up from my plate.

Roscoe's parents smiled kindly at each other, a simple look I had never seen between my own parents. I turned and looked at Roscoe who gave me two huge thumbs up with a dopey smile and then mouthed the words, *told you*.

I nodded gratefully, still terribly embarrassed about the whole thing but relieved to know that I had a place to sleep for the night.

That night, I asked to use the phone to call my house, and I pretended to be a telemarketer. My mother answered, and I asked her to get to a place where she could talk without arousing my dad's suspicion. She was relieved to know that I was okay and had a place to stay. She also told me that Rachel Ellis had called for me, which was a surprise. She didn't leave a message though.

I had my gym bag in my car, so luckily I had enough toiletries and clothes to make it through a night at Roscoe's and school the next day.

My mom negotiated for me to come back home for half an hour after school the next day to grab a few of my things. My father stayed locked in his room for the time I was there. Mom prepared a bag of sandwiches and snacks while I loaded up an old suitcase with clothes, a mason jar filled with quarters, my makeshift survival kit, and my shoebox of photos. Downstairs, I grabbed my .22 caliber rifle and some ammo from the gun cabinet. I wrapped it in a sweatshirt before my mother saw it.

"Here's some money to give to Mrs. Martin, to help pay your way. You be on your best behavior over there, okay?" my mom said as she handed me some cash.

"Thanks, Mom. Will I see you at church?"

"Your father thinks it's best if I stay home until this whole thing gets resolved. When your father gets like this, there is just no reasoning with him. I'll wait till things calm down, and then I'll talk to him."

"You really think that will do any good?"

"I think it will. Things will get better. It just takes time. I love you, Sylas."

"I don't believe it."

She was astonished. "You don't believe I love you?"

"I don't believe you think things will get better. They never have before."

She let out a sigh, knowing that I had called her bluff. She had been married to the man for over twenty-five years. She knew him better than I did, and she knew that I was right.

"I love you, Mom." She began to cry. "I don't blame you," I said in a whisper, dropping my belongings and squeezing her tightly. "I'll call soon. I will always call at exactly 7:30 in the evening. That's how you'll know it's me."

"I don't blame you either, Sy." She sniffled as I picked my things back up and left.

Part of me had always prepared for this day. I had always

known my father's love came with strings and conditions. I also knew that my mother had been left by her own father in the past and therefore, she was not able to stand up to her husband for fear of being left a second time. I knew she was deeply hurt to be disregarded by someone she truly loved. It seemed as though through her own self-preservation, she had allowed her son to suffer the same fate.

I stayed at Roscoe's the rest of the week although I didn't call my mom again. I knew she must have been worried, but it was nice to live in a house of peace and quiet with no eggshells to walk on. I was living in a dream world, and I had no desire to wake up from it.

When the weekend came I was on the living room couch reading the book Mr. Oakridge suggested for me, and Mr. Martin was in the nearby laundry room. Since no one else seemed to be around, he asked if he could have a word with me.

"We've really enjoyed having you here for the week, Sylas," he said as he stepped further into the laundry room.

"Thank you, sir," I replied.

"Any word about how the extermination is coming?"

"No, sir."

"Have you spoken to your parents this week?"

I broke eye contact and looked down at the floor. "Just my mom, but she didn't know when it would be safe to return home yet."

Roscoe's father leaned back on the washer. I felt as if he was a bit unsure of what he wanted to say next.

"There were never any roaches, were there?"

I paused for a second and then said, "No, sir."

He sighed deeply and softly spoke, "Sy, are you okay?"

I couldn't stand to look at him. I was too ashamed.

"Sylas."

I gritted my teeth and clenched my hands tightly.

"Sylas?"

I felt my face grow hot and my eyes fill with tears uncontrollably. No one had seen me cry since middle school. For at least four years I had hidden my tears from view; they had all been stoppable - until now. I put my face in my hands and wept. Roscoe's father didn't say another word. He moved in close and wrapped his arms around me. He didn't try to silence me. He didn't try to calm me; he just allowed me to feel everything that I had been holding onto. I cried it all out – everything - until all the hurt and anger had left me. It was only then that he began to speak.

"I think I need to have a talk with your father," he said.

I never told him anything. He just knew.

"It won't do any good."

"How can you be so sure?"

"I just know."

"It won't hurt to try will it?"

"I guess not, but it won't do any good."

"We'll just see about that," he said with a reassuring smile.

I smiled back at him, hoping against all odds that he was right; although, in my heart I knew he wasn't.

I stayed with Roscoe for another week. We carpooled to school together and had an all-around great time hanging out. But one Sunday morning when I awoke early to use the restroom, I heard Roscoe's parents speaking quietly downstairs. I walked backwards a few steps and stopped to listen.

"Are you going to talk to him now?" Roscoe's mom was asking.

"Yes," his father answered. "I'll take the van. I think he's serious about buying it. I'll see you and the boys at church."

"Remember to tell him that the gas gauge can kind of stick once it gets below a quarter tank. He needs to fill it up before then."

"Yeah, of course. I already let him know about it, but I'll remind him again."

"Good luck, dear."

"Thanks honey. Say a prayer for me."

"I will, it's just--"

"What's wrong?"

"You don't think Sylas feels like he is unwelcome here do you?"

"No, but his father has to realize that we have kids of our own to take care of. We can't afford to take care of his, too."

"Just be careful how you talk to him. He sounds like he's a difficult person."

"I will, hun. I'll see you at church."

I returned to bed for another ten minutes before getting up again to use the restroom. I didn't want Mrs. Martin to know I had heard their conversation. Mr. Martin's request for prayer humbled me, knowing that he was going to confront my father on my behalf. I hadn't prayed in months. It felt weird, considering I wasn't sure of its effectiveness. But out of respect for Mr. Martin, and partially out of desperation, I said a prayer. I prayed all morning until I fell back to sleep.

I sat patiently with Roscoe and his mother in the sanctuary, waiting for church to begin. About five minutes before the service started, I saw Roscoe's father sneak into our aisle. His family always sat on the same row every Sunday morning. He sat down and whispered to Mrs. Martin who in turn shook her head. Then after a few minutes, he turned to me.

"Do you need to grab anything else from your house on the way home?" he asked.

I knew what that meant. He had lost. He lovingly wanted to know how he could still help me, but as kind as it was for him to take care of me, I realized I was my own man now. It was time I started taking care of myself.

I waited until nearly sunset that day after Roscoe's father left for his restaurant to set up for a busy Monday lunch hour before I gathered my things and headed towards the door. I was trying to make my exit as swiftly as possible.

"Alright, well, I'm outta here." I said.

"You are?" Mrs. Martin asked.

Roscoe came downstairs after using the restroom. I was trying to make it out before he had finished. "Where ya goin', buddy?"

"Back to my house."

"Your house?" Mrs. Martin echoed.

"Yeah. I called my folks after church, just kinda talked things over with my dad. We were able to get it worked out."

"And he's letting you go back?" Roscoe replied. "I mean, like all the bugs are gone and everything."

"Yep, but hey, thank you so much for everything, really." Roscoe's mother still stood in disbelief. I knew I needed to wrap things up quickly. "Roscoe, it's been awesome man. I really appreciate it. I know you're gonna tear up that I'm leaving."

"Tears of joy maybe. I'm tired of smelling your farts every night."

"You loved it."

"Alright, man, I'll see you at school."

"Alright, well, bye everybody," I said. "Bye bye, Lily!" I waved to her as she played in the corner with her dolls.

"Bye bye," she echoed, completely oblivious.

The wind almost took the door out of my hand before I was able to close it behind me. The nervousness of my next move hadn't fully set in yet. I was very thankful for everything that Roscoe's family had done for me, but I no longer wanted to burden them with my problems. I saw their life as perfect: a beautiful house, a beautiful family, and a beautiful story. In a way, I felt like I had been an imperfection. The last thing I ever wanted to do was ruin their perfect story. As I pulled away from their home that evening, I grew more afraid than I had ever been. In spite of all the dangerous and stupid things I had done growing up, this was the first time I had ever genuinely feared for my well-being.

It was also the first time I ever felt completely alone.

CHAPTER 21

I pulled up to the house with an overwhelming sense of vulnerability and depression. Never did I think that I would have started this school year so rich in potential and friendships only to end up homeless and alone. The wind bullied me around as I searched for the key in my pocket. I slid my key into the lock and pushed open the door. Inside it was dark, cold, and empty.

Chernobyl was my new home.

The light and heat were fading fast. It took me several trips from my car to unload all of my stuff onto the cold, cement floor. The wind wasn't letting up and seemed to enjoy making my task even more difficult. Roscoe would've certainly helped me move in and probably even generously donated many home furnishings to help make my stay more pleasant. But he couldn't know. No one could. This was more than just embarrassing. It was defeat. I had lost the battle with my father, my school, and ultimately myself.

Digging into a duffel bag, I found my flashlight. I had accumulated a small collection of camping gear over the years and was glad to have it at a time like this. My .22 rifle was also a very welcome tool and probably my most guarded treasure. I'd kept it locked in the trunk while I had stayed at Roscoe's. He didn't need to know I had taken it from home. The sun had set about twenty minutes ago, and dusk was quickly turning to darkness. I slid the flashlight in my hoodie's front pocket as I started to hang several of my shirts in an unfinished coat closet. I spent the next hour or so neatly organizing what little possessions I had along the open studded walls. The wind was howling heavily outside and had found a loose piece of Tyvek to slap around. The vacant house heaved and croaked against the bluster.

The old familiar couch that I had so many fond memories of was now my bed. I first dusted off the loose pretzel and potato chip remnants and draped my sheet and comforter set over the worn cushions. The couch caved in the middle, which made sleeping on it feel more like a hammock than a bed. I decided to stay in my clothes that night, feeling too vulnerable in pajamas. Placing my .22 underneath the couch, I crawled into the blankets. The wind outside was still angry and continued to attack that piece of home wrap. I turned off my flashlight, rested my head on the pillow, and without thinking, began to pray.

It's funny how people turn to prayer in times of desperation. People who never think about God or even believe in Him otherwise often send up a prayer in desperate times, hoping that it might be heard somewhere. Like tossing dice in the dark, their lives are already at the bottom. Taking any kind of gamble doesn't seem to hurt. If I were God, I think that would annoy me.

"God," I began. For years, I usually opened prayers with the lines, 'Dear Heavenly Father,' but tonight if He was even up there, He was just 'God.' "I'm not sure if you're listening. I'm not sure who is up there. I hope someone can hear me. It would sure be nice. I only got two things to ask of you or whoever might be listening. One: please get me outta here. I guess my dad was bound to do this sooner or later, but please help me go home. I want to see my mom and just go home. Let this be the only night I spend here. And two: please give me an answer to this question: why are evil people running a Christian school? If you're real, why would you allow people like that to be in charge? They're harming you in more ways than I even realize. Why would you be okay with that? I guess the more appropriate question would be; who are you? Because if you're not who I think you are - who I thought you were - then I guess that answers my question. So, God, or gods...who are you? Oh, and let me get some sleep tonight. Amen."

I inhaled deeply, trying to relax. My eyes were closed, and I tried to drift asleep with the memories of the fond times that I enjoyed in this very room. It didn't work.

An hour later, that darned piece of Tyvek sounded like a flag on a roller coaster and still wouldn't let me sleep.

Upstairs a broken window was leaking cold air into the house. The old groans from the house seemed to get louder. I got up and did some pushups and jumping jacks to warm up and release any excess energy. I jumped up and grabbed a cross-brace to one of the studs and tried to do a pull-up. I managed one, but my lower body weight must've outnumbered my upper body strength. It must have been around 11:30 when I jumped back into my blankets and tried to fall asleep again.

It took me about twenty minutes or so before I finally succumbed to slumber; although it was only half an hour before the cold woke me back up.

The wind was still screaming outside, and the sheer noise was enough to keep a person awake. But the cold sealed the deal. I buried my head in my blankets trying to trap any excess body heat and lay like that for another hour.

That's when I heard some scratching noises upstairs. At first, I thought it was just the wind, but as I listened closer, the sounds were coming from inside the house. I quickly reached for my gun under the couch and jumped out of bed.

The scratching noises were getting louder and moving about upstairs. The entire house was completely open, so I knew that whatever was up there could easily come down here. There were no doors and no walls. I placed my flashlight under my gun like a SWAT officer and cautiously moved upstairs. A hurried scratchy, scampering noise shocked me, and I almost dropped the flashlight. It was an animal, but I wasn't fortunate enough for it to be a pesky mouse. This creature was much bigger. Taking the safety off of my gun, I kept pushing forward. It scampered again and stopped. Through the open walls I caught the eerie glowing eyes in my flashlight.

It was frozen, just watching me. Bringing the gun to my eye, I was ready for a shot, hoping that my .22 caliber bullet would be enough but expecting that it wouldn't. Then it moved again, it's bushy striped tail catching the light of my flashlight. It was a raccoon.

Finding the broken window it came from, it quickly climbed the 2x4 walls and escaped. My heart was beating fast. He was probably just trying to get out of the wind like I was. We were both homeless, although he had a much better chance at survival. In that moment, I realized what I had become. I was just an animal struggling for survival. We were on the same level. I had no more right to occupy this shelter than the raccoon did. I was just merely the one to claim it.

I didn't get any more sleep that night. I alternated between shivering and exercising until the dawn started to slowly appear. The sun never fully had a chance to rise before I left Chernobyl that morning. The sun's rays would have brought warmth and subdued the winds, allowing me a chance to sleep. But I didn't have the luxury of waiting for that. I had errands to run.

Cherrywood was eerily quiet in the early mornings. It felt like a funeral parlor. About an hour before homeroom, I sat in the locker room pitifully eating a cold bowl of instant oatmeal. I turned on one of the showerheads to let the water warm up.

The usually bustling locker room was also vacant. Solitude was becoming my new normal. I grabbed the nearest locker to the showers and unpacked my school uniform and old beach towel along with my new bottle of generic, all-purpose shampoo and body wash. The locker room would be where I'd be taking all of my showers for the foreseeable future.

Homeroom and yearbook were the only periods that day where I kept my eyes open for the entire duration. In a few classes, I did some embarrassing head bobbing trying to keep my head up in the face of fatigue. My growling stomach was also a source for humor among several of my classmates. For the rest of the classes, though, I boldly just set my head down on my desk and slept. School was a blur that day. Sadly, I don't remember much of it. I know I talked to people, but I didn't remember who.

I went to work after school and then the grocery store. Grocery shopping was new for me. Usually the only time I would buy food at a grocery store was when I was going on a road trip or wanted some late night munchies with friends. My mom did all the grocery shopping in our house...well, my parent's house now. I had only one sandwich left from the bag my mother made me, which had spoiled by the time I returned to my new home. It's remarkable what little food choices you have available if you don't have a stove or a refrigerator. I picked up a few cheap canned goods and the staple ingredients for PB&J sandwiches. Tonight's dinner would be cold pork and beans out of the can, an apple, and some peanuts. I also invested in a gallon of spring water. That would be my clean water source at home that I would replenish each day with a couple of empty Gatorade bottles from my gym bag.

God didn't answer my prayer, since I didn't go home that day.

I stayed there for the rest of the week, and by the end of it, I had a cozy little home set up. I purchased a used propane grill, kerosene heater, and some pots from a thrift store to function as my heat and cooking source. And in order to trap in the heat from the kerosene heater, I created a small greenhouse-type room out of plastic paint drop cloths, a space blanket, and some loose pieces of Tyvek, all held together by duct tape. It was really nothing more than a grownup fort, but it kept the heat contained in the unfinished living room and allowed me to sleep comfortably. My meals consisted of mostly canned goods because they were cheap and wouldn't require refrigeration, but I was still able to enjoy barbecued chicken and scrambled eggs every once in a while by simply storing the ingredients in the community fridge at work and cooking them as soon as I got home. The $346.00 I had in my savings account before being banished had now dwindled down to $29.00. I liked to think that I could've made that last another week until payday, but I knew that my car's gas tank and my stomach would be empty long before then.

I had never been broke before. I wasn't the greatest with money, but even when I was a little kid, I could always find a quarter or something hidden in a secret jar I had squirreled away. But I saw the writing on the wall. I'd be penniless within two days, and it was the worst feeling of desperation and hopelessness I'd ever experienced. Asking my parents for money was out of the question, and I had too much pride to let my friends know what was going on.

That led me to pick up the phone at work one day and place a call.

"Hello?" the voice on the other end said.

"Hi, may I speak to Dillon, please?"

"This is he."

"Dillon? This is Sy," I said, putting the scrap piece of paper with Dillon's phone number back into my pocket. "We met at CCC about two months ago. I helped you on one of your cooking…"

"Oh my God, hi! Yeah, of course I remember you. Thanks for calling. How you been?"

"Umm...well...you know when you offered to lend me a hand for helping you out that one time?"

"Yeah. Why, what do you need?"

"I kinda ran into some hard luck, and I won't have any money until next week. I was just wondering if you ever have any leftovers from your cooking class, would you be able to save them for me? If it's not too much trouble."

He muttered a curse word then followed it with, "You're out of food?"

"Funds are getting low."

"Well yeah, I can help you out. It's the least I can do after that 'A' you helped me get. Come by The Starboard tonight around nine. Can you do that?"

"Yes, of course. Thank you so much. I'm really sorry to put you out like this. I'm just going through a bad time right now. Please don't go out of your way."

"Just stop. Can you be there at nine?"

"Yeah, I'll be there."

"Ok. I don't know who the greeter is tonight, but just ask them to get me and I'll be out."

"Thank you so much, I really appreciate it."

"Hell yeah. Don't even sweat it. I'll see you tonight."

My stomach was churning when I walked into The Starboard that night. Soft music and expensive décor graced the dining room. I felt too insignificant to be there but found the black-tied greeter anyway.

"Hi," I said as I approached the greeter. "Dillon from the kitchen is expecting me."

"Dillon Alexander? Sure, wait right here. I'll go get him."

"Thank you," I said taking a seat on the ritzy leather bench. I ran my fingers through my hair and fixed my jacket. An older woman sipping a glass of red wine caught my eye-line and quickly looked away. I shook my head, completely embarrassed. A few minutes later Dillon came out carrying a large paper to-go bag.

"It's so good to see you," he smiled giving me a side hug with one arm and holding the bag with the other. "Here, there's about a week's worth of dinners in here. There are several of the same dish because I just grabbed a few of last night's unsold entrees, but there's some new stuff, too, that I just whipped up tonight. Think this will hold you over?"

Completely stunned at the overly kind gesture I replied, "Oh my gosh, Dillon. Thank you so much! You didn't have to do all this."

"Look, you didn't ask me for money; you asked me for food. That's serious."

He leaned in closely to whisper, turning his back to the rest of the restaurant.

"Are you okay? Like seriously? It's supposed to be cooler the next few days. You're electricity is still on and everything, right?"

"Yeah," I lied. "Yeah, everything is good." I was relieved to know that with the cooler temperatures, at least I would be able to keep most of these meals at Chernobyl without them spoiling. "Thank you so much, Dillon. This was way too nice of you."

"It's fine. Don't sweat it. Keep my number, okay? Let me know if you need help with anything else."

"Thank you. Really. Thank you." My stomach snarled.

"Oh my God, honey, just go eat! You're starving! Just grab a table and eat. I gotta get back to work, but just sit anywhere."

When Dillon left, I opened the bag to find seven plastic to-go boxes stuffed with all kinds of seafood, steaks, side dishes, rolls, plastic silverware, and more. I almost got choked up in that moment. Dillon didn't even know me, but he had not hesitated to help me when I needed it. Why should he have shown me more love than the majority of Christians I knew? How did that make sense?

I called my mom every so often from the gas station pay phone. I told her that I had gotten my own apartment, but didn't have a phone line hooked up yet so I couldn't receive calls. I think she bought it. It took me about a week before I had a relatively stable home set up for myself and only another week before I figured out how to add some creature comforts. There had always been a drain and some other pipes sticking out of the floor in the unfinished main-level bathroom of Chernobyl when the contractors stubbed them into the foundation eight or so years ago. I was getting used to whizzing outside and trying my best to hold any bowel movements until school or work when a formal toilet was an option.

But one night while reading, I thought about the bathroom drain. If the builders had full intentions of completing this house, surely they would have gotten all the necessary groundwork completed before pouring the slab and raising walls. I put down my book and walked over to the drain in the floor. After unzipping my fly, I gave it a test. Everything seemed to disappear so I decided to take my experiment one step further by dumping about three gallons of creek water into the hole, which also just vanished. That's when I realized I had something to work with.

The next day, I visited this typical Carolina hillbilly house that I had known about from my drives to Mr. Oakridge's. The front yard contained about five cars up on blocks, couches, a deer skull from a bygone hunting season, countless Busch beer cans, and a whole collection of other rusted weathered nonsense, including an ugly, dull pink toilet from God only knows where. I had become too crotchety for manners, so I just walked right into the junk pile and grabbed hold of the thing by the tank, immediately wishing I had a pair of gloves. It was much heavier than I expected. Putrid rainwater and filth fell out of the tank, drenching my t-shirt as I dragged it back to the car.

When a greasy guy wearing a Nascar T-shirt and dirty swim trunks walked onto the porch, I didn't even care. I just asked him to help me load it in the trunk.

Later that day, a rude little girl interrupted me at the public library when I was taking notes from a book called *How to Plumb*. She said, "Mommy, that man smells." I told her it was lots and lots of poopy while her mother glanced at me in disgust and quickly ushered her daughter away.

After I grabbed a wax ring from Sanderson's, I bear hugged the God-awful porcelain throne from my trunk and into the house to get it in position. It was about 7:30 on a Friday evening, and my camp lantern was the only light I had to work by. Grizzled and dirty like an Alaskan trapper, I didn't think I'd ever smelled so bad in all my life. I was on my knees, fiddling with the wax ring when I first noticed the noises outside.

It sounded like laughing. Then suddenly, a scratching at the doorknob and the front door was instantly thrown open. I shouted and jumped up from the floor, startling the two figures in the doorway who also screamed.

"Sy?"

It was Cam and his flavor-of-the-week girlfriend.

"What's up, Cam?"

"Dude, what are you doing here?"

"Just...Just hanging out. Doing a little work, ya know." I said awkwardly as if someone had thrown open the curtain while I took a shower.

"What are you working on? I kinda need the place right now," he said slyly motioning to his girl.

I looked at my half-completed project. "Welp. I'm installing a toilet. Pretty sweet, right?"

He looked at his brunette, public school girlfriend who was covering her nose. "That thing reeks," he said. "Why are you installing a toilet now? And...is it pink?"

"Yeeup. This place has been plumbed for it the whole time! Why not?" I said smiling.

My embarrassment had faded, and I began to own the moment, no longer giving a crap about what Cam thought of me. He looked at me with confusion and disgust.

"So...what are you doing here?" I asked, even though I already knew what his plans were.

"We were just gonna hang out. Did you deck this place out, too?"

"Yeah."

"What are these photos you got hanging up?" he asked pointing to my string of photographs that I had suspended with paperclips from one of the beams.

"Uhh...Nothing. Just a project I'm working on."

Cam paused for a moment. Then he said to his girlfriend, "We'll go somewhere else. You mind waiting in the car for a minute? I'll be right there."

She agreed and headed back out of the door. Cam closed it behind her. He looked back at me with concern as I started to pull some of my photos down.

"You're living here, aren't you?" he softly said. I remained silent. "Why?" he asked.

My overconfidence had faded with the strange girl out of the room. Now that it was just Cam and me, I felt my insecurity begin to creep up on me, along with a lump in my throat.

"It's all I got," I said.

"What do you mean, it's all you got?"

"My dad kicked me out, okay?"

I think that shocked him. He was at a loss for words for a moment. "You got no place to go?"

"Nope."

"Dude...I'm sorry."

"It's cool."

"Why'd he kick you out?"

"He thought it would be better for everyone if I wasn't around. I brought the Devil to his doorstep, as he put it. Maybe he was right."

Cam shook his head. Cam and I were different people now, but in this moment, I could still feel our friendship; some things like that never really go away.

"You got enough to eat?"

"Yeah, I'm good."

"You got a place to take a shower?"

"Yeah."

"Clean your clothes?"

"...Yeah."

"Ok." We stood in silence for a moment. Then he continued, "I'm gonna go, man. She's waiting. You alright?"

"Yeah, I'm good. Don't tell anyone, okay?"

"Alright," he said apprehensively. "Take care, dude. Good luck with the toilet."

He paused for a moment before grabbing the doorknob.

"Thanks."

He turned around and slowly shut the door behind him. I should have been utterly embarrassed, but I wasn't. I actually felt relieved. Someone finally knew where I was. If there was a God who should take me in my sleep that night, someone would know where to look for me.

CHAPTER 22

A few days later, I was walking to seventh period History when a voice begged my attention.

"Hey Sy," it said. I didn't recognize it at first. After looking up, I saw Grady Sites staring at me.

"Oh hey, Grady."

Grady Sites, the grandson of the principal at Cherrywood, was well known by everyone at the Academy, at least on the surface. He lived a life of privilege and was being groomed to take over the family businesses and legacy, but to me, Grady was just a normal guy. He just wanted to live as normal a life as possible, so he tried to stay out of the spotlight whenever he could.

Grady grabbed my arm and pulled me beside the drinking fountain while everyone else hurried to get to class. In a quiet voice he asked, "Hey man. Is it true that you're livin' at the old Glenwood Estates?"

"Who told you that?"

"Cam told me before first period. He sounded worried about you. Is it true?"

I breathed an exasperated sigh. "I'm staying there for a bit while things cool down at my place, but it's pretty humiliating, so keep this between us, okay?"

Grady nodded and then added, "I overheard what happened to your mom."

I looked at him, confused by his statement. I hadn't told anyone about what my mother had been going through.

"It's my grandfather, isn't it?" he continued.

I still searched his face for answers to understand where he was going with his remarks. He shook his head and looked up at the ceiling.

"It is," he added. "You don't have to say it. I heard him talking on the phone the other day. He mentioned a Helen Ernst. That's your mom, right?"

"Why are you telling me this, Grady?"

"Because what my grandfather is doing is not right. I don't know what you did to upset him, but my guess would be that he probably deserved what was coming. Every family has its own share of dark secrets, but I would wager to say that my family's secrets are darker than most. Your mother doesn't deserve this," he said, pausing for a moment. "Neither do you."

"Ok," I said. "What do you think I should do? My own father said no one would trust the words of a backsliding kid over a man as powerful as your grandpa."

"Is that why you're at the Glenwood Estates? Your dad kicked you out?"

I nodded, looking down at the floor.

Grady sighed and began again. "I'm not sure, Sy. I've known that man my whole life, and even when I was young, I knew that there was something off. I'm not sure if there is anything we can do to keep him from hurting your family, but for what it's worth, I wanted to let you know that I don't agree with him. If there is a way to help, I'll do what I can for ya."

I stopped for a moment, realizing the significance of what Grady was actually saying. "I really appreciate it, but don't jeopardize your future just for me," I warned him.

"There is no future for me here, Sylas. My grandfather's legacy is built on a foundation of greed and manipulation. This empire will die with him."

His words humbled me, knowing that Grady was willing to sacrifice his own family, and possibly his future, to help me and to do what was right.

"Thanks, Grady," I said extending my hand for a shake. He grabbed it and pulled me in for a hug.

"I'll be in touch," he said, as he jogged down the hall to make it to class on time.

That weekend I cleaned myself and my clothes in the empty locker room shower. I made myself presentable, and an hour later I was knocking on Mr. Oakridge's door. This was the second time I had dropped in unannounced. I felt bad that I hadn't called beforehand, but it was kind of difficult when you don't own a phone. Gracie answered again.

"Hi, there. Is your dad home? You can tell him that it's Sylas Ernst."

She simply took the information and ran back inside, not saying anything. A few moments later, Mr. Oakridge appeared at the door.

"Sylas. How's it going? Again."

"I'm sorry to drop in again Mr. Oakridge. My phone got disconnected, and I won't be able to call for...a little while, so I figured I'd just swing by. If this is a bad time, I can..."

"No, no. This is fine. Do you want to come in?"

"Well, I don't have to. I know you weren't expecting anybody."

"No, now come on in."

"Ok, thank you," I replied as he led me into his home. It was a humble place with kid's toys, drawings, and other paraphernalia hanging around.

"Here, have a seat," he said directing me to the couch. "Do you want something to drink? Water, Sprite, cranberry juice, milk. I think that's about it."

"A Sprite would be great. Thank you," I replied, anxious to taste something other than water.

"Ok," he replied heading to the adjacent kitchen. While opening the refrigerator he said, "So what's on your mind?"

"Oh. Quite a bit at the moment, but I'll just stick with why I came here."

I chuckled. So did he.

"I've actually been reading and studying science a lot, and the origin of life and all that stuff, and it seems to me that this world cannot be an accident."

"Did you ever think it was?" he replied re-entering the room with my can of Sprite and his glass of water.

"No, not really. But obviously that's what modern science teaches, so I wanted to look into it. This world is too impossible to be an accident. I mean, Earth is just the right distance from the sun and moon, it rotates at the right speed, there is just enough water, hydrogen, oxygen, and nitrogen to support life, and the list goes on and on. The probability that this world randomly happened from nothing is just mathematically and logically impossible, so therefore, it was created by something or someone, right?"

"Have you not been listening in my classes?" he joked.

"No, I have. I just like doing independent research. I guess I'm kind of a nerd."

He laughed again. "No, that's good. Good for you."

"Ok, so there is a Creator. So what? Most people on Earth believe in some sort of Intelligent Designer. The reason I'm here, though, is to ask - why does that have to be the God I've been taught it to be? Why not Allah or Brahma or Zeus or any one of them?"

He cocked his head back and leaned back in his chair. After taking a sip of water, he replied, "Because you and I are lucky, Sy. We're lucky because we were born in the twentieth century. And I'm sure that people who are born after us will be even luckier. There has been a litany of really significant scientific discoveries made before we came along that give us insight to the God of the Bible like never before. For example, are you familiar with the Book of Job?"

"Yeah, kinda."

"Of course. We've all learned about poor Job, right? Well, Job is the oldest book of the Bible, written between 1900 - 1400 B.C. That's a verified fact. You knew that, right?"

"Yeah, I knew it was the oldest."

"Ok. Well, this ancient book makes a lot of interesting statements. For one, it says, 'He hangs the earth on nothing,' so it references Earth as free-floating in space. But during that time, ancient people believed that a large turtle, an elephant, or even the Greek god Atlas held it up. Job also mentions the 'springs of the sea,' but it wasn't until deep diving equipment was invented in the 1970's that we discovered that there are actually live springs on the ocean floor. The book also mentions the 'weight of the wind,' which wasn't discovered until modern times that air actually does have weight to it, and Job, Isaiah, and Zechariah, mention that God 'stretches out the heavens.' And Mr. Hubble didn't discover that the universe was expanding until the late 20's."

He paused for emphasis, then when he saw that I was thoroughly captivated, he continued. "The book of Jonah mentions that there are mountains and valleys on the ocean floor, which they didn't know about during his time. They just thought that the ocean floor was flat, like what you see at the beach. Why would they think anything otherwise? Isaiah talks about the earth being round in a time when everyone believed the earth to be flat, and Job, again, mentions that light can be separated before Isaac Newton discovered it with a prism. Pretty bonkers, huh?"

"Wow," I said flatly.

"Yeah, wow is right. How would the writers of those old books have known that stuff?" It all *contradicted* the scientific knowledge of the day, but we know, sitting here in the twentieth century, that it's all accurate. But that's not even the best part about being born when we were. We happened to come along after this guy named Jesus of Nazareth. Maybe you've heard of him," he said with a smirk.

"See, Jesus was a real, historical figure just like Napoleon, Alexander the Great, Julius Caesar, and all those guys," he continued. "There are people who don't like to admit that He lived, but He did. In fact, there's more evidence to support His existence than most of the other ancient figures you read about in history books. So Jesus came onto the scene, interestingly enough, around one thousand nine hundred ninety-six years ago. Our calendar is even based off of His life. No one else gets that kind of treatment. He did something really bizarre though, something that very few people have ever done. Jesus didn't just claim to be a Messenger from God or a prophet or anything, like founders of other religions have. He claimed to *be* God.

"But here's the craziest stuff of all. This guy had not one, but four full biographies written about His life, the latest appearing roughly seventy years after his death. This was in a time of mostly oral traditions, so for anyone to take the time to write out an entire biography about anybody was pretty unique. To put it in perspective, Alexander the Great, who lived just a few hundred years before Jesus, had only one biography written about him, and it came about four hundred years after his death. And he had to conquer most of the known world in order to get that kind of treatment. Jesus, though, was...you ready?" He paused for humorous emphasis: "a carpenter," he finished.

I was hooked on Mr. Oakridge's story, even though I knew half of the information. Mr. Oakridge had a way of captivating his pupils through his lessons. He taught with the information of an encyclopedia, but presented it with the entertainment of children's story time.

"So here's this poor, basically homeless, carpenter who walks around the country-side with a bunch of fisherman claiming to be

God," he continued. "Sounds like a complete nutcase, right? But for some reason, we're still talking about Him to this day. Why?"

He paused again. I stayed silent, partly because I was waiting for him to continue, but also because I had no idea how to answer.

He never gave me the answer to the question but left me wanting it, as any good teacher will. Mr. Oakridge excused himself to start preparing dinner. He invited me to stay, but I declined not wanting to wear out my welcome. He had given me even more to think about. How could one Man change the world so drastically? Who was this Man who changed the face of time?

I had been keeping my head low in school, just trying to push through to graduation. The Academy had won. All of the stuff they threw at me, whether intentional or not, was an attempt to control me...to silence me.

And it had worked. I stopped raising my hands in class, stopped caring about my grades, and volunteering for anything. I did everything I could to stop calling any kind of attention to myself. I tried to disappear, and sadly, I was successful. The rumors were eventually forgotten, and so was I. My birthday came and went. Shawn and Roscoe still invited me to hang out regularly, but half the time I would just lie about having some difficult classes and needing to study a lot. We would hang out every once in a while, but we made it a point to never spend any money, and I strategically tried to bum as many free meals off their parents as possible. I felt less and less like myself. The solidarity shrunk my soul like a raisin. I spent hours alone working in the yearbook room. My love of photography was the only thing that had not changed, but I was barely able to afford it. That was the only sort of connection to Cherrywood I tried to keep.

On Easter Sunday, Cherrywood Baptist Church bloomed with freshly picked baskets of lilies and colorful guests. The women were wearing their bright Easter dresses, and the men were decked out in pastel polos. Easter morning was the Super Bowl of church. It was the big event, the crux of that which our faith rested on.

Finally, the weather had turned. It was getting hot - too hot, actually. My little hut had to come down last week because its greenhouse effect was too effective. I was sleeping in my boxers and wife-beater again and listening to the crickets, as I had done on so many of our summer camping trips.

My motives for going to church that morning were different from everyone else's. They wanted to celebrate our risen Lord. I mainly just wanted a nice place to take my morning poo and brush my teeth. When I came out of the bathroom, a middle-school kid approached me all hyped up on saving the world.

"We're starting a ministry to serve the people in need," she said, rehearsing her lines with notebook in hand. "Would you like to donate to help the homeless of our community?"

"I *am* homeless," I replied matter-of-factly, knowing that sadly she wouldn't take me seriously. I was right. She awkwardly chuckled thinking it was just a crude joke. She walked away just like I had expected. I guess I hadn't looked homeless enough to receive empathy.

I kept moving through the foyer toward the sanctuary when outside the large glass windows, I spotted Pastor Samms' BMW parked quietly near the side entrance. I don't know why I didn't think of this sooner: Mike Bradshaw, owner of Bradshaw Toyota and local celebrity famous for his cheesy TV ads, went to our church every so often. He wasn't a regular, but more of a Christmas and Easter kind of guy. He didn't know me at all, but I knew him from his annoying local commercials. He was talking with someone else when I walked up and quietly interrupted.

"Excuse me, Mr. Bradshaw. You don't know me, but I've got a completely odd question for you."

"Ok," he asked very confused.

"See Pastor Samms' Beemer out there? How much do you think that would cost new? That's last year's model."

"You're right. That is an odd question," he chuckled. "A '95 Beemer like that probably cost around thirty-eight thousand. You don't want a German car though; you want a Japanese."

I politely laughed. "Ok, thank you, sir. Have a nice day."

He was befuddled as I walked away, but my head was crystal clear. That vehicle expense on Cherrywood's taxes last year - the one that they started taking the depreciation on around the same time Joel received that car as a gift from the church board - was the company vehicle. That's where our tithes and offerings had gone.

"What's up, Sy?" Roscoe asked, catching me by surprise as I made sure my toothbrush and toothpaste were shoved securely in my pocket.

"Oh hey, man!"

"Dude, where were you yesterday?" he asked. "I tried to call you all day, but your mom kept saying you weren't there."

"Oh yeah. I was fishing."

"By yourself?"

"Yeah."

"Why didn't you tell me? Where'd you go?"

"Uhh...this guy from work invited me to his private pond. I couldn't really be rude and invite anyone else."

"Did you catch anything?"

"Got a few largemouth. Nothing huge."

"Nice. You sitting with your mom this service?"

"I haven't seen her yet. We drove separately.

"Oh. You can sit with us if you want."

"Yeah, okay. That sounds good."

Truth be told, I wanted to sit with my mom that day. I wanted to see her, that is, if my father allowed her out of the house. As I sat with Roscoe's family that Easter Sunday, I kept looking around for her, but I never found her. Pastor Samms was back, and he was more chipper than ever. The worship team led some beautiful praise music, and the service was nothing short of a triumphant Broadway performance. Nearly two thousand years ago, Jesus had risen from the dead. Throughout the service, I wondered where He went.

Before leaving church, I grabbed my camera from my car and snapped a photo of Pastor Samms' Beemer. I'd need it for the project I was working on. On my way home, I happened to drive past an estate sale that looked as though it was just wrapping up. A few men loaded an old antique sofa onto a flatbed truck when I pulled up to the curb. Walking up the driveway, I hoped I might find some treasure I needed to help make my home more livable. An old set of beautifully kept carpentry tools, the kind with the oak handles, sat out on one of the tables.

I asked the old woman running the event about them, and we struck up a small conversation, which led to a purchase. The old tools were her late husband's, and she couldn't part with them for much of a discount, but she did offer to throw in another item for the same price, to help sweeten the deal. It was an old, beat up Victrola, one of those antique gramophone things, that ran with a

wind-up crank instead of batteries or electricity. She assured me
that it still worked and even included a few old records, since they
were as good as useless without the old machine anyway. She did
ask one thing of me though - to listen to *It Never Entered My Mind*
by Miles Davis. It was her husband's favorite.

I got to what I was calling my home around four o' clock and
rearranged my plastic crate shelf to fit the old machine. Wagner,
Beethoven, and Bach were included in the old record collection,
along with Dizzy Gillespie, The Rat Pack, Billie Holiday, and Miles
Davis. Thinking of what the old woman had told me, I pulled the
Miles Davis record from the sleeve and cranked the player. Putting
the needle on the far outer edge immediately filled the old
abandoned house with the sweet sound of jazz. Life filled the dead
air, breaking the stale quiet that surrounded that old place. I
looked at the back of the sleeve and scrolled down the playlist to
track four. *It Never Entered My Mind* crackled and drifted through
the walls. I could imagine the happy times the old woman and her
husband spent together listening to this sweet song.

Music brought a new dimension to my existence that I wasn't
aware was missing. Hands down, it was the best twenty-five bucks
I'd ever spent. I switched the record over to The Rat Pack to get
my creative energy flowing as I sat down to continue working on
my project. I opened the manila folder on the coffee table,
spreading out the photos, documents, and notes that were inside. I
lifted off the East Creek game program from last fall and found
the Cherrywood Baptist tax return. Flipping through, I located the
$37,000 company vehicle expense and circled it with my Sharpie.
Once the photo I had taken earlier was developed, I'd have another
piece of the puzzle complete.

Then, without warning, there was a knock at the door. I
panicked, thinking it must be the police, and quickly stuffed
everything back into the manila folder and shoved it in a couch
cushion. I looked outside to see a car I didn't recognize but was
relieved to know it wasn't a cop, so I slowly opened the door.

"Grady?"

"Sylas! Good to see you," he said visibly winded, almost like
he had run instead of driven. His joy then turned to a frown as it
all sank in. "So it is true."

I stared back at him.

"Mums the word," he said, twisting the key to the imaginary

lock on his closed mouth. "Is that Dean Martin?" he added, catching his breath.

The music from my Victrola echoed through the walls. I was so used to it now that I barely even noticed it.

"Uh, yes, actually."

"You like big band?"

"No - I mean - yes. I just very recently began to appreciate it. Why are you here?"

He pulled an envelope from his back pocket and pushed it at me. "This is for you."

"What's this?"

"The least I could do to help. Use it how you wish. But don't go down without a fight."

"What?" I said, beginning to open the envelope before he stopped me.

He glanced down at his watch, noticeably in a hurry.

"I'm not like my family," he said. "I was never here, okay? We never spoke. Good luck."

"Grady, I -"

But it was too late; he had already headed out the door.

I looked back down at the envelope while he got into his car.

When he drove away, I walked back inside and opened the seal. What I found inside was a darkness that I was too naïve to think even existed.

Chapter 23

To whom it may concern at Southern Hope Ministries,

It has been several months since we have last heard from you and pray that you and your organization are well. We are hopeful that you are still interested in funding our orphanage project but fear that, since we have not heard from you in quite some time, God may have other plans for your resources. Our facilities and living conditions are still in desperate need of financial assistance, so if you are still interested, our need is growing. We have been primarily operating out of homes located within the village, but the humble huts are barely suitable for the owners' families and cannot house all of the nearly 100 orphans that we care for. Please find some of my enclosed Polaroids which are meant to help illustrate the living conditions that these children face on a daily basis. My intention in sending these is not to make you uncomfortable in any way but to merely illustrate the needs of our community. If the orphanage project is too lofty for you at this time, I humbly ask for your hand in aiding with food and medical supplies. Many of the children are frightfully malnourished, and sadly, we have lost three infants this year to diseases and malnutrition, which includes lack of acceptable drinking water. No donation is too small, so if you are no longer interested in a larger building project, perhaps you would consider making a small offering. I trust that God is granting you the wisdom necessary to manage the resources He has placed under your control and pray that you may still be interested in sharing some of His gracious gifts with the children of the Kobansi village here in Kenya. To God be the glory.

Sincerely,
David Hisham
Humble servant of our Lord

I leaned my head back in disbelief. I couldn't move. I only had enough energy to operate my racing mind. I gently set the letter on the table and picked up the three photos that accompanied it. One featured a child with protruding ribs. The next was a young teenager sleeping under a tree. The final photo showed a child covered in mud drinking muddy water from a bucket. I stared at the photos, my face lacking expression. I set the photos back down on the table and just dropped my head into my hands.

Then without realizing the anger for what it was before it had come to the surface, I slammed a fist on the table and jumped to my feet.

"There is no orphanage!" I exclaimed to myself. "There never was!"

The orphanage that Pastor Samms was always telling us about, the one that they were always raising money for and we were giving to, doesn't exist. They were playing the missionary in the letter just like they were playing all of us! Brandi and the volunteers couldn't visit the orphanage on their trip not because of civil unrest, but because it wasn't there! What had become of those donations? That money is somewhere, but like Jeremy, did not go to Kenya.

This was the darkest curtain of the Academy I had pulled back, and if there were others, I couldn't bear to unveil them. I had seen enough and soon, so would everyone else.

I unclipped a few of my photos from the hanging string and placed them on the table. I arranged them with the three new photos that accompanied the letter, and after I studied them for a moment, I ripped a loose-leaf piece of notebook paper from my Biology Trapper and started to draw.

As soon as Mrs. Turner finished our class prayer, I was out of my chair and headed towards the computers.

"I see that most of you already know the drill," Mrs. Turner said. "Final page layouts must be submitted no later than the end of class on Wednesday. We'll be editing each other's work on Thursday and then going over the final draft of the yearbook in class on Friday. This week is a work week so please stay focused."

Most of us had stopped listening, as we were already into our editing programs and working on our pages.

My backpack was in my chair, reserving my place at a computer. I stood above it and slowly pulled out the envelope Grady had given me. I glanced around me. The students were all busy with their work. There were eyes everywhere, but they were so focused on their own projects that they wouldn't even notice me. The yearbook room had one scanner for us all to use, and luckily, it was available. I opened the lid to the scanner and placed the three photos on the glass. Pressing the green 'Scan' button, I watched as the light moved slowly from beneath the lid and the images visibly appeared on the computer screen. The haunting photos of the starving orphans stared out into the classroom for all to see. I anxiously watched the classroom. Everyone was too busy to notice.

Then I removed the photos and placed the letter in their place. I pressed 'Scan.' Like the photo, the letter materialized on my computer screen for all to read. Mrs. Turner got up from her desk and started walking towards me. I waited impatiently for the scanner to finish its task, and the second it did, I quickly snatched the letter from inside. I also grabbed the floppy disk it was now saved to and jumped back to my computer. Mrs. Turner stopped to see how Jessica Baldwin was progressing on her layout. Any second she'd be glancing over my shoulder.

I pressed 'Save' on my screen. The irritating hourglass symbol appeared indicating that I had to wait while my images saved. The letter was still as clear as day while I sat there helplessly. Mrs. Turner smiled at Jessica then looked at me. I smiled back and quickly turned back to my screen. The hourglass was still there.

"How is your page coming along, Sy?" she asked as she approached. She hadn't seen my screen yet. Finally, the words 'Save successful' appeared, and I instantly opened another window.

"Pretty good. Just putting the last finishing touches on," I replied.

She leaned over my shoulder to inspect my work. "That's clever," she said. "Saintly Skirmish.' I love the dichotomy in your headline, how you've got the Saints football players here, and the photo of this big tackle. Is that your picture?"

"Yes, ma'am."

"Very nice," she remarked. "Great timing. Looking good there." She then stepped away to the next student along the row of monitors.

"Thank you." I replied. I waited until I saw that she was engaged in Steven Dalrimple's computer screen before I opened up the other page layout I was working on. Some photos of Jeremy Maitland and Dr. Sites appeared. I looked around to find that once again everyone was too busy to notice. I clicked 'Insert Image,' and after opening the photo of the starving African child drinking muddy water, I dragged it into my template. There was no turning back now. No matter the cost to me, the truth would be heard.

When I got to work that evening, I walked straight into Mike's office. I tapped on the side of the door, waiting to be asked inside.

"Hi Sy. Come on in," he said.

"Thank you, sir. Actually, I just wanted to let you know that I accepted an offer for a summer internship, so unfortunately I'd like to put in my two weeks notice."

"Oh, well, congratulations! We'll certainly miss you."

"Thank you, sir," I said with a smile. Mike had manipulated me in the past, demoting me to a lower position and lowering my pay at the whim of Mr. Winters. I knew he cared nothing about me, but he lied through his teeth with a pasted-on 'God bless you' smile. He fooled no one.

"Thanks for everything you and Mr. Winters have done for me. I'm so glad to have gotten to work here and will hopefully continue to work with Winters' Printing in one way or the other in the future."

"Of course, of course. We'd love to have you as an employee or a client. We'll be happy to give you high recommendations if you need them. Thank you for your time here. We're really going to miss you."

"Thank you, sir. I'll miss ya'll, too."

We talked about my fake summer internship for a few more minutes before I left his office. I didn't know where I was going to be in two weeks, or even what would happen to me. But I knew that after two weeks time I couldn't be anywhere near here.

It was Friday and the entire yearbook class was huddled around Mrs. Turner's computer screen. We were systematically going through each page of the yearbook from the front to the back cover. We took turns laughing at some of the photos, congratulating each other for exceptionally clever writing, and fondly reminiscing on bygone highschool days.

"And the back cover," Mrs. Turner warmly said as she reached the last page of our final proof. "Does it look good?" A few of the girl's were teary-eyed. We all applauded. I donned a smug smile.

"Nice job, everyone," Jessica Baldwin said.

"The page about Cafeteria Cathy was so sweet," Angela Nyalas mentioned.

"I like the page about Coach's hair," Michael Timons stated to which everyone answered with laughter.

"Should I place the order?" Mrs. Turner asked.

"Right now?" Jessica asked.

"Yeah, now," Mrs. Turner smiled while she reached for the phone.

"Oh my gosh, guys. We're finally done!" Brittany Clemons said.

Mrs. Turner had picked up the phone and punched in a number. With all of us huddled around her she said, "Hi, could I speak to Mike, please?" We all kept quiet and listened. "Hi Mike, this is Janette from Cherrywood Christian Academy. I'd like to place an order for five hundred and seventy yearbooks, please." She turned and smiled to the class. A few of my peers silently smiled at each other and hugged.

"Yes, I'll send the final proof over first thing on Monday...Yes, I did...That's correct...Ok, great! Thank you very much! Bye-bye."

When she hung up the phone with my boss, the class erupted in applause and cheers. I took the opportunity to try to seem upbeat and helpful.

"You want me to take the proof tonight when I go to work?" I offered.

"Are you going to Winters' Printing after school? Why, sure! That would be great!"

At the end of class, Mrs. Turner slipped a stack of floppy disks into an envelope. "Okay Sylas, here is the final copy of the yearbook. Take good care of those."

"Yes ma'am." I replied, placing the hardshell case in my backpack. "I can't wait to see how this turns out."

After school, I headed directly to Winters with a sense of duty and power.

"I have something for you, Mike," I announced when I marched into his office.

"What's that? Oh yes. That's what I was waiting for. This is the whole yearbook?"

"Yes, sir!"

"Let's just pop it in and have a quick look."

"Actually, sir would you mind if I set it up in the program? I know I'm not in this department anymore, but since this is my last two weeks and all, would you mind if I programmed it in the system? For old times sake."

Even with the questionable sense of trust, I knew Mike had gained a newfound respect for me over the last several months. He saw that I could stick it out through thick and thin and then finally elevate myself to move on to bigger and better things.

"You still remember how?"

"Of course! I just want to make sure everything is perfect."

"Then I don't see why not. You'll be done in about an hour right?"

"If that," I joked.

"Well that should give me time to run out for a quick bite and use the bathroom. Here, have a seat. Don't get too sentimental and start crying on my keyboard," he laughed.

"I'll try not to." I took out the disks while he stepped out of his office. Opening up the computer program that I was all too familiar with, I quickly imported all three hundred and twenty-one pages. I checked my surroundings. Then I popped in another disk...one that I had made.

Some time later, I stepped into the break room to see Mike drinking a coffee and chatting with a guy from shipping and receiving.

"You all done?" he asked.

"All set up. Thanks for letting me do that, sir. It actually meant a lot."

"Yeah, no problem. Let's go have a look."

"Now?"

"Sure."

"Uhh...ok."

We walked back to his office and he took a seat in his chair. I watched nervously from the doorway.

"Oh, those are nice graphics. Did you do those?" he asked, referencing the front cover of the yearbook on the screen.

"No. That was another classmate."

"Oh ok." He clicked through some of the pages and laughed at several of the photos. Then he went through the order line sheet on his desk. He clicked a few buttons on the screen. His brow furrowed. Then he looked back at the sheet. "Hmm," he mumbled.

"What's wrong?"

"Well your teacher said there were three hundred and twenty-one pages, so that's the quote we gave. But it looks like there are actually three hundred and twenty-four."

"Oh?"

"Yeah, the page count seems to be off."

"Maybe Mrs. Turner forgot to include the front and back cover?"

"Mmm...no. That's not it. Those are included. Hmmm. She wrote a check for three hundred and twenty-one color pages. We'll just need to make her aware that there will need to be a supplement check for the extra three."

"Three pages, how much could that cost?"

"Three actual pages, not much at all, but three pages printed in five hundred and seventy books would be about $150," he said picking up his phone. "Maybe I'll just give her a call to let her know."

I quickly tried to interject, "Well, she's gone for the day."

"She gave me her home phone just in case. I'll just try her on that."

I was helpless to stop him as he punched in the phone number and started speaking almost right away. "Janette," he said. "Hi, this is Mike, at Winters' Printing. I'm fine, how are you? That's good, that's good. I'm just going over your order now, and the page count seems to be a little off."

I was standing in the doorway more nervous than ever. "Yes

ma'am, three pages. Three hundred and twenty-four pages total, and you have three hundred and twenty-one written down. Yes ma'am, do you know what they--. Well, I can go ahead and print it if--. Uh, yes ma'am, it says 1996 on the envelope and files. Oh, you are. Alright, so go ahead and print it as-is. I will do it. Now there is going to be an extra charge of about $150 or so. I can't give you an exact number right now. Is that alright? Perfect. I will get to work then. Yes ma'am. Thank you, have a good evening."

With all of that said, he hung up the phone.

"Okay, we're all set," he said, giving me a smile. "Let's print some yearbooks."

CHAPTER 24

I peeked at Page 217 only once when the first book came off the line. They were printed correctly. All three hundred and twenty-four pages. I came up with the idea of individually wrapping each one with brown Kraft paper sealed with a red wax stamp. When I pitched the concept to Mrs. Turner and the yearbook team, I explained that it would make each book seem special and unique. In reality, I just didn't want anyone to discover what was printed inside before the books had been fully distributed. Everyone loved the concept, so for two days in the packaging department, I individually wrapped and sealed all five hundred and seventy yearbooks. It was the most efficient I'd ever been at my job. No one from Winters' ever saw them.

It was an excruciating two weeks to wait. Summer had long since arrived, and Senioritis was infecting everyone. There were only two and a half more weeks to go before I was done with Cherrywood forever. This week, our final reports and papers were due for various classes. On Friday afternoon, we would receive our yearbooks, next week were final exams, then graduation.

Friday finally came, and we all huddled into the gym. "Please find your homeroom teacher," Coach shouted over the crowd.

Across the gym, I saw Roscoe move in with his group. Cam did the same. Everyone was full of excitement. I was feeling a different emotion. No one knew what they were about to see. Our homeroom teachers all stood along the walls on various ends of the gymnasium with the large cardboard boxes I had packed sitting patiently at their feet. The concentrated crowd began to disperse joyously to their respective teachers who were all also waiting with excitement. The only order to the chaos was when our homeroom teachers took roll call.

My heart was beating a mile a minute. Mr. Hadenfield read down his student roster to which we all acknowledged that we were present. Nobody was missing. No one wanted to miss this.

Mr. Hadenfield leaned into the box and pulled out a stack of brown packages. One by one, he doled them out as each one of his students snatched them up and tore open the wrapping. The gym was eagerly filling with joy as all of the other teachers did the same thing.

The ominous red seal stared back at me as I slowly tore the book's paper cloak. My sweaty palms almost couldn't grasp its smooth, shiny surface. The front cover read *Cherrywood Christian Academy of 1996*. I opened to the first page and immediately felt uneasy as I stared at a photograph I had somehow overlooked before now. There I was, staring back at me. A group photo of that year's yearbook staff graced the front page with a simple heading that read 'The Memory Preservation Team' and a quote from Louisa May Alcott that read:

Preserve your memories, keep them well. What you forget, you can never retell.

I looked at myself standing there in the front row, the third from the right. When the photo was taken, I had no way of knowing what memories my future self was going to preserve, but even so, my face resembled a look of complacency as if I did.

I had tried to predict this moment in my head, and I guess I'd thought that there would be an immediate reaction. But there wasn't. For a good fifteen minutes, the whole gym was buzzing with people signing each other's books, sitting Indian-style on the floor perusing every page and sharing a few laughs and tears with friends. Of course, I knew what was on Pages 217-219. I had been working on them for the past two months, planning them out at Chernobyl, and then carefully designing them in the yearbook lab in between my other assignments.

While everyone was paying attention to something else, I quickly turned there. There they were, in living color. The first image was the one I had taken of Jeremy Maitland speaking at the Southern Hope fundraiser, dated Saturday, October 14th, with his quote that read, "On Wednesday, we returned from a month-long assignment in Kenya…"

Directly underneath that was the photo I found of him at the homecoming game with a date marked "Friday, October 6th." I expanded from there. The photos of him at the East Creek away game talking to Fitzpatrick, his alleged $21,000 per year salary on the Southern Hope books, my notes of Topher's failing English quiz, pictures of Pastor Samms' new car, and the circled matching vehicle expense on Clanton Baptist's tax returns, his salary paired with the polarity of that malnourished African child, Governor Hawkins and the money Clanton Baptist donated to the government, the tax returns for Southern Hope and Clanton Baptist, my mom's suspension letter, the letter from the Kenyan missionary, and much more. It was all there. I had quotes, diagrams, circled images, computations, and all of the questionable facts I had discovered that year. I made no judgments and wrote no remarks.

I had only presented photographs and graphics. The facts easily spoke for themselves.

Jessica Baldwin, my yearbook neighbor and homeroom peer asked, "Sy, can you sign my yearbook?"

I immediately shut mine and responded with a flustered, "Uh, yeah sure." Propping the book against my knee I wrote, *This book turned out great. Have a good summer. Sy.'* That would be the only yearbook I signed that year.

When I gave the book back to her, I heard the first murmur in the crowd. About twenty feet away was a sophomore girl with a concerned face pointing to a certain page in her yearbook. They looked at the page with confusion then reached for their own books to see if these pages were also in theirs. They were, and upon that discovery, they showed their friends. I tucked mine under my arm and started to move toward the door.

As I moved across the floor, the mumblings got louder. I overheard some gasps and witnessed a rapid dampening of the jovial mood. Several teachers also consulted their own yearbooks. Word was spreading quickly. I made it to the hallway and out the front door in less than thirty seconds. A minute after that, I was in my car. Slowly pulling out of the parking lot, I saw Dr. Sites jogging through the courtyard to the gym like the building was on fire.

In a sense, I guess it was.

I slid the key into my door at Chernobyl and shut it quickly behind me. I didn't know where else to go. There were only a handful of people in the world that knew I lived here, so I felt it was still the safest place for me to be right now. I wouldn't have dared to come home at a time like this if I still lived with my parents. I threw my backpack on the floor and dropped my yearbook on the coffee table. Plopping myself down on the couch, I opened the book again to page 217. It was a reprehensible masterpiece. The pages were laid out like a crime file, and they told the whole story. Photos I had taken and that no one had ever seen before were on display for all to remember - calling out students, teachers, and leaders for what they really were. It was raw and uncensored. The truest piece of journalism in the entire book.

I laughed and looked out the window. For a moment, I felt as if I would be able to put this all behind me. But then the cold bite of reality hit me, as I realized the worst may be yet to come. The woods were quiet, and the bright sunshine invited anyone to come outside and enjoy its warmth. But I didn't. I stayed hidden inside for an hour, picking up on some long neglected chores. After a while, I heard the sound of a car engine pulling up and then cutting out.

I peeked through a window on the opposite side of the room, making sure to avoid the exterior walls and staying concealed in the center of the house. It was Shawn's 4Runner. Shawn and Roscoe were approaching the front door, checking their surroundings for followers.

In no time, their fists were pounding at the door.

"Sy, let us in," Shawn spoke from outside.

I quickly opened the door and hurried them inside.

"You've been living *here*?!" Roscoe said. "The whole time?"

"Yeah," I said.

"Dude. Why? My house is right there. Why'd you lie to me?"

"Sorry, man. Pride, I guess."

"You're cooking on a gas grill. Seriously? You're homeless, bro! Why didn't you just knock on my door? You coulda kept staying with us this whole time!"

"Ok, as crazy as it seems, we've actually got bigger issues here," Shawn interjected. "Dude. What...the heck?" Shawn emphatically stared at me until he broke out a huge smile. "You are a freakin' legend!" he said as he held up his hand for a high-five then moved in for a man hug.

I started to cautiously smile and accept the high-five. "I cannot believe you did that," he said.

"You got major cojones, man," Roscoe added. "Your

fireworks idea was crazy, but this was insane."

Shawn released me from the one armed hug and said, "You started a riot, dude. We gotta get you outta here."

"A riot?" I asked.

"Yeah, it's getting real. The bigwigs are looking for you."

"What are people saying?"

"Words like lawsuit, cops, jail, stuff like that," Roscoe said as he rummaged through my shirts that hung from an old broom handle in my makeshift closet. "What clothes do you want to take?"

"Jail for Dr. Sites and those guys though, not me, right? Do people understand why I did what I did?"

"Some of us. But we're not the ones with the deep pockets and connections."

"But do people get it? Do they see what's going on?"

Shawn and Roscoe didn't answer while they feverishly threw some of my things in boxes and bags.

"Shawn! Do people understand what's been happening? For years?"

With my books in hand about to walk out to his truck, he stopped and said, "They do now. I'm gonna take these out to the truck, is that cool?"

"Is all this really that urgent?"

Shawn stepped back away from the door, letting Roscoe squeeze through with a handful of my clothes. "Yes. It's urgent." Shawn looked down for a moment, trying to find the words to say. "Now that a bunch of people - powerful people - might lose their jobs, businesses, and everything else, they want your head, literally, so yes it's very urgent. Come on, grab a bag and help us pack."

I paused realizing the unintended consequences of my actions. I always thought of my plan as a mischievous way to reveal the truth and do what was right. I never intended it to harm so many people, including myself. But as I've discovered many times before, intentions are meaningless.

"So where we going?" I asked.

"Haven't gotten that far yet. Roscoe, you think we should head to your house?" Shawn asked.

"People will know to look there," I said. "I'm not putting his family through that."

We thought for a moment more, and then Shawn posed an

idea. "My dad's garage for now. No one would think to look for you there."

"His garage?"

"Yeah, he's got a sweet little set-up out there. He likes to tinker around on his Jag, so he's got a mini fridge and some other stuff. We'll set you up out there for a little bit until we can figure something out."

"He's the Academy's lawyer!"

"Exactly. That's why no one will look for you there."

"Why can't I stay here? No one knows that I'm here."

"We do. Cam and Grady do. Word's out, man. You gotta move. Last thing you need is a few gorillas like Topher and Joey showing up with baseball bats because you killed their scholarships."

I stopped for a moment to reflect on my situation.

"Grab some stuff, man," Shawn said. "We're sticking our necks out for you here. Come on!"

After packing the majority of what I owned into the back of Shawn's 4-Runner, I drove my car to the very end of Glenwood Estates and backed it behind some large shrubs, effectively hiding it from the road.

It was still daylight when we arrived at Bruce's garage.

"So, he's not here?" I asked.

"No," Shawn said. "He'll probably be working overtime tonight when he gets the call from Sites."

"So I'm squatting in the garage of the guy who's going to try to put me behind bars. Perfect."

"Not sure if he's trying to put you behind bars or keep Sites and the others out of them, but either way, yeah, you're about right."

Shawn opened up the side door of the garage and flicked on the lights. Inside set a sleek, black Jaguar, a whole wall of assorted tools, road signs, a mini fridge, and that little blue moped scooter with white-wall tires. It was a brilliantly stylish and completely masculine workspace, except for the scooter.

"Home sweet home," Shawn said.

"It's a step up from your old place," Roscoe added.

"What do I do if I need to use the bathroom?"

"Depending on how late it is, you've got your choice of some bushes outside, the clubhouse, or a five-gallon bucket," Shawn answered.

"Where's the bucket?"

"I dunno. You'll have to find one."

"I'm gonna start grabbing some of his stuff," Roscoe said.

"Where should I sleep?" I asked.

"I dunno. Maybe behind the Jag."

"Maybe I can just run back to Chernobyl and grab the couch cushions."

"Nope. Too risky. You can't go back."

"Where should we put this stuff?" Roscoe asked coming back in with some of my bags.

"It's pretty warm in here. You got a fan or anything?" I asked Shawn who had already come back in with a load of stuff under his arm.

"I can get you one."

"What happens if I have it running in the middle of the night and your dad comes in?"

"He probably won't," Shawn answered. "He usually only works on his car when he has free time, and something tells me he is not going to have much of that."

"So are we setting all this up and leaving Sy here now?" Roscoe asked Shawn.

"Yeah, probably. It's kind of an Anne Frank situation right now."

"You cool with that, buddy?"

"I guess I'll have to be. You guys gonna swing by tomorrow morning?"

"Yeah, we'll be back by. We'll get you outta here. Stay low tonight though. We'll see you tomorrow."

"Ok, see ya."

The fellas left me alone in the garage. It seemed that none of the neighbors realized yet they had a wanted man hiding in their cul-de-sac. I glanced out of the rectangular windows of the garage door to watch Shawn's tail lights fade. I grabbed an old blanket from the work bench, unfolded it to shake out the dust, and laid it on the hard concrete floor. This would be my bed for the evening.

It was another night of sleep deprivation for me. I didn't

know what was going on in the outside world or who might be the first to find me. I desperately wanted to sleep on the comfy leather seats of the Jag, which taunted me all night. But I couldn't risk it. I knew Mr. Lessner would kill me if I even touched it.

The next morning I was reading one of the books that Mr. Oakridge had let me borrow. As I was reading, a hornet distracted me as it buzzed around the garage in circular patterns throughout the rafters. It banged its little body against each pane of glass, looking for an exit. I opened the back window to the garage to let the little trapped insect find its way out and noticed the tip of the Ferris Wheel peeking over some trees on the distant side of a fountained pond.

The annual Clanton Fair had come to town already, and like a prisoner in his cell, I could merely dream and reminisce on the life I once had outside these walls. As I looked out to the Ferris Wheel, I heard the unmistakable sound of Cam's rattling truck muffler pulling up. It made me very nervous. I hadn't spoken to Cam in quite a while, and I couldn't help but feel like his loyalty still was with the jocks and not with me.

"Open up, Billy the Kid!" I heard Roscoe shout. I nervously cracked the door, unsure of what to expect. Shawn and Roscoe stood at the door, each holding a soda. Cam stood behind them.

"What's going on you guys?" I said. "Hi Cameron...Long time."

"I'm glad to see your living conditions have improved," he joked.

"Yeah, thanks. At least I've got electricity now."

"Look...Roscoe talked me into coming by here today," he said lowering his head in a way I had never seen before. Then he offered his hand for a handshake and remarked, "Dude, what you did was insane. That took guts."

I accepted his handshake. "Thanks."

"So where to?" Shawn interjected, trying to change the uncertain mood.

"Dam!" Roscoe shouted.

"What?" I asked.

"No, we're going to the dam."

"Oh!" I said. The dam was on Cape Fear and was another little retreat we had frequented in the summer to do some swimming, fishing, and general misbehaving.

"We figured that would be one of the only places that we wouldn't run into anyone who might want to kill you," Shawn joked.

"Do you think people really want to kill me?"

"Bro, you changed the entire face of the Academy and basically the entire city of Clanton. You realize that, right? The cops already got a formal investigation going. They're looking into everything. A lot of people are going to lose their jobs and businesses because of what you put in the yearbook. They're not going to love you for that."

"I never meant to hurt anyone, though," I said. "I just got backed into a corner."

"You don't have to explain it to us," Shawn said. "Actually, there are a lot of people hailing you around town as a hero, a martyr of sorts - giving up your high school diploma for disclosing the truth."

"My diploma?" I asked.

"That's just a rumor."

"Yeah, but you know it's going to happen." Cam shot back. "You don't honestly think they're going to give a diploma to the kid who potentially closed the Academy, do you?"

"Closed the Academy?!"

"You dropped a bomb of...of poo on the place! And now that poo hit the fan, and it's smattering anyone and everyone."

"Okay, enough with the poo." Shawn said, grossed out.

"Poo," Roscoe chuckled.

"Look, there's a lot of rumors flying around, but several major contributors have already pulled their funding from Cherrywood. Also, kids are transferring out of next year left and right. Teachers are quitting, too. Mrs. Turner already hung up her yearbook camera. She's gone. No one wants to be tied to this sinking ship. The Academy's going down."

I walked away from the group, unsure of what to say next. I leaned on Cam's truck. I couldn't believe how my simple idea had spread like wildfire so quickly. I thought that Principal Sites may have been fined or asked to step down, but I never meant for things to be blown so out of proportion or for innocent people to be affected. What would happen to my teachers or friends? By trying to save my mother's career and my own future, I had destroyed the lives of countless others. I very quickly began to realize the severity of the mistake I had made.

"I'm not sure I'm feeling up to going to the dam today. You guys go on without me."

"What?" they said in unison, pleading.

"Why?" Cam asked. "Because of this whole thing?"

"What's done is done man," Roscoe said.

"And nothing can be done about it now," Shawn added.

"You've already knocked down the house of cards," Cam said, "and nothing is going to change about how they fall."

"Guys, let's quit talking and start moving," Shawn said. "My dad'll be back soon. Let's go."

Begrudgingly, I grabbed a towel and my swim trunks from the garage. Looking back, I am very glad I went with the guys that day. I had no way of knowing then, but it was the last time we would all be together.

We spent the day on the bank of the river by the dam, just like countless days before. We fished, swam in the calm waters far away from the dam itself, and soaked in the warm sun. No one would bother us here. We were on the other side of the tracks, a different place entirely from Clanton. I thought it strange that such a city could be so small and yet so divided. Inside Clanton, there was Cherrywood, and then there was everything else. That day I enjoyed resting on the fringes of what was deemed acceptable society for Cherrywood.

Like always, we talked about girls, life, and school. Roscoe and Cam talked sports while Shawn and I discussed a road trip after high school to the Outer Banks. Little did we know that as our carefree day drifted by, the consequences of my actions would continue to unfold upon both the guilty as well as the innocent.

The rain had just started when Cam dropped me off at my temporary living arrangement. It was a bit depressing to call a garage home, but still I was thankful for someplace dry. I was amazingly exhausted from the day. I had been able to push the thoughts of what was happening in town out of my mind. But that changed when my head hit the pillow of my makeshift bed. My mind began to race again, and I couldn't turn off my brain. Some of the thoughts were so strong that I could've sworn I heard the voices talking inside my mind. A grumble of sorts, groans, and accusations blended into a sea of meticulous thoughts and confusion.

The darkness was broken by the dimly lit street lamps shining in from the end of the street, but even then, there was just barely enough light to see a hand in front of my face. Then without warning, a bright light turned on overhead, and a thunderous grinding sound began to open the garage door. Startled, I hunkered down lower into my position behind the Jag. Surely Shawn's father would not be taking out his pride and joy convertible in this weather. I thought it might've been a glitch. I lay motionless as the overhead door came to a stop, completely exposing the garage.

No one was there. Nothing was happening. Looking through one of the wheels and through the downpour, I saw a figure standing in the right upstairs window of the condo across the street. The figure did not move, nor did I. Wrapped in blankets behind the old convertible, I prayed that my body would blend in with the old tarps lying around the garage.

I counted the seconds passing in my head. Three minutes went by, then six. I began to wonder if the figure I had fixed my eyes on was nothing more than a coat rack or perhaps a suit Mr. Lessner had retrieved from the cleaners. I slowly turned my gaze toward the garage door opener once again and noticed a manual close button on the underside. I was pretty sure I could reach it if I used a broom handle.

Slowly, I began to rise from my place. I felt stiff, like a dog that was trapped in his kennel all night. On my hands and knees, I stretched out my hand to grab the broom, but then the machine on the ceiling roared again and the garage door began to close. Without thinking, I jerked my head back and looked up at the right upstairs window. The figure was gone, and once again, I was left alone lying in the darkness.

CHAPTER 25

I was jarred awake by the mechanical grinding of the garage door. The same sound that had startled me and kept me up worried for most of the night was testing my nerves again. I pulled the blankets over my head, leaving one eye exposed to observe my surroundings. Birds chirped from outside and the morning sunlight filled the garage. Concealed behind the convertible, I listened closely as the sound of footsteps appeared from outside. They grew louder as their owner came closer. Eventually, the sound of feet on asphalt turned into the sound of feet on concrete as the person entered the garage. Then, it stopped.

Someone was standing in the garage, just on the other side of the car. Presumably, it was the same figure I had seen the night before.

"Sy."

The sudden voice startled me even more. I recognized it at once. It was Mr. Lessner. "Sylas. I know you're in here. If you want me to look behind the car, I will."

I was busted.

Slowly, I uncovered myself from the blankets and stood up from behind the car. Mr. Lessner was standing at the entrance of the garage with a look of stone on his face. I bashfully made eye contact.

"Is anyone else in here with you?" he coldly asked.

"No, sir," I meekly said.

"Good. Come on in the house," he ordered, as he turned and walked back into the street.

I didn't move from my makeshift bed right away. I looked behind Mr. Lessner to see who else was with him. I saw no one, so I grabbed my shoes from the floor next to me and slid them on. After he silently escorted me from the garage to his condo, he invited me to have a seat at his kitchen table.

"What time is it?" I asked.

"Around eleven."

"Oh," I said, as I rubbed the sleep from my eyes. I thought it was earlier than that.

"You want some breakfast?"

"No, that's okay."

"Come on. Have a bowl of cereal or something. Cereal's in that cabinet there," he said pointing to the cabinet next to the fridge, even though I already knew where he kept it.

On the kitchen table sat a cup of coffee, some legal paperwork, and the Sunday edition of the Clanton Chronicle. I immediately noticed the front page photo. It was a picture of a mob of press interviewing a highly inconvenienced Governor Hawkins on the steps of the state capitol. The large, bold headline read: *State Scandals exposed in School Yearbook.*

"You made the paper," Mr. Lessner said, noticing me eyeballing it. I looked away. "You want some coffee or anything?" he asked.

"Sure. Black," I replied. I normally didn't drink coffee, but I felt like I could use the extra boost of energy today of all days.

"Here you are," he said, handing me a cup of coffee. "Grab your cereal and come have a seat. I got something I want to run by you."

I obeyed and got up from my chair to retrieve a bowl. I prepared a bowl of Frosted Mini Wheats and returned to the table. Mr. Lessner had already sat down and was glancing over some of the legal documents that were sitting there.

"Thank you," I said.

"For the cereal or living in my garage?"

"Both," I said embarrassed. "How long have you known?"

"Since yesterday. How long have you been there?"

"Just since Friday night."

"Oh okay, so not long. Did you find my nudie mag collection?"

"No."

"Good," he smiled. I couldn't tell if he was joking or serious, although my gut told me that it was the latter.

"Okay, so here's the deal, Sy," he started. I got very nervous. "Everyone is looking for you. They all know it was you. Just be glad I'm the one who found you instead of someone else, okay?"

I started to sweat and the bowl of cereal in front of me went forgotten. I knew there were people after me, but no one had told me how many.

"The little stunt you pulled is going to bring down some very powerful, very important individuals. It's already starting to. Pastor Samms stepped down this morning. I just got a call that he's already announced it at the first service. Some of these guys are going to want your head and - take it from me - some of them can probably get it."

My palms were sweaty, and my eyes were wide open.

"So here's what you're going to do. You're going to sign these papers hiring me as your attorney representing you. I'm doing this pro bono. No charge," he said as he slid over the paperwork and a pen. I was shocked. I glanced at the paperwork which was an employment contract written in legalese. My brain quickly thought over all of the information that had just been dumped into it.

"You can stay at my place here if you'd like. You don't have to stay in the garage. It'll be sort of a protective custody type thing, if you will. I'll negotiate with the school for you to take your final exams here. You don't have to go back there if you don't want to. I wouldn't recommend it right now anyway."

"Why?" I simply asked.

"Because I'm not sure how many friends, apart from my son and a few others, you actually have left at that school."

"No, I mean, why do you want to represent me?"

"Because you're going to get nailed for all kinds of lawsuits, not to mention other personal attacks if you don't have adequate legal representation."

Still processing all of the information, I bluntly asked, "You're doing this to protect yourself, aren't you?"

Mr. Lessner stopped and looked at me a moment. I knew I had taken him off-guard, but his poker face seemed impossible to crack. "You want the truth, Sylas? Well, I can give it to you. I am using you, and in return, you get to use me. Separately, the growing mob in Clanton will burn us both to the ground, but together, I might be able to get out of this ordeal with my firm and maybe, just maybe, you will get out of this alive. Have we got a deal?"

He was trying to save his own skin, which was slimy, but he was exactly what I needed. I was once again backed into a corner. I felt that part of me was agreeing to make a deal with the Devil, and another part of me wondered if my willingness to allow Mr. Lessner to represent me was just as twisted and deceiving as many of the crimes committed by the executives I had outed in the yearbook.

"Yes, sir," I replied.

"Call me Bruce."

"Knock, knock," a female voice said from below in the entryway. This must have been Bruce's mysterious girlfriend who we all knew existed but had never seen. Bruce winced, then I looked over the table to see her face, completely shocked at who it was.

"You up yet, sleepyhead?" she said, starting to walk down the stairs. Now, it was Bruce who knew he was busted. Janelle Samms, Pastor Joel's wife, walked up the stairs into Bruce's living room.

Bruce dropped his head.

"Have you met Janelle?" he embarrassingly asked me.

I paused and then nodded, my face growing red.

She seemed shaken as well. "Hi, how are you?" she asked me, trying to cover up the awkwardness. They both knew I had already put two and two together: Janelle had left Pastor Samms for a guy, and that guy was Bruce.

"Sy, it's not what it looks like," Bruce said. "Joel and Janelle's marriage was over a while ago. Joel's not who you think, but you already figured that out."

I stayed silent, not knowing what to do or say. This morning, all of us had been caught in one way or another.

"Just sign the papers," he told me.

I obeyed, grabbing the fancy pen with which to sign, thereby hiring Bruce as my attorney.

"Good. Now let's get to work. Tell me your story. Start from the beginning," he said getting up to grab a legal pad to write on. "Don't leave anything out."

Not wanting to judge someone I didn't know, and realizing that I was the last person to point a finger, I turned over to Janelle.

"My name is Sylas Ernst."

"Pleasure to meet you, Sylas. Janelle Owens."

"Nice to meet you, too," I said smiling, "I really like your scooter."

The afternoon had turned a bit overcast. No rain had been indicated in the forecast; just some low-hanging clouds. I spent about five hours talking with Bruce, helping him put together all the puzzle pieces, and working on our case. He recommended that I pay one last visit to Chernobyl, to clean up as much evidence as I could so nothing could be used against me.

I pulled into Glenwood Estates, like I had been doing every day for the past month, and parked in front of my former home. From the outside, I could tell it had been disturbed since I had last been there. Several of the windows were broken, and there was more debris in the overgrown yard than normal. I searched for my key in my pocket, but before I could locate it, I noticed the door was already ajar.

Slowly pushing it open, I could see that the house had been ransacked. What possessions I had left, like my barbecue grill, food items, and miscellaneous other goods, had all been overturned and strewn about the concrete floor. Stuffing from couch cushions blew about the corners of the room and our coffee table lay overturned and dismantled. It was hard to say who did this, but I had a pretty good idea of what they wanted, and more specifically, who they were after.

As I slowly took inventory of what was left, I noticed my overturned Victrola pinched below the palette that had served as my coffee table. I lifted the palette and dragged the sad machine out. The cone was dented, but from what I could tell, it might still be salvageable. Most of the records had been broken, but I did find one that was still intact. Placing the machine upright on the floor, I put the record on and wound up the old, creaky machine, curious to see what it would do. After a few pops and scratches, the sweet voice of Frank Sinatra began. The second half of *Old Man River,* a soulful old song, filled the house and soothed my mind as I picked up the fragments of my life.

In my rush to escape just two days before, I had left behind a few envelopes of photos, which unfortunately, had been discovered by the vandals. I collected the photos, mostly torn and crumpled, scattered amid the debris and wet from last night's storm. I also gathered a few other odds and ends and put them and the salvageable photos together into a milk crate. As I stood to carry out the first load to my car, I caught something out of the corner of my eye.

I doubt I would have ever noticed movement like that before had the windows not been broken. But with no glass or glare to obstruct my view, I caught a quick glimpse of a figure rushing through the woods about twenty yards away. It was moving parallel to me. It wasn't coming towards me, but I could tell he was carrying something.

The person was moving as quickly as he could while trying to negotiate the brambly woods. I stepped towards the window for a closer look. After I watched him for a second, I made two startling realizations: the first was that the object he was carrying was a gun, and the second was that it was Roscoe.

I rushed to the door and stood outside, still just watching. He wasn't stopping. In fact, he was getting faster. Roscoe and I had gone squirrel hunting from time to time, but never back in these woods, and at the speed in which he was moving, he was not hunting.

"Roscoe!" I yelled. He didn't stop.

He finally broke through a thicket and onto one of Glenwood Estates dirt roads where he revved into a full-out sprint.

"*JAKE!*" I yelled again, this time using his real name and starting to run in his direction. His back was toward me and his shirt was torn by the branches and thorns he had just escaped from. He was wild with furry, not listening to a word I said.

Roscoe continued his sprint onto the only paved road in Glenwood Estates and headed in the direction of the only finished house on the street.

"Edmund," I whispered out loud to myself.

"ROSCOE!" I called, now in a sprint to catch up with him. Frank Sinatra's voice grew more powerful even as I ran through the trees away from my old home. "Stop!" I yelled. Again, he didn't respond.

As he got closer and closer to Edmund's, I could hear him yell something, but I couldn't make out what it was. While he continued to run closer to the house, Edmund came to the door, eating what looked like a Popsicle. He just stood there, seemingly unfazed by the man running towards him with a gun.

"*JAKE!* What are you doing?!" I shouted again.

Roscoe shouted again with what sounded like "Giver back," although I still couldn't quite tell. He was about fifteen yards away from Edmund's front porch when I saw him start to raise the gun.

"JAKE!" I shouted again, about thirty yards away from him. Still, my cries were ignored.

It was at this time when Edmund turned around and commanded someone inside the house to "stay inside." I would later tell the cops that he then looked downward. That's when I heard the unmistakable ratcheting sound of the pump action shotgun.

In one last plea of desperation I cried, "NO!"

My cry was muffled by a blast that mutilated Roscoe's face.

It's an image that I'll take with me to the grave. One that would forever haunt me and affect me in ways that I could never know.

The sound was not a gunshot. It was an explosion. The shotgun that Roscoe had brought to his cheek in an attempt to shoot Edmund had blown up, fracturing it into pieces and dropping him immediately to the ground.

"ROSCOE!!!"

I cried out his name, beginning to sprint towards the scene. A female scream came from inside the house. My heart was racing as a million questions flooded my head. The closer I got to the house, the more pronounced the images were. Edmund was on his knees with hands over his head, crying. Roscoe was barely moving. When I reached him, the terror of what I saw ripped my soul from me, as I fell to my knees at the site.

The right side of Roscoe's face was unrecognizable, his temporal lobe was visible, and his right eye was missing. Teeth delicately hung from his shattered jaw while the other half of his face was covered in blood. Splinters of the wooden gun stock were embedded in his neck and shoulders and his left eye stared past me in a shock-like state. I shook him, for him to look at me, but his gaze was fixed. I will never forget the sound of my friend drowning in his own blood. His body, seized in my arms as life continued to escape him, formed a broadening crimson pool beneath us.

A woman's cries still came from inside the house as Edmund cowered on the front porch, his face speckled with red and green spots. The red was blood from a few shotgun pellets that hit his shoulder. The green was the remainder of his Popsicle.

"Are you hit?!" The woman inside shouted. "Beeker, are you hit?!"

Edmund's mother finally came outside and dropped on top of her crying child. When she saw Roscoe, she was just as horrified as I was and screamed again, through heartbreaking tears.

"Why did he do that?" Edmund asked. "Why did he do that?" He kept repeating it over and over, like a confused chant.

"Call an ambulance!" I shrieked, knowing in my heart it was too late.

I collapsed on the ground beside my friend who lay mangled and dying. His father's shattered 12-gauge sat on the ground next to him.

Roscoe's body fell limp in my arms as one last gargling breath escaped him. I put my hand over his face to close his eye that was gazing up to heaven as I wept uncontrollably. It was the most devastating pain I had ever felt.

I was sobbing, as was Mrs. McBryer, huddled over her terrified adult boy with her cordless phone in hand. " I'll call 911," she said.

My heartbreak had quickly turned to denial. "Roscoe, you stupid fool. Don't die like this. Please don't die. Please."

"The police are on their way," Mrs. McBryer said.

It was around 6:30 p.m. on May 26th, 1996 when Jacob "Roscoe" Martin died.

The first officer on the scene comforted me and gave me the courage to let Roscoe go. I never got his name. In that moment, though, I experienced the very last emotion I ever expected: hope. The officers were followed shortly by the ambulance. It wasn't until later that evening that I would learn the whole story of why this event actually happened.

The church service earlier that day had been a bit unusual. Because of the recent allegations that I had uncovered and that the community was now investigating, Pastor Samms gave the shortest sermon of his life. Only about half of the usual congregation was in attendance, including Roscoe and his family. However, there was no shortage of press sitting in the front row on Edmund's bench, creating disorder and causing him extreme discomfort. The entire church service lasted only ten minutes. It was comprised of some apologies and news that Pastor Samms would be stepping down as senior pastor of Clanton Baptist, along with several other church leaders who would also be retiring. For able-minded people, an experience like this isn't hard to comprehend. But for people suffering from autism, like Edmund, big changes and chaos of this proportion were very uncomfortable and almost impossible to understand. I was told that Edmund was extremely unsettled by the empty auditorium, the press, and the short service. It had gotten so bad that his mother and a few deacons had to work to calm him down. And sometimes when Edmund got nervous, he looked for a friend.

Meanwhile, as empty as the sanctuary was, someone who wasn't usually in attendance did show up. I guess my dad had a change of heart when he learned of my yearbook stunt and happened to go to church that day to see how the community was reacting. He drove his new van, Roscoe's family's old one. Poor Lily must have made an honest mistake when getting out of children's church and had gotten into the old family van like she had done every Sunday for the past several years. She climbed inside, and when my dad arrived most likely pleasantly surprised by his delightful passenger, he offered to take her home.

My dad made a few innocent mistakes that day. One was not attempting to first find Lily's parents at church before he drove her home. It was an honest mistake, but one that could have saved Roscoe's life. The second mistake was not leaving a note when he found the Martin's house empty after he arrived there. They must have still been at church looking for Lily when my dad pulled up to their front door. And instead of leaving a simple note, he decided to turn around and drive Lily back to the church. But finally, and probably the worst mistake of all, was forgetting about the sticky gas gauge on the van that Mr. Martin had warned him about. On the way back to church, my dad ran out of gas. He spent nearly an hour and a half with Lily, walking to the closest gas station, and then returning to the abandoned vehicle. But in the hours that she had been missing and her family had frantically searched for her, Roscoe came to the hasty conclusion that Edmund - simply wanting a friend after the unsettling church service - must've taken her.

In his uncontrollable, emotional rage, he rushed back home. He grabbed his dad's 12-gauge and a handful of shells from that infamous blue box of leftovers. He must not have checked to see what ammunition he had grabbed because the cops determined that he was in possession of three 12-gauge shells and a 20-gauge.

What happened to Roscoe is called a 12-20 burst. Loading a

20-gauge shell into a 12-gauge shotgun can cause it to jam and obstruct the barrel, which is exactly what happened. Roscoe accidentally loaded the 20-gauge shell first, and when he approached Edmund who appeared to be commanding a child to stay inside the house, Roscoe absent-mindedly cocked a 12-gauge shell into the already jammed chamber and pulled the trigger, causing the gun to backfire and literally blow up in his face.

It was more than just a string of misunderstandings and outlandish, coincidental circumstances that killed Roscoe. It was the result of the unjust rumors and slander initiated by the Academy about the man who was Edmund McBryer. Yes, he was mentally challenged and at times obliviously inappropriate. But he was not a pedophile or a creep or a retard like we all had been conditioned to believe. He was just a churchgoer who didn't fit in with the rest of them. He never kidnapped Lily or any child. When he looked downward and told someone to "stay inside," he wasn't ordering Lily around, like Roscoe probably thought.

He was trying to protect his mother, who happened to be sitting in her rocking chair.

CHAPTER 26

Edmund was treated at the hospital for the shotgun pellets that had lodged into his arm. Other than that, he was fine. Aside from Roscoe, Edmund's vinyl siding suffered the most damage. The fractured pieces are still there to this day - the one imperfection of the house - which Edmund never fixed.

I called my mom from Bruce's house the night of Roscoe's death to let her know that I was okay. My dad was being held for questioning and potential kidnapping charges, but it was too soon to determine what the outcome would be. Mom and I talked for hours—about what I had been doing for the past two months, about life, about family. I apologized for not calling her more often. Through everything that had happened, I never realized how much I had missed my mother.

It was very hard for me to sleep that week, which was unfortunate as it was the week of exams. Bruce negotiated with the school to allow me to take my exams in the safety of his condo. He kept me honest though, and took all of my books and notes away so I had no way of cheating.

He also did something else really nice for me: with Janelle's permission, he gave me that scooter. She had only used it a few times, but wasn't in love with it, and I don't know if Bruce had ever personally turned it on. It was a wonderful gesture and one that forever changed my views of Shawn's dad.

Shawn came over once in a while to keep me company and talk things out. He also told me that Rachel Ellis had come to school looking for me after she found out about the yearbook and Roscoe. I gave her a call to let her know that I was okay, not realizing that she was in her ninth month and would be a mother any day now. We ended up talking for hours, mainly discussing our fears about life and the future. It was really nice talking to her. I think we both felt safe as we listened to one another.

My discussions with Shawn brought a sense of healing as well, but as much as we tried, our conversations still didn't satisfy my many questions. Praying didn't seem to either. So I took my new scooter, and I made a visit to one of the two men I needed to see.

———————————

"Sy. I'm so sorry," Mr. Oakridge said, coming out through his front door and meeting me on his porch that Tuesday. He must have been watching for me out of his window. This was one of the few times I had called before coming over. I really needed to see him and wanted to be sure he'd be home.

"Thank you, sir," I said as I accepted his open embrace.

"Jake was a good man," he said, patting me on the back.

"One of the best," I answered. We quickly finished the consoling hug, and then he invited me to come inside.

"Do you want anything to drink?" he asked as he walked me into his living room.

"I'll just take a water if you don't mind."

"Not at all. Not at all. Be right back."

"Thank you."

When he returned with a glass of water for me and a glass of iced tea for himself, he said, "So, you seem to have gotten yourself in a little trouble."

I smiled. "Yes sir, I guess I have."

"You figured out a lot more than I did. I'm not sure I would've been brazen enough to take the approach you did, but I'm glad someone exposed the truth."

"So you knew what was going on then?" I asked.

"Some of it. Why do you think they fired me?"

I nodded. He took a sip of his tea. I put my head down in thought for another minute, not quite sure how to begin. He allowed me the time.

"I saw Jake die two days ago and I've been asking 'why' ever since," I said. "I've legitimately asked myself this, and I just don't know. Why did this have to happen? Why would God allow it? I mean, the circumstances were just so bizarre, ya know? Lily got into the wrong car, my dad's a little weird, Edmund's even weirder, and then Jake made a hasty judgment call based on presuppositions, and a shotgun literally blew up in his face. That's so...so arbitrary. There could've been a million things that could've interfered with this whole random collection of events, but nothing ever did, and now he's dead. So my question is, simply, *why?*"

"Why did this happen or why did God allow it to happen?" Mr. Oakridge asked.

"Why would God allow it to happen? Jake was a saint, and his family is made up of the most wonderful people I've ever met. Why would God allow them to suffer like that?"

He thought for a moment, and then responded, "I know the pain you're feeling is still very raw, and there is nothing I can say to make that go away. But, to answer your question, God gave us free will, Sy. With the ability to make our own choices comes the ability to receive our own consequences. And if you think God allows some suffering to happen, wouldn't it be reasonable to think He also prevents some from happening? Don't you think it would've been even more unfortunate if the gun hadn't backfired and actually killed Edmund? Then *his* family would have had to live with the consequences of a free will choice made by someone else. Not to mention, Jake would be imprisoned for murder. If you ask me, wasting life behind bars is a worse sentence than the fate Jake suffered. Could it be possible that God actually *did* intervene and *allowed* the shotgun to explode because if it hadn't, circumstances might actually have been a lot worse?"

Mr. Oakridge's words fell hard into the pit of my stomach. It was certainly a perspective I hadn't thought about before, but through the anger I felt come over me, I couldn't help but think that perhaps he was right. It still felt so senseless, but perhaps I was simply too close to see the big picture. Then I remembered another theological dichotomy that I had been struggling with recently, and in attempt to swallow the emotional lump in my throat and press forward with the conversation, I began to share my thoughts again.

"Ok what about this?" I responded. "Topher Landau asked me this question once, and to this day, I still don't know the answer. You live in a nice house with running water, indoor plumbing, and a grocery store down the street with everything you'll ever need. But in places like Africa, for example, people live in extreme poverty with no food, with diseases, and they're dying every day because they don't even have *access* to water. Your kids can bathe with toys in gallons of clean water, but all those impoverished kids die because they can't even find it. So can you please answer, why would God allow *that?*"

He sat back in his chair, amused by the difficulty of the question. "Topher asked that? Hmm, he's smarter than I thought. Don't tell him I said that." He had a chuckle and then continued. "In some parts of Africa there is hardly any rain. But you know where else there is hardly any rain? Las Vegas, Nevada. But Vegas has a gluttony of water. They shoot it hundreds of feet into the air with powerful fountains and have swimming pools inside of hotel rooms. Does God love the people of Sin City more than the people of Africa? Hardly. Then what do you think the difference is?"

I stayed silent. I didn't know.

"The difference is us. It's the society. See, here in America, we have a system that allows people to be creative, to build things, to prosper, to advance. But in some parts of Africa, the leaders have not established that. In America, the leaders try to empower the citizens to improve society. But in some parts of Africa, the leaders make the free will choice to oppress their citizens in an attempt to gain more power for themselves which in turn leaves their people struggling for survival and often dying. See, God has given the people of Las Vegas and Africa the same amount of resources. But *people* make the difference, Sy. It's not God's responsibility to make every corner of the globe perfectly habitable for humans, but He has given us the brainpower to use what resources have been provided. It's not God's fault that those people don't have water...It's man's.

"Perhaps you and I have the obligation to help provide those people with water, because we realize how precious their lives really are. Then we are doing God's will, and in a sense, He provides for even those who are oppressed by their very own government."

I remained silent. The answer was so unique but so elegantly simple. Just like most people, I was hoping for someone or something to easily blame. And now I had it, although the answer was not what I had been expecting.

"In the Garden of Eden, what did God say would happen to Adam and Eve if they ate the forbidden fruit?" he asked.

I thought for a moment and replied, "They would die."

"Exactly. And what did they do?"

"They ate it."

"And what happened?"

I shrugged my shoulders.

"They began to die. We don't know how much time Adam and Eve spent in the garden before they disobeyed God. We just believe that it happened. They began to age. They also began to suffer pain and hardships. Evil entered the world with a choice, and with it came a lot of hurt for the innocent, the good, and the undeserving. But God loved us, and so He made a way for us to choose him by sending His Son to bridge the gap between our shortcomings and God's perfect will. There is still a lot of pain and hurt in this life, but the life we have here is very brief. I believe Heaven will be eternal."

Mr. Oakridge was finally helping me understand some things that I had always wrestled with. Still, though, my heart was broken. Mr. Oakridge was right. There was no reason or logic that could ease the pain.

"I just don't see what good can come from all of this."

He looked at me, then back down at his hands which he contemplatively rubbed together.

"Let me tell you a story. I grew up poor. Really poor. Never had a dad. My mom raised my brother and me on her own. We lived in downtown Atlanta in one of the roughest neighborhoods. My mom worked as a waitress to put food on the table, but it was a rough childhood; I'm not going to sugar coat it. She was robbed probably once a month because people knew she was walking home with cash tips. I knew she got raped a few times, although she still tries to hide that from my brother and me to this day. Gunshots and ambulances were my lullabies. You get the idea. As I got older, several of my classmates joined gangs. It was an animalistic environment driven by fear. They were all scared, so they thought safety was in numbers. A few of 'em ended up killing each other, but the ones who didn't attempted to hide their fear by trying to intimidate others. I was one of the others. I got beat unconscious several times and knifed in the back all before the age of sixteen. But through all of this, I got good at one thing: running.

"I ran for my life on several occasions. I developed stamina and speed. I was fast. No one could catch me. And I kept it up. I joined the track team in high school and broke several school records. I still hold the school record for the one hundred and four hundred meter. I was so good that WVU gave me a full scholarship to run for them. So I took the opportunity seriously and graduated college with a 4.0. The first in my family to ever go to college, much less graduate. I met my wife in college and used that diploma to get jobs that my family could only dream of. Granted, it was always middle-class wages, but it was still the kind of money that people from my area only knew how to make by dealing drugs and pimping.

"Now I've got a beautiful, smart wife and kids, live in a great house, don't ever have to worry about having enough food for them, and we can all sit out on the porch at night and watch fireflies, not firefights. Most of the kids I grew up with are either still struggling for survival back in Atlanta, in prison, or dead. Did God allow me to suffer growing up? You bet He did. But I thank Him every day for that, because now I know why."

As usual, Mr. Oakridge had left me speechless. I dropped my head in reflection. So did he.

"Thank you, sir," I humbly said as I looked back up. "You were a runner?"

"Yes."

"You don't look like a runner."

"Hey now!" he said laughing. "That's what married life does to you as I'm sure you'll find out one day."

I chuckled as well.

"I hope that answers some of your questions, Sy," he said with a smile. "I'm sorry about Jake. When's the funeral?"

"Friday at five."

"Ok, I'll be there."

I visited Mr. Oakridge, the first man I had needed to see, on Tuesday. On Wednesday, I visited the second.

I pulled into the driveway and cut the engine. My father's car was not there, but my mother's was. I looked around briefly to make sure I did not see anyone from the press or individuals with cruel intentions. I didn't even make it to the front door before it opened and my mother captured me in her arms, snatching my breath away in the process. It was good to see her again. She didn't say a word. She just hugged me and cried.

"Hi, Ma. I missed you," I said as I sunk into her embrace.

I didn't rush her. I knew she had been waiting for this

moment for a while. I had, too.

"I missed you, too," she said, laughing through tears. "Reporters have been here every day looking for you."

"Huh," was all I could say.

"You've lost weight!" she said.

"I have?"

"There's hardly anything left of you. Let me make you something to eat. What do you want?"

"I'm fine, Mom. Is Dad here?"

"He just ran to the store. He'll be back soon."

"How's he doing?"

"He's different."

"Different?"

"He's doing better. Come on in. What can I get for you? You sure you don't want something to eat?"

"Maybe a sandwich?"

"Of course. I just picked up some peppercorn turkey."

She headed for the kitchen to make a sandwich, and I headed upstairs to collect a few more clothes, along with some odds and ends. From the upstairs window, I saw my father pull in. He looked around cautiously, not recognizing the blue scooter in the drive way.

I took a deep breath and folded a few more shirts as I heard him enter the door downstairs.

"Is he here?" he asked my mom.

I didn't hear her respond. Then I heard his footsteps start to climb the wooden stairs. I put my shirt down on my old bed and walked to the doorway. As he rounded the corner of the stairway, he caught my gaze.

"Sylas."

"Hi, Dad."

My father didn't say another word until he walked over and wrapped his arms around me. He had never held me so kindly before. I felt like I was a young boy again. The world melted away, along with the lies and loss I had experienced over the past year.

"You, okay?" he asked.

"Yeah," I nodded. "I'm good. How are you?"

He took a moment before he said anything. "I'm so sorry, Sy. I'm so sorry."

"Dad, it wasn't your fault."

My father sat on my bed and looked out the window. I sat beside him as he continued.

"What I did to the Martins', what I did to them...how could they forgive me for that?"

"I'm sure they will, Dad. It's just going to take time."

He looked down again. I could tell his eyes were starting to get teary. It was the first time I ever saw my dad show empathy without judgment. There comes a time in every child's life when the role of child and parent becomes reversed - when the provider needs providing and the protector needs protecting. I put my arm around him as he continued.

"They already did," he said. "Jake's father came to the jail Sunday night. He dropped all charges."

He wiped a tear from his eye.

"What did he say?"

"He's blaming himself for storing mixed shotgun shells. He knows it was all an accident. Just a big accident...He knows God...more than me. I'm sorry, Sy."

"It was just an accident. You said it yourself."

He stood up from the bed, slumped his shoulders, and put his hands in his pockets as he leaned against the wall.

"I'm sorry about what I did to the Martins, and I'm sorry about what I did to you," he said. "I thought I had lost you for good. I felt like I had completely failed you as a father, but I couldn't find the words to tell you. But after spending the day with Lily, I realized that I was the only person standing in my way, and that I needed to let go of the past hurt and pain in my life. She's such a little angel. She loves unconditionally, as a child, and trusts fully, believing the best of each person she meets. That's what the love of God must be like, I think. If I was ever able to help anyone as a pastor, it should have first started with you, son."

I dropped my head and quietly muttered, "Thanks, Dad."

I had longed for that moment, to know that my father's love for me was unconditional for as long as I could remember. Now that it had happened, I was speechless. My mom was right. My dad was different. Somehow, a simple child and the love of her father showed him what was most important in life. His love was once tied together with conditions, fairness, and each person sharing equal halves, as a way to protect himself from hurt. He had been afraid of sharing his heart for fear of someone breaking it. The intimidating exterior of my father hid a scared and hurt young boy inside. He had always believed in the Scriptures before, but somehow still believed God's love came with conditions. He never felt worthy enough to accept grace fully, and therefore, he could never reciprocate that grace to others.

"Sylas, I realized that when you let go of all the hurt and pain of this life and trust in God to the fullest, He takes away all of that hurt and somehow changes it into something for the good. He will give you a peace nothing in this world can offer. That's why Jesus died to begin with, because we have all been hurt. And at times we hurt others, even if it is simply passing along the pain and suffering given to us by another person. Jesus died to show the world grace and that we could know what it truly means to forgive and to be forgiven. I learned that on Sunday. I should have learned it years ago."

I gave my dad another hug. "That's awesome, Dad. Thank you."

"Thank you, Sylas. I'm glad you're back. I tried to come see you at Bruce Lessner's but I couldn't get past the front gate."

"Sorry about that," I said with a slight chuckle. "I'm glad to be home."

"Where are you going now?"

"Right now, or when the dust settles?"

"Both."

"Right now, I'm heading back over to Mr. Lessner's house at Locksboro Country Club. He's my lawyer. Maybe after graduation, I might visit Grandpa in Pennsylvania or maybe hike a bit of the Appalachian Trail."

"The Appalachian Trail?" my father said, laughing.

"I know, it's crazy. But I want to be able to be alone with my thoughts for a while, ya know? Figure some things out."

"That sounds great, Sylas. Really great."

A brief silence filled the room as my father grew somber. "So Jake's funeral is Friday?" he asked.

"Yeah. At five."

"And graduation is the next day?"

"Yeah, but I don't think I'll be there."

"Well, is it okay if I see you Friday at the funeral?"

"Yeah, that would be great."

In my wildest imagination, I never would've guessed that the person who I would feel the safest with on one of the toughest days of my life would be Mr. Lessner. Even before the three of us exited his sleek, leathery BMW, I felt all eyes from anywhere on campus fixed on me.

"You ready for what's coming?" Bruce asked. I wouldn't realize how coincidental that question would be until twenty years later.

"Security?" I asked, noticing two large armed men at the front of the church.

"My idea," Bruce replied. "This day is about Jake. I didn't want anyone to detract from that."

"I'm ready," Shawn answered from the passenger seat.

"How 'bout you, Sy?" he asked into his rearview mirror.

I took one last glance at my notes then tucked them into my jacket pocket. "Yeah," I answered.

He nodded and unbuckled his seatbelt. We all exited the car and made our way up to the formidable church steps. Roscoe's parents were outside on the porch greeting people as they entered the sanctuary to offer their condolences. Roscoe's mom and sister were crying while his dad maintained a brave face.

Bruce was the first to reach Roscoe's dad. The two men shook hands and Mr. Martin thanked him for coming. Then he saw me and his face filled with more emotion. The two of us never cried. I was too nervous to cry, and he'd already seen me do it once before.

He gave me a hug and whispered, "We're here for you, Sy." It was the only time I got choked up for that entire day. In their time of loss and mourning, they would be here for me, and that meant everything.

"I miss him," was all that I could muster while still controlling my emotions.

"We do, too," he said. Then he reached out to hug Shawn. Shawn shed a few tears during all of it, but still maintained his self-control. Interacting with Roscoe's mom and Lily was actually easier for me. As a man, I felt a sense of duty to remain strong for them, even though it broke my heart to see them both in tears.

I kept my head down as the three of us walked toward the middle of the sanctuary to find a seat. Flower bouquets and baskets filled the stage, along with one oddly out-of-place custom cookie arrangement. Through my periphery, I could hear whispers and see faces turn toward me. This was the first time in a week I had been in public.

I saw my parents, sitting along the aisle, looking back at me. I smiled and moved toward them as they slid over in their pew to make room for Bruce, Shawn, and me. All of us exchanged pleasant and silent nods to each other.

Sitting next to my dad, I tried to muster a smile, given the situation. I took a deep breath, trying to ignore the stares and gossip around me.

"The cookie bouquet is from Edmund," my father whispered, seemingly reading my mind. "He bought them for Lily."

I winced my face at the sweet gesture and looked back at my father as we both chuckled. It felt good to laugh with him again.

Pastor Tom, the Youth Leader, was the first to move to the podium. He opened with prayer and told the uplifting story of when Roscoe accepted Christ during his sixth grade retreat. There were very few dry eyes in the building when the story finished. Then he said the words that I'd been preparing for, but fearing, for that entire week.

"One of Jake's best friends has been asked by the family to say a few words." He looked directly at me, nodded, and turned to leave. I swallowed the large lump in my throat and stood. Bruce nodded at me in encouragement.

Shawn merely whispered, "You got this."

Whispers blanketed the closed-casket ceremony as I stood. Standing up in front of the crowd, I felt like I should be the last person who deserved to be up there. I took the stage, and took a moment to collect my thoughts. My heart was pounding. Then a thought popped into my head that seemed equally appropriate, as well as inappropriate, but one that Roscoe would have appreciated me starting with.

CHAPTER 27

"Jake still owed me four dollars when he died," I began.

A few people in the audience let out a guarded chuckle. The rest of them were silent.

"Jake kept to himself most days," I went on. "His friends knew him to be an introvert, and because of this I consider myself lucky to have known him as I did. He wasn't perfect, but he always kept his promises. The only time he didn't was when he promised to pay me back those four dollars he borrowed to buy a sandwich. It would seem the only thing that could make him break his promises was death."

"Most of you called him Jake. That's the name we all used to call him. But over the last few years, his closest friends called him by another name: Roscoe. Our freshman year, Jake found a postcard at the flea market of snow-capped mountains below a blue sky and above rolling plains. *That is where I want to live,* he said. I took the postcard out of his hands and flipped it over. It was a picture of the Beartooth Mountains, just outside of a town called Roscoe, Montana. We started calling him Roscoe after that and the name stuck. I always thought it curious how such a little thing could change a person's life. I used to wonder what his nickname would've been if he'd picked up a postcard to Slicklizzard, Alabama or Sandwich, New Hampshire."

I briefly looked up to see Roscoe's mom in the front row, smiling and teary-eyed. I smiled at her, and then refocused my attention back down to my paper. The words grew blurry through tears. One dropped to the paper below.

"I've been one of the fortunate ones to call Roscoe one of my best friends since sixth grade, the year that I started coming to Cherrywood Christian Academy. We both went to Clanton Baptist, attended Lighthouse youth retreats, and both got our first kisses on this campus, although his was two years before mine. And since I feel like I don't have much else to lose, I don't mind telling you that two years ago after Halloween, we smashed pumpkins in the parking lot by dropping them off the Eastman Hall roof."

The crowd snickered. A baby cried. I looked up from my paper and into the crowd attempting to zero in on where the noise came from. Tucked securely in her carrier basket, I saw a child being gently rocked by her new mother, the glowing Rachel Ellis. Rachel smiled at me, and I smiled at her.

I lost my train of thought. I quickly looked back down at my paper and tried to re-center myself, but I couldn't quite do it. There were only a few paragraphs I had left to read, but they felt stuffy. Continuing on just didn't feel the same. I folded my paper and began to speak from the heart.

"I spent Christmas with Roscoe and his family last year. I will spare you the details, but suffice it to say, my family situation was less than ideal over the holidays. When I was with them last Christmas, I realized that whatever they had as a family - whatever unconditional love they shared with each other - was exactly what I wanted and was exactly what Christianity is all about.

"Roscoe was one of the best men I've ever known. He made a foolish final choice; however he made this choice out of love, to protect his sister. It is not my job to judge what was in his heart that night. I have no right to look down on him simply because he sinned differently than I do. This is what I learned most from Roscoe: to love first, without question and without prejudice. The one time Roscoe lost sight of that because of fear and anger, it cost him his life. It is not our responsibility to put limitations on the grace of God. It is not our place to decide who can obtain forgiveness. Love others, the way Christ loved us."

I grabbed my paper and walked back to my seat as the crowd grew silent. Shawn patted me on the back when I sat down, but I kept my eyes forward.

After the funeral was over, I said goodbye to my parents and walked straight for Mr. Lessner's car, talking to as few people as possible. I knew that they just wanted to ask me questions about the yearbook. They didn't want to talk about Roscoe.

I sat in the car waiting for Shawn and his father who had not been as quick to escape the crowd and was left holding obligatory conversations. I looked over to see Rachel Ellis sitting under a shade tree. She had spread out a blanket for her and her daughter. Another young mother sat on the blanket beside her with her toddler son. Rachel looked up to see me through the tinted back window of the car. She waved with a smile.

That was the last day I ever lived in Clanton. I packed up my car that afternoon and headed for my grandfather's house in Pennsylvania the next morning.

A formal police investigation turned up felony charges of embezzlement and money laundering against several members and directors of Clanton Baptist and Southern Hope, including Joel Samms. Governor Hawkins hired a team of attorneys to help him deny any allegations of bribery or involvement with Cherrywood or its members. He was acquitted but lost the next election by a landslide and never returned to politics. Dr. Sites was indicted on a whole slew of charges including bribery, embezzlement, coercion, and others and was sentenced to four years in the Mississippi State Penitentiary.

It turned out that even though Jeremy Maitland was an unsuspecting pawn in the Southern Hope scandals, he wasn't totally innocent. Sites had been paying Jeremy under the table with donations collected through Southern Hope to help scout good football players and bribe them into coming to Cherrywood. Once they were there, Sites incentivized a few of the faculty to make sure those players didn't fail any courses and lose playing eligibility. He also turned a blind eye to their drug use and encouraged a few of them to make life hard for me when I started to piece that together. The football team alone brought in over $200,000 in profits that year through sponsorships, advertisements, tuitions, and prize earnings.

As I had suspected, the orphanage in Kenya was never really built. Rather, a church somewhere in Oklahoma that actually did start its own orphanage was awarded a judgment for copyright infringement on many of its photos that Southern Hope had been illegally using in its promotions.

Mrs. Yelski, along with several other teachers, were blacklisted from the Teacher's Union for accepting bribes to manipulate student's grades. Winters' Printing, along with a handful of other businesses, was forced to close its doors after it was convicted of money laundering involvement with Clanton

Baptist. Mr. Winters had alerted Dr. Sites about my investigation of their tax returns, and in an attempt to limit any more of my discoveries at work, I had been demoted. Winters had been keeping an eye on me; cutting my pay was just another way for them to maintain control.

Although it was several months later, Bruce Lessner became a Christian. He admitted that since he regularly lied in his profession, he thought that if he adopted religious views and started to feel guilt and moral accountability for those decisions, then his income would suffer. Therefore, he had tried to justify a way around religion. Religion was an inconvenience for him. To his surprise, though, he opened his own practice after his publicity with the Cherrywood case and is doing better than ever. He helped get all lawsuits against me dropped and arranged for me to finally receive my high school diploma.

I was in the last class to ever graduate from Cherrywood Christian Academy. They closed their doors shortly after, but reopened under the name Faith Christian Schools about five years later. They claim to have no affiliation with Clanton Baptist anymore but we all know they still do. The Southern Hope Foundation, on the other hand, closed its doors for good.

My father continued to become a completely different man than the one who raised me. Time and distance have a way of changing things, smoothing over rough edges, resolving arguments, and finding forgiveness. My father finally came to realize the true meaning of the poem by Ellen Sturgis Hooper:

> *I slept, and dreamed that life was Beauty;*
> *I woke, and found that life was Duty.*
> *Was thy dream then a shadowy lie?*
> *Toil on, sad heart, courageously,*
> *And thou shalt find thy dream to be*
> *A noonday light and truth to thee.*

With the help of time and reflection, my father understood that although life is made of obligation and duty, our dreams and our goals help to guide us and give us direction to help us find our way.

I shared Proverbs 16:9 with him. "In his heart a man plans his ways, but God directs his path." He was saddened that he never fulfilled his dream of becoming a pastor. His harsh tone and character had mellowed over time like a fine bourbon, but his message was no less than one hundred proof potent. There comes a time in every son's life when he realizes that his father is not perfect. I thanked my father for the lessons he taught me growing up, and I told him that although he was not able to personally share his faith with a congregation as he had hoped, he had shared it with me and with Buck, and perhaps that was all that God intended. I may not have always agreed with my dad, but I was still able to glean wisdom amongst his faults and love in spite of his judgment.

Last Christmas, he and I sat down to talk about the future. He is growing older now. I invited him to come stay with me when he felt the time was right. My father had never experienced unconditional love as a child, and therefore was unable to accept it or share it freely with others. It is my hope that in his final years and in his growing weakness, he will be able to see God's unconditional love through me.

My dad allowed me to take our dog Buck to my grandparent's farm the summer after I graduated. Buck was twelve years old and around Clanton had become quite slow, but on the farm Buck became like a puppy again, living out his last days chasing rabbits and squirrels.

I spent a few months in Pennsylvania collecting my thoughts. About a month after arriving at my grandpa's, I decided to look up Joe Knowles and gave him a call. I had not heard from him after Dr. Sites had told me he was not interested in working with me. I figured that at very least, he would have some pointers or advice for me. I was only able to speak to his agent who gave me his address, so I sent him some of my best recent photographs - pictures of my grandpa, strangers I met in the rural towns of Pennsylvania, and my companion Buck.

Two weeks later I received a phone call from Joe. He told me Dr. Sites had never shown him any of my work but that he had heard what had happened and agreed to take me on as his assistant. I paid my dues and eventually got my first break shooting editorial pieces for Relevant Magazine.

I lost contact with a lot of my peers from Cherrywood. Shawn and I still talk on the phone every once in a while. Grady distanced himself from his family and moved to Seattle where he opened up his own insurance agency and Natalie got married shortly after college and is now living in Scottsdale. There is one person from the Academy who I see quite frequently, though.

Rachel Ellis and I kept in touch while I lived with my grandfather. Then when I moved back down to Charlotte where Joe's studio was located, I learned that Rachel had taken a position in Raleigh. She worked her way through college, and we started to hang out every once in a while. After three years of commuting to see one another, I finally got the courage to pop the question. We married in the spring along the shore of the Outer Banks. Rachel had been the light beside me to guide me through the darkest of times. As I often wondered where God was in my life, Rachel never did. She said that He had always guided her through her dark points, and without His intervention, neither she nor my adopted daughter Hope would be alive today.

Over the past twenty years, I had been assigned to photograph important people and events all over the world, but out of all the assignments I had ever been given, the one that Mr. Oakridge gave me that day in Bible class was the greatest one I've ever received. That's why, when I moved from Pennsylvania to Charlotte, North Carolina in the fall of 1996, I passed through Clanton to deliver a report that I had been working on all summer. It was long overdue but one that I was glad to finally complete.

Dear Mr. Oakridge,

Last year, you gave me an assignment to write a report on Christianity. On the surface, this assignment seemed simple. Although I know you meant for this to be a challenge, I don't believe you realized how complicated it actually would be for me to complete.

While I was taking your class, I began to truly take notice of my surroundings. I observed how Cherrywood Christian Academy preached love, forgiveness, and acceptance but then expelled a certain student when she needed those things the most. I saw how on Sunday mornings, Pastor Samms would preach about generosity and helping others, but then behind closed doors, he would accept our generosity to help himself. I saw how some students would get reprimanded for using foul language, but others would not for using cocaine. There were so many hypocritical and, frankly, sinful things that went on at my Christian school that it made it very easy for me to believe that all I had learned there was a lie.

For months I was reluctant to take on the role of a Christian, even in class, until I could say in my heart that I actually believed it. That's what made your assignment so difficult for me. I knew it required me to write an argument in defense of the faith, but in my heart, I didn't have one. In the months following your dismissal, Pastor Samms' resignation, and Jake's death, I have begun to find some answers. This is what I have learned so far:

I first tried to explain away the concept of Creation, along with the notion that there was something bigger and much greater than myself. The idea of life evolving from nothing and therefore meaning nothing was oddly comforting. If there was no rhyme or reason for my existence and no consequences or condemnation for my actions, I was free to live without purpose. But the more I photographed and the more I learned about biology, the human body, and the universe, the more questions I had.

If there are billions of species on this planet that have been evolving for billions of years, shouldn't there be zillions and zillions of transitional forms? Why have we not found *one*? Why does our most advanced technological achievement resemble mere child's play when compared to the complexity of the most basic living cell? We have the blueprints and designs to billions of different plants, animals, minerals, and objects that occur in nature but in all of the time that humans have been on this earth, and even when we work with the basic ingredients that are already here, we have not been able to independently duplicate, much less improve on any of them.

So why should we believe random chance can do what our own intelligence can't?

Natural selection and mutation are the main drivers of the Evolutionary Theory. Natural selection though, occurs within a species and does not provide the additional genetic information required to go from one species to another. Mutations on the other hand, whether natural or experimental, are always destructive and cause diseases like cancer, Down Syndrome, and Spina Bifida. So wouldn't the theory of "de-evolution" make more sense? Why wouldn't life have started with superhumans, and as genetic information got lost and things became more disorderly, we are only left with us? Evidence suggests that humans used to live for hundreds of years, but now even with cutting edge technology, we are lucky to live to age eighty. From everything I have seen and studied, we are in a state of decay and not of improvement.

I have come to understand that to accept the Theory of Evolution in its rawest form, you must accept the notion that at one time something literally came from nothing, and through a series of random, causeless events that violate all mathematical probability, that something was a universe so complex that its mechanics literally defy human comprehension. It is a theory that violates several scientific laws, common sense, mathematics, archaeologically, science itself, and one that its own founder, Charles Darwin, even questioned in the *The Origin of Species* - the very book in which he proposed the theory.

"Long before the reader has arrived at this part of my work, a crowd of difficulties will have occurred to him. Some of them are so serious that to this day I can hardly reflect on them without being in some degree staggered."

Evolution attempts to explain life in a very organized approach using phylogenetic trees based on physical and genetic similarities of creatures to illustrate how they could have evolved. However when I look at these items, I can't help but see the handwriting of a common Designer who delicately stitched life together with organization and purposeful intent. Evolution does a dreadful job explaining how we came to be and does not, in any sense of the word, explain *why*. It does, however, attempt to explain away the concept of a Creator, the realization that we were made for a purpose, and it makes a futile attempt to explain away our very souls.

Evolution isn't taught in mainstream media and schools because it's scientific. Science is the study of the natural world through observation and experimentation. Evolution is neither, since it has never been observed and all of its crucial experiments have failed. Evolution is taught because it is our best attempt to explain the world around us without considering a Higher Power as an option. It's taught because it doesn't involve a Creator, and therefore, is thought not to involve religion. But just because it doesn't involve a Creator doesn't mean it's not religious. It takes more faith to believe in evolution than in an Intelligent Designer, and just like religion, the Theory of Evolution brings people hope. It brings them hope that deities, the supernatural, and religions are not true.

I clung to this hope for a brief time. But it was a hope that I have long since abandoned.

I have come to realize that there is a Creator of this world, and He did either one of two things: He either kept Himself hidden from us so we can't know who He is, in which case, we're all in the same boat and there's nothing we can do about it. Or He has given us information about Himself and it's our job to find it. If the latter is true, this information is probably contained in one of the world religions, which claims to possess it.

Christianity is the world's largest religion and one that should be extremely easy to debunk if it were false. Christianity started with a historical figure named Jesus of Nazareth, or Jesus Christ; however, Jesus didn't claim to be a messenger or a prophet from God like so many other religious founders have. Jesus of Nazareth claimed to *be* God.

That claim should be easy to disprove if it were wrong because it leaves us with only three options. C.S. Lewis put it very neatly when he said that Jesus was either a "liar, a lunatic, or Lord." If he wasn't who he claimed to be, then he was either crazy or deliberately trying to deceive people by offering sinister claims like the forgiveness of their sins and the ability to rise from the dead. If he wasn't certifiably insane - which there is good evidence to support that he wasn't - he was evil. Unless of course, he was telling the truth.

The life of Jesus of Nazareth has been feverishly studied by scholars for the past two thousand years and proved completely accurate, while his death by crucifixion is an undeniable historical fact. The burial site of Jesus has been known since his crucifixion, but curiously, his body has never been found.

Over five hundred people claimed to have personally met him *after* his death, and many of his most prominent persecutors while he was alive, renounced their unbelief and were willing to face martyrdom, some gruesomely torturous, after his resurrection. The Old Testament contains over three hundred prophecies concerning the Messiah that were fulfilled in Jesus Christ, and mathematics states that the probability of just eight of these coming true would be one in 100 quadrillion. Our calendar is based on His life, He originated the largest religion in all of history, He's got more information written about Him than any other ancient ruler, and millions of people over the past two thousand years have been willing to die for His cause. And none of it would've happened if someone just exhumed the dead body of a vagabond carpenter.

Christianity should have been easy to debunk. I was hoping I could do it. I was hoping I could think my way around things I didn't like, just like humans try to do. We can clearly witness that some creatures just cannot understand all of the knowledge contained in the universe. A goldfish only has the capacity to comprehend its contained fishbowl environment. So why do we arrogantly believe that we are the species who can comprehend anything outside of our fishbowl understanding of this world?

We don't always know why God allows or disallows certain things. There may even be some difficult passages in the Bible to understand, possibly due to translations, customs, and philosophical reasoning. However, even though some passages may be confusing or even seem contradictory, amidst all the names, places, descriptions, and great detail in the sixty-six book Bible, there is not one proven fallacy and modern archaeology continues to validate its credibility on a daily basis.

We don't like the idea of suffering, but if God disallowed suffering, hardship, and pain, we'd be like spoiled brats and life would ultimately be meaningless. Everything would be easy; we'd have nothing to work at, and relationships, efforts, and actions would mean nothing. We would be bored. But since boredom is a form of suffering, we'd need to be reduced to robots to not notice our discontent. God gave us our own free will. He loves us and has given us the ability to love Him back.

The world God created for us to live in is a beautiful place, and while it is not perfect, that was not His doing: it was ours. Dictators who slaughter millions of people, rapists, liars, pastors who steal from their congregations, and church members who ostracize someone for being different; no one is exempt. That's our fault. It's who we are. It's not who God is. I used to believe that intentions were meaningless. In this life, people care about what you do, who you are, and what you create instead of your intentions. Not so with God. To God, intentions are everything. People look at what is on the outside, what a person actually does. God looks at the person's heart, and with that, God shows his love and grace first. Jesus died so that we may obtain grace...so that the consequences of our actions could be made into something good, that our evil intentions to hurt others might be forgiven. Even Jake Martin's. Even Principal Sites. Even my own.

So many times, people believe that what they have been told is true. They'll go with what their parents have taught them, what society says, or with the group that seems the most certain. There are very few things that I am certain of in this life. It is because of these few certain things, that I encourage others to search for the truth so they may come to understand the hope and joy which I have obtained. It is not my place to force my beliefs on others, nor is it my intention for others to assume my words are absolute truth.

It is, however, my responsibility to represent the best truth I have yet come to find.

Your Student,
Sylas Ernst

Acknowledgements

Ryan Mix

I'd like to thank my beautiful wife, Janine, for her love and support as I worked on this project. When I needed to sacrifice our time on weekends to brainstorm, the early mornings and late nights you were kept awake by my keyboard typing, and the marketing ideas you helped me develop for the finished project – thank you for your belief in me and your support.

To my parents...the only people to have read three different versions of this book. Thank you for the time you've spent proofreading to help me fine-tune and perfect the story. Your encouragement and support was invaluable. And thank you for teaching me the values and principles Sy had to learn on his own.

I would also like to thank my sisters, Becky and Katie. Becky, thank you for your very sharp editing eye and the time you devoted to this project. I'm sorry that I do not use commas as well as you do. Your scrutiny has made me a better person. And Katie, thank you for your encouragement and your word-of-mouth marketing. Even though you didn't get to read the book before it was published, I know you were one of its biggest fans.

Thank you to the people who inspired many of the characters and circumstances and thank you to those who helped turn this collection of words into an actual product. To Kevin Scharfe and Britney Higgs for your creative time and energy. To the web designers, editors, and proof readers who helped complete the project. Thank you for your time and skills.

Lastly, I'd like to thank my co-author, Josh. In spite of the schooling and time-restraining activities you were committed to over the last three-and-a-half years, you still saw this project through to the end and never quit. Thank you for your diligence, your belief in this book, your hard work, and your friendship.

J.T. Payne

First, having the best intentions in mind, and not wanting to leave anyone out, I believe it is appropriate to begin my thanks where the inspiration for this story began. Daniel M., Chad H., Eric R., Mr. Woodard, and Mr. Schwedt; thank each of you for being a positive inspiration for Sy's friends, teachers, and mentors. Rianna, Suzanne, Lisa, and Cassidy; thank you for collectively inspiring the integrity of Rachel's character. A special thanks to our senior class at Lynchburg Christian Academy. Thank you for letting me photograph your every move. I considered myself very blessed to be with you.

Thank you to all of my friends in Nashville, in particular: Beth Z., Terry Z., Matt S., David J., Stef M., & Steve I. Thank you for being there for me always. Pastor Ken Wetmore, thank you for your insight during the final stages of completing The Academy. A huge shout out to my classmates at MTSA! (To answer your question, this book was largely written before school began.)

Special thanks to my siblings: To my sister, Crystal, for her courage and wisdom, and to my brother, Jeremy, for literally and metaphorically using his left hand in a world that uses it's right. You taught me to ignore the approval of the narrow-minded. You're a brave man. I love you both.

On a somber note, the character of Buck, the Ernst family's German Shepherd was originally a tribute to my father's German Shepherd who lived a full happy life. Sadly, my 16 month-old German Shepherd, Asher, died tragically 3 weeks before The Academy was scheduled to publish. I would also like to dedicate Buck's character to the memory of Asher and to anyone who has lost a pet before their time.

At this time, I would like to acknowledge the Christian giants in my personal life. I cannot think of a more appropriate word than to call them my heroes. These men and women of integrity have sharpened my mind and molded my character as I continue to discover the truth on a daily basis.

Billy Gillespie, a crazy college student from the south was my first and most influential youth counselor. His passion for the youth he leads, even to this day, is second to none. Tim Grandstaff, my high school youth pastor was an advocate for my brother and me. He led by example as he walked by faith, leading a group of teens through the streets of Atlanta and New York to witness to the lost. Aaron Bryant, you were the pastor I came to at my darkest hour in life, and you helped me find hope. Aunt Jo and Aunt Viv, thank you for your selfless generosity to me throughout the years. Your love for Christ is reflected in the joy you bring to others. I always feel at home when I'm with both of you. I love each of you dearly. Mom, you are the most selfless person I have ever known. Your giving is only outweighed by your humility in the face of hard work. Most of all, I would like to thank my father, a God-fearing man with conviction as tough as nails, a passion for truth, and a mind filled with wisdom. Thank you for sharing your faith with me at such an early age. I am proud to call you my dad.

I would like to thank Ryan Mix, the man who helped to make The Academy. You pushed me and challenged me to create the best story possible. Thank you for your patience, for your dedication, and for staying by my side since the sixth grade. Thanks to your family for being there for me, no questions asked. Thank you for making me a better person and for helping to make this dream a reality.

Above all, thank you Lord for my salvation, for your grace, and for second chances.